For every science fiction enthusiast out there, dreaming of distant stars and quantum quirks—may this story spark your imagination as much as those tales have sparked mine.

And to the brilliant scientists at Fermilab, who so graciously welcomed me into your extraordinary facility, answered my endless (and most assuredly annoying) questions, and showed me the real magic behind the mysteries of the universe. Your passion and patience made this book possible. Thank you.

I0687659

Here's an video preview of what the book is about that you can download by scanning the QR code with your phone, or typing the IP link into your computer.

https://www.youtube.com/watch?v=056pUCUNC7A

Paradox

(Forging the Keys To Hell)

Randy Benjamin

© Randy Benjamin Music
Intguide Publications
BMI 2026

350 Felt King Road
Suite 101
Vincennes, IN 47591

1st Corinthians 1:19

"For it is written, I will destroy the wisdom of the wise, and will bring to nothing, the understanding of the prudent."

Prologue

The first sign that something wasn't quite right came a few days before Christmas, around December 22nd, if memory serves. Most of the scientists and their families had already left for the holidays, leaving an eerie quiet in their wake.

Winter had descended upon Illinois with unusual haste that year. Frost whitened the landscape long before the echoes of "Trick or Treat" had faded from the countryside. In a cluster of brightly colored buildings—more reminiscent of Disneyland than the world's center for particle physics— a most astonishing discovery was about to take place. Questions that had eluded theologians and theoreticians alike were on the brink of being answered.

This groundbreaking revelation might just as easily have occurred at Cal-Tech, Stanford, or any of the prestigious European universities. The Japanese had been at the forefront for years, and the Russians, too, were searching for their own Rosetta Stone—the skeleton key that would unlock the secrets of creation.

Even so, it seemed predestined that this discovery would take place in the United States. After all, the world's most ambitious particle physics project, Fermilab's **Proton Improvement Plan-II (PIP-II)** and the **Deep Underground Neutrino Experiment (DUNE)**, was underway here. Within the vast underground tunnels and state-of-the-art facilities, the keys to unlock the universe's mysteries were being patiently forged.

Prominent scientists in the fields of quantum mechanics and cosmology had been coaxed from their respective universities to work solely on this project. They came from all corners of the globe: Steven Tyco from the CERN Laboratory for Particle Physics near Geneva, Maxwell Bruiner from the DESY Institute in Hamburg, William Scott from the "Brain Trust" at Stanford's Linear Accelerator in Palo Alto. Even Professor Yamamoto, now in his 80s, the founder of Japan's famed Fifth Generation AI Lab, had seen fit to join this hallowed assemblage. After years of research and billions in funding, the triumph these brilliant minds so diligently sought was finally within reach.

Why was Tim Collins associated with such intellectual giants? Probably because his article, "In Search of the Elusive Monopole," had won last year's coveted Pillanger award. Nova's decision to turn it into a PBS documentary hadn't hurt either. In any event, as the science editor for Future Technology magazine, it was going to be his job to document the discoveries taking place at Fermilab as they unfolded.

He would bear witness to nature's hidden wonders, observing the obliteration of protons as they smashed into their component particles—quarks, gluons, tops, bottoms, color, charm, spin, and all the other yet-to-be-discovered particles—born of massive collisions at relativistic speeds, swimming in fields of synchrotron radiation.

Tim would record the merging of new technologies, the marriage of matter and anti-matter, the quest that would lead to the confirmation of the Theory of Super-symmetry and the key to creation itself. Like a scribe in the days of the ancient Pharaohs, his task would be to chronicle the activation of the most complicated machine the human mind had ever devised—Fermilab's new accelerator complex, the heart of the DUNE experiment, the most powerful and sophisticated particle physics facility in the world.

At least, that was his intention. Had he any idea of what really lay ahead, he would have run as far and as fast as his spindly legs could have carried him. Never looking back. Never stopping to catch his breath. Never once turning his head to chance a glimpse of whatever it was that was making those God-awful moaning sounds behind him. And when he could run no more, he'd walk. When he could walk no farther, he'd crawl. If nothing else, he'd just fall forward. Anything that would put one more inch between him and the images that would dwell in his mind and haunt his memory forever.

Truly, the light of discovery was burning brightly at Fermilab, but some things are better left in darkness. Some doors should never be opened; they should be bolted shut, FOREVER. That giant accelerator not only unlocked the secrets of matter and energy; it punched a hole through the very fabric of space and time. What emerged from that hole was not of this world, maybe not even of this universe.

The trouble with having a skeleton key is that you can never be sure of what's standing behind the door it unlocks. And as that door creeps open, you may just find that no matter how hard you push, something on the other side pushes back—just a little bit harder. And there's nothing you can do to close it again.

Here, then, are the events as they unfolded, as Tim Collins recorded them before the demons were unleashed and the darkness fell.

1st Corinthians 1:19 "For it is written, I will destroy the wisdom of the wise, and will bring to nothing the understanding of the prudent."

Forward

The soft glow of an LED bulb cast long shadows across the study as General J.T. Russell (retired) sank deep into the cushions of his twenty-year-old recliner. The worn leather creaked softly, a familiar sound in the quiet room. A reading lamp hung low over his right shoulder, illuminating the stack of papers lying in his lap, their crisp edges a stark contrast to the comfortable disarray of the general's sanctuary.

On a nearby marble end-table, a crystal snifter of Courvoisier XO cognac caught the light, its amber contents promising warmth and comfort. Next to it, the sleek remote to a 70-inch OLED television lay within easy reach, a gateway to hundreds of high-definition channels and a meticulously curated collection of streaming favorites.

Most evenings, the rich strains of a Beethoven symphony or a Mozart concerto would fill the air, courtesy of his prized Bose stereo system. This was his hideaway, a place where he could shed the weight of responsibility and bask in hard-earned solitude.

But tonight was different. Tonight, duty had followed him home.

As Russell's calloused fingers leafed through the papers, a small smile tugged at the corner of his mouth. "It feels good to be needed again," he murmured, his voice a low rumble in the quiet room. Like the rest of the world, he had been captivated by the unfolding events at Fermilab. Now, he found himself on the inside track, privy to truths others could only guess at.

Earlier that day, DARPA—the Defense Advanced Research Projects Agency—had pulled him out of retirement. The project they'd presented him with wasn't just classified; it had the potential to rewrite human history. Russell, never one to shy away from a challenge, had accepted without hesitation.

Now, three hours later, he held in his hands one of only four existing copies of Tim Collins's daily ledger. Collins, a chronicler of Fermilab's cutting-edge technologies, had vanished four days ago along with his precious notes. The recovered document, its pages warped and stuck together from exposure to the elements, had been found at an undisclosed location. A dedicated restoration team had worked tirelessly to salvage what they could.

Russell's mission was clear: unravel the mystery of Collins's disappearance and locate him and his companions. DARPA's top brass were convinced that the answers lay hidden within the ledger's pages.

He skimmed the opening sections, glossing over the mundane details of Collins's appointment at Fermilab. Time was of the essence, and Russell's instincts told him the real meat of the story would be found near the end. As he delved deeper, the general's brow furrowed. The final entries were a far cry from the meticulous notes at the beginning. Here, Collins's thoughts meandered, whole paragraphs dissolving into incoherence. It was as if the writer had intended to fill in the gaps later, perhaps when he found himself in safer circumstances.

What Russell did manage to decipher, however, sent a chill down his spine despite the warmth of the cognac. Portals. Aliens. Monsters. No wonder the public was being kept in the dark. For a moment, the general wondered if he was reading a classified report or if someone had slipped a draft of the latest sci-fi blockbuster into the file.

Collins spoke of concepts beyond Russell's comprehension, and the abrupt, mid-sentence ending to the ledger only deepened the mystery. Who were these people Collins mentioned? What forces were at play? Intrigued, Russell focused on a particular passage:

"Shsssss Shsssss Shsssss" Everyone turned, trying to figure out where the hissing noise was coming from. "Shsssss Shsssss Shsssss" Then they saw it. Fifty or sixty feet ahead of them, the tunnel seemed to get blurry. It was as if they were looking through air rising off a hot section of highway. The image shimmered as they watched. Within a few seconds, a portal appeared, and the hissing sound stopped.

Russell paused, his mind struggling to process the information. What does he mean... a portal? He continued reading, his curiosity piqued.

It was a huge portal blocking the tunnel entirely except for a small space next to the bottom of the inside wall. A few more feet and it would have cut into the beamline itself. All hell would have broken loose had that happened.

Depina's curiosity got the better of him, and he walked over to investigate the phenomenon. As he approached, he could see the desert scenery that some of the others had talked about. It was like looking through a giant window, only there wasn't any glass. He felt like he could jump right into it and walk around. It was tempting. Then he remembered the things under the sand and the bent crowbar. Maybe later!

Again, the General was lost as to the meaning of what he'd just read. Who were the others? What deserts? Glassless windows? Crowbars? What the hell is he talking about? But he continued, drawn deeper into the bizarre narrative.

Several of the others came to join him, their curiosity overcoming their fear. They gazed, wide-eyed, into that alien landscape.

Off in the distance, Depina thought he saw something move. He pointed, and the rest of them saw it too. By the time the rest had joined them, the object had grown larger as it stopped and started in quick, jerky movements.

"What is that?" Carol said, not to anyone in particular.

It continued these strange movements as it steadily drew closer. It was still too far away for them to tell what it was or what it was doing.

"Damn, I wish I had a pair of binoculars," someone said from the back.

They watched, mesmerized by what they were seeing.

Suddenly, a shadow appeared in their peripheral vision, about a hundred yards away to their right.

A few seconds later, the object that cast the shadow appeared. It looked like a cross between a spider and a starfish. It was about the size of a Volkswagen, and the sound it made was a low rumbling moan. It was moving in the same manner as the thing they'd been watching for the last few minutes.

It was running across the sand as if in pursuit of something. It would stop and stand for a few seconds, turning its head much like a robin does when it's listening for a worm. Then it would start up again. After a minute or so of these exaggerated movements, it stopped and plunged its two protruding tusks deep into the sand. For the next few seconds, it didn't move at all. It just stood there, rigid as a statue. Then it raised its head, throwing sand everywhere.

Impaled on the tusks was some kind of animal. It resembled a huge mole. It was still alive and squirming as the creature shook it violently. The mole was making a grunting sound as it tried to free itself. The grunts didn't last long though, as the tusks suddenly separated, tearing it in half.

"My God!" Carol gasped. "Did you see that?"

Depina was looking at the same gruesome scene. "Yes, and from that moaning sound, I think it might have been what we heard behind us earlier."

The entire group was maneuvering, trying to get a better view. This caught the attention of the creature. It turned and faced them. It seemed to sense their presence more than actually seeing them. It started towards them but without that jerky motion it had shown before.

The group started to back up, slowly at first, eyes riveted on the thing in front of them. Then they turned and ran like hell, all but Depina. He just stood there, riveted to the floor. By the time he finally turned to run, the creature had closed the gap between them to less than fifty yards. Its legs were throwing sand everywhere as it moved. It was fast for its size.

The others practically climbed over each other getting through the maintenance room door, which they locked using a heavy steel bar that wedged between two braces. Someone remarked, "Why would a door have this kind of lock on it? It's made to keep something out, not to protect something inside from being stolen."

Two of Singleton's men climbed the ladder leading into the hatch only to find it was already occupied. It was confining with four men in such a small space, but they didn't really have much choice. Bill shut the hatch and shoved the bolt into the lock. They couldn't see into the beam tunnel with the door shut. But they could hear.

When Depina finally got there, everything was locked down tight. He panicked. Looking around, there was nowhere to go. He tried to squeeze into a small opening behind one of the giant magnets, but there just wasn't enough space to hide his 170-pound frame. He could hear the sounds of the monster's feet as they echoed off the tunnel floor. Then he heard another sound, just as loud and just as clear. Bells—he heard the sound of bells. But that was impossible. It must be the rush of adrenaline causing him to imagine things.

He was terrified. His mind was racing. Then a voice popped into his head. It was as clear as if the speaker was standing right beside him. He glanced to both sides, expecting Bill or Singleton to be standing there.

Use the hose to kill it.

Then it dawned on him. He was standing next to the leaking liquid nitrogen line. He pulled off his shirt and wrapped it around the hose. Then he turned the valve governing the refrigerant's flow to the off position. Richardville had deliberately left the connector loose, so it was easy to unscrew.

When he turned around, the creature was standing between him and the outer wall. It was glaring at him through four compound eyes. His heart nearly stopped. In his worst nightmare, he couldn't imagine anything so ugly. It was waving its tusks in the air menacingly. They were pointed and serrated. Anything impaled on them wasn't getting off.

He pointed the hose at the creature's head but waited to turn it on. The creature took a few steps towards him and stopped. It seemed to sense that something was wrong. What was this thing in front of it? Why was it just standing there?

The people inside the maintenance room gathered around the two overhead monitors. Depina had uncovered the cameras earlier, and they were working again. As they watched in horror, they realized there was absolutely nothing they could do.

The creature took its time approaching Depina. It had never seen anything like him before and wasn't sure if he was even edible. As it neared him, it detected the heat from his body—this triggered its instinct to strike.

Depina stood there, his left hand holding the hose, his right hand on the valve. He knew he only had one shot at this. It had to be timed just right. He didn't want to drive the monster back into the tunnel; he wanted to kill it.

The creature sensed that it had the advantage and eased towards him, tusks ready to tear him to pieces.

It was time. He turned the valve all the way to the left, and a plume of liquid nitrogen shot from the end of the hose, dousing the creature before it realized what had happened.

Its eyes froze instantly as soon as the liquid hit them. It reared up on its four back legs, trying to clear the cold from its eyes with its front pair. It was trying to get away, but with its vision destroyed, it didn't know which way to turn. Tissues froze at the touch of the liquid nitrogen. The creature blindly lurched forward, trying to spear whatever was attacking it.

Depina stepped out of the way, the short hose not allowing him much leeway, but it was enough. He was careful not to touch the creature's frozen flesh as it thrashed in agony. He sprayed the head, covering it with a thick layer of slush. This stopped any motion wherever it landed.

In less than a minute, it was over. He shut the valve, and the hose went limp immediately. He'd let Richardville hook it back to the magnet later. Right now, he just wanted to catch his breath. The door to the maintenance room flew open, and everyone rushed out to see if he was alright. They couldn't believe he'd actually killed this thing. They also realized how lucky he was to have been near the liquid nitrogen line. Had he been anywhere else, he'd be dead.

The scene was surreal as the liquid nitrogen warmed and turned back into a gas. The bubbles caused the hair on the creature's body to move as though it were still alive. It was a thoroughly disgusting sight.

"That was sheer genius using the liquid nitrogen. How in the world did you think of it?" Carol asked. "I'd have been too scared to even move."

Depina stood there for a few seconds before answering, "I didn't think of it. I heard someone say, 'Use the hose to kill it.' I'd have never thought of it myself. When I heard the voice, I just did it."

"What do you mean—a voice?" Carol asked.

"That's exactly what it was, a voice. I swear it was like someone was standing right beside me. I remember something else too. I heard bells. I'm sure of it."

"You had to have imagined it. We were watching the whole time. You were alone."

"Somebody was here—and they saved my life."

Depina looked back toward the other side of the beam tunnel.

"I just hope there aren't any more of these things down here."

No one spoke. They had all heard those same moans before. But right now, they needed to—

General Russell looked up from the page, pondering what he'd been reading. The last sentence was never finished.

One thing was for sure; he wasn't going to solve anything until he knew what had taken place at the beginning.

With his cognac to keep him warm, he straightened the stack of papers and started to read, but from the beginning this time. He would still be reading when the sun came up.

At this point, we're going to leave General Russell. We aren't limited to those original sketchy pages that he has to work with. What follows is the complete story of the days before and after...the key was forged, and the door was opened.

Chapter One

Tim Collins was pleasantly surprised when he received an invitation from the White House Press Secretary to attend an event of national importance. As the science editor of "Future Technology" magazine, Tim was intrigued. The event they were inviting him to was the commissioning of the newest addition to Fermilab's Particle Research Facility: a sprawling, state-of-the-art accelerator complex known as the **PIP-II**—the Proton Improvement Plan-II. This new facility, together with the **Deep Underground Neutrino Experiment (DUNE)**, would soon be the most advanced particle physics project in the world, capable of sending the world's most intense neutrino beam deep underground to detectors a thousand miles away.

Actually, the invitation couldn't have come at a better time. Tim was long overdue for a vacation, and the DOE (Department of Energy) was going to be picking up the tab. How could he refuse? Besides, he was pretty sure this would be a first-class operation. After all the hoopla surrounding the cancellation of the Super Conducting Super Collider, the last thing the DOE wanted was to be the brunt of any more bad press. He could certainly tolerate being wined and dined at the government's expense for a few days.

With a smile, Tim signed 'yes' to the enclosed reply. Nine days later, he received a special delivery package containing first-class plane tickets, accommodations at Chicago's famous Pine Estates, and an engraved invitation personally signed by Sharon Ashton, the President's Science Advisor.

He arrived at Chicago's International Airport on a Tuesday morning. His old friend and college roommate, Dan Parker, greeted him at the terminal. Dan was a top-notch reporter for the Chicago Daily News and was also attending the PIP-II commissioning.

"Bribed you too, huh?" Tim quipped as Dan helped him with his luggage.

"I wish! The only person that gets any bribes around here is my editor."

Thirty minutes later, they pulled into the Pine Estates parking lot. When Tim checked in, he found that the DOE had already taken care of his expenses, including a charge account for dining and drinks in the lounge.

"I wonder how many others got invitations," Dan mused as the elevator doors slowly parted.

"I don't know, but I'll bet we aren't the only ones."

Dan's official title was Political Correspondent, but he'd been known to cover everything from UFO sightings to weather reports. Still, Tim wondered why Dan had been chosen for the Fermilab assignment. He doubted if Dan could tell a neutrino from a neutron. Science had never been his forte.

After getting Tim settled into his new surroundings, they headed for the hotel's restaurant. They reminisced about their days at Florida State, trading stories that neither of them had given any thought to in years. The waiter brought the check just as they were finishing their third glass of wine.

"I'm ready to call it a night," Tim said as he signed the tab, adding an overly gracious gratuity. "We've got a busy day ahead of us, and I'm pooped."

"I know how you feel. I'm tired too, and I've still got a half-hour drive home. I'll meet you in the morning at eight sharp. We may as well go together; there's no sense in both of us driving."

The DOE had provided Tim with a rental, but he'd rather ride in Dan's Mercedes. Besides, it would give him more time to spend with his old buddy.

"Sounds good to me. I'll see you in the morning."

Dan pulled up to the lobby ten minutes early and found Tim already waiting. They loaded Tim's luggage into the Mercedes, checked the map one last time, and headed west. It looked to be about an hour and a half drive to Fermilab.

Tim was quite surprised when they arrived. It wasn't anything at all like he'd expected. The complex is situated on 6,800 acres of what looked to be prime rangeland. There was even a resident herd of buffalo grazing on the long grasses blanketing the grounds. The first thing he noticed as they turned onto the main road was a unique new-age sculpture. Other similar sculptures greeted them as they drove on.

At the first intersection, they saw a sign that read "FERMILAB LIBRARY" with an arrow pointing to the right. Tim looked and could just make out the corner of a building partially hidden behind the trees at the edge of a large wooded area. In many ways, this place resembled a theme park more than the home of particle physics' most advanced accelerator complex. They drove on. Houses were scattered about in a random fashion.

He had to admit; it was a pleasant change from the bastions of science he was used to working in. Most of the time, he was stuck inside some giant square structure made of steel and cement—modern wonders that were either skinned in colored glass or had no windows at all. They were usually located in the middle of college campuses or hidden in sheltered underground sanctuaries, a reflection of how much of their research was controlled by the military. Most of these facilities had sterile, antiseptic feelings about them and were known by three or four-letter names such as CERN or MIT. This was definitely not the case here.

Tim's overall impression was that of a small Midwestern town plucked right out of the last century. Quaint little houses with closely cropped yards contrasted sharply with the brightly colored buildings he could see in the distance. It was a strange mix of the old and the new. At any moment, he half expected Ronald McDonald to come darting out from behind one of those surrealistic sculptures, waving a Big Mac in one hand and a Coke in the other.

And buffalo. Now that's something new for a research facility. "This place reminds me of a cross between Knott's Berry Farm and Little House on the Prairie," Tim said, as he pointed to the buffalo grazing lazily on the prairie grasses.

"It was called Weston before the State purchased the land from the townspeople," Dan explained. "It was donated to the Federal Government in the early '60s. The Feds gave it to the DOE, which broke ground for the Research Center in 1968. Those large white houses we've been passing belonged to the early farmers. They were left almost intact on the outside, but the insides were remodeled to accommodate the needs of the visiting scientists. The clusters of brightly colored houses are all that remains of the village of Weston proper. They painted the houses in bright colors to keep a lively air about the place. They didn't want this to be just another dull-looking research facility. I think it worked."

Tim had a quizzical look on his face. "What the hell are you doing, moonlighting as a tour guide?"

"No," Dan laughed, "I've just been reading the press release while you were driving."

As they neared the center of the complex, Tim could see that this wasn't quite the Ma and Pa version of Elementary Particle Physics he had first visualized. Ahead stood one of the most futuristic structures he had ever seen. A sign outside the building read "ROBERT RATHBUN WILSON HALL," and it looked enormous. It towered 16 stories above the prairie grass. Its design was magnificent, built in the shape of an inverted V.

They found parking to be their first inconvenience. There were over 2,000 people working at the center, and even though there were plenty of empty spaces, none of them were close to where they were going. They parked in the closest spot they could find. As they got out of the car, they noted a few of the other buildings nearby.

One was the Feynman Computing Center. It, too, had an unusual design. It was three stories high and built in a semicircle. The front was sheathed in cold black glass. Dan produced a pamphlet showing the sides and back of the building. The back was very unusual, consisting of vertical stone pillars that contrasted sharply with the ultramodern glass adorning the front of the building. Tim had always been a computer enthusiast, having three computers at home as well as the laptop he carried with him.

He remembered reading somewhere that Fermilab was home to one of the most advanced computing centers in the world, with access to a range of government supercomputers and AI-driven data analysis platforms. These were among the most powerful systems made.

He'd also heard that Fermilab had recently installed a new generation of high-performance, massively parallel computing clusters, designed specifically for the DUNE experiment. Instead of using one extremely fast processor, these systems combine thousands of smaller processors, all working in parallel. This was the kind of cutting-edge technology that Tim was really interested in investigating while he was here.

Since they were parked a little closer to Wilson Hall than the Feynman building, they decided the larger of the two buildings looked like the best place to start exploring.

Robert Rathbun Wilson was the first director of Fermilab. Not only was he a famous physicist, but he was also an accomplished artist and sculptor. He was intimately involved in the design of many of the buildings in the Fermilab complex. Wilson Hall, which bears his name, was intended to be a showplace from its inception.

It is unique both inside and out. Part of its allure is that it houses one of the world's largest atriums. As they walked up the steps leading to the entrance, a sign above the building's glass doors confronted them:

Welcome To Fermilab
Operated by Universities Research Association Inc.
For the U.S. Department of Energy

As they entered the building, they were immediately impressed by the large expanse of open area between the inwardly sloping sides of the inner walls. The trees of the atrium occupied most of the central floor. Located in the center of the building, directly behind the information desk, hung a Foucault pendulum. Tim had seen a similar one at the Chicago Museum of Science and Industry. The ball of the pendulum swung from a wire attached to the top of the 16-story structure.

Foucault Pendulums are used to prove the rotation of the earth. Looking up, they could see crossways joining several of the staggered floors high above them. These allowed workers on the upper floors easy access from one side of the building to the other. Toward the back of the building was the main dining area, a cafeteria.

"How about some coffee and donuts?" Tim suggested.

Looking around, they noticed several people talking at the end of the counter. Dan caught a glimpse of a name on one of the briefcases. "L.A. Times" was lettered in gold. Three people seated at a nearby table were probably technicians. They were wearing light blue lab coats with nametags attached to the pockets. Had he been in another place, he might have mistaken them for doctors.

Breaking his concentration, Dan said, "I'm going to go back into town and talk to some of the local folks. This shindig won't start until two o'clock anyway. I'd like to cover this story from a human-interest aspect. I'll let you scientific types fill in the boring details. I might skip the afternoon ceremony altogether. I can get all the biggest, newest, and fastest crap from the press release. I'm more interested in knowing what the people who live around here think about all of this high-tech wizardry."

"Just don't get lost! I'll need a ride back to Chicago," Tim replied. "The presentation runs from 2 until 3:30. Then there'll be Q&A for another half hour. There's a cocktail party this evening with a string quartet for entertainment. I'll save you a seat."

It was then that Tim realized why Dan's editor had chosen him for this assignment. Of all the reporters covering this story, Dan was probably the only one who would be writing a completely different slant on it. The rest of us might just as well write one story and all of us sign the byline.

When two o'clock rolled around, the place was packed. There were scientists and journalists from every part of the world. The DOE had spared no expense in making this commissioning a success. Actually, the presentations were quite informative and interesting. Of course, Tim's idea of interesting was somewhat biased. His whole life revolved around science.

Dan missed all of the afternoon's activities, but he did make it back for the evening finale. By 9:45, things started to break up, and they decided they should be getting back to Chicago. As Tim was saying his goodbyes, a young man wearing a black suit and tie approached him.

"Excuse me, Mr. Collins?"

"Yes," Tim said, as the man extended his hand.

"Mr. Collins, my name is David Jenkins; I'm an aide to Senator Walker. He would like to see you in the security office. Could I take you there?"

Wondering what the hell he'd done now, Tim said, "Sure, let's not keep the Senator waiting."

The security offices were located on the second floor next to one of the emergency exits. As they entered, Tim noticed two very large men giving him the once-over. Obviously, they were the senator's bodyguards. Senator Walker had been one of the featured speakers earlier in the afternoon.

With a huge grin on his face, the Senator introduced himself. "Mr. Collins, I'm Senator Walker, and I have a proposition for you." Tim was more confused now than ever. At least he wasn't under arrest or being audited.

"What can I do for you, Senator?"

"Well, Tim, I've read several of your articles in Future Technology magazine, and I saw the PBS special you produced. (Tim hadn't actually produced it, but apparently the Senator thought he had.) We are going to be bringing the PIP-II accelerator online soon, and we need someone with your talents and background to document it."

"I'm flattered, but I don't think I can get away from my other commitments. Being the science editor—"

"No, no, no, don't worry about that. It's all been taken care of. Everything has been cleared with your publisher. You'll be 'on loan,' so to speak. Actually, we've made a deal with your editor to let Future Technology have exclusive rights to what you'll be covering here at Fermilab. So you'll be receiving your usual salary plus a very nice bonus for the work you'll be doing for us. Just say you'll accept my offer, and you'll be a part of our team immediately."

Tim was stunned. He was beginning to wonder if somebody had spiked the punch.

"I'll need to fly back and—"

"Not necessary," the Senator interrupted him again. "You can go into Batavia tomorrow and purchase anything you think you'll need. You'll be given a DOE credit card. We'll provide you with an office, secretary, and a computer. Whatever you need in the way of clothes and personal items can be charged to your credit card.

You'll be sharing a house on the premises with Steve Turner. He's a senior research scientist from MIT. He'll show you around and help you with everything you'll need to know to bring you up to snuff. We're planning some very important experiments when the PIP-II accelerator goes online. Being able to document the results and explain them in layman's terms is an absolute must. Your job will be to make that happen."

The Senator went on to explain some of the projects that were scheduled for the new accelerator. To say that Tim was excited was an understatement. Finally, the Senator motioned for Mr. Jenkins again. "David, would you accompany Mr. Collins back to the party and see to it that he has something to sleep in tonight? He'll be staying with us for a while."

As they left the elevator, Tim realized that he'd been upstairs for over an hour. The party had cleared out, and the only people left were the custodians. They were cleaning up the mess and getting the building back in shape for tomorrow. One of the custodians handed him a note written on the back of a torn press release. It read:

I was waiting for you when one of Senator Walker's aides told me you were going to be working with the Senator on a special project and would be spending the night. I'm sure everything is OK, but, if you don't mind, would you give me a call in the morning just to let me know that you weren't kidnapped and taken to China or something! Seriously, I missed this afternoon's meetings and I need to borrow your notes. Dan.

What a strange turn of events this had turned out to be. Tim felt like a character in a James Bond novel. One thing was for sure: this was going to be an interesting change from his previous lifestyle.

Chapter Two

Bill Scott's greatest passion is fishing. Who would have thought that one of the best places to catch a trophy bass would also be the site of the world's most advanced particle accelerator? Early on, Fermilab's designers decided to set aside a large portion of the main complex for recreation. A 1,000-acre lake was dug and stocked with some of the largest bass in the entire state. Other game fish—crappie, bluegill, striped bass, and catfish—were also included.

The lake is located directly in the center, just inside the new accelerator's ring system. Since its creation, over a dozen seven-pound-plus bass have been caught. Bill was planning on catching the next seven-pounder.

Even though it was still early in April, Bill had a feeling that this just might be his lucky day. Bass usually go on a feeding frenzy when winter starts to wind down. The cold slows their metabolism, so they don't feed much during the winter months. As the water starts to warm up, the bass become more active. The best time to go fishing this early in the season is late afternoon. By then, the sun has had all day to chase the chill from the water.

Unfortunately, Bill is working the nine-to-who-knows-when shift, and about the only time he can find to fish is early morning. Right now, most mornings are still downright cold. On this particular morning, the air was chilly and noticeably damp. A thin layer of fog looked like smoke as it crept across the lake's surface. He rifled a few casts into the perfectly still water.

The sun had inched over the horizon a few hours earlier, and it was getting hard to shade his eyes from its brilliance. Like a dummy, he'd forgotten to wear his hat again. Now he was getting a double dose of sunlight. The sun was not only glaring down from above, but it was also reflecting off the water's surface like a mirror. Even so, this had actually turned out to be a pretty good morning. He'd been lucky enough to catch two decent bass, one of them tipping the scales at just under three pounds. It was the biggest bass he'd caught this year. Of course, this was only his third time out.

He had about an hour left before he'd have to get ready for work, and the action seemed to be slowing down. He decided to experiment. I think I'll try a deep diver, he thought to himself as he unsnapped the smart swivel from the surface lure he'd been using. He opened his tackle box—now with a built-in digital scale and weather sensor—and selected a shiny black lure with beady white eyes and a set of stainless steel treble hooks—his all-time favorite lure, a Bomber. He'd been using Bombers since he first began fishing as a little boy. Normally, he wouldn't use such a fast-moving lure this early in the season; the bass were still too sluggish. You just about had to bounce the lure off their nose to get one to hit it. But time was growing short, and besides, fish don't always react like they're supposed to.

On the third cast, he had a strike that nearly pulled the rod out of his hands. Strikes on a Bomber are often violent because of the speed of the retrieve, but this one was something else altogether. He was using a Shimano Stella reel, medium action rod, and thirty-pound spider wire fishing line. When the bass struck, the rod nearly doubled, almost touching the water. He had the drag set a little too tight for a fish this size, even with thirty-pound line, so he quickly backed it off, keeping pressure on the fish while being careful not to give it too much slack. Bill doubted that any fish in this lake could break thirty-pound spider wire, but if it managed to tangle him on a submerged stump or some other obstruction, he could easily lose it. He wanted to get the fish to shore as soon as possible. This is the one, he thought, as he gave the rod a second jerk just to make sure the treble hooks had a good bite.

The bank along the water's edge was smooth; the grass dead and still matted from the winter's heavy snows. The ground sloped towards the water at a slight angle, making it easy for him to walk along the shoreline. The fish pulled hard and to his right. By walking along the water's edge, he could apply just enough tension on the line to keep it taut without the risk of its breaking. He was thoroughly enjoying the fight. Then, just when he was sure he was getting the best of it, something happened.

"Crap!" he muttered as the line went limp, "I've lost it!" The line lay dead in the water. At first, he thought it had broken, but as he continued to reel, he could still feel a weight on the other end. Had the fish snagged him on something? If so, it wasn't very solid. He could still reel the line in. The fish had probably wrapped him around an old tree limb, getting off in the process and leaving him with the proverbial stick fish. It felt like about an eight-pound stick fish.

He pulled the rod back, then, dipping it down until it almost touched the water, he reeled up the slack.

After about thirty seconds of this pulling, dipping, and reeling, the fish broke the surface. What in the hell is that? he thought to himself. Startled, he flipped the bail on his reel, letting the line slip back off the spool and allowing whatever he'd caught to sink back below the surface. By now it was almost eight o'clock. Looking around, he saw Tim Collins getting out of his car—an electric Ford, gleaming in the morning sun. "Tim," he yelled loudly, waving his right arm high in the air to get Tim's attention. "Get your butt down here! There's something I want you to see!"

Tim wasn't much of a fisherman, but he knew that Bill had been trying to catch a trophy bass since he first met him. He figured he must have finally caught it. He cautiously made his way down the twenty or so feet to the lake's edge, expecting to see Bill grinning from ear to ear. As he approached, the only thing he saw was Bill staring down at the limp line dangling in the water.

"What'd you do, lose it?" Tim asked, a quizzical look on his face.

"No, that's the problem; I caught it. I thought I had a monster bass hooked, but when I reeled in my line, I found this."

With that, Bill reeled up the slack, and as soon as his fish broke the surface, Tim gasped. "What the hell is that?"

"Beats me! I've fished my entire life, but I've never caught anything that looked like this. If I were in the Keys, I'd say it might be a Moray Eel." Grunting, he pulled the creature up on the bank where they could study it more closely.

Bill poked at it with the butt end of his rod. "It's dead. It must have died while I was trying to land it. It looks like an eel, except eels have eyes. This thing doesn't seem to have any."

"It looks to me like a giant hotdog with a mouth," Tim said.

"Feel the skin; it's smooth like a catfish. Did you notice the splotches all over its body?" Bill asked.

"Yeah, they look like dimples. Where are the gills?"

"I don't see any," Bill said, while turning the fish over. "There are fins and a tail but no gills. Maybe it's some kind of a water snake?"

Tim was now bent over, examining the shape of the head. "How big is it?"

"I don't know. Get the scales out of my tackle box and I'll weigh it."

Upon opening Bill's tackle box, Tim was amazed to find dozens of brightly colored lures, each in its own compartment. There was also an assortment of hooks, lines, sinkers, screwdrivers, etc. It was obvious that Bill took his fishing seriously. At the bottom of the box, he saw a small blue nylon pouch with the words "Fenwick - Digital Scales" silk-screened on the front in white letters.

"Is this what you're looking for?" Tim asked, holding up the object so Bill could see it.

"That's it. Bring it over and we'll see how much this thing weighs. Eight pounds nine ounces exactly."

"I really would like to know what it is," Bill said again. "I'm going to store my gear and put this thing on ice. I've got a cooler in the trunk. I'll show it to a couple of the guys at the lab and see if they can identify it. You've heard of Nessie, haven't you? Well, this is 'Fessie.' Fermilab's version of the Loch Ness Monster—in miniature, of course.

Let me get my lure out of its mouth. Hmmm? This is weird. There aren't any teeth, but there's a tongue and it's rough as sandpaper. Mercy! This thing's got a tough mouth. I can't get the hook out. I think I'll just unsnap the swivel and cut it out later when I have more time. I don't want to lose my best Bomber."

Turning, Tim said, "I'll get you some ice from the cafeteria. Why don't you gather up your things and I'll meet you back at the car. I'm kind of curious to know what this thing is myself."

Tim scrambled up the slope, being careful not to slip on the dew-covered grass. The cafeteria in Wilson Hall had been open since 6:00 A.M. Many of Fermilab's personnel arrive long before the building officially opens at 8:30. Finding what he needed, Tim grabbed a couple of bags of ice and headed back to the car where Bill had just finished stowing his gear. Bill was fumbling with a cooler that was wedged between the spare tire and the left side of the trunk. Once he got it out, Tim poured in the first bag of ice. It covered the bottom completely. Bill had to fold "Fessie" at the middle. Even folded, the big fish just barely fit inside the confines of its plastic coffin. Tim added the second bag as Bill chuckled, "Fessie on ice."

It was nearing 8:30 now, and people were starting to fill the parking lot. Seeing the commotion Bill and Tim were making, a couple of technicians meandered over to see what was going on.

Eyeing the empty ice bags and the cooler, Harvey Connors, a systems engineer and fellow fisherman, smiled and said, "You must have finally caught a big one."

Bill and Tim just looked at each other and grinned, "Sure did; want to see it?"

"Sure," said Harvey. "You knew I caught one last year that went seven pounds five ounces, didn't you? On ten-pound line too."

"Well, Harvey my boy, I beat you by over a pound." Lifting the cooler's top, Bill beamed like a proud father seeing his new baby for the first time, "Check this out."

"What the hell is that?" Harvey said, as he pointed a finger at the cooler. "I ain't never seen anything like that before."

"Any idea what it might be?" Bill asked.

"I haven't the foggiest."

Harvey studied the fish for a little while and then said, "I know where you can find out though. There's a big aquarium just off Lake Shore Drive in Chicago. It's only about an hour and a half from here. I'll bet they could tell you in a heartbeat. You think there's any more of those things in here?"

"If there's one, there's got to be others."

"Say, Harvey, have you done any fishing this week?"

"No, it's too cold for me to get out here; I'm waiting till it warms up, why?"

"I'd swear the lake has risen several inches in the last few days. I'm sure I was standing higher up on the bank this morning than I was last week. We haven't had any rain, I just don't get it. The aquarium's a good idea. If you do happen to go fishing, keep an eye on the water level."

Bill closed the trunk, and the four of them headed on in to work.

Bill was pretty laid back to be the 'Director of Operations' at Fermilab, but he was a good one. He was well-liked and good at his job. It was unusual for the director to also be one of the top scientists. Few people could have held both positions so effectively.

By noon, Bill's curiosity was getting the better of him. He decided he might as well drive on into Chicago and meet with the people at the aquarium. He couldn't keep his mind on what he was working on anyway. One nice thing about being a big shot is you can pretty much come and go as you please. His secretary was familiar with the Shedd Aquarium; her cousin works there. He had her make a phone call and was immediately given an appointment for three o'clock that afternoon. That's perfect, he thought; with any luck, I'll be there and gone before the rush-hour traffic hits.

Bill had never been to the aquarium even though it was virtually next door to the Adler Planetarium, which he'd visited on several occasions.

As he was leaving, he ran into Tim again, "I have a three o'clock appointment at the aquarium with a Connie Baker." Anxiously, he sorted through the jumble of papers he had wadded up in his pocket. "Here it is; Dr. Connie L. Baker, G.O.A. Marine Biologist. Say, what have you got going on this afternoon?"

"Not much. I'm pretty well caught up on everything here. I was thinking about revising an article I've been working on—but I'm not much in the work mood right now. How about this, let's get your fish ID'd and then go chow down on some Chinese cuisine at the Baby Panda."

Bill replied, "That sounds fine, but I need to get back here no later than seven o'clock. They're bringing the PIP-II accelerator up to 90% of full power tonight. I'd like to be there when they do. I missed last week's test. They might even try for full power if everything goes alright."

"Damn, I almost forgot. I need to be there too," Tim said.

"We're getting to the point now where things are getting interesting. I heard they might go for full power too."

As they talked, they walked over to Bill's car.

"I'd better check on the ice," Bill said, as he stowed his briefcase and jacket in the back seat.

"Don't want a bunch of cats climbing around on my trunk." He hit the button between the seats and the trunk popped open. Removing the lid, he found the ice had barely melted. "Polypropylene, what would we do without it?"

It was 1:15 by the time they gassed up and pulled Bill's Chevy—now a self-driving hybrid—onto I-88. It was interstate all the way once they left Batavia. They took the toll roads as they neared the suburbs, but traffic was light. They were both glad to be getting out of the sticks for a while, and Chicago was about as far out of the sticks as you could get.

The aquarium was located on McFetridge Drive, just off Lake Shore Drive. Bill was right in his assessment about getting there by three o'clock. It was late enough to miss the lunch hour traffic and a couple of hours before the evening rush. A little over an hour later, they pulled into the aquarium parking lot.

The cooler was quite heavy, so they both took hold of a handle. It was a 50-yard hike to the main entrance. Once inside, they asked a guard where they could find Dr. Baker's office. He told them to take the elevator to the second floor, turn left, and it would be the second door on the right.

As they peered into the office, they saw a smartly dressed young woman sitting at a mahogany desk. It was piled with papers of every size and description. Bill knocked on the sill as they entered, "Dr. Baker?"

Looking up, the young lady smiled warmly, "No, I'm sorry, I'm afraid Dr. Baker's running a little late. I'm Caroline Tanner. You must be the gentleman from Fermilab? Dr. Baker asked me to make you comfortable until she gets here. I might be able to help you while we're waiting. I'm assisting Dr. Baker in classifying new additions to the aquarium. Your specimen, it's a freshwater variety, is it not?"

Bill was disappointed that he'd been shuffled off on an undergraduate. He was used to talking with the head honcho. But after all, this wasn't brain surgery; he just wanted to find out what he'd caught, have a great meal, and get out of Chicago before the rush hour traffic began.

"Yes, I caught it in the lake at Fermilab about eight o'clock this morning. None of us have ever seen a fish like it, and we were curious as to what it might be."

"Let me have a look, I'm familiar with most species native to this part of the country." As Bill opened the cooler, Tim watched the young girl's face closely. He wanted to see if she would register any reaction when she saw "Fessie."

"Mercy!" she said, definitely surprised. "Are you quite sure you caught it here? It looks more like something that came from the ocean, possibly a Gymnothorax Javanicus."

Not being used to having his word questioned, Bill straightened up and asked rather sternly, "When do you think Dr. Baker will be back, Miss Tanner?" Sensing the sharp tone of his voice, Caroline realized she'd made a mistake by asking such a doubting question. Now was the time for her most disarming smile.

"I'm sorry, Dr. Scott. I didn't mean to question you like that. It's just that—I'm completely taken aback by what you've brought in. Actually, Dr. Baker was hoping that I would be able to identify your fish and send you on your way without her having to change her busy schedule. I think she'll want to see this. I'll have her here in a few minutes." With that, she picked up the phone and dialed the number to Dr. Baker's other office.

"Dr. Baker, the two gentlemen from Fermilab are here with a rather unique specimen. Could you please help me in identifying it? Yes, surely, that would be fine. We'll be right down."

"Down?" Tim asked, his curiosity piqued.

"Yes, Dr. Baker is on one of the lower levels. We have four levels here in the aquarium. The main floor where you entered is the only area open to the public. All of our displays are located there. The heart of the aquarium is our display area. We have over 3,500 different species of fish and other exotic marine creatures behind the glass partitions. The lower levels house the things needed to keep the aquarium running—maintenance, acquisitions, security, print shop, etc. This level contains mostly administrative offices. We also have a top-notch oceanographic research department of which Dr. Baker is in charge. She's waiting for us in the large examining room. If you'll follow me, we'll take the service elevator."

In a matter of minutes, they were standing before what looked to be a large metal garage door. Caroline pressed a lighted green button on the side of the wall, and the door silently began to rise. She wasn't kidding when she said large examining room. The room appeared to be at least forty feet wide by sixty feet long. In the center was a stainless steel platform big enough to hold an elephant. Surgical lights hung overhead on moveable gurneys. There were racks of electronic equipment lining the walls and a bank of video monitors, all displaying the same message: "OFF LINE." The place was spotless. If not for the platform and the overall size of the room, they could well have been in one of the "detection chambers" back at Fermilab.

"We perform surgery here on creatures as large as killer whales," a voice said from far off and to their left. A little startled, they turned just in time to see the speaker picking up a new pair of surgical gloves. She was dressed in a doctor's gown. It had what looked to be blood splashed in a narrow arc over her right forearm and upper shoulder. "I'm Dr. Baker. I'm sorry I couldn't meet with you earlier. I thought I'd be finished with my surgical duties long before three o'clock, but I had a few more problems than I'd counted on."

After introducing everyone, Miss Tanner suggested that they set the cooler on the operating table where they would have plenty of room to examine the fish in detail. Upon opening the lid, Dr. Baker exclaimed, "Oh, my! This is not what I expected at all." She gently picked up the specimen, laying it fully outstretched on the stainless steel table.

"Be careful of the treble hooks," Bill said. "I couldn't get them out of its mouth, so I just left them there, lure and all." With a puzzled look on her face, Dr. Baker turned to Bill, "What treble hooks are you talking about?"

Bill was standing a few feet away and couldn't get a good look at the fish's head. As he moved closer, he could see that there was no Bomber attached to the fish now. "Well, I'll be damned! I know it was there this morning." He looked in the cooler and lying on the bottom underneath the remaining ice and water was what was left of his lure.

He reached in and retrieved the remains of his Bomber. About a third of it was missing. His first thought was that it had somehow melted. The back part of the lure including the treble hooks was missing. The lure was made of plastic and the hooks were stainless steel. The more he studied it, the more amazed he became. As he ran his finger over the end of the lure, he realized it didn't look melted after all, it looked—dissolved. As if someone had dipped it in some kind of acid. The whole back section of his lure, hooks and all was just—gone. He handed what was left of it to Tim. "Well buddy, what do you think of this?" Tim, dumbfounded, just stared.

Dr. Baker looked baffled as she examined the specimen. Turning it from side to side, she'd prod and poke, jot down a few lines in her notebook, and then start the whole process over again. After about ten minutes of this, she stopped. "Gentlemen, please don't think me rude, but as I don't really know you, or if what you're telling me is true—can I see some identification please?"

Normally, Bill would have been offended by that request, but under the circumstances, he didn't mind at all. He showed her his Fermilab digital ID. When Tim handed her his press card, she visibly grimaced. "I feel like a fool; I should have recognized your face right away, Mr. Collins. I've subscribed to Future Technology for years. You look just like your picture.

I'm sorry for the formalities, gentlemen, but I thought some of my colleagues might be trying to play a practical joke on me. Caroline, would you mind getting my dissecting kit for me? I don't know what this thing is, but I can tell you a few things about it. Do you see that gray fleshy object at the back of its mouth? It looks like a tongue, doesn't it? It's not. I think it's part of the stomach. I'll tell you for sure when I open it up. With your permission, of course, Dr. Scott. I mean, it is your fish."

"You're the expert; go for it."

Miss Tanner handed Dr. Baker the scalpel.

"Damn, this is like cutting leather with a plastic spoon. Caroline, there's a bone knife in drawer A-4, would you get it for me?"

Trying to get a better view of what he had thought was the tongue, Tim pried the fish's mouth open with his index finger. Quickly pushing his hand away, Dr. Baker exclaimed, "I wouldn't do that if I were you!"

Tim about jumped out of his shoes. "Why not?" he asked, looking at his finger as if he'd just been bitten.

Dr. Baker opened the mouth a little wider with her pencil. "I was just thinking about that fishing lure. Mr. Collins might be right about the acid. Something dissolved that lure. Unless you're carrying hydrochloric acid around in your cooler, whatever dissolved that lure must have come from inside this fish."

"Here's the bone knife, doctor." The bone knife was normally used to cut through bone and cartilage, but it would work equally well on the tough outer hide lying before them. "This is absolutely amazing!" Dr. Baker exclaimed as she peered into the unfamiliar insides of the specimen before her. "I can hardly believe what I'm seeing! Caroline, get the camera. I want to document all of this." With that, she laid open the specimen's carcass, splitting it right down the middle.

"Well, what's the verdict, Doc?" Bill asked, looking over her shoulder.

"To start with, it's not all here; most of the organs are missing. There's no heart, bladder, or kidneys. The only thing I recognize is the air sack, and it's ruptured. The air sack has expanded so much; it must have pushed the vital organs out of the mouth. It is a fish, however. But it's not like any of the fish we have around here. I've seen air sacks rupture like this before.

When I was an undergraduate at USC, I worked one summer on the 'Sea Ray.' The Sea Ray is a deep-sea research vessel. We were investigating marine life along the edge of the continental shelf, about 60 miles off the coast of California. We used to drag nets along the ocean bottom to capture marine life.

"The only problem was, as the nets were pulled to the surface, the fish they had snagged were usually dead. On dissection, we found they all had one thing in common. Their air sacks had ruptured. The sacks act like a float valve. The more air in the sack, the higher the fish rises in the water. It's similar to ballast in a submarine. As a fish rises to the surface, the pressure diminishes and the sack expands. If it rises too quickly, the sack can literally explode. This rarely happens in nature. Deep-sea divers have a similar problem with nitrogen expansion in the blood. We know it as 'the bends.'"

"Are you trying to tell us that this thing died from a change in pressure?" Bill asked, his brow furrowed.

"Yes, I'm almost sure of it."

"How deep would this fish have had to have been in order to experience this kind of pressure change?"

"It's hard to say for sure, but I'd guess somewhere in the neighborhood of eight to nine hundred fathoms would do it."

"In English, Doctor."

"One mile, maybe more!"

"Dr. Baker," Bill was getting upset now. "Are you trying to tell me that there is a hole in the lake that I've been fishing for almost four years that's a mile deep? In a lake where I've never found a spot deeper than ten feet! A lake that's really more like a large pond? Have you lost your mind?"

"No, Dr. Scott, I didn't say anything about your lake in particular. What I'm saying is this—what we have here is a fish of unknown origin, a fish that lives at great depths and pressures, and a fish that probably died from a quick change in that pressure. Caroline, would you douse the lights for me?"

"What are you going to do now, show us home movies of Sea Hunt?" Bill snipped. "I really don't think we have time for—" As the lights went out, he stopped short.

"Do you see that, Dr. Scott? Almost all the creatures that inhabit the deep oceans have one thing in common. Because of the absence of light at those depths, they are luminescent. They glow!" Sure enough, coming from the table was an eerie glow that resembled the luminous hands on a day-glow watch. The dimples scattered about the fish's body glowed brightly like tiny yellow LEDs.

"I'll be damned. If I hadn't seen this with my own eyes, I wouldn't have believed it! How could something like this get into the lake at Fermilab?" Bill said, his voice a mixture of awe and confusion.

"I assure you, I haven't the faintest idea. As to what kind of fish it is—I just don't know. The texture of the skin, the lack of internal organs—there doesn't seem to be any skeletal structure either, though that's not unusual in deep-sea creatures. All these things together add up to one big question mark."

As Caroline turned the lights back on, Bill looked at his watch. "Four thirty. We've got to get back to the lab."

"Would you allow me to keep the fish here, Dr. Scott? I'd like to run some tests on the tissues and get a DNA sample. I'm sure that either myself or one of my colleagues will be able to identify it pretty quickly. If not, I'll send a picture and description of it to the Woods Hole Oceanographic Research Center. I'm sure someone there will be able to identify it."

"That will be fine as long as you promise to call me as soon as you find out what it is." With that, they exchanged phone numbers. Bill and Tim were more puzzled than ever.

They figured they still had time to make it to the Baby Panda, so they took the chance, and things went exactly as planned. It's too bad the rest of their night didn't turn out as well.

Chapter Three

It was about 9:45 when Bill and Tim got back to Fermilab and pulled into one of the parking spaces overlooking the lake. As the headlights played across the water, Bill remarked, "I've been fishing this lake for almost four years now. If there was a hole deeper than ten or eleven feet, I'd know it."

Leaving the car, they stood on the bank and gazed down at the stars undulating in the water's reflection. A gibbous moon provided just enough illumination to detect a slight ripple creeping across the inky surface. Bill could make out the reflection of the Orion constellation in the water. The three stars in its belt shimmered like diamonds flung against a velvet background.

"I wonder what else could be in this lake," Bill said, as he bent down and picked up a small stone.

"I've been wondering about that too. Is there anything taking place here that could possibly be contaminating the lake, or fish? I mean, this is the world's most advanced particle accelerator complex. You know—cutting edge technology and all that stuff."

"I haven't noticed any of the buffalo glowing if that's what you mean," Bill said, as he tossed the stone, hitting the reflection of Betelgeuse, the red-giant star in Orion's shoulder almost dead on.

"What about the lake? Doesn't part of it lie directly over the accelerator's primary rings?"

"The lake is located in the center of the ring system. I doubt if it comes within fifty yards of the tunnels."

"Have you ever seen anybody dumping anything into the water?"

"No! Never! There are a couple of creeks that might overflow into the lake if the water got high enough. There's a spillway on the backside that connects to an underground storm drain. It was put there to keep the lake at a safe level. I don't remember ever seeing the water high enough to go over it though. There are also three smaller lakes on the grounds. Most of the research here is at the subatomic level. We don't work with plutonium or other highly radioactive isotopes. The medical center uses some radioactive material, but nothing out of the ordinary. Besides, the EPA and DOE keep us under constant surveillance. They're always running some kind of study, using us as the guinea pig. They can be a real pain in the ass sometimes."

"Listen, how sharp are you on particle physics anyway?"

"Not as sharp as I'd like to be," Tim said as they turned back toward Wilson Hall. "I mean, I know the basics; I learned a lot about the field while researching 'Magnetic Monopoles,' but most of what's going on here is way beyond me. Why?"

"Well, there's a group, including a couple of Congressmen, coming down here next Tuesday from Washington to hear Max Bruiner's lecture on what we're doing here. You might want to attend. He's one of the best I've ever heard at explaining the inner workings of the accelerator. He's the one the DOE calls when it's time to convince the Bureaucrats that we need some newfangled piece of expensive equipment. He knows this place like the back of his hand. He designed most of the collision/detection circuitry and wrote nearly half of the analysis software for the DUNE experiment."

"That's a good idea. I'll make it a point to be there. I guess the DOE has to scramble as much as any other department to get funding."

"That's an understatement. We have to fight tooth and nail. The problem with particle physics is—the public just plain doesn't understand it. It doesn't generate the glamour that many of the other sciences do. Take the James Webb Space Telescope—when people see those beautiful photographs, it's something they can appreciate and relate to. They may not understand the implications of what they're seeing, but those pictures offer proof that the telescope is doing what it was designed to do. Then there's the Mars missions. The free coverage the Rovers get while driving around on the Martian surface is worth millions in future funding. Hell, the post office even issued a stamp with the Rover on it. People could watch it on their phones. And the fact that they've kept on going all these years has added even more interest. A three-month expected life has turned into decades.

"We just don't generate that kind of glamour in particle physics. One of the greatest discoveries of the 21st century was the confirmation of neutrino oscillations and the detection of cosmic neutrinos. Did the networks cover the story? Sure, they spent about thirty seconds on it. Physicists had been searching for these signals for decades. It was a momentous discovery, but who cares besides a bunch of scientists? It's not that the networks don't want to cover us, but they know the public interest is just not there. Lady Gaga is a lot more interesting to the average person than a neutrino!"

Bill shrugged his shoulders and continued, "Particle physics takes place on such a small scale that for the most part, only physicists can appreciate it. We have pictures too, but they look like a bunch of squiggly lines drawn by a five-year-old. That's probably why the Super Conducting Super Collider was canceled. The public just didn't understand what it could do. It's a shame too. There are tremendous benefits that come from particle research.

"MRI (magnetic-resonance-imaging) is the most recognized. We can look inside a person's body with such detail it's like looking at a cutaway photograph. The MRI can detect extremely small tumors and lesions without the risk of radiation or surgery. We can image muscles and bones alike. I'm sorry; I get carried away—let's see what Tyco's doing. They should be bringing the PIP-II accelerator up to speed by now."

Upon entering Wilson Hall, they found it occupied by dozens of technicians all wearing the same light blue full-length lab coats. "You can always tell the Techs," Bill said. "If anyone ever doubts that cloning humans is not possible, just bring them in here when the big gun's being fired. These guys all look like they came out of the same test tube."

"It looks like a medical AI convention," Tim said, a big grin on his face.

Standing next to the elevator, Bill spotted one of the senior systems administrators. "What's up Don, they paying triple time or something?"

Don stared at his smart watch as he checked off items on a digital clipboard and replied without ever looking up, "Weren't you here when they made the announcement? There could be a full power test tonight. We're bringing her up to 80% right now. If everything looks good, we'll take her to 100% after midnight."

"Tim and I went to Chicago a little before noon. We just got back."

"Yeah, I heard. Something about having a fish mounted."

"Not exactly, but close enough. We're getting ready to head over to the DUNE detector. I want to see what they're targeting tonight. I hope it's less of a zoo than this place is."

"You may as well take the tunnel. You'll miss all the commotion on the first floor, and you're at the elevator anyway," Don mumbled, still not looking up from his clipboard.

"Good idea. I've only been in the beam tunnel a few times. It's a straight shot to DUNE."

Fermilab employs almost two thousand people and it seemed like one thousand nine hundred and ninety-nine of them were here. In reality, probably only about a hundred people were directly involved in tonight's test, excluding the security and maintenance people. But in the rush and furor of the moment, it seemed like a whole lot more.

"What happens next?" Tim asked, as they entered the elevator. Bill pressed the L-2 button and the elevator shuddered slightly as it began to descend to the second underground level. A female voice announced, "Level L1," from a speaker hidden behind a wall panel. About thirty seconds later the same voice declared, "Level L2," and the doors opened. There was no vibration at all to reveal that the elevator had stopped.

Exiting, Bill looked dismayed as he surveyed the situation. "Damn, there's supposed to be some self-driving carts here, but it looks as if they've already been taken."

This was the first time that Tim had ever been in the tunnel housing the new accelerator rings. It was about twenty feet wide and fifteen feet tall. The walls were made of concrete and painted a slick grayish color. There was a row of orange-colored lights running along the ceiling as far as he could see, spaced at twenty-foot intervals. They were enclosed in wire cages that hung down from the ceiling. They reminded him of the new street lamps that were showing up in great numbers around the neighborhood. The idea was that the orange color was supposed to be more pleasing to the eyes. You couldn't prove it by him though.

Lying close to the inside wall of the tunnel were the accelerator rings. They were smaller than he had imagined. The rings themselves were only about six inches in diameter. The magnets that surrounded them were huge in comparison. They were painted in bright shades of red and blue. He could see the line that carried liquid nitrogen to the magnets running in parallel just above the rings.

Turning to Tim, Bill said, "We've got about a half-mile walk ahead of us. With any luck, we'll catch a ride before we get there. I'll give you the two-dollar tour along the way."

"Where are we going anyway?" Tim asked.

"To the DUNE detector module. That's where the real action happens. If everything is running on schedule, that should happen about midnight. This is how it works in laymen's terms:

"There are several stages involved in the acceleration process. The first stage takes place in the ion source, where we generate protons from hydrogen gas. These protons are accelerated in the PIP-II linear accelerator, reaching energies of over 800 million electron volts.

"From there, the protons are injected into the Booster ring, which boosts their energy up to about eight billion electron volts. At this energy level, the protons are ready to be loaded into the Main Injector. The Main Injector is the heart of the accelerator complex.

"Protons race inside these long tubes. This is where the real action starts.

"See those square casings? Those are the superconducting magnets. There are over a thousand of them equally spaced around the ring. They bend and focus the proton beam, keeping it inside the tube. This synchrotron cranks the energy up to a little over 120 billion electron volts. The Main Injector replaced the old Main Ring. The Main Ring had been in operation since the 1970s. We used a lot of its parts in building the Main Injector. We're still running evaluation tests on it. It's actually a little newer than the Tevatron was. They work in unison. It provides a lot more protons than the old Main Ring. By providing more protons, the luminosity of the DUNE experiment is increased. The more protons we can generate, the greater the chances of meaningful collisions and neutrino production.

"Now, what you came down here to write about takes place in the last stage. The protons are sent to a target, producing a beam of neutrinos that travels underground all the way to detectors in South Dakota. The DUNE experiment is designed to study these neutrinos and answer some of the biggest questions in physics—like why the universe is made of matter instead of antimatter, and whether protons eventually decay.

"Are you following any of this?"

Tim got a serious look on his face, "Sure; well, almost. I understood everything you said up until the time we left the elevator."

"Thanks a lot. Hey, I think I hear something up ahead." Bill cupped his hands to his ears and they both stopped and listened.

"You're right. It's one of the carts."

"Dr. Scott, is that you?" the driver of the cart shouted as the cart slowed, finally coming to a halt. "I didn't expect to see you here tonight. I heard you were going to Chicago for a seafood feast."

"Hi, Kevin; are we ever glad to see you. I was about to give up on getting a ride to the detector. Do you know Tim Collins?"

"No, I've seen you around the cafeteria but I've never had the opportunity to meet you. I'm Kevin Grayson. I work with Steven on the DUNE detector. You're the journalist, aren't you? I heard we had one onboard."

"Yes, how close are they to getting the test underway?"

"I just came from the control room. The PIP-II was running at 82% when I left." With that, Kevin turned the cart around and they headed back to the DUNE detector.

Looking puzzled, Tim glanced over at Kevin and asked, "How did you know we were coming?"

"Someone saw you on a monitor as you stepped out of the elevator. I just now had a chance to come and get you. The AI-driven monitoring system in the beam tunnel keeps track of all personnel for safety. Most of the cameras are pretty well hidden. If you didn't know where to look, you'd never see them. Anytime you need a ride, use the phone in the white box on the wall next to where the carts are parked. There's a directory inside that lists the number of each department in the complex. DUNE is 21. All you had to do was call and we'd have come and got you."

"Nice of you to tell us now," Bill said. "You know, I've been the director here for almost four years and this is only the third time I've been in the beam tunnel. I've always entered DUNE from street level."

"It's nice when it's raining outside or if there's a test going on and the place is busy as hell."

As the cart picked up speed, Tim began to notice the distinctive hum that accompanied the operation of the accelerator. It came from the magnets. The power being consumed by over a thousand superconducting magnets was enormous. It was a low, almost inaudible sound. A sound that could be felt more than heard. There was something he didn't like about being around those magnets when they were in operation. There was no known danger associated with them, but it still gave him the creeps. The cart's path kept them at the outer edges of the magnetic flux. The heart of the magnet's power was generated at the center of the coils.

Not everyone could 'feel' the energy surging inside the coils, though most people could hear the hum.

Even though he had never been this close to the rings before, he could usually tell when they were being tested. As the tests reached ever-increasing power, this feeling became more pronounced. He couldn't explain it, but it caused a tingling sensation throughout his entire body. Being this close to the rings was a little frightening.

A few minutes later, they arrived at the elevator that would take them to the DUNE control room.

Kevin brought the cart to a halt. "This is where you guys get off. I'll see you in an hour or so. Tell Steven that I'm going to make a final check of the tunnel, just to be sure that our water problem hasn't returned." With that, Kevin swung the cart back into the main aisle and slowly disappeared around the bend.

"What water problem was he talking about?" Tim asked as they entered the elevator.

Bill sighed, running a hand through his hair. "That's what we'd all like to know. Three times in the last four months we've had a problem with water leaking into the tunnel. I think the first time was just before Christmas. The last time it was a real mess. The only thing we can figure is that there must be a spring located somewhere below ground. You'd think it would have been discovered when the tunnel was built, though."

He paused, frowning slightly. "Funny thing is—the water has shown up in three different areas of the tunnel. The first two times were hardly worth mentioning. Just enough water to get the rings and magnets wet over a 10 to 15-foot section. It didn't hurt anything, but it shouldn't have happened. I'd guess there was probably less than a few gallons total. But the last time, water covered almost a hundred-foot stretch. Everything was wet, and water was standing on the tunnel floor. They found a crack in the concrete where it looked like the water might be coming through, but when the repair crew broke through the wall, it was bone dry on the other side."

The whine from the cart's electric motor faded as it headed back in the same direction they had just come. Tim turned around when he heard the chime signaling that the elevator had reached the lower level. The doors opened, and a familiar voice greeted them, "Level L2."

Tim punched the lobby button, the doors closed, and they slowly began to rise, leaving behind the mysterious water problem and the humming energy of the tunnel below.

Chapter Four

This was the first time Tim had ever been to the building that housed the detector. From the outside, it was one of the most impressive structures in the complex. He couldn't wait to see what it looked like on the inside. When the elevator doors opened, he wasn't disappointed. He felt like he was stepping into Arthur C. Clarke's "2001: A Space Odyssey." Engineers, technicians, and AI-driven workstations were everywhere.

On the west-facing wall were four rows of what looked to be 80-inch ultra-high-definition monitors, continuously updating the condition of each of the thousand superconducting magnets surrounding the PIP-II accelerator's tubes. Each screen was flashing the status of the 50 magnets it was monitoring, showing them as either green for "good" or red for "problem." Other monitors displayed the coolant temperatures of the liquid nitrogen and helium surging through each magnet's frozen coils. All of the magnets were under AI-assisted computer control and could be individually shut down if necessary. Several magnets could fail, so long as no two were adjacent to each other. If that happened, the whole system would have to be brought down.

The heart of the control room revolved around a complex of quantum computers and high-performance servers. They monitored the 200-ton DUNE particle detector itself. These systems were networked directly to the Feynman Computing Center's exascale cloud. Before the advent of electronic detectors, particle collisions were photographed on glass plates. Each plate had to be individually inspected by a physicist—a slow and laborious process. In contrast, the computers humming all around him were capable of analyzing millions of collisions a second in real-time, with no human intervention at all.

These systems incorporated the latest in AI programming to separate the various particles produced in the collisions into a series of known and unknown events. Collisions that met the theoretical criteria they were looking for were separated from the rest of the data stream and recorded in special files. Physicists could review these recordings in-depth at a later date. It was evident from the congestion in this area that this was where the bulk of the action was taking place. Tim had met Dr. Tyco on several occasions, but he'd never been around him while he was at work. Watching him now reminded Tim of seeing old news clippings of General Schwarzkopf conducting operations in Desert Storm.

The wall on his left was glass from ceiling to floor. It looked out over a cavern that housed the DUNE detector. Tim walked over and peered into the chamber below. He hadn't realized just how big the 200-ton detector was until this moment. The floor of the chamber was almost five stories below him. Technicians working there resembled toy soldiers as they administered to the massive detector that towered over them.

Running through the center of the chamber, he could make out the main PIP-II beamline and one of the superconducting magnets. They had snaked along their journey only to appear at the gaping mouth of the beam tunnel. The tubes ran directly into the center of the detector. Targets made of exotic materials could be lowered into implosion chambers placed directly in the beam paths. The beams of particles circling in the tubes could be magnetically deflected into different targeting areas where the collisions were to take place. The shower of particles given off by the colliding beams is what particle physics is all about: the higher the energies, the greater the chances of discovery. The DUNE detector at Fermilab acts like a giant microscope, so powerful that it's capable of detecting the building blocks of which all matter is composed. This miraculous apparatus is the focal point of the research being conducted.

Looking along the periphery of the detector, Tim could make out the blue cooling lines that carried the liquid nitrogen and helium. Many of the devices in the detector needed to be cooled to almost absolute zero. As you near absolute zero, electrons move with little or no friction. Because there is no resistance, these devices become hundreds, sometimes thousands of times more sensitive than they would be at room temperature.

Most sections of the giant detector looked like a plumber's nightmare. Each wire was in its own shielded metal tube. These tubes were bent in every shape and angle that could be imagined. Tubes were color-coded and numbered. Large clusters of tubes were joined together with elaborately fabricated binders and marked with warnings such as "Danger – High Voltage" or "Danger – Cryogenic Liquids." On other sections, he saw warnings he didn't understand: "Danger – Proton Deflection Stream" and "Danger – Asynchronous LASER Staging Area." He knew what LASER stood for (Light Amplification by Stimulated Emission of Radiation), but what the hell was an Asynchronous Laser?

Technicians were busy at computer consoles feeding data into the detector or reading it out. There was a network of high-speed solid-state storage arrays standing at one corner of the detector, their status lights blinking in rapid patterns as they received data from the detector's sensors. This was a temporary holding area where data was identified and cataloged before being transferred to permanent cloud storage in the main computing library. The amount of data being produced by the accelerator was almost beyond imagination. Only distributed storage has enough capacity to hold the raw data before it can be processed. The neural nets comprising the sophisticated pre-analysis routines reduce this data by almost a factor of 100,000. Even then, the remaining data would fill a hundred petabyte drives after a 24-hour run. All of this was at less than half the power they would soon be working with.

Several speakers hung from the walls, and as he watched, he could hear Dr. Tyco directing two technicians sitting at a console marked "Upload DM3." He was stepping them through the process of loading a diagnostics program into the terminal's quantum drive. Apparently, there was a problem with either the terminal or the drive.

The entire chamber was bathed in the same orange-colored light that lined the ceilings of the beam tunnel. If it had been up to him, he would have used a few dozen good old LED bulbs and forgotten about all this orange crap. Looking down into the DUNE chamber was making him dizzy. Turning back towards the center of the control room, Tim noticed a huge flat-screen monitor hanging on the far wall. It must have been eight or nine feet across. This was obviously one of the new ultra-thin OLED displays. They could be hung on the wall like a picture and were only a few millimeters thick.

Only three lines of text were displayed on the monitor. The first line had bright blue letters that were easily seven or eight inches high. They read, "Elapsed Time of Run: 6 Hours - 33 Minutes - 12 Seconds." The next line was the same size and stated, "Collisions X 1000K: 0000." The last line was flashing slowly in brilliant red letters that took up the whole lower half of the screen. All it said was, "88% Power." The accelerator was operating at 88% of its full power potential. He remembered one of the technicians saying earlier that they might go to full power tonight. It's a good thing they got back when they did because it looked as if they were well on their way.

Chapter Five

Back in the beam tunnel, Kevin drove the self-driving cart slowly down the corridor, his eyes trained on the walls and floors, looking for any sign of water. He couldn't help but notice the low, resonant humming coming from the vicinity of the accelerator tubes adjacent to him. He wondered if it was being produced by the superconducting magnets or by the tubes themselves. He didn't like being so close to the rings when the PIP-II accelerator was in operation. The cart wasn't moving much faster than a walk. At this pace, it would take him almost an hour to travel the four miles of tunnel stretching out before him.

It was spooky being in the tunnel alone. The LED lighting gave everything a strange, clinical glow. A flashlight was attached to the dash, just in case of a blackout. He felt a little claustrophobic. Because the tunnel was a perfect circle, he could only see about twenty yards ahead before the curvature cut off his line of sight. It was boring too. If not for the identifying markers on the wall and the three elevators that led to the upper floors, you wouldn't have the slightest idea where you were. All three of the elevators were located in the southwest section of the tunnel. The first to the last was separated by about a mile and a half of tunnel. This was the section he was in now. The really boring part of the tunnel was the stretch between the Computing Center and the DUNE detector. It was two and a half miles of nothing. At least the silence was broken by the hum of the accelerator and the sound of the tires as they rolled on the concrete floor.

Suddenly, Kevin felt an intense pain in the right side of his chest. He had never felt anything so excruciatingly painful. His first thought was, I've been shot. His left hand instinctively pressed against the pain, hoping to appease it if he pushed hard enough. It didn't work. He looked down and saw blood oozing between his fingertips and slowly spreading out around his palm. In his confusion, the cart veered into the concrete buffer that held the tubes up and off of the tunnel floor. It stopped abruptly, throwing him into the steering wheel where he banged his face. He bit his lip. Blood was now dripping from his nose and mouth, as well as from his chest.

He had enough sense to look around him. If someone—some lunatic—had shot him, he needed to get away, fast. Get to safety and help. He floored the cart. It lurched forward, but its top speed was only five, maybe six miles an hour. If someone wanted to, they could easily catch him without even breaking into a sweat. He didn't see or hear anything. Terrorist, or maniac, raced through his mind, as he sped on through the tunnel. Then he realized he was still going in the same direction he was traveling in when he was shot. He might be running right back into whoever had shot him. He'd gone 40 or 50 yards and nobody had jumped out at him yet, so he continued. He looked at the wall, trying to remember what the last marker had been. Thirty-one, he thought to himself. The Computing Center's elevator is just a few minutes ahead. From there, he could get help. Fermilab has one of the most advanced medical centers in the Midwest, but they didn't have much of an emergency center. They specialized in MRI imaging and cancer research. Still, with over two thousand people working here, there was always someone in need of emergency medical attention.

"I wonder if any of the doctors have any experience treating gunshot wounds?" He was talking to himself—out loud. He needed to stay conscious. Hearing the sound of his own voice helped. The pain in his chest had subsided into a dull but throbbing ache. Only a few minutes passed before he saw the lights of the Computing Center's elevator. He stopped the cart next to the elevator and looked for the phone box. He was glad they didn't hide the phones like they did the cameras. So this is what it feels like to be shot, he thought, as he staggered out of the cart. He was afraid to look down at his hand, but he did and soon wished he hadn't. Blood was everywhere. His lab coat was soaked. Blood was all over the cart, even on the backrest. He hadn't thought about the bullet going clean through him, but it must have. The white of the seat's backrest was now streaked with dark crimson splotches. Seeing all this blood and knowing it was his, was making him nauseous.

I can't believe this is happening, he thought to himself. I must be dreaming. But he knew he wasn't. I've got to pull myself together. Get to the phone. Get help. His vision was beginning to blur. He set his sights on the phone box and pushed himself in its direction. He opened the box. There was a handset and keypad. On the inside of the door was a directory with the extensions of the various departments. Two of the names were written in red, MEDICAL #1 and SECURITY #2. He pressed #2. The phone rang in the Security office.

"Security, Sgt. Madison speaking."

"This is Kevin Grayson;" (coughing up the blood in his throat) "I'm in the beam tunnel next to the elevator, under the Computing Center, Level L2. I've been shot, and I'm bleeding badly. I need a—doctor." He was blacking out.

"Captain Rider! We have a situation," Sgt. Madison shouted into the other office. "Line one, Sir."

"This is Captain Rider. What's your problem?"

"I've been shot, and I need help. I'm in L-2, under the Computing Center."

"Who is this?

Kevin Grayson. I've got to sit down I'm dizzy—I'm—

"We're on our way. Was more than one person involved in the shooting? Mr. Grayson? Mr. Grayson!"

Kevin stumbled backward, nearly falling into the cart. Though he was pressing as hard as he could against the pain in his chest, it wasn't doing much good. His right lung had collapsed from the gaping holes in both sides of it, and when he tried to breathe, blood was being sucked into his lungs along with the air. He couldn't see it, but the back of his shirt was soaked in blood. There was even a hole going through the backrest of the cart. In a matter of minutes, he wouldn't be able to breathe at all. He lay back, sprawling across the seat, gasping for air. It seemed like forever, but in reality it was only a few minutes, before the elevator doors opened. Three security guards and two paramedics stepped out. The paramedics immediately began working on Kevin. They administered CPR, attached two IVs to his arm, and a cardiac monitor to his chest. What he needed most now was oxygen, and then he'd need blood, lots of blood. He was fitted with an oxygen mask, but the blood he needed would have to wait until he could be taken back to Fermilab's hospital. The saline solution would have to do for now.

Of the three elevators servicing the L-2 level, Federal officers had already secured two of them. The third would be secure within a matter of minutes. Next would be the job of finding, and eliminating, any intruders. The security staff at Fermilab was top-notch. Since the DOE was responsible for managing the facilities and protecting visiting dignitaries and scientists, Federal authorities provided on-site security. For the most part, these were seasoned ex-military men under a competent commander, with access to advanced surveillance, biometric scanners, and anything else they might deem necessary. Each was picked because he was the best at what he did. Guarding a multi-billion-dollar facility was an enormous responsibility. These guys didn't take it lightly.

As the men were being deployed, Captain Rider was deep in thought. Of all the nights to have problems, why tonight? Had someone been monitoring the progress of the accelerator? Did they know that we might be going to full power tonight? From a terrorist point of view, this was probably the perfect night for an attack. What part did Dr. Grayson play in this? Did he surprise them, or was he just in the wrong place at the wrong time? What was he doing in the beam tunnel anyway? Was someone trying to sabotage the project?

His plan was to first seal off all exits to the beam tunnel. There were three elevators and two escape hatches leading to the surface. He'd do this by stationing a man at each exit. Next, he'd send three-person search teams to investigate the tunnel.

The teams were to leave one man at the base of each elevator, while the other two would split up, one going left and the other right. Anyone still in the tunnel would be trapped somewhere between the team members. Upon finding an intruder, they would seal him off, taking whatever steps were necessary to control the situation. They were in constant radio contact with each other and with headquarters. Each man had a digital map of the tunnel and knew from the wall markings exactly where he was in respect to the tunnel and the other men. It took less than twenty minutes to cover the area between the three elevators. That's where they hoped to find their quarry, but they didn't. Not a hint of a person, no shell casings, no smell of gunpowder. The confinement of the tunnel should have left a powder smell lingering for hours. Nothing seemed unusual. Nothing, except the scattered splotches of blood that clearly defined the path the cart had made as it zigzagged along the floor.

"We know that Dr. Grayson's been shot," came Captain Rider's voice in their headsets. "What we don't know is who did it. It could be one person or several. There's a good chance that whoever shot him is still in the tunnel. I want you to check every possible place that someone could squeeze into or stand behind. We don't know what their reason is for being here, but if they were serious enough to shoot someone, they were probably trying to sabotage the accelerator. Be on the lookout for anything that might resemble a bomb. If you see anything you can't identify, locate the nearest ID marker and I'll send an explosives expert down to check it out. Be very careful. One person has already been wounded. We don't want any more casualties."

"Captain," Johnson here. "Hanson and I are at midpoint, between Wilson Hall and the DUNE detector. We haven't seen a thing."

"Same here Sir. This is Tom Blake. I've just met up with Lieutenant Wolf. It's clear between Wilson Hall and the Computing Center. It will take the two officers covering the outer perimeter of the tunnel at least half an hour to meet midway. Should we stay put until we hear from them, or return to our original positions?"

"Listen up; I want all of you except those men covering the outer perimeter to go back to your original starting positions. Check every inch of that tunnel along the way. I've put in a call for a bomb-sniffing drone. We're not going to take any chances. They'll be here in about an hour."

"Hanson here Sir, we're starting back."

"Blake Sir; Lieutenant Wolf and I are heading back too."

"Captain, this is Lieutenant Lane. I'm in the outer loop at marker L-174. I figure I'm about a mile and a quarter from midpoint. Nothing out of the ordinary so far."

"Same here Captain, this is Terrance. The Lieutenant is making a little better time than I am. I'm at L-315; I've probably got a little less than a mile and a half to go before midpoint."

"Let me know when you meet. You can come back together. Remember, what you're looking for will probably be small. Plastic can do a lot of damage and it doesn't take up much space."

"Captain, Johnson here again. I was just thinking, we didn't find anyone in the tunnel, and I don't see how anybody could have gotten by us. What if Dr—what's his name, wasn't shot by a person at all? Maybe he tripped a booby trap of some kind. That would explain why we haven't found anyone in the tunnel. Assuming they're not in the outer section that is."

"That's a possibility Johnson. You heard him, men. Be on the lookout for anything that might be part of a booby trap or triggering device…a cord possibly, or a wire, anything out of the ordinary. Be especially careful around the area where Dr. Grayson was attacked. Get back to me when you've reached your starting positions."

Chapter Six

Tim stood by the door when a young engineer burst in, shouting that terrorists were in the beam tunnel and three people had been killed. Soon, a group of seven or eight wide-eyed technicians gathered around. At the same time, an announcement boomed over the intercom, warning people not to use the elevators. Tim didn't recognize the voice, but it indicated a problem with one of the cryogenic lines and that both the elevators and the beam tunnel were off-limits. Everyone should use the stairs for the time being.

Tim hurried back to the wall overlooking the detector chamber. The mouth of the beam tunnel was clearly visible below. Nothing looked out of place, and the technicians working next to the tunnel didn't seem worried about anything. He wondered if they had heard the announcement.

The engineer was busy telling the crowd how the state police and National Guard had been called in because there weren't enough security guards to deal with the situation. He didn't know exactly how many people had been wounded, but he was sure that at least three had been killed.

Something here didn't wash. Tim pushed his way to the front of the crowd and began questioning the engineer, "Were you there when they brought the dead and wounded out of the tunnel?"

"Well, no, but I talked with someone who was. He was also there when they stormed the elevators, guns drawn."

"Doesn't it sound a little strange that there could be an armed conflict going on and we wouldn't have heard any gunfire? I thought there were cameras in the beam tunnel. Has anybody seen anything on the monitors?" The small crowd looked puzzled as they shrugged their shoulders.

The fact was, everyone had been too busy working to have been paying any attention to the tunnel monitor. Now they all started looking. There was only one monitor, and it switched every few seconds between each of the three elevators. As they watched, they saw two armed men standing in front of the doors, looking like they were guarding them. One of the self-driving carts could be seen next to the Computing Center's elevator, and it looked as though something had been spilled all over the seats. Because of the orange overhead lighting, it didn't look like blood. It looked more like someone had spilled a pitcher of chocolate milk all over it. It didn't appear red at all in the camera's eye.

"Well, that's what he told me—I didn't actually see it myself. Didn't you hear that announcement? The elevators and beam tunnel are off-limits."

"I heard an announcement, but I didn't hear anything about anyone being killed. It said there was a problem with one of the cryogenic lines."

"I just came from the Computing Center, and everybody there is talking about it. It started about forty-five minutes ago. Bill Ramsey was standing next to the elevator when two paramedics brought Dr. Grayson up on a stretcher. He was covered in blood. There was even blood on his shoes. Bill heard one of the paramedics say that Kevin had been shot to death and that security officers were sealing off the tunnel and looking for more casualties."

By this time, Dr. Tyco had joined the group. "Do you guys see that monitor over there on the wall? We are at 94%. That's only six points away from full power. Now get the hell back to your stations! I don't want to hear another word about anything that doesn't directly concern this test. Is that clear? And you, Mr.—"

"Boyer, sir, James Boyer."

"Mr. Boyer, is there any reason for you to be in this building other than to cause a commotion and generally screw things up?"

"A—well—no sir."

"Then I suggest that you get the hell out of here before I use you as one of the targets in the detector."

"Yes sir, I'm leaving right now."

"And Mr. Boyer—don't let me see you around here again unless you have a very, very good reason for being here."

"Yes sir, I have—I mean, if I'm here, I will have—"

"Just go, Mr. Boyer!"

"Yes sir; goodbye, sir."

With that confrontation over, everyone returned to their work. The monitor on the wall clicked over to 95%. Before Tim could do anything else, the intercom sparked to life again, "Tim Collins, report to the security office please. Tim Collins, report to the security office."

Now what the hell's going on? Tim thought. He wanted to be here when full power was achieved, not sitting in some stupid security office. He stormed out of the control room and looked for the elevator that would take him to the ground floor. Then he remembered—no elevators. The stairs were right next to the elevators, and both were just a few steps away. Standing directly in front of the elevator were two men dressed in military fatigues. One of them looked right at him. Then, glancing at a picture he'd pulled from his pocket, he said, "Mr. Collins?"

Approaching him, Tim answered, "Yes," astonished that they seemed to be waiting for him.

"Mr. Collins, I'm Sgt. Madison of the Illinois National Guard. I've been ordered to accompany you to the security office in Wilson Hall. Captain Rider would like to talk to you, sir."

"What about, Sgt.?"

"I don't have any idea, sir, you'll have to ask him. I'm just supposed to take you there. Would you please step into the elevator? A car is waiting for us."

"I thought the elevators were off-limits?" asked Tim.

"Not to us."

A few minutes later, they were on their way to Wilson Hall. As Tim walked into the security office, Captain Rider rushed over to shake his hand.

"Am I ever glad to see you. We have a problem."

"I heard; a leaky pipe or something. I'm not a plumber; what do you need me for?"

"I'm afraid it's more serious than that, Mr. Collins."

Tim couldn't believe it. Maybe there really were terrorists in the tunnel.

"We have had a breach of security, and there's been a shooting in the beam tunnel. We don't know what else might have taken place; I have three armed teams in the tunnel right now. We've also had a casualty. Dr. Grayson was killed. Since you are our, how can I put this, our in-house press agent, we'd like you to handle the media when they come around to investigate."

That really pissed Tim off. "I'm nobody's press agent. I'm a journalist, and I'm here to document the research that's going on, not to play nursemaid to a bunch of reporters."

"I realize that, Tim. May I call you Tim? But this is a very serious matter, and I don't want the press to get any wrong ideas."

"What kind of ideas might that be?" Tim asked, glaring at the head of security as he fumbled nervously with the stylus he'd pulled from his shirt pocket.

"There are projects underway here that are vital to our national defense as well as to the scientific world in general. Scientists and dignitaries come and go all the time; I'm sure you've seen and talked to many of them during your stay here. I wouldn't want them to feel concerned about their welfare while they're visiting our facilities. This is a terrible tragedy, granted, but it's also a fluke that I'm sure will never happen again. Just the same, things need to be brought to light in the proper way."

"You're doing a piss-poor job of that so far," Tim sneered. "There was an engineer over in DUNE just a few minutes ago telling everyone that there had been a riot in the beam tunnel and three people had been killed."

"That just goes to prove my point," Rider retorted. "What I need right now is someone who can stop this kind of misinformation before it starts. That someone has to be familiar with both Fermilab and the media. You, Tim, are the only person I know of who meets both of these requirements."

"This isn't what I really want to do but, under the circumstances, I guess I could help you out...on one condition."

"What's that?" Rider asked.

"I want to know everything that happens, as it happens. No bullshit, and no need-to-know secret agent crap. I'll handle the press as long as you're straight with me. Deal?"

"Deal."

"Tell me about the shooting; was there more than one person involved?"

"No, we don't think so. This is probably the act of one man, most likely a disgruntled employee. But we're not taking any chances. We're investigating this matter as if it really is a terrorist attack. Of course, we'd like this to be played very low-key to the media. If there really is a threat, we'll be more than happy to let you expose it. We just don't want to alarm anyone unnecessarily. I'll know more about the situation as soon as my men report back."

As Tim turned to leave, he asked, "Can you get me back to the DUNE building? They're probably close to full power by now, and I still have a job to do there. I'll also need a file on Dr. Grayson."

"I'll have Sgt. Madison drive you back. The file will be on your desk by 7:30 tomorrow morning, along with a report on anything else we find out tonight. There's a press conference being called for 3:00 PM tomorrow. That will give us over fifteen hours to pursue our investigation. I'd like you to attend a 10:00 AM briefing tomorrow morning."

"Fine. I'll see you then."

Tim started to leave, then, half mumbling to himself, he said, "Wait a minute."

"I'm sorry, did you say something?"

"Who did you say was killed in the beam tunnel?"

"Dr. Grayson," Rider said.

"That wouldn't have been Kevin Grayson, would it?"

Captain Rider shuffled through some papers on his desk. Finding the one he was looking for, he answered, "That's right. Dr. Kevin Grayson. Did you know him?"

"I just left him in the beam tunnel not much more than an hour or two ago. He gave Bill Scott and me a ride to DUNE in one of the carts. Someone had noticed us walking on one of the monitors, and Kevin decided to give us a lift. We were on our way to the detector from Wilson Hall. He let us out at the elevator and said he was going back into the tunnel to check for water; something about a leak, I think. I just can't believe that he was the one that was killed."

"I logged the time of his call on the emergency line. It was exactly 87 minutes ago. Did you know him very well?"

"No, that was the first time I'd ever met him. That's why it took a while for his name to ring a bell. I think he might have been a friend of Bill's though."

"Maybe you'd better have Bill come in tomorrow, too. He might remember seeing something that could help us. I'll see you both in the morning."

Tim left the office in a fog, forgetting even to close the door. Knowing how close he had been to the murder left a very bad taste in his mouth. Things had happened so fast, and there was so much going on, it hadn't even dawned on him that he might have been the one killed. On the way back to DUNE, Tim didn't say a single word. He was completely lost in his own thoughts.

Chapter Seven

"I'm hit!" The words rang in the team's headsets. Everyone stopped dead in their tracks. Then silence as several seconds passed.

"Who said that?" Rider's voice crackled.

"It sounded like Blake, Captain."

"Blake! Blake!" The Captain waited, as more seconds passed with still no answer.

"Blake's in trouble. Everybody converge on the section between Wilson Hall and the Computing Center. Lieutenant Wolf, you should be the closest, so watch your step."

The next few minutes were extremely nerve-wracking. With the curvature of the tunnel limiting the officers' view, they didn't know what they might run into. They were almost upon their fallen comrade before they realized it.

"I see him, Captain," Wolf yelled into his microphone as he stopped to catch his breath. "Something's wrong. He's not moving. He's about 15 yards in front of me. It looks like he's slumped over something."

"I see him too!" It was Don Nelson. He had been guarding the elevator at the Computing Center. "He's motionless. His gun's lying on the floor. This is really weird. It's like he's suspended in mid-air. His feet are touching the ground, but there's no weight on them. Something else is holding him up, but for the life of me, I don't know what it could be."

They were standing beside Blake now, frantically looking around, but there was no one else to be seen. "It's Wolf, Sir. I think he's dead! I'm not getting a pulse. There's blood on his vest and on the floor. There's a hole in it too. I thought these things were bulletproof. And Nelson's right; he's just hanging here. It's like he's floating. I can wave my arm over his head. There's no wire holding him up. Nelson, grab his arm and let's see if we can move him."

"He ain't moving, Captain, and we're pulling pretty hard."

"Get the hell out of there. Somebody's got to be in there with you. He didn't shoot himself!"

"One second, Captain," Wolf said. "Let's try pushing him forward. You grab his arms and I'll push and lift on his vest."

Blake's body dropped to the floor with a thud. Both men jumped back. Their eyes were wide open, but they didn't see a thing.

"Let's get him the hell out of here," Nelson said, as he motioned to Wolf who was still trying to figure out what had been holding Blake up. "We're heading back to the elevator, Captain, bringing Blake with us."

"Get back there as fast as you can. The medics will be waiting for you when you get there."

"Listen up everyone, get your asses back to the elevators and stay there. Don't let anybody into the beam tunnel without my authorization."

The phone in the security office rang loudly. Captain Rider, startled, jumped back. "Damn, what else can be happening?" He picked up the phone, "Security, Rider speaking."

"Hello, Captain Rider. This is Dr. Tailor. You asked me if I could determine the caliber of the bullet that killed Dr. Grayson. Well, I've performed a preliminary autopsy scan, but I don't believe it was a bullet that killed him."

"What's that supposed to mean? Everybody said he was shot. Hell, he even said he was shot. I talked to him myself."

"He probably thought he was shot. When you first look at it, it looks like a gunshot wound. But there's no way that a bullet could have caused the damage he sustained."

"Are you positive?"

"Absolutely, and for several reasons. A bullet expends energy when it hits muscle and bone. There are always tears in the surrounding tissue. Two of his ribs were punctured. A bullet would have fragmented when it struck a rib and there would have been shrapnel and bone fragments in the wound. It was clean. The exit hole should also have been larger than the entrance, but it wasn't.

Whatever went through his body took the tissues with it when it exited. The ribs didn't shatter. They looked more like a hole had been drilled through them and the bone removed. It reminded me of an apple corer. It's as though somebody took a 1/2 inch core sample out of his chest.

There wasn't the slightest indication of any trauma, anywhere. Whatever passed through his body did so without disturbing so much as a hair."

"I don't know what to make of what you're telling me, Doctor. If it wasn't a bullet, then what the hell was it?"

"I wish I knew. I've never seen anything like it before. I'd like to call a colleague in Batavia and get a second opinion, maybe run the data through the AI for anomaly detection."

"No, not yet; I'd rather keep this under wraps for now. Besides—another man has just been killed."

"You've got to be kidding. What's going on here? Two deaths in less than an hour! I suppose he died in the same manner?"

"I don't know. I want you to do an autopsy just as soon as they get him there. I need answers, Doc, not speculations. Answers! People are dying! It's bad enough that I don't know who's killing them; I don't even know what's killing them! Get me some answers!"

Captain Rider hung up the phone and tried to relax. "He's right. What the hell is going on here?"

Chapter Eight

Ninety-six percent! The monitor in DUNE clicked over another number, but the technicians were too busy to notice. Things were really beginning to get hectic as the accelerator neared full power. There were hundreds of controls to tweak and gauges to monitor. Fortunately, the computers took care of the majority of the mundane tasks. But people were still needed to make sure the computers were doing what they were supposed to. In the future, neural networks would take over this monitoring process completely.

The last thing that Steven Tyco needed at this critical juncture was for a security officer to interrupt his concentration.

"I don't have time for this now," he told the officer as they stepped outside of the control room in order to gain some privacy.

"I'm sorry," answered Sgt. Madison, "but there've been some things happening that may cause the Director to have to call off your test. Things that are...out of our control."

"Are you crazy? We're at 96% right now. I can't just shut this thing down like it was a giant video game. What could possibly be wrong that could cause us to cancel now?"

"There has been an incident in the beam tunnel. We think at least one, and possibly even more people might be involved. A colleague of yours has been killed, along with a security officer."

"Who was killed, Sgt.?"

"I'm sorry, Sir, I'm not at liberty to impart that information. You'll need to ask Captain Rider."

"Very well, but I still don't think that shutting down the accelerator before we have completed our tests is a good idea. Can't you place guards at the entrances to the beam tunnel and the detector?"

"We already have. There are two men about thirty yards inside of each entrance, just out of view of your technicians. You've probably already heard that the elevators are off-limits. I'm not ordering you to stop the test yet, Sir. I have every reason to believe that we can get this situation under control. If things should deteriorate, I'll need your cooperation in getting the PIP-II shut down and under wraps. How long will it take you to close everything down and clear the building if an emergency situation arises?"

"That depends. I guess about an hour. That's a best-case scenario though. It could take upwards of two if we're having trouble, especially if it's with the injector."

"That's what I needed to know. I'll report this back to Captain Rider. You can continue with your testing, but if it becomes necessary for you to stop, I'll expect you to do so as quickly as possible."

"I understand, Sgt. I didn't realize that people had been killed. As far as I knew, the only problem was that something was wrong with one of the cryogenic lines. Now, if you no longer need me, I'll get back to the control room."

"Thank you for your patience. We're doing our best to contain this problem."

With that, Sgt. Madison turned and headed anxiously back to Wilson Hall.

Captain Rider was picking up some papers he'd dropped when Sgt. Madison walked into his office.

"I have the information you requested, Captain. The accelerator can be offline and the building evacuated in at most, two hours, and at best, one."

"Good. How are the tests going?"

"Dr. Tyco didn't give any indication one way or the other. I gathered that there had not been any problems though. He definitely didn't want to stop."

"Well, if he didn't complain about any problems, I doubt that anything that's happened in the tunnel has affected the tests. Are they still going to full power?"

"They were at 96% when I left. Yes, I'd say so."

The telephone rang, interrupting their conversation. "Security, Rider speaking."

"Captain Rider, this is Dr. Tailor. I haven't completely finished with my examination, but I've found some things that I thought you should know about."

"Fine, Doctor; I'm glad you called. I'm going to put you on the speakerphone. What can you tell me?"

"The cause of this man's death was almost identical to Dr. Grayson's. There was one major difference though. Whatever killed Dr. Grayson passed through his body in a perfectly straight line. Your security officer had multiple wounds, but all coming from a single source."

"I'm not following you. What do you mean by multiple wounds from a single source?"

"This is hard to explain over the phone. It would be much easier if I could show you. Could you stop by my—"

"I can't leave now, Doctor, you'll have to explain it to me. Just go slowly."

"OK. Let me start from the beginning. I don't know what the object was that killed these men, but for simplicity's sake, I'll call it a ring."

"You've lost me already, Doctor. How does a ring kill anybody? Why not a bullet?"

"It's not like a bullet at all. It's like—a ring. It leaves a perfectly circular hole and—"

"OK, OK, I've got the picture."

"All right, this ring penetrated the officer's vest from the front and traveled approximately three inches into his body cavity where it stopped. The officer probably thought he'd been shot. At this point, he must have turned to his right because the ring moved laterally inside of his body. Only this time, it didn't cut at all. It tore. I don't know how this ring could move at right angles through the body, but that's the trail it left. Each time it moved in a direction other than forward, it tore the tissue in a very fine slit. Just like a ring or disk would do if it were being pushed sideways.

It obviously didn't have sharp edges, because the tissues were stretched until they tore. When the ring moved forward, it cut, or dissolved everything it touched. Remember me saying it looked as if a core sample had been taken? In a forward direction, there are no tears or strained tissues at all, just a hole about the size of a dime. At one point, it even went up, again tearing the tissues as it traveled until it stopped, apparently lodged under the right shoulder blade. The strange thing is, it exited out of the front of the body, only a few inches from where it had entered. But it traveled almost thirteen inches in between, including several 60-degree or greater turns."

"How sure are you of all of this, Doctor?"

"Quite sure. The only thing I'm not positive of is which hole was the entry point and which was the exit. Since there was no trauma to the surrounding tissues or clothing, I can't be certain if I'm looking at an entry wound or the exit."

"Thank you, Doctor. I appreciate all you've done, especially on such short notice. I did take your advice about getting a second opinion. I have a forensics expert, a Professor Riley, coming in from Chicago. I'd like for you to assist him if you don't mind. He'll be here in a couple of hours."

"I'd be happy to, Sir. I'll have everything ready for him when he arrives."

"In the meantime, I'd like you to document everything you've found and send it to me as soon as possible. I'll get back to you when Professor Riley arrives. Goodbye, Doctor."

"Goodbye, Captain Rider."

"Well, Sgt.? You heard...what do you think could have killed those men?"

"It's the strangest thing I've ever heard of, Sir. It almost sounds—I mean—the way this ring or whatever it is seemed to stop and then start up again in a different direction. It's as though it were being controlled by something."

"Something is right," said Captain Rider. "Listen, what if this 'ring' wasn't moving at all? What if these men just happened to run into it?"

"I don't understand, Captain."

"Suppose that there was a spike suspended in the air somehow, magnetically maybe. Someone comes along and runs into it. Could we tell from looking at the wound whether it was the spike that was moving, or the man? We assume that whatever it was that killed these people was moving because that's usually the case. How could anything make right-angle turns inside of a body without bouncing off of something first?

What if it was the man that was moving—while the object remained stationary? Wouldn't that produce wounds similar to the ones Dr. Tailor was describing?"

"If it was solidly anchored to something, sure, but nothing was seen. Besides, it would take a hell of a lot of pressure to drive a spike clean through someone!"

"Or the spike would have to be unbelievably sharp!"

"See if this makes any sense," Captain Rider said.

"Do you remember when Wolf and Nelson said that Blake's body seemed to be floating in mid-air? The first time they tried to move him, he wouldn't budge an inch?

Dr. Tailor said that the ring had lodged under his shoulder blade. Maybe whatever killed these men was stationary. Maybe this ring was inside Officer Blake and wedged under his shoulder blade, holding him up. Dr. Grayson was traveling much faster in the cart than Officer Blake would have been since he was walking. Dr. Grayson would have passed through this ring, (or it through him), before he even realized it. But Officer Blake might have stopped as the ring cut into him. At that point, he may have tried to turn and run. Trying to get away from what he must have thought was a sniper.

The ring, being inside of him was immobile and wouldn't let him go. As he moved, it tore him up from the inside, finally killing him. In death, it held him up, lodged under his shoulder blade until Wolf and Nelson lifted him over it. Why it seems to cut in one direction and not in the other is beyond me. I know this sounds fantastic, but I'm just trying to come up with something that might explain what Doctor Tailor was talking about. I think I might know of a way to find what killed those men. I have an idea."

"What's that, Captain?"

"I'm going to make a ring detector."

"How are you going to detect something when we don't even know what it is we're looking for?"

"True, we don't know what it is, but if it's a stationary object, I think I might know of a way to find it."

"How's that, Captain?"

"With a balloon—or rather, several balloons."

"You have definitely lost me now, Sir."

"Sgt., I want you to go down to the gift shop. I'm pretty sure I've seen balloons in there."

"Yes Sir, they say Fermilab and have a picture of the atom on them. They're a big hit with kids. I think there's also a tank of helium gas used to blow them up."

"I want you to blow up about 100 of them. Then tie them together, so they won't float away."

"I'll do it right now, Captain. Should I bring them up here?"

"No, wait. I have a better idea. Bring all of the balloons you can find along with the helium tank over to the elevator in the Computing Center. We'll blow them up there. I'm going to get someone in here to answer the phones. Can you meet me in the Computing Center in about twenty minutes?"

"Yes Sir, twenty minutes at the Computing Center."

After making arrangements for the security office to be staffed, Captain Rider headed for the Computing Center. Along the way, he picked up a few additional items: some duct tape, string, and the frame from a reclining lawn chair that was sitting on the patio outside of the cafeteria. These should come in handy, he thought to himself, as he opened his rear car door and placed his bounty in the backseat. If this doesn't work, some people here will be ready to have me committed. He was still thinking about how he was going to assemble his ring detector as he started his car.

It only took a minute or two to reach the Computing Center. He found the place abuzz with people. The test was still going full-bore and data was streaming into the center's computers. Two officers were standing in front of the elevators. When they saw him, they looked at each other, then back at him. He figured they must be wondering why he was carrying a lawn chair frame under one arm and a bunch of duct tape and string in the other.

Wait until Sgt. Madison shows up with the balloons, they'll think we've both gone off the deep end!

"Captain Rider?" asked one of the guards, a look of astonishment on his face.

It was Lieutenant Wolf, and Nelson. They were the two officers who had found Blake. At least something was going right. These were the officers he wanted to see.

"Have you seen Sgt. Madison?" the Captain asked.

"No Sir, is he supposed to be here?"

"Yes, he's bringing the balloons."

They looked at each other, and then back at the Captain, "Balloons, Sir?"

"I'll explain later. I have an idea as to what might have killed Officer Blake and Dr. Grayson. Well, I don't really know what killed them, exactly, but I may know how to detect it. It's complicated. Did you see anything unusual when you found Officer Blake?"

"Seeing someone hanging in midair was unusual enough," answered Norton. "Other than that, I didn't see anything else out of the ordinary."

Lieutenant Wolf was fidgeting, staring down at the Captain's feet, almost as if he didn't really want to say anything. Then he blurted out, "Sir, I did see something. It was just after Blake's body fell to the floor."

"What was it, Lieutenant?"

"Damned if I know. We grabbed Blake and started running towards the elevator. I just wanted to get the hell out of there. But as I looked back over my shoulder, back to where Blake's body had been hanging, I thought I saw something floating in the air...something very small. I've been telling myself that it was just my imagination. I was scared. I half expected someone to jump out from behind one of those concrete dividers and shoot me at any moment. Seeing Blake hanging there like that, it had my mind racing. But I did see something, something that didn't belong there.

Don't ask me to describe it though. All I can tell you is—it was just this tiny little silver spot suspended in the air. If I hadn't been looking right at it, I'd have probably never even noticed it."

"There's Sgt. Madison now, Captain." Nelson pointed towards the entrance. Sgt. Madison was carrying a big box of something. The top of what looked like an oxygen tank was sticking up out of it. The building was full of engineers, but they barely noticed him as he made his way to the elevators.

"I brought the whole box of balloons, Captain, and the helium tank. There must be a couple of hundred at least."

"Good. I don't think we'll need that many, but you never know. I picked up the metal frame from a lawn chair; I think I can use it to hold the balloons. I want to make a square shape big enough for a man to hide behind. Let's gather our equipment and get down to the beam tunnel. Officers, I'd like you to go with us. I'll send whoever is guarding the beam tunnel now back here to take your place."

With that, they entered the elevator and pushed the L-2 button. The familiar voice announced each floor as they descended. In about 30 seconds, the elevator stopped. Level L2. They were in the beam tunnel.

Chapter Nine

The two officers stationed in the beam tunnel were surprised when the elevator doors opened and Captain Rider stepped out. They didn't know what to think when they saw his lawn chair frame and assorted whatnots. Looking around, Captain Rider told the officers to take the elevator back to the main level and not to let anyone pass. "Be sure and keep an ear to your comms," he said. "We may still have intruders in the beam tunnel."

"Yes, Sir, we'll be ready if you need us."

With that, the two officers stepped into the elevator, leaving the four men alone in the tunnel.

It was one thing to hear the reports of what had happened earlier in the beam tunnel; to actually be there brought about entirely different feelings. Something had killed two people, and they had no idea what it was. Something strange was happening in this tunnel—strange and deadly—and the low hum of the accelerator was enough to try the nerves of anyone.

Captain Rider looked at Lieutenant Wolf and Officer Norton. "You haven't heard the results of Blake and Grayson's autopsies. While the Sgt. fills you in, I'm going to assemble what I hope will help us find the cause of their deaths."

With that, Captain Rider took the lawn chair frame, duct tape, string, balloons, and helium tank over to where the carts were parked. Within about fifteen minutes, the object he had envisioned started to take shape. By the time Sgt. Madison was finished, the "detector" was assembled.

"We give up; what is it?" The security officers looked dumfounded as they stared at the contraption Captain Rider had jerry-rigged. It looked like something a kid might have thought up.

The rectangular frame of the fold-out lawn chair was approximately 30 inches wide by 5 feet long. Tied to one side, covering the entire surface of the lawn chair, were several dozen helium-filled balloons. The balloons were tied side by side with no gaps between them. The frame could be held in an upright position by grasping the legs that were attached to the side opposite the balloons. With the frame in this position, a man could stand behind it and be completely hidden from view. The whole thing only weighed a few pounds.

"You did a fine job, Captain, now, what the hell is it?" Even Sgt. Madison was at a loss as to what the Captain had built.

"This may end up being even more stupid than it looks, but if I'm right, this might be a safe way to find out what killed those men. I think there's something in this tunnel that's suspended in mid-air and Officer Blake and Doctor Grayson ran into it. I also think Lieutenant Wolf may have glimpsed it when he looked behind him as they were extracting Blake's body. I have serious doubts that these men were the victims of a shooting. Not after what Doctor Tailor told me. He alluded that something in the shape of a ring had killed them. I don't know what the hell this ring is, but a bullet it's not! From the way Doctor Tailor was talking, I think we'll find this ring, or disk, suspended above the tunnel floor."

"Lieutenant Wolf, you and Norton said you didn't see anyone else in the tunnel when you found Blake's body. I think that whatever killed him was either so small that you missed it, or it was translucent, almost invisible. Doctor Tailor said that the tissues in the wounds were cut so cleanly that he couldn't tell the difference between an entrance and an exit wound. Whatever cut through those tissues also cut through a Kevlar bulletproof vest! If that's so—we could easily walk into the same thing."

"I don't think we would be safe holding a metal shield in front of us. This ring might go through the metal just as easily as it went through Blake's vest. What I've made here isn't a shield; it's a detector. When this ring hits a balloon, or more accurately, when a balloon hits it, the balloon will pop. At this point we stop, back up a few feet and look to see which balloon popped. Whatever popped that balloon should be right in front of us. It's not exactly hi-tech, but, if it works, that's all that matters."

It was easy to tell by looking at their faces that the other men didn't have anywhere near as much faith in Captain Rider's detector as he did. But no one had any better ideas and at this point, no matter how odd it sounded, it was better than nothing. It's just that—well, a lawn chair with balloons tied to it seemed a little far-fetched, even under these circumstances. "What do you want us to do?" Sgt. Madison spoke for the three of them, as they stood there nearly motionless in the tunnel.

"I guess it's time to see if this thing's going to work. I want all three of you to walk in a line directly behind me. Try to stay in my path, step in my footsteps if you can. Keep your eyes open too. Hell, for all I know there could be somebody down here with some newfangled type of weapon. I may be barking up the wrong tree entirely. You guys don't look like you have much faith in this contraption."

"Let's just say we're reserving our opinion," Officer Norton grinned, as he lined up directly behind Captain Rider.

"Sgt. Madison. I want you to go last and bring along the box of goodies I brought with me. You'll find a couple of cans of black spray paint and a few other things in it. I want you to spray a foot-long marker once every ten to twelve feet on the floor where we've walked. That way we'll be able to retrace our path by following that line when we return. If we find what we're looking for, there's a yellow can of spray paint in the box as well. We'll mark the ring's location with the yellow paint. I would have rather had red, but there wasn't any in the supply room. OK gentlemen, as they used to say in the army—fall in!"

What a strange sight this was. Four men crouched over, walking in a tunnel as slowly as they could. The leader peeking out every few seconds from behind the frame of a lawn chair with a bunch of balloons tied to it. Every ten to twelve feet, Sgt. Madison would spray a line about a foot long on the floor.

"Captain," Lieutenant Wolf whispered, as they crept along at a snail's pace. "I was just thinking. Where was the wound that killed Dr. Grayson?"

"You mean Grayson. He was hit in the upper right torso. I think his lung was penetrated. Whatever killed him passed clean through his body. It even went through the back seat of the cart. Why?"

"Wasn't he sitting down when the attack occurred?"

"I imagine. What difference would that make? My God— you're right! He was sitting down. How tall a man was Officer Blake?"

Norton, not catching the first of the conversation but hearing the Captain's last question answered, "He was a big man, Sir, probably six foot three, maybe six four. Funny how easily we carried him when we were heading back to the elevators. I guess the adrenaline had kicked in. He didn't seem heavy at all. I think we could have carried him—"

"You see what I'm getting at, Captain?" the Lieutenant cut in, his voice much louder this time.

"Yes, Blake was standing up, but Dr. Grayson was in a sitting position. Either whatever we're looking for is moving, or there's more than one object. I didn't expect this. I thought that since both people were killed in the same area, they had both stumbled into the same thing. Blake was wounded at least 18 inches higher than Grayson was. If this thing is moving, it could be anywhere."

"And if there's more than one, there might be dozens. Who knows?"

"What are you guys talking about?" interrupted Officer Norton. "What do you mean, there could be dozens? Are you talking about the ring?"

Screeee- Screeee-

Something ran across the toe of Officer Norton's right shoe, making the damnedest noise any of them had ever heard. It was grayish-white in color, furry, and really strange looking. It was about the size of a small dog, a poodle maybe. It had stubby legs, a short hairless tail, and a long snout. A very long snout! It must have been half as long as its body. It had apparently been hiding in one of the numerous cracks and crannies that were scattered everywhere along the sides of the tunnel walls. It was gone in a few seconds.

Screeee- Screeee-

They could still hear its shrill screeching as the sound faded into the depths of the beam tunnel ahead. From the time the thing first appeared until it was nothing more than an echo took about ten seconds. They had all jumped when the animal appeared, especially Officer Norton. The sound it made resembled a policeman's whistle. It was that shrill. It scared the hell out of them!

"I think we were just attacked by Mighty Mouse," Captain Rider managed to utter, while trying to catch his breath.

"I think I just peed my pants," it was Officer Norton. "Look at the toe of my shoe. That thing put a gash in the leather when it ran over it. What the hell was it anyway?"

"I didn't get a very good look," said Captain Rider.

"I did." It was Officer Norton again. "It looked like a miniature anteater. You know—long, thin, pointed nose—hairless tail. Maybe we should get out of here and get some reinforcements."

"Get serious," Captain Rider answered in a ridiculing tone of voice. "We're just jumpy because of the circumstances. What are we going to say—Help! We've been attacked by a two-pound, long-nosed rodent? Send backup immediately? Are you kidding?"

"You might not feel that way if it was your foot it ran over. I guess it would sound kind of stupid though."

"OK then, let's get back to doing what we came here to do. Let's find that ring, or rings, or whatever the hell it was, that killed those men."

Chapter Ten

Ninety-nine percent. The main operations monitor in the DUNE control room would soon be signaling that the accelerator was functioning at full power. So far, everything was working exactly as planned. The technicians had installed the first of a series of targets into the primary implosion chamber inside the massive particle detector. The AI-driven control systems were online, the power grid was stable, and data would soon be flowing by the terabyte into the buffer area. There it would be presorted and streamed to the exascale clusters in the Feynman Data Center.

No one in the control room was aware of what was really happening in the beam tunnel. As far as they knew, the only thing wrong was a cryogenic line had leaked. During the power-up of the accelerator, there were so many things to be concerned with that a bomb could have gone off in the entranceway and I doubt that anyone would have noticed. Tonight was especially stressful since this was the first time they might actually achieve full power. As this event neared, everyone began to feel the pressure of the moment. This was the test that they had been working up to for months.

The control room was alive with activity. It was a virtual carnival of sound and light. Buzzing, beeping, and electronic chimes mingled in a menagerie of sounds that seemed to float in the air, defying anyone to pinpoint their exact location. Row upon row of dynamic LED panels chased each other in a choreographed dance from which a trained eye could immediately discern a problem. Colorful displays of graphs and digital gauges adorned the dozens of monitors throughout the room. So many, in fact, that it was hard to imagine how anyone could possibly be watching all of them.

There were dozens more monitors than there were technicians to watch them, but all of them were being watched—if not by a technician, then by an AI. If a piece of equipment that a display was monitoring went out of tolerance, the screen would flash between bright red and black at one-second intervals and an alarm would sound. You couldn't miss it. Almost every section of the particle detector had a sensor reading being displayed on one of the monitors in DUNE's control room. The most important devices had more than one system monitoring them. Redundancy was common at Fermilab.

PIP-II had been operating at 99% of full power for about ten minutes. Everything had checked out perfectly. Dr. Tyco was just about ready to order the technicians to bring the power up to full. One last check with the systems coordinator at the Feynman Data Center, and he would issue the order.

Or, should I say, he would have, if someone hadn't already issued it for him. At least, that's what he thought. Because the next thing he knew, the main systems monitor, the one that showed the combined power being generated by PIP-II, was showing 100%. Full power! Full power and he hadn't given the order? What was going on here?

He didn't have time to question anyone because in the next few seconds, the digital readout climbed to 101%, then to 102%. As he stood there amazed, his eyes frozen on the flashing red and black numerals, a flurry of numbers raced across the monitor stopping at 120% and staying there. How can this be? We can't possibly be operating at 120% of full power. The generating stations are set up to limit electrical power to no more than 1.25 megawatts. At that level, the maximum beam power that can be achieved is no more than 105%, and then only for a few minutes. A safety factor of almost 15% had been designed into PIP-II. Even if this were breached there wouldn't be any chance of a nuclear accident, but running at this rate could do insurmountable damage to the heart of the accelerator, the superconducting magnets. How could all of the safeguards have been circumvented? Who was running this show, if anyone?

Dr. Tyco was abruptly snapped out of his trance by the sound of his chief engineer. He was yelling at the top of his voice to STAND DOWN. This meant to immediately stop whatever you were doing and start shutting down the accelerator. Another flurry of activity and lights began to dim, monitors flickered on and off, and the control room grew strangely quiet. Reflections of monitors and gauges could be seen in the glasses of many of the engineers.

They looked dumfounded as they tried to figure out what was going on. This shouldn't, no, couldn't be happening. There were numerous safety devices that automatically triggered a stand-down condition if power exceeded 100% without the system's manager issuing a coded control sequence. That sequence has not been issued. Of that Dr. Tyco was sure, because he was the only one on the site who knew the sequence. Yet, here they were at 120% and holding.

That brought up another thing. How could they possibly be holding at such a high energy level? They had to be using more electricity than the power grid was designed to deliver. At this level, the neighboring town of Batavia was probably experiencing a blackout. Technicians were pulling the plugs, but the accelerator was not shutting down. In fact, he thought he could hear (or feel) a decidedly low-frequency hum as the accelerator propelled its load of protons into ever-higher energy levels. One thought kept coming back to him. How are we going to stop something that can't be happening in the first place?

"Numbers, everyone, I need numbers! Johnson, give me the power coming in from the generating station."

"It's 0.57 megawatts, sir."

"Are you sure? We can't be operating at 20% above maximum with that amount of power?"

"I'm reading the power from two different sensors, sir, and they both agree, 0.57 megawatts."

"Run a diagnostic on the power grid and get me a printout showing the average power consumption since we first brought PIP-II online—no, make that since noon today."

"Yes sir, I'll have it for you in a few minutes."

"Stevenson, you and Bradley start running diagnostics on the superconducting magnets. I want to be sure that they haven't been damaged. I'm not seeing any warning lights, but this can't be doing them any good."

"Phil, I'm not so sure that we really are in a full power plus condition. We might have a faulty sensor somewhere that's causing the computers to think we are red-lining when in actuality, we're not. It's not likely with all the redundancy that's built into this system, but it's worth looking into. Hell, it's no more unlikely than what seems to be happening right now. Check it out and get back to me as soon as possible. Come on, everyone. Don't think of this as a screw-up, think of it as an opportunity!"

Even though he was acting like he was in control, he knew that he wasn't. From the second that the power had increased to 100%, all he could do was watch. He was not going to just stand around and let this happen. He was one of the three or four people who had been in on this project from the beginning and he knew as much or more about the internal workings of PIP-II as anyone. In a way, that was what bothered him the most. He knew in the back of his mind that this wasn't an act of sabotage; something very wrong was going on here. Something he didn't understand at all.

Even if somebody could have overridden the built-in safety precautions, what purpose would it serve to take the machine up to such a high level? There was no way that this could be happening because of a programming error, yet to go past the 100% level was impossible unless a definite series of sequences were followed. The most important of these sequences was the entering of the encrypted control code.

"Dr. Tyco?" It was Bill Stevenson and his voice was a bit shaky, "Here is a printout of the entire energy consumption since we first powered up the system at 9:45 this morning. I also started a diagnosis on all of the cryogenics systems including production and delivery. I should have a report ready including everything that's under computer control within 20 minutes."

"What's your initial reaction, Bill?"

"It doesn't make any sense, sir."

"Details, Bill, we're in a hurry here."

"Well, I run these same diagnostics every time we test PIP-II. There is a given amount of power needed to cool the magnets to almost zero Kelvin. Once that level is reached, very little additional power is needed to keep them there. I would have thought though, in order to operate at 20% over full power, we would have needed a significant boost in electrical power. To explore these limits, it takes a prodigious amount of electricity."

"The point being?"

"Well, see for yourself. The power consumption is less than half that needed to keep the magnets in a superconducting state. Theoretically, they can't be functioning in a superconducting state. It takes more power than they're using. It's impossible!"

"What's the temperature in the magnet cores?"

"Minus 353.4 degrees Kelvin, and steady as a rock. The graph doesn't show a variation of more than a tenth of a degree since we went to 100% power."

"Dr. Tyco!" Tony Johnson came running over to where the two men were standing, breathing heavily and pointing to some papers he held in his hand. "You're not going to believe what just happened."

"Tony, at this point I'd believe anything."

"I was monitoring the power grid as it comes in from the generating station in Chicago; it's been steadily climbing towards 1.05 megawatts since we started the test. About, (looking down at his watch), three minutes ago, the power level dropped to 0.57 megawatts. No warning, no sliding down, just bingo—0.57 megawatts. I've never seen anything like it. I'd better get back to my monitors; I just wanted you to know what had happened. If anything else happens, I'll inform you immediately. Maybe PIP-II is shutting down. That might account for such a sudden drop."

"If it is, the computers don't know it. They still say PIP-II is operating at 120%. Phil, how are you coming with the sensor diagnostics? Any chance of a component failure?"

"A complete diagnostics will take hours, but the main systems are functioning OK, other than showing overload conditions! I heard what's happening with the magnets and the power grid. I don't understand it either."

The control room wasn't cornering the market on confused scientists. All you had to do was look out of the control room window onto the floor of the detector and you could see technicians running around everywhere. Some were pointing, some yelling, most were just standing around with an amazed look on their faces. Alarms were going off on every console that had an alarm connected to it.

Things weren't much better in the Feynman Data Center. The AI clusters were trying to sort out the billions of bits of data arriving every second, most of which didn't make any sense. The interface to DUNE's detector was being overloaded to the max. Both the primary and backup systems were operating at full capacity. In fact, the main processing CPUs had automatically gone into a "hibernation" mode because of an "information overload." All activity was now being diverted to the chore of just recording the massive amounts of data arriving over the detector uplink. Processing would have to be delayed until a later time.

Such a situation had been deemed possible when the interface software was written, but I'm sure the software designers didn't think it would be needed so soon, if at all. Every last byte was being recorded. It might take days, even weeks, before this enormous amount of data could be analyzed. If a reason for the events of the last few minutes could be found within it, at least they would have the data in its entirety for the analysis.

Normally there was very little human communication between the data center and DUNE's control room. AI handled almost all of the interactions between the two. But when the main computers went into "hibernation," the technicians immediately called DUNE to see what the problem was.

When they did, they found that DUNE was every bit as much in the dark as they were. If there were answers to their questions, they wouldn't be coming from DUNE, at least not then. The answers might be found in the stream of data pouring into their systems, but until the flood of information slowed, they couldn't even attempt to try and coax the answers from the data. For the time being, all that these expensive computers could do was to act like a giant sponge, soaking up the waves of data emanating from DUNE's detector.

Even though most of the activity was taking place in the main detector, there were other, smaller groups of technicians scattered throughout the complex who were just as worried. The operation of PIP-II involved dozens of highly skilled people. There were cryogenics experts, electrical engineers, structural engineers, chemists, carpenters, laborers, maintenance, etc., all of them hand-picked for their prospective positions.

Backup support was everywhere. When problems came up, there was a wealth of people who could be counted on to come up with solutions. There were also physicists from around the world staying here on a semi-permanent basis. Some of them were Nobel Prize winners.

How could things have gotten so out of control? Steven thought to himself.

What had he missed? What had they all missed?

Then, the unthinkable happened. The lights went out! All electrical power to the complex was broken. Not only was Fermilab in the dark. There wasn't a light visible, for several miles in any direction. The whole town of Batavia was in the dark. The backup lighting system should have come on the second the main power failed, but it didn't. There were battery-powered lights in the halls and elevators of every building in the complex. They were equipped with sensors that activated the lights if a loss of power was detected. They never came on. One of the technicians in the control room felt his way back to his desk and fumbled with the drawer, finally finding his flashlight. He switched it on—nothing.

The silence was deafening. Just seconds ago, every piece of equipment that had any kind of buzzer, ringer, flasher, or siren was buzzing, ringing, flashing, or whining. Now there was nothing but the sound of breathing. No one wanted to say a word. No one knew what to say! Everyone just stood there in the dark, listening. Then they heard it, each in his own way. Some with their ears. Others, in the pit of their stomachs. The sound was ever so slight, ever so soft. No louder than a cat purring. It may have been there all along, just unnoticed as it blended in with the rest of the sounds normally found in the busy control room.

A scary picture started forming in Steven Tyco's head. What is that sound? It reminds me of—bells.

Then, after nearly two minutes of total darkness, the lights came on. There was a cacophony of noise as hundreds of pieces of equipment fired up at once. Whether it was on before the blackout or not, everything was powered up. Lights, monitors, computers, even the shopvac, a little barrel of a sweeper that resembled a red R2D2 was energized and ready for action. It was as if these things were never really turned off, they were just waiting—switched to standby mode until somebody gave them the order to, WAKE UP!

As Steven's eyes adjusted to the returning light, he was astonished to find that the monitors were all showing normal. No overloads. No excessive power fluctuations. No overheated magnets. Nothing. There wasn't any sign that anything out of the ordinary had even happened—business as usual. Every monitor showed exactly the same thing—normal operating conditions. The power monitor, the biggest and most important display of all, was reading 35%. Not the 120% it had read just a few minutes ago. Everything looked exactly as it did before the test had begun.

If it hadn't been for one thing, one undeniable little item that was displayed on the readout of every monitor in the complex—if not for that one telling item, they might have gone home believing that none of these events had taken place.

But they had taken place. The proof was in the icy blue numbers framed in a cold gray rectangular box, defying you to miss it.

In the bottom right-hand corner of every monitor was the elapsed time clock. Every monitor's clock showed exactly the same thing, 00:00:21, and counting. According to the computers, only 21 seconds had expired since the test had started. What had happened to the last eleven hours?

II – Portals

Chapter Eleven

Captain Rider's group had also been plunged into total darkness when the power was disrupted.

He was the first to speak, "Sgt., feel around in the bag you're carrying. There should be a flashlight and a bundle of light sticks. I don't think the backup system is going to kick in."

Before the Sgt. could find them, the main overhead lights came back on. It took a few seconds for everyone's eyes to adjust from the pitch black of the tunnel. They stood there, unmoving, until—

"Did anybody else feel it?" Norton asked, his normally husky voice just barely audible above a whisper.

There was a long pause—nobody wanted to be the first to answer. Then, finally—

"I did," said Sgt. Madison. "I think I experienced that feeling once before. When I was about ten years old, I remember my Dad taking a bunch of us boys to the county fair. We usually spent most of our time on the rides, but on this one particular day, we decided to check out some of the exhibits. Most people called them sideshows back then. Anyway, I remember this guy, a carnival barker. He was standing on a podium in front of a dark blue tent with lightning bolts painted all over it. He was pitching his line to everyone that passed—

'Two Bits; just one quarter of a dollar and you can witness a modern marvel of science. Only two bits—see the amazing Marko, the human lightning rod—'

Something like that, anyway. I can still remember hearing the sounds of electricity and seeing bright flashes of light pouring through a tear in the tent. It was pretty scary to us boys. We were only about nine or ten at the time. We gave the man our money and went in. It was dark and the place had a pungent smell to it. I later learned that it was ozone. It was hard to see inside. I think one of us must have bumped against the stage when all hell broke loose. It was like an electrical storm on a hot summer night, only it was happening right there, just a few feet in front of our eyes! When they brought the lights up, I saw that it was coming from some kind of machine."

"A Van de Graaff generator," Captain Rider interjected.

"Yes, I think you're right. I remember seeing a smaller one years later in a high school physics lab. It was a little different, but it accomplished the same thing. I can still remember how awed I was at the guy on the stage. He was standing in a shower of sparks and lightning bolts were dancing all around him. He placed one hand on this giant chrome ball then reached out and bolts of electricity would jump from his fingers. He picked up a light bulb and it lit up at his touch.

They asked for a volunteer from the audience and of course, I volunteered. I climbed up onto the stage and when he took my hand a strange feeling shot through my whole body. My hair stood straight out, just like in those cartoons when someone sticks his finger in a light socket. It gave me the weirdest feeling—having all that electricity flowing through me. I felt like—if I were to touch someone, I'd burn them to a crisp. I had that same feeling a little while ago, when the lights went out. But it's gone now."

"I think we all had it," Officer Norton's voice chimed in from the rear, though this time with a little less vibrato.

"What happened to the backup lights?" Captain Rider asked, as he inspected the contraption he was hoping to find the ring with.

"I don't know. There's a backup light every 40 or 50 feet on the outside wall. Look, there's one on the wall just in front of us now," Norton said. "They're the good old halogen lights too. Not these day-glow orange globes that everybody is going crazy over. They look like an electrified DreamCycle."

"I thought the backup lights were supposed to come on when the main system failed?"

"There's probably not been anyone down here when the main system failed to test them."

"Remind me to include that in our report. No emergency lights."

"Tell them to bring a couple of giant-size rat traps down here too while you're at it. I think they've definitely got a rodent problem," Officer Norton added.

"I don't like this," said Captain Rider. "Not one bit. I don't like it that the lights failed and I really don't like it that the backup system failed too. I only brought the flashlight and light sticks because they were on the table next to me. I didn't think I'd really have to use them. I'm also worried that four of us might have to rely on just one flashlight. Turn that thing on, Sgt., I don't even know if it works."

Sgt. Madison pushed the on/off switch. The eight-cell flashlight threw a beam bright as a car headlight.

"Well, that's a relief. I'd hate to think I packed an emergency flashlight and it was a dud. With only the one flashlight and a few light sticks, it might be better if only Sgt. Madison and I continue with this expedition. If we find what we're looking for, I can call in the cavalry. Officer Norton, why don't you and Lieutenant Wolf go on back to the elevator and wait for us there. I'll call you on the radio if we find anything. If I call you, come running. Just be sure you stay on the line the Sgt. spray painted."

"I'd be happy to, sir; this place gives me the creeps. We'll head back to the elevator and wait for you there."

"Here, take a couple of the light sticks just in case the lights go out again. Do you know how to work them?"

"I believe all you have to do is break the glass."

"That's right. When you bend the stick, two chemicals are released and when they mix, they glow. There's no heat, just a greenish colored light. Each one will burn for about an hour at full brightness and then they'll begin to dim considerably."

The two men turned and started back to the elevator.

Captain Rider looked at Sgt. Madison. "I'd love to have a picture of this to show to my grandkids. You look like some kind of subterranean Santa Claus, carrying your box of goodies. Me, with my lawn chair and balloons, who knows what I look like? An idiot I imagine."

"Who cares what it looks like as long as it works? Are you ready?"

"I'm as ready as I'll ever be. Let's get going."

With that, the two men started down the beam tunnel. Captain Rider made a little opening between two of the balloons. He wanted to be able to see where he was going without having to look around the edge of the "detector." Sgt. Madison was walking so close he was about to push Captain Rider down the tunnel.

"Sgt., if you were standing any closer, you'd be in front of me. Do you think you could back off just a little?"

"Sorry sir, but you said to walk in your footsteps."

"Yeah, but wait until I get out of them first."

They walked on for another 50 or 60 yards, Sgt. Madison stopping to spray a foot-long black line every 15 feet or so.

Suddenly, Captain Rider froze.

"What's wrong? Did you see some—"

"Shhhhh. Listen. I hear something up ahead."

Both of them stood there listening, barely breathing.

"It sounds like running water."

Captain Rider had crouched down and Sgt. Madison could easily see over his head. "I hear it, but I don't see anything." The sound was coming from around the bend and neither of them could see what was causing it.

Captain Rider stood back up and started walking forward, slowly. "There's been a problem with water showing up in the tunnel for several months now, though it has never been enough to hurt anything. It's usually just a wet spot on the floor except, there was one time when a large section of the tunnel was soaked. It's strange that the source was never found. We might get lucky and find where this water is coming from. The structural boys would love us if we do."

"How about we don't, and say we did," Sgt. Madison snickered.

"You're not afraid of a little water are you?"

"Water, no, things that swim in it, maybe."

"I don't think we're going to be finding enough water for anything to be swimming in."

The men walked on a few yards farther, Sgt. Madison stopping every so often to spray a stripe behind them. Captain Rider was holding his "detector" out in front of him, trying to figure out how near they were to the water they were hearing.

POP! "Did you do that?" Sgt. Madison asked, bumping into Captain Rider.

"No, I mean, I don't think so. One of the balloons just popped. I think it was one about waist high. Back up a step or two. I'm going to put this thing down. Stand very still and look directly in front of me. Ok, let's do it."

With that, the two of them took two small steps backwards. Captain Rider turned to his right and laid the detector on its side on the tunnel floor. Before he could straighten back up, Sgt. Madison was already blabbering.

"I see it. I can see the damn thing as plain as day! Look— right there—waist high, just like you said. If we hadn't had that stupid looking do-ma-jiggy of yours, we'd have walked right into it sure as hell. You, Captain, are a genius."

Sure enough, when Rider looked at where Sgt. Madison was pointing, he could see it too. It looked like— a hole in the air. It was round, like a ring. They had that much right. But it was little more than a hole in the air. They approached it carefully. It was about an inch in diameter. Much bigger than what had killed the two men earlier. It was about forty inches off of the floor.

"I'm surprised I didn't see it before I ran into it. I guess I was paying too much attention to the sound of the running water."

The two men were now standing directly in front of it. They bent down and studied the object. They could almost see inside. The hole was translucent, but it also had some color to it. It was shifting, from a pale gray to a light tan. As they looked, they thought they saw movement. They both stepped back. Had they imagined it? It almost looked like blowing sand.

"Get the yellow paint can out of the bag. I want you to spray a circle on the floor under this thing, and a couple of lines horizontal to it, at one-foot intervals. I don't want anyone to run into it by mistake. You'd better stay back at least two feet. Who knows what it is? It might be able to move. We better look around a little more before we do anything. There could be more of these things."

Captain Rider picked his detector back up and while Sgt. Madison waited, he crisscrossed the area within ten feet of the object. No more balloons burst, so he figured they could safely continue with their investigation. Sgt. Madison took the can of yellow spray paint and started shaking it furiously.

"All we need is a marker so we'll know exactly where it is."

With that, Sgt. Madison began spraying a line on the floor. He started about two feet in front of the object and moved in a circle to his right. He continued, not taking his eyes off of the object for even an instant. Suddenly, he startled the Captain when he cried out, "Captain, it's gone!"

"What are you talking about? I'm looking right at it."

Sgt. Madison took a step back and to his left.

"I don't believe it. When you look at it from the side, it totally disappears."

"Let me see."

Sure enough, as the Captain approached the object from the side, it disappeared. He quickly moved back in front of it and there it was again.

"Let me have your spray can, Sgt. I'm going to put an X right under it. Remember, it's directly above the X on the floor."

After drawing the X, Captain Rider said, "I want to try something. Walk around to where you're directly behind the object and see if it reappears."

Sgt. Madison carefully stepped in a circular motion until he was directly behind the X on the floor.

"No sign of it Captain, nothing. Not even a glimmer. I must be looking right through it."

"Stand right there. I'm going to perform a little experiment. I know this thing is solid, because it burst my balloon. At least the front of it is. Let's see if the back and sides are solid too. I'm going to touch the side of this thing and see if I can feel it. Let me get something from the box. I put a wrench in there to open the valve on the helium tank. I'm going to tap on the edge of it. I'll just barely touch it."

"Wait a second; I think I'd rather be standing there with you when you start banging on this thing."

"No, stay there. It might become visible when touched. I'll tell you when I'm hitting it."

With that, Captain Rider took the wrench and slightly tapped on the outer edge of the object in front of them.

"Any sign of anything?"

"No, all I saw was you tapping the air. What did it feel like?"

"It's solid. You may not be able to see it, but I can sure feel it. Let me tap it a little harder—solid as a rock. Here, I'm going to hand you the wrench. Tap on it from the back."

"I can't see it."

"I'll guide you. I'll tell you when you're getting close."

"OK, I've got a good idea where it is. I should be pretty close right now."

"You are. You're about two inches high, and just a shade to your right. Move a little bit to your left. Stop! Now, come straight down."

"I hit something." Sgt. Madison was amazed that he was touching something solid, something that he couldn't see. "I'm going to hit it pretty hard this time. Let's see if it will change shape or color."

"It didn't do anything at all. I just realized that we aren't hearing anything either and it looked like you came down pretty hard with that wrench."

"I did. It was like hitting an anvil."

"Hand me the wrench. I'm going to try something else."

"Wait a second. I'm coming back around to the front."

"On second thought, give me your ink pen."

"What are you going to do?"

"Watch."

With that, Captain Rider took the ink pen and poked it directly into the hole. Nothing happened. They could see the ink pen in the hole and it didn't appear that anything strange was happening to it. Then he pulled it out and examined it. It was the same old ink pen. Next, he tapped on the hole from the top and sides. No noise and as solid as before. Then, he tried to tap on the front of the hole.

"Did you see that Sgt.?"

"Yeah, my ink pen just broke in two pieces."

"No, the part that was touching the front of the hole just disappeared into it. All I'm holding is the top of the pen."

"I don't get it. Where did the rest of it go?"

"I don't know. I didn't feel anything. It just disappeared. Hand me that wrench. I'm going to try the same thing with it."

With that, Captain Rider placed the steel crescent wrench into the hole and then moved it to where it was touching the inside edge. As the wrench touched the inner edge, it just disappeared into it.

"Did you see that? The edge of the hole seemed to cut through the metal like it was nothing. I mean, literally, like nothing. I didn't feel a thing. Look at this. The cut's as smooth as a baby's butt."

"Does it feel hot?"

"No, it's not even warm."

"Now what do we do?"

Captain Rider plucked his microphone from the Velcro holder on his shoulder, "We're almost ready to go back, but first I want to find the source of that water. It has to be just around the bend. I'm going to call in and report what we've found and let everyone know we're all right. Let's go a little deeper into the tunnel to see if we can find out where the water is coming from."

After a few minutes on the radio the two of them took up their positions. Captain Rider and his detector in front, Sgt. Madison bringing up the rear, paint can in hand. They started moving slowly, deeper into the tunnel. As they walked, the sound of the running water grew louder. They had only gone about fifteen yards when Sgt. Madison grabbed the Captain's shoulder.

"Look, over there by the lower tube, about 20 feet ahead. I think I see a puddle of water."

"You're right. It's not much, but it shouldn't be there. Let's make our way over to it. Stay behind me."

In the orange glow of the overhead lights the puddle took on the color of jet black. It wasn't much of a puddle. In fact, it was more like a little stream that was inching along the wall under the lower of the two tubes that made up the accelerator's beam guide. As they neared it, they could see that it was indeed moving, but very slowly.

The source of the water was still ahead of them. As they crept forward, the sound of running water grew louder. They had to be getting near the source. The strange thing was—how could such a loud sound produce such a small trickle of water? Another 25 feet or so and they found the answer. Every so often there was a drain in the floor of the beam tunnel. These weren't big drains. They were just a little bigger than what you'd find in the average shower.

As they got nearer, they could see a large volume of water flowing into one of them. What they had been following for the last 20 or 30 feet was the overflow that the small drain couldn't handle. The water had backed up into an area covering a good half of the floor of the beam tunnel and was probably at least a half an inch deep near the tunnel wall. The sound of splashing water filled the tunnel in front of them, and they knew that they had to be very near the source of the leak.

Then they saw it—a very small stream of water gleaming as it reflected the overhead light on the arched ceiling. No. Not one stream—but three. They were shooting from three distinct sources, like someone had punched holes in a dike. The water shot out into the air in a horizontal arc, traveling about five feet before splashing on the tunnel floor.

The streams were only about a half an inch wide, but they were strong and never seemed to falter. One of the streams was splashing against the accelerator's tubes, but the other two were aimed directly towards them.

The three streams varied in height between waist and shoulder level. As they approached the streams, their faces revealed the shock in what they were seeing.

The Captain was the first to speak. "I can see the water clear as day, but I can't see where it's coming from."

"Unless there are three ghosts taking a whiz, I don't think it's coming from anywhere. It's coming right out of the air. There's nothing else there."

"Let's get closer, there has to be something there. Maybe there's a broken cryogenic line, or something like that. We might be seeing some kind of condensation coming from a clear glass or plastic tubing."

"I'm telling you Captain, there ain't nothing there. That water is shooting straight out of nowhere."

Before they could get much closer, something else caught their attention. Another dripping sound had started coming from just behind and to their left. They wheeled around, and only a few yards from their heads water was starting to drip. Right out of the air! In a few seconds, it turned from a drip into a stream, exactly like the three that were up ahead of them. This stream continued to grow until it was at least an inch in diameter and was shooting out with such force that it was landing ten or fifteen feet away from them. If they were to return the way they'd come, there was no choice but to duck under it. Before they could do that though, it abruptly stopped.

"I want to get a sample. Is there anything in the bag that will hold water?"

With that, Sgt. Madison fumbled through balloons, string, a short length of wire, six or seven light sticks, and the flashlight. "No, sir, there's nothing in here."

"The flashlight, give it to me along with a couple of light sticks. Put a few sticks in your pockets, just in case the lights go out again."

"What are you going to do with the flashlight?"

"I'm going to take the batteries out of it. The tube should hold several ounces of water." With that, he unscrewed the end holding the light bulb and turning the tube section to the ground, let the batteries slide to the floor. Next, he held the tube under one of the streams, filling it to the top. Then, he screwed the top part back on. The flashlight held eight 'D' size batteries. That was probably equivalent to at least a pint of water, maybe more.

"Now, let's see if this thing's as waterproof as the manufacturer claims it to be." With that, he turned the flashlight in several directions, shaking it as he did so.

"You must have been watching MacGyver reruns with all the devices you're coming up with."

"I don't know why I thought of this, but it seems to work. Let's get the hell out of here before something else happens."

They turned and started back towards the elevators at a fast walk for the first few yards, but soon, they were almost at a full run. Captain Rider was still holding his detector, but down to his side. He'd completely forgotten about the danger of any new rings they might have missed along the way in. They did have the presence of mind though to stay on the line that Sgt. Madison had laid down. As they reached the point where they encountered the original ring, they stopped.

From this end of the tunnel they were looking at the backside of the ring and it should have been invisible. Now, they could plainly see it—and it had grown, considerably. In fact, it was about the size of a softball. They looked on in total amazement as they approached it. When they were within a few feet, they could definitely see that there was movement inside of it. It was like looking into faintly colored glass. The movement definitely looked like sand being blown across a desert landscape.

They noticed that it was exactly where they'd left it; the X was still directly under it. It had just grown in size. It also seemed to be rotating, oh so slowly. They went around it, one on each side. Just as before, it disappeared as soon as they passed to the side of it.

At this point, Captain Rider got a grip on his emotions and without saying a word, brought his detector up in front of him again. He walked quickly towards the elevator. Sgt. Madison was in close pursuit. They resembled a scene from an old Marx Brothers movie, where Groucho is bent over doing his duck walk and Harpo is right on his heels.

Within ten minutes they were stepping inside the elevator. They turned and reached for the lobby button together. For a few seconds they just stood there—eyes glued to the bend in the tunnel. Listening, they strained to hear the sound of anything that might be following them. "Close, damn it, close," Captain Rider whispered to himself.

The look on their faces betrayed their thoughts. Neither of them said a word as the elevator doors finally drew shut. There was just the hint of a vibration as the elevator started to make the ascent to the upper levels. They were going to make it back to civilization after all. The only thing they wanted to hear now was the sweet lady's voice as she said, "Lobby." That wasn't going to happen any time soon!

Chapter Twelve

"Are we moving?" Sgt. Madison asked, almost in a whisper.

"I think so. I'm sure I felt some vibration just after the doors closed." But Captain Rider wasn't quite sure about anything at this point.

As several more seconds passed, it was evident that they definitely were not moving.

There was only one thing to do. "Captain, I think you should push the open button and see if we're still in the beam tunnel."

"I have a very bad feeling about this, Sgt., but I guess you're right." With that, Captain Rider touched the illuminated door open icon on the touchscreen panel. The doors opened—slowly.

They both moved to the back of the elevator as the gap between the doors inched wider. Sgt. Madison had drawn his service revolver, just in case. What they saw as the doors inched open was something they would never forget. About forty feet away stood a creature the size of a St. Bernard. No, it was more like a Shetland pony. It was about four feet tall and covered in heavily matted hair, almost snow white in color, except for the tail, which was hairless. Even though it was facing away from them, they knew exactly what it was. It was the same thing they'd seen earlier. Except this one was a much larger version.

Screeee Screeee Screeee.

It stood up on its hind legs and threw its long neck and head into the air. They could see the narrow, hairless snout, probing the air for a scent. After a few seconds it whipped its head around and looked squarely at them. They froze, neither wanting to breathe. Then Captain Rider took a single step towards the elevator's control panel. The creature detected the movement and charged.

What happened next took place so quickly that neither was entirely sure of what really did happen. The creature's first lunge must have covered about a fourth of the distance to the elevator. Captain Rider started pounding on the close door button. Sgt. Madison dropped to a kneeling position and raised his weapon. The dim LED light of the beam tunnel didn't offer him a very good view of his target. Sighting along the barrel he took aim at the creature, but it was moving so fast and its head was so narrow, he knew he'd be lucky if he hit it.

In just a few more seconds the creature was within a dozen feet of the doors, which had finally started to close. He might not get a head shot, but he could still do plenty of damage. These were .357 magnum hollow points and they could stop a bull. Sgt. Madison squeezed the trigger and the explosion of the discharging bullet sounded like a cannon going off in the confined space of the elevator. The concussion of the expanding gas around the gun's muzzle almost ruptured their eardrums.

Unfortunately, he missed. His nervousness had caused his aim to be off to one side. He just grazed the creature's right ear which only made it madder. The only thing the bullet did was knock a chunk of concrete out of a brace attached to one of the cryogenic lines. Before he could get off another shot, the animal lunged again. It was only a yard or so in front of the closing doors, its long snout almost in the elevator with them when a brown blur streaked out from their right and snatched the creature from sight.

It was incredible. This thing had to weigh at least two hundred pounds. Even with all of its forward momentum, one second it was there and the next, it was gone. As the doors shut, they could hear its wailing cry.

Screee Screee Scr—

The last screech was cut short. Then, through their pounding ears, they heard what sounded like boards being broken. But they knew it wasn't boards at all, it was bones. There was a slight vibration as the elevator finally started its ascent.

They pressed themselves against the back wall of the elevator as the sounds of the breaking bones grew fainter. The elevator vibrated a second time.

"I think we really are going up this time," Captain Rider said, never taking his eyes from the elevator's doors.

Sgt. Madison didn't say a word. He just stood there, still pointing his weapon toward the doors.

Several seconds passed when there was a sudden jarring of the elevator. They both knew that its upward motion had stopped. The light above their heads flickered, but stayed on. Nothing happened for ten, maybe fifteen seconds. It was like being in a tomb. Then they heard it. At first, it was just a light scratching on the floor below their feet. If the elevator hadn't been so completely silent, they might never have even noticed it. They leaned over, almost to a bow, turning one ear to the floor trying to make out what the sound was.

WHAM! Something smacked the floor so hard the elevator must have jumped an inch or two in its shaft.

WHAM, a second time!

This blow not only jarred the elevator, it buckled a section of flooring near the control panel. They grabbed at the slim, reinforced railing attached to the wall, almost falling, barely managing to keep their balance. All of their senses heightened. Every nerve and muscle fiber on full alert.

Sgt. Madison's revolver was now aimed at the floor only he didn't know which part of the floor to aim it at.

Then—silence. The beating of their hearts was the only sound they were aware of. Several seconds passed. Then, half a minute. They were afraid to move, afraid to even breathe. God, don't let that light go out, Captain Rider thought to himself. I can't imagine being here in the dark. He stood there, trembling in the silence.

Then, just barely above the sounds of their breathing, scarcely above the threshold of their heartbeats, they heard a sound resonating from the floor. It sounded like the noises an old house makes late at night. Noises you only hear because the rest of the world is sleeping. They both realized what was causing the sound at the same time. They could see it. The floor was pushing up. A slight bulge had developed at the center. What they were hearing was the stress of composite and steel, as it was being pressed out of shape by some unseen force. The floor was tiled, not carpeted.

"Tiled floors are easier for the maintenance bots to clean," Captain Rider half spoke and half whispered.

Sgt. Madison looked up at him. "What?"

He realized how stupid that must have sounded. A few of the tiles were beginning to pop up around their edges now, and he could see a layer of material beneath them. It looked like it might be plywood, but he had no idea what went into the construction of an elevator's floor.

Whatever it was, it was being stretched out of shape as if a giant hand were pressing against it. In a few more seconds the center of the floor was at least four, maybe five inches higher than the outer edges. More tiles popped as low groaning noises erupted from the overstressed composite and metal.

Then, as suddenly as it started, it was over. The floor was frozen in this convex position. The creaking and groaning noises ceased as the pressure was taken away. Captain Rider inched his way to the control panel staying as close to the walls as was humanly possible. He pressed the lobby button for the fourth time that night. Once again the elevator vibrated, this time violently, but it started its rise to the next level. It was a jerky ride, the undercarriage no longer fitting properly in its track.

It seemed like forever, but it only took about 20 seconds before they heard, 'Level L1' over the elevator's speaker. There she was, that beautiful voice they had been waiting for. The one they thought they might never hear again. 'Lobby.'

When the doors finally opened another surprise was awaiting them. People were working, talking, joking; everything was business as usual. How could that possibly be? How could anyone have not heard all the commotion in the elevator? Where was the rest of their team? Where were the police?

Then, one of their colleagues passing by happened to look over at them. "What happened to you guys?" As his gaze drifted to the floor he said, "And what the hell happened to our elevator?"

Chapter Thirteen

It was getting close to 2 A.M., and Dr. Baker was still studying the fish that Bill Scott had brought in earlier. She was so excited about what she was finding (or not finding) that she just couldn't stop herself. There were plenty of other things she should have been doing, but this fish was so incredible, she had completely forgotten about her other duties. Caroline, her assistant, was just as amazed as she was. They had both lost track of the time—

"Caroline, how would you like to take a little vacation? Paid, of course."

"Are you kidding? Just tell me when and where."

"Well, it's not very far, but we could be gone for three or four days. Can you check if there are any hotels in Batavia? I want to look at that lake where this fish was caught. I think it's time we impose on Dr. Scott and find out if there have been any other unusual catches there. I'd like to leave as soon as possible, before noon tomorrow if possible."

"I want to get tissue samples out to a couple of colleagues before we go. I'll start prepping the samples, why don't you book us some rooms. We'll be gone at least four days. Get us two rooms— no, make that three rooms. One for each of us and another we can turn into a mini-lab. I want to run tests on the lake water and any surrounding streams."

Caroline pulled up her phone and started searching for Batavia hotels. Within a few minutes, she had three rooms reserved at a hotel just across from Fermilab's main entrance, all booked and confirmed digitally.

"There are a few options, but I found a place right across from Fermilab. Three rooms, no problem," Caroline said.

There was still a lot of work to be done. The tissue samples had to be labeled and packed in dry ice. They would be shipped out by overnight courier in the morning. Physically preparing the samples was the easy part. What would take time was organizing the notes she'd taken, and then writing a detailed report on what she'd discovered.

They finished at 3:30, dog-tired and hungry. They were so wrapped up in what they'd been doing that they forgot they hadn't eaten in over twelve hours. Eating would have to wait. Right now, what they needed most was sleep.

"Let's meet back here about 10:30 in the morning," Connie said. "There's no sense in getting here any earlier. I think it's only a few hours' drive. We can take care of the rest of the paperwork before we leave. I'll have to write up something to excuse our absence for the next couple of days and get someone to cover for us. Bring some old clothes. We'll probably be getting wet. I plan on doing a little fishing while we're there."

"I've got plenty of those," Caroline said.

With the fish in the deep freeze, they said their goodnights and headed home for a few hours of well-deserved rest.

They met on schedule the next morning, though they didn't get out of Chicago as early as they'd have liked. It always seems to take forever when you put a trip together on the spur of the moment. Once they arrived in Batavia, they couldn't wait to get started. Their lack of sleep was overcome by the excitement that lay ahead of them.

The hotel clerk thought it a little strange that they requested three rooms since there were obviously only two of them. Of course, they didn't mention the third room was going to be a makeshift lab. The rooms were small, but clean and nicely furnished. Best of all, they were right across the street from Fermilab.

Dr. Baker looked at her watch—it was 2:05 in the afternoon. By the time they checked in, unpacked their equipment, set up two laptops and a portable cooler, it was almost 3:30. They figured they still had plenty of daylight left, so they decided to use the time to investigate the layout of the Fermilab complex.

Fermilab is a very public area. There are no guards at the gate and you don't have to have any special pass to get onto the grounds. You can wander around most of the complex to your heart's content. At least, that's what the brochures said, and they soon found it to be the case.

Other than the actual lab areas, the grounds and main buildings are open to the public. As they entered the main gate, they noticed what looked to be armed men off in the distance. Driving a little farther, they realized they were security of some kind. Nothing seemed amiss. There wasn't any visible sign of trouble, but uniformed men were everywhere. As they approached the congestion, a State Police officer directed them to the side of the road.

"Good afternoon, ladies," the officer said, as he signaled to the car ahead of them to move forward. "Are you here on business, or are you just touring the facilities?"

Caroline was driving, but it was Dr. Baker who spoke from the passenger's seat. "Actually, we're here on both accounts. This is not quite the welcome we were expecting. Is there some kind of problem?"

"I really can't say, but the facility has been temporarily closed to all except staff and scientists. It may be open by tomorrow. This has happened a couple of times since the 9/11 terrorist attack. If you give me your names, I'll check and see if you're on the list."

"I'm afraid you won't find us, officer. We came in this morning, unexpected from Chicago. I'm Dr. Baker, and this is my assistant, Caroline Tanner. We are marine biologists with the Shedd Aquarium in Chicago. We were brought this incredible fish yesterday that was caught in one of the lakes here, and— it's a long story. We're staying at the hotel across the street. I think it would be best if we just go back to the room and call someone in authority that can get us invited to the party."

"That's probably the best thing to do. Nobody gets in without an invitation. Sorry!"

With that, the two women turned the car around and headed back down the winding blacktop. Not far in the distance, they could see the digital security gates that marked Fermilab's entrance.

"What do you think that was all about?" asked Caroline, more thinking out loud than actually talking.

"I don't know. I wonder why they don't just block the road at the gate instead of letting people drive so far only to have them turn around and leave again?"

"It doesn't make any sense, does it? There sure were a lot of police on hand for nothing serious to be happening."

It was Dr. Baker who made the call to Fermilab. Bill had given her his card, so she dialed his number first.

"Hello Dr. Scott, this is Dr. Baker from the Shedd Aquarium. We talked yesterday."

"Hello, Doctor, this is a surprise. I didn't think I'd be hearing from you this soon. Have you identified my fish already?"

"Well, not exactly. I sent specimens to several of my colleagues and I expect to have an answer any time. Actually, I thought I might take a few days off to test your lake and see if there's anything unusual in its chemical makeup. Carol and I checked into a hotel near Fermilab a few hours ago."

"Great! How long do you plan on staying?"

"That depends on what I find. We just tried to get into the complex but we were stopped at a security check. Has something happened? The place isn't about to blow up or anything, is it?"

Bill had to choke back a laugh, but he wasn't sure if he should tell her about the deaths that had occurred. "No, nothing's going to blow up, but something happened during a test last night...an accident of some kind. Anytime something happens involving the DOE, the State and Federal boys show up. This facility is supported by the DOE, you know."

"I guess I'm just not used to seeing so many police at one time."

"And you're from Chicago! I'd think this was an everyday occurrence there."

"OK, you got me on that one. Now, how do I get on the grounds?"

"I'll take care of that, but I doubt if I can get you a pass until tomorrow. Do you need anything? Computers, internet access, maybe dinner and a martini?"

"Why, Dr. Scott, how nice of you to make the offer. Actually, I do need something. I'll need a boat. I brought my fishing gear. Caroline is with me so any dinner invitation would have to be for the both of us."

"I can take care of both requests. You can use my boat. How about 7:30 this evening for dinner?"

"That sounds wonderful, we've only eaten once in the last 24 hours. I have a lot of questions about your fish so I hope you won't mind if we talk shop at dinner. I took some slides of your specimen after you left that I'd like to show you."

"Great. I'm just as interested in finding out about it as you are. Would you like steaks, seafood, or pasta? I'm game for whatever you ladies feel like."

"Surprise us. You know the area. We can eat at McDonald's if you'd like. But a steak sounds awfully tempting. We're staying at the Drothers Inn, just across from the Fermilab entrance. 7:30 sounds great. We're in room 15. We'll see you then."

The evening had gone smoothly and everyone had enjoyed the steak and cold beer. Bill was telling them about the monster bass that thrived in the lake when his phone rang. It was 9:30, and he wasn't happy about having his evening disturbed.

"Hello."

"Bill, it's Tim. Where are you?"

"I'm in town having a steak. I tried to find you earlier. I wanted you to join us. Dr. Baker and her assistant are here from Chicago."

"Sorry, I've been tied up all day. We have more problems."

"More? I was planning on coming back in another hour or so..."

"You'd better come back now. More people are missing."

With that, the call ended abruptly. Bill sat there for a few seconds, dumbfounded.

"More people are missing?"

"Who's missing?" Caroline asked, breaking his concentration.

Bill hadn't realized that he'd repeated those last words out loud. He looked at Caroline, then at Dr. Baker. Things were beginning to take a turn for the worse. He didn't know if he should tell them what little he knew, or let someone with more authority clue them in. After all, they didn't have anything to do with what had gone on last night. He knew that rumors had been floating around all day.

First, it was terrorists. Then it was just a problem in the beam tunnel and that could have been almost anything. There was also that weird thing about the accelerator not wanting to shut down. That was no rumor. He also heard that someone had been killed. Now, Tim says that more people were missing? Inferring that the rumor of someone being killed earlier must be true?

"I'm sorry, ladies, you remember Tim Collins? He was with me when I brought you the fish. Well, he said that something is happening at Fermilab that needs my attention. So, I guess I'd better get back and see what he's talking about. I'm too full to eat anymore anyway. I imagine you ladies have had a pretty big day yourselves. Why don't you finish your drinks. I'll take care of the bill and then take you back to the hotel."

"I almost forgot. I talked to the head of security just before I picked you up. You'll be able to come and go as you wish. A few areas will still be off limits because of hazardous chemicals and electrical dangers. I can't even get into cryogenics without special authorization."

"I imagine that things will be shut down to the general public for a few days at least. If you'll give security your names in the morning, they'll have your ID badges ready allowing you to go most anywhere."

"That's great news. I don't know about Caroline, but after last night's marathon I didn't get nearly enough sleep. I'm all for hitting the sack and getting an early start in the morning." After paying the tab, Bill drove them back to the hotel. As they approached, they could see a soft bluish glow just topping the crown of trees surrounding the Fermilab complex.

"What's that light?" Dr. Baker asked.

"You know, I don't remember ever seeing it before. It must be something the security guys have set up. They probably have the place lit up like a Christmas tree. What time is it, anyway?"

"It's only a few minutes after ten, but I feel like I've been up for a week. I guess all this excitement has taken more out of me than I realized."

"Why don't you ladies get some sleep and I'll see you tomorrow. Call me when you get ready to come over. I'll show you the sights. If you're serious about catching some fish, I'll take you on a guided tour of the best spots in the lake."

"You've got a deal."

"The water's still pretty chilly, there's no sense in getting on the lake too early. You'd probably rather sleep in a bit anyway. How does 9:00 A.M. sound? There's a boat ramp just past the main parking area next to Wilson Hall. I'll double check with security and make sure your ID cards are ready. Do you need any fishing gear?"

"No, I brought everything I need. I'll see you in the morning. Thanks for a wonderful dinner. The food was excellent."

Carol chimed in, "Yes, thank you Bill, I really enjoyed the evening. We'll have to treat you before we leave."

"You're on. Connie, I'll see you in the morning around 9:00. Carol, I'll have someone give you a tour of the facilities while we're out on the lake. Good night, ladies."

As the two of them watched the car pull out of the parking lot, Carol smiled at Dr. Baker and said, "Bill seems like a really nice guy. If I were a few years older, I might just—"

"That, young lady, is the difference between a twenty-one year old and someone who's...well, a lot more mature." Then, smiling, Dr. Baker said, "He is a hunk though, isn't he?"

Grinning, Carol said, "Who's the twenty-one year old? Besides, I'm almost 24." With that, the two women retired to their rooms. Tomorrow morning would come soon enough. As Bill turned into Fermilab's entrance he wondered, where is that blue light coming from?

Chapter Fourteen

Bill had risen early to get the boat and gear ready for the morning's fishing expedition. The night before, he'd loaded his rods and digital tackle box into the boat and hooked up the battery charger to the lithium trolling motor. The sun was well above the tree line as he backed his electric SUV into one of the storage sheds. While fumbling with the trailer's smart hitch, he noticed that the trolling motor battery wasn't fully charged—the charger's display still showed one amp. That meant the battery was close, but not quite topped off. It shouldn't be a problem, though; they wouldn't be out all day. This trip was just to collect water samples and maybe catch a fish or two. A few hours would be plenty.

He wanted to double-check his sonar depth finder. This was the one item he knew Dr. Baker would be interested in, though he expected she'd be disappointed. He was sure she was expecting to find a bottomless pit, while he'd be amazed if they found anything over three meters. Then again, who could blame her? The fish he'd brought to the aquarium could hardly have come from a shallow lake in the Midwest. Yet it had. The problem was, he'd been over every inch of this lake for years, and the deepest spot he'd ever found was just over three meters. She would soon see firsthand that this lake was just like any of the thousands of others in northern Illinois.

He thought it might be a good idea to bring along a paddle—just in case. If the battery died, he didn't want to be stranded in the middle of the lake. Better safe than sorry. Next, he temporarily hooked up the trolling motor and depth finder. The lights on the finder came on and the propeller spun, so they seemed fine. He unhooked them.

Life jackets and the compressed air horn (why the state still required a horn on a 14-foot Jon boat in 2030 was beyond him) were next on his list. Once everything was loaded, he dropped the trailer's tongue over the SUV's hitch, fastened the safety clasp, and was ready to go. The boat launch was about a quarter mile away. When he got there, Dr. Baker was already throwing casts from the shore.

"Good morning," Bill called out. "How long have you been here?"

"Morning. I just got here a few minutes ago. This is only my fourth cast."

"What type of lure are you using? I caught Fessie on a Bomber. It's a deep—"

"Deep diver. I know, I saw it. Or what was left of it, anyway. I've been using Bombers, Hot-N-Tots, and other deep divers for years. I'm surprised the fish will hit such a fast-moving crankbait this early in the year."

Crap, Bill thought, she's a marine biologist; she's probably caught more fish than I ever will.

"Have you tried a Devil's Horse?" he called out.

"What's a Devil's Horse?" Smiling, Bill thought, there may be hope for me yet!

After launching the boat, Bill parked the SUV and came back with a small waterproof basket.

"Is that lunch or breakfast?" Dr. Baker asked.

"Neither, I'm afraid. I always keep my phone, wallet, sunblock, etc. in here. But I did pack a snack or two."

Bill climbed into the back of the boat. Dr. Baker would have to push them off because he'd be running the trolling motor. The rear of the boat needed to stay in deeper water so the prop wouldn't drag bottom. She pushed the boat away from the ramp and jumped into the bow in one fluid motion, barely making a ripple. It was obvious she knew her way around a boat launch.

The water was still cool. The air temperature was a chilly 65 degrees, but climbing quickly. Bill checked the water temp—just 62. The water was as clear as glass. When the sun rose to its highest point, you'd be able to see the bottom in many places. Bill maneuvered the boat out toward the middle of the lake.

"Are you familiar with this type of depth finder?" he asked.

"It looks like a Lowrance. What's its range?"

"There are three settings: eight, thirty, and a hundred meters. I rarely use the deeper settings. I think I've only used it once while fishing Kentucky Lake above the dam. I keep it on the lowest setting here. It's reading just over a meter and a half right now. See the little blips between the top line and the bottom?"

"Yes," Dr. Baker said, scooting toward the back to get a better look.

"I'm sure you know all about depth finders, but this one's pretty new, and it might be a little different than what you're used to. The bottom line is the lake bottom. The top is the surface. For the most part, it'll stay between the one and two-meter mark while we're this close to shore. Those blips that pop up every so often are fish. As a rule, the bigger the blip, the bigger the fish. This unit sends out acoustic waves in a cone shape, with the point of the cone at the transducer." He pulled up the transducer mounting, showing how it could be lowered or raised by hand. As he did, the display went wild with blips, then went blank.

"How big an area does the cone cover on the bottom?"

"Well, I'd have to check the manual, but I think it's about three meters wide at the deepest point here. I caught a five-pound catfish once and let him swim under the boat to see what size blip he made. He was about two meters down and made a blip almost an inch long. Pulled him up closer, and the blip covered the whole screen. It's hard to tell how big a fish is when it's close to the transducer."

"Where were you when you caught the fish you brought to the aquarium?"

"Other side of the lake, near Wilson Hall. I was fishing from shore, so it couldn't have been very deep. Watch the depth display and we'll cruise around before we go over there."

Bill made a cast with another Bomber and wedged the rod between the transom and a brace holding the trolling motor. He flipped the switch to #3 and started trolling. The depth finder never varied more than a few feet as they pulled out farther. It approached three meters at one spot, but quickly came back to two and a half. They trolled for about fifteen minutes, zigzagging to cover as much of the lake's bottom as possible.

"Here, let me show you something neat about this finder." He turned the trolling motor off. "Keep your eyes on the display," he said, fiddling with the transducer rod. He pulled the lever to a 45-degree angle and several new blips appeared. Then he changed the finder's depth setting to maximum—thirty meters. Dozens of blips appeared.

"What did you do?" Dr. Baker asked.

"The transducer can be aimed at any angle. By lifting the lever, I turned the acoustic cone horizontal. Then I set the power to max. What you're seeing now are echoes from fish up to thirty meters away. I have it aimed at that big tree on the other side. By swiveling the rod, I can look for concentrations of fish in any direction. Any big blips, especially at the farthest depths, are big fish. Look, there's a pretty good one now, about twenty-five meters out."

"That's a great feature; I don't think I've ever seen anyone do that with a finder this small. I've used side-scanning radar for anomalies on the ocean floor. I remember finding the wreck of a Spanish galleon off Venezuela using a similar technique."

Bill switched the transducer back to vertical and reduced the power to the lowest setting. "Two and a half meters as usual," he announced.

As they trolled out to the middle, Bill noticed a slight change in the water's color. It reminded him of the way water looks when a drop of oil is mixed in—a shiny rainbow appearance.

"I brought several sample jars. Let's stop here; I want to get a sample of this water. It looks like it's contaminated with something."

"Sure," Bill replied. "While you're getting your sample, I'm going to make a few casts."

Before Bill could cast, the finder's alarm sounded.

"What the—" Bill said, staring at the display. "This doesn't happen often, and never this early in the year." Almost as soon as the alarm sounded, it stopped.

"What is it? What triggered the alarm?"

"For a moment, the finder was reading a depth greater than its selected range. When that happens, the alarm goes off. Then, as we coasted a little farther, it came back to the usual two and a half meters and the alarm turned off."

"That may be the hole we're looking for."

"I doubt it," Bill said, suppressing a laugh. "What probably happened is we passed over something that's a poor reflector of the acoustic signal. The finder can't get a return echo, thinks the bottom is out of range, and sounds the alarm. Probably a patch of moss. I've seen this in southern lakes, but moss doesn't usually grow much up here; it's too cold. Let me back up and see if I can find it again."

He put the trolling motor in reverse and retraced their path. Sure enough, they'd just backed up a few feet when the alarm went off again. Then, before he could stop—silence.

"That's got to be moss! It's soft and slimy and doesn't reflect sound waves worth a damn."

"I've got my sample, let's go to where you caught your fish and do some fishing."

"Ok, we're off. Cast to your right and I'll cast to my left. We may as well troll on the way. We might catch something out here in the middle."

Bill turned the motor to #3. The battery didn't seem down at all. He figured they could run at this speed all day. It was #5 that really drained the power.

They'd only gone about a hundred yards when the alarm went off again. This time, things were different. The alarm stayed on. Bill brought the boat to a standstill. The alarm blared.

"It's hard to believe there could be this much moss so early in the year. Let me crank up the power and see if that won't find the bottom. Even if only a small part of the signal gets back, it'll at least shut the alarm off."

He clicked the switch to the thirty-meter level. The alarm still blared.

"Ok, I give up. I could get a reading off a piece of carpet at three meters when at full power. This should do it."

The second he flipped the switch to the hundred-meter setting, the alarm fell silent.

"That must have done it. I don't hear that raucous noise anymore," Dr. Baker said.

"You're not going to believe this, but I'm still not showing any bottom. It's still flashing, OUT OF RANGE."

"But the alarm went off."

"There's no alarm on the hundred-meter setting. Otherwise, it would never shut off in the ocean or next to a dam. What I don't understand is—where the hell is the bottom?"

Then, all at once, there it was. But on this scale, the space between the surface and bottom markers was hardly readable.

"Something's screwy here."

He realized that while they'd been talking, the boat had drifted in the breeze. He put the trolling motor in reverse and slowly started backtracking.

Sure enough, the display flashed OUT OF RANGE again. Only this time, there was more. This time he could see other blips, some big, some small, dozens—hundreds maybe. These blips were mostly very deep, starting at the forty-meter level and going down until they were out of range.

"This can't be right. I must be picking up some kind of temperature inversion. That's got to be it. At this time of year, the water on the bottom is a lot colder than near the surface. The finder must be picking up a thermocline."

"Well, there's an easy way to find out," Dr. Baker said, bringing Bill back to the present.

"Sorry," he said. "I was just thinking. What are you going to do?"

She opened her tackle box and brought out what looked like a jumbo red sinker. Which, in fact, it was. It weighed eight ounces. Then, she picked up a fishing pole that looked like it might have belonged to a child, but the reel was enormous.

"That," Bill said, "looks like the kind of rig they use to catch giant catfish below the dam on Kentucky Lake."

"This isn't a fishing rig. This is what I use to measure water depth when I'm not sure if my sounder's working."

"How much line is on that thing?"

"Seven hundred feet of ten-pound test on this spool, but I have others. It changes color every hundred feet. There are markers at five, ten, and fifty-foot intervals. I'll be able to tell within a few inches the exact depth by converting these colors to feet. If we were in the ocean, we'd be converting to meters."

"That's a pretty neat outfit, but I'm sure we're just over some moss or detecting a thermocline."

"We'll know soon enough."

Dr. Baker attached the weight to the line with a swivel. Bill could see why the pole was so short and stiff now. There was no need to do anything but let the line out. The pole only had to be long enough to get the weight over the side. You didn't have to cast it, just press the release and let it drop. A longer pole would droop with the weight.

"Here goes nothing," Dr. Baker said, pressing the release. The sinker dropped immediately. "This will fall at about a foot every three seconds initially. As more line leaves the spool, it'll speed up a little, but not much. The weight of the line in the water helps pull it down, but the resistance cancels some of that. It stays within a foot every two or three seconds most of the way."

Before she finished, the line passed the first ten-foot marker.

"Bill, try to hold the boat in this exact position."

"I'll throw out the anchor. There's hardly any wind, so we shouldn't drift much."

He dropped the anchor. Its twenty feet of rope became taut in a few seconds as it failed to touch bottom.

"What the—that's a twenty-foot anchor rope! We really are in a deep spot," Bill said, astonished.

"I've got sixty feet of line out now and it's still going."

"Let me see if I can find your sinker on the display." He looked, but doubted the sinker would bounce a signal back at that depth. He did see the anchor, hanging straight down, about twenty feet under the boat.

"One hundred feet."

They both sat there, stunned, as the reel continued to play out line.

"One hundred fifty. Bill, get me a sample of the water here, would you please?"

That suited him fine. He needed something to do besides watch that spinning spool. He filled a sample bottle, labeled it, and returned it to her bag.

"Two hundred fifty."

"What happened to two hundred?" Bill asked.

"We passed it fifty feet ago," Dr. Baker said, smiling.

For the next twenty minutes, neither said a word. Bill watched the colors change as the line played out, until, finally—

"Six hundred feet!"

With that, Dr. Baker clicked the windup crank forward, stopping the falling weight. Even so, the weight would continue to fall another foot or so as the line stretched.

"Why'd you stop?" Bill asked.

"I don't know. I think I'm a little frightened. This isn't right. We're not off the continental shelf; we're in a Jon boat in northern Illinois. This can't be happening."

"It can't be, but it is. Maybe there was an old mine shaft that's been here all along. Maybe the fish I caught lived at the bottom of it."

"Mine shafts don't go straight down," Dr. Baker said. "For a little bit, maybe, but then they go off horizontally."

"A well could go that deep."

"An oil well could, easily," Dr. Baker replied. "But oil wells are never more than a foot or so wide. What's the chance that when this place was built, they drilled some kind of test hole, an exploratory shaft? I mean, this place is run by the government, isn't it?"

"I don't know why they would have, but it's possible, I guess. There has to be some explanation. Maybe someone was thinking of using this lake as a dumpsite for nuclear waste. A hole in the bottom would be hard to find."

"We work with nuclear materials all the time, though they're just low-grade isotopes. Maybe someone was afraid we might discover some exotic new form of matter and this hole was bored as a precaution—a safe place to hide something in."

"How could it be so wide? It must be twenty to thirty feet across. How could I have missed it? I've been over this lake dozens, probably hundreds of times, and I always have the sounder on."

Without thinking, Dr. Baker pressed the trigger on the reel again and the line began playing out. Two minutes later—

"Six hundred fifty feet," she said, in a monotone. Then, after what seemed like an eternity—but was only a few minutes more—the spool stopped spinning and the tip of the pole bounced as the line tightened. The spool was empty.

"Seven hundred feet," they said in unison.

Dr. Baker repeated it, as if that would change something. "Seven hundred feet and still no bottom."

Between the sinker, the line, and the reel, the pole was beginning to feel heavy. At this point, there was nothing left to do but reel it back in.

"Here, let me do that," Bill said, offering to trade places. "Take over the motor, and I'll spell you on the pole." Just as Bill started to get up, a look came over Dr. Baker's face that caused him to stop. She was staring at the display. Along with the dozens of small blips, there was one huge blip, close to the bottom of the display.

"What is that?" she asked, pointing toward the back of the boat.

The way she said it startled Bill even more.

"What is what?" Bill asked, looking out over the water. He half expected to see the neck of some gigantic sea monster.

"That!" she said, this time pointing vigorously at the depth finder. She was still holding the pole tightly.

Finally, Bill realized she was pointing at the sounder. The display was showing dozens of blips, almost all of them deep. There was one blip that shouldn't be there. Not as large as this one. How could it be so big and yet so deep? As they watched, they realized the blip was rising quickly toward them. It was now in about forty meters of water.

"Let me have that pole," Bill said.

He grabbed it and started reeling in furiously. After about thirty seconds, he stopped.

"Why did you stop?" Dr. Baker asked.

"It won't come up anymore."

"What do you mean, it won't come up anymore?"

"I mean, it's hung up."

"But there's nothing for it to get hung up on."

"Well, it's stuck on something. Look!" He pulled up on the pole as hard as he dared, afraid he might break the line. The pole, stiff as it was, bowed about six inches. Sure enough, the line had caught on something—something very deep down in the hole. All he was doing was stretching the line; the sinker wasn't coming up at all.

"Oh my God!" Dr. Baker gasped. This time, she not only looked scared, she sounded scared. Like a yawn, he caught her fear. "Look at the display now!"

The blip was much closer, and it was getting bigger. It was only about fifty meters from the surface, and moving upwards with ever-increasing speed. Fifteen seconds later, forty meters! At this rate, it would reach the surface in just under two minutes.

"Here, take this. I'm getting us the hell out of here." He handed Dr. Baker the pole. She instinctively pressed the trigger, letting the spool go back into free fall. This took the pressure off the line. Bill had only reeled in about thirty meters. It wouldn't be long before it reached the end of the spool again. Bill flipped the trolling motor into high, but he'd forgotten it was still in reverse. He wasted precious seconds getting the boat turned around and headed toward the bank. His gaze was transfixed, between the display and where they were headed. They'd only gone a few feet when the normal two-meter bottom popped back onto the display.

"OK! We're over shallow water again. At least we're not over that hole anymore." Whatever was coming up from the depths had only been about thirty meters below them when they reached the edge. Thirty meters, yet it had taken up the whole bottom of the display. Bill couldn't even imagine how big it was. He only knew it was huge. This wasn't a fish; this was a whale, or a monster!

A few seconds later, the boat, which had just started to pick up speed, suddenly jerked hard and to the left, the bow dipping almost into the water and nearly capsizing them. The boat had reversed directions. They were facing back toward the hole again. The trolling motor pushed them ever closer.

Dr. Baker cried out, "It's the anchor! You still have the anchor out!"

Sure enough, the anchor must have caught on the edge of the hole, and when the rope tightened, it jerked the boat back toward it. Bill never moved faster. Grabbing the fillet knife from his tackle box, he tossed it to Dr. Baker.

"Cut the rope," he said, as he turned the trolling motor to the right, trying to get leverage on the taut rope.

He didn't have to tell her twice. Dr. Baker took the sharp knife and slashed the rope in one motion. As soon as the pressure was released, the boat immediately swung around under the urging of the trolling motor. They were headed toward shore again.

Several people standing on the bank verified what happened next. They had been watching the boat with interest, wondering why two people were fishing in the middle of the lake with what appeared to be a kid's fishing pole. These last antics with the trolling motor had really gotten their attention.

The boat was still moving toward the shore, but the 20-pound thrust trolling motor didn't have enough oomph to get it there quickly.

Suddenly the pole with the weight attached flew up from where it was laying in the bottom of the boat as the line pulled tight! The pole wedged between the depth sounder and the rear bow light. The line stretched to its breaking point, broke with a 'crack' that sounded like a gunshot, and the pole fell to the bottom of the transom.

From behind them, the water started to rise.

It was as if someone had turned on a powerful hose. Or a huge water main had broken under the lake and the pressure of the escaping water was causing the surface to rise slowly.

Nothing broke the surface, but it was definitely taking on a convex appearance. In the next few seconds, it rose more sharply, changing from a small mound into an ever-growing hill of water. Still, nothing broke the surface. As it grew, it started to churn. Tons and tons of water erupted up out of the depths. The water was being pushed with incredible force by whatever they had seen on the depth finder. Fortunately, whatever was pushing it was apparently too large to fit through the hole itself. But it was forcing thousands of gallons of water through that hole. And who knew what else.

The mountain of water struck the Jon boat and lifted it like a surfboard. The boat rode the wave right onto the shore, landing only a few feet from the startled spectators. Not just to the shore—but on the shore. The trolling motor acted like a rudder, plowing into the ground. The spectators were drenched as the wave washed over the shoreline.

As the water ran back into the lake, fish were stranded everywhere. Some of them didn't look like any fish either of them had ever seen before.

"I think we found what I was looking for," Dr. Baker said, half in a state of shock.

"I don't know what we found," Bill said, as he fumbled to turn off the motor that was still spinning, the shaft bent beyond repair. "One thing's for sure though, my fishing days in this lake are over."

Chapter Fifteen

Almost 72 hours had passed since all hell broke loose at the normally placid Fermilab complex. Three days— just enough time for the powers-that-be to decide that, no matter what had gone wrong, it wasn't serious enough to shut things down for long. Oh, there wouldn't be any "full power" tests right away. Not until the previous problems could be fully understood and corrected. But testing would begin again, and soon. The Department of Energy paid the bills. When the DOE said to power the systems up, they would be powered up.

You couldn't really blame them. Sure, some very improbable things had happened. Still, many of the reports being filed were so utterly ridiculous, hardly anyone at the DOE believed them. As if the problems encountered at DUNE weren't weird enough, when they read what Captain Rider and Sgt. Madison had turned in (water flowing out of thin air and being attacked in the elevator by a monster), that was the icing on the cake.

Accompanying the official "White House" report and affixed to the outside of its cover was a memo, signed by Dr. Slater, head of DOE's investigative team. It stated: "Due to the stress and nature of the events that took place on the night of May 12th, 2030, I suggest that the report filed by Captain Rider and Sgt. Madison regarding their experiences in the beam tunnel be stricken from the record. It is suspected that being in such close proximity to the intense electromagnetic fields, generated by the superconducting magnets, caused them to suffer hallucinations." There was no mention of the condition of the elevator.

Harder to explain was the fact that two men had died. (Several more would turn up "missing.") That was the real reason the tests were on hold. As far as the DOE was concerned, they were sticking to the story that someone had infiltrated the complex; most likely a "disgruntled" employee, sabotaged the test, and was the primary cause of the strange events that had transpired. Several congressmen already thought that more than a few of Fermilab's scientists were riding that fine line between genius and just plain nuts—it wouldn't take much more for them to believe that someone had stepped over it. All the DOE wanted was for the testing to get started again.

Unfortunately, State authorities had been called in and they were apt to want to run their own investigation. State and Federal law enforcement agencies are notorious for having problems when it comes to working together. This is pretty much true everywhere, and Illinois is no exception. It's only when something like 9/11 happens that all the branches of government pull together. When all was said and done, the DOE (Federal usually wins out in these matters) ended up with complete control over the investigation.

The State Police were basically delegated to the ranks of traffic control. They patrolled the roads leading into and out of the complex, turning back those who didn't have the proper clearance. They set up a roadblock near Wilson Hall where they looked like they were doing more than they actually were. For all practical purposes, they had been left out of the loop.

The E in DOE stands for energy. For a while at least, the PIP-II accelerator had been operating at more than its designed capacity while using less than half of the energy it should have consumed. Everyone wanted to know how this impossibility could have happened. And how to make it happen again!

As much as the DOE was pushing for the go-ahead, others, namely Steven Tyco, were dragging their feet. Steven didn't want to do anything until he was satisfied that he had a handle on what had actually happened. Even three days after the event, he still didn't have the slightest idea of what had gone wrong. Part of his problem was that in order to find out what had caused the runaway, he needed to bring PIP-II back online and at the same power level as when the problems began. He didn't think that this was such a good idea though, DOE or not!

Truth be known, he was scared. While it was happening, he didn't have time to think about the consequences of what was going on. Now, in hindsight, he wondered what would have happened had the accelerator continued to accelerate? When you pull the plug and nothing happens, what do you do next?

He was trying to figure out what had caused PIP-II to overrun by combing through massive amounts of digital logs and system data. This was the only safe way he knew to come to any conclusions. The more he learned, the more confused he became. He was not alone. Every scientist involved in the test that night was doing the same thing. Strong coffee and protein bars had become the food of choice. You could choose your own poison—caffeine, sugar, or both.

The thing about it was—most of the test went just fine. On first examination, nothing seemed to be out of order. Even when things began to go crazy and PIP-II just kept on accelerating, there was nothing in the logs that indicated anything was wrong. Two days after the incident, one of the AI clusters was taken offline and programmed to cross-reference the data from the various instruments in operation that night.

Records were run against each other. Whole banks of instruments were compared on a second-by-second basis to see if a malfunction in one instrument might have caused something down the line to malfunction. This was commonly known as the "ripple" effect. Simulation after simulation was tested. But even a modern AI wasn't powerful enough to explore all of the scenarios that could have happened that night. There were just too many variables.

Thousands of instruments are involved in a major test of this sort, all of them working in unison—the output of one instrument feeding the input of the next. There are millions of connections, many with backup capabilities. A wiring nightmare Freddie Krueger might have designed. As if that wasn't enough, there were things to consider outside of the Fermilab complex. Only a few weeks before serious testing had begun, sunspot activity increased to the point where the Aurora Borealis could be seen as far south as Houston. This rarely happens. That's why they call them the "Northern Lights."

When the electrical activity in the Earth's upper atmosphere is this strong, it can play hell with the power grid. A large part of Canada was blacked out in 1999 by unusually strong sunspot activity. A huge solar flare was detected that was aimed directly at the earth. As the electrically charged particles carried by the solar wind lined up along the Earth's magnetic field, they started interacting with the power grid, forcing voltage transients that eventually shut a large part of the grid down. It was several days before the problem could be rectified. Even then, there wasn't much the engineers could do—the problem pretty much fixed itself when the sun's activity lessened. Could that have been part of their problem?

One thing that hadn't been checked was the power transmission lines running the length of the beam tunnel. There were miles of electrical connectors. The valves controlling the flow and amount of liquid nitrogen pumped into the superconducting magnets needed to be checked and verified too. Maybe there was something wrong with the magnets themselves? The science behind this technology (superconducting magnets) has been around for years, though the number and size of magnets like these had never been tested before. As far as he could tell, they were operating well within the safety limits predicted by computer simulations. He was trying to think of anything that might have been responsible for their problems.

Why was the beam tunnel still off limits? He'd heard rumors, everything from terrorists to monsters. Whatever it was, it didn't look like he was going to be getting any reports on the magnets anytime soon. The technicians were locked out too. He didn't really feel that the magnets were the source of the problem anyway. They were under computer control and he had the logs of each magnet's performance during every second PIP-II ran free.

Nothing he'd seen so far implied that there was anything wrong with either the beam tube or the superconducting magnets.

A week had passed and there were still no answers. Since no harm had come to the equipment and no damage was done to the surrounding neighborhood, the DOE got its wish. Work began again to bring PIP-II online. The next test was scheduled for May 20th.

Preparations were underway to monitor every aspect of the test, including the installation of one hundred and forty-four new surveillance cameras in the beam tunnel. The grounds above the tunnel, the entrances to Wilson Hall, the Feynman Center, and DUNE had additional cameras installed as well. All were interfaced into Central Command's security system.

Armed security personnel guarded the technicians installing the cameras. The work crews were never officially told of the events that had happened earlier, though they had all heard the rumors.

Once the cameras were installed, they were connected to a bank of twelve monitors at the security center. Each monitor was connected to twelve cameras, arranged in a matrix of four wide by three high. The images on the monitors were programmed to scroll in several different ways. The data on the cameras was recorded using a technique pioneered for high-speed data streaming and AI anomaly detection. It was really quite ingenious.

The displays were being watched by computer for any changes in the normally static images. If the AI's scanning algorithm found anything out of the ordinary, an alarm went off and 'human' intervention was called for.

Within a few days, these cameras would be recording images that seemed to be coming from a horror movie instead of the usual emptiness of the beam tunnel.

Chapter Sixteen

Bill Scott had just gotten to his office when his AI assistant pinged him: "Dr. Baker is on the line."

"Hi, Connie. You must have heard something about my fish?"

"Good morning, Bill. Sorry, I still haven't had any luck in identifying it, but I received an interesting call from Tom Cooper at Woods Hole about an hour ago. He wanted to talk to you and anyone else who might have been there when you caught it. I guess the sample I sent them is causing quite a stir. I told him how busy you were and that you didn't have much free time. He understood and left me his private number, just in case. I assumed you wouldn't have time to talk to him right now."

"No, I've got too much on my mind to worry with that right now. I sure would like to know what it is though. Did he have any idea at all?"

"No, but I could tell it was bothering the hell out of him. I've worked with him enough to know how he thinks. When he can't figure something out, he'll work on it until he does. And believe me, this has got his full attention. He's checked the DNA against every known type of fish in their database. There's nothing that even comes close. He did agree that it's a creature that lives at great depths. Not just because of the luminescent splotches but because the cell tissues had adapted to withstand great pressure. He said he has no doubt that this creature lived in the deep oceans."

"It may be deep alright, but it wasn't the ocean."

"I didn't even bring that up. It's bad enough that I bring him a fish he can't identify. If I told him it came from a small lake in Northern Illinois that had an average depth of less than three meters—well, he'd probably think I was trying to put something over on him. If I told him what happened when we found that hole, I don't know what he'd say."

"How are you coming with the other fish we captured?" Bill asked.

"Same thing, they all drew a blank. I thought I'd wait a week or so then send a few of them to Tom as well. If he hasn't ID'd our first fish by then, that will give him something else to work on."

"Listen, Connie. We're going to be bringing the PIP-II accelerator online again Friday afternoon."

"I thought you said that no more tests would be run until the problems had all been worked out? When did that happen?"

"It didn't. That's what I wanted to talk to you about. We're supposed to keep the testing time secret until the actual day of the test, but I was hoping you might do me a little favor."

"Sure. What do you need?"

"I'd like for you to watch over the lake while PIP-II is running. Maybe you and Carol could have a picnic and just keep an eye out over the water. I'd like to know if anything looks strange, or out of place. I'd especially like you to watch over the area where we found that hole. If you see something unusual, I want you to call my cell immediately."

"I don't see any problem with that. I could use an afternoon off. Since the DOE arranged for Carol and I to share a house here on the grounds, I've been putting in 15-hour days."

Bill was shuffling through his digital schedule as he talked. "I never dreamed that they'd act as fast as they did. I told them about catching the fish and taking it to your lab at the aquarium. I mentioned that you were here now, inspecting the lake. Before the day was out, they were inviting you to stay and join our project."

"I really didn't mind. Something like this comes along once in a lifetime, if at all."

"Good, that settles it. I'll make arrangements for you and Carol. Security will be extra tight during the day of the test. I'll also see that you get two pairs of binoculars and spring for your picnic lunches. The test will start about noon, but it will take several hours to get all of the systems online. I'd say, if you can get there by three, and stay a couple of hours—that should be enough time to see if anything is going to happen. I checked the weather and it's supposed to be around 75 by then. Not the warmest, but it will only be for a few hours."

"Sounds fine to me, but do you really think something might happen?"

"No, not really. I'd just like to keep an eye on the area over that hole. If anything should show up, you're the only one that would know what is going on."

"I wouldn't count on it. If it's anything like our past experience, I'll be no more help than the janitor."

"You did fine the last time. Don't kid yourself. If the DOE didn't respect your abilities, you wouldn't be here. Everyone here is the best at what they do."

"Thanks for the compliment. Carol's shopping in town; I'll let her know of our plans when she returns. I'm sure she'll be happy to get out of here for a while too. Living upstairs over the lab beats driving to work each day. The downside is, we usually end up working twice as long as we normally would. Let me know if I need to bring anything special, otherwise I'll be picnicking Friday while everyone else is working. Since you're buying, get us a bucket of the Colonel's best. Extra crispy, with coleslaw, rolls, and a six-pack of diet Coke."

"You got it. All you need to bring is yourselves. I'll let security know that you're still on the clock, even though you're picnicking. It's a zoo here now and will continue to be so until after the test. If I don't see you before Friday, have a good time. Maybe we can get together with Tim and Carol over the weekend. We could all unwind with a show and dinner?"

145

"Now you're talking. You know where to find me. Give me a call Saturday morning if you want to get away for the evening. I know some wonderful places in Chicago, or we could just catch a movie and relax here."

"It's a date. I'll call you before noon. Have a nice picnic and tell Carol I said, Hello."

"Talk to you Saturday. Goodbye."

As Bill hung up the phone, he wondered to himself, am I being stupid, thinking that revving up PIP-II might stir up something in the lake? And if I really am serious about that happening, why the hell am I sending Connie and Carol out there? It could be dangerous. I've already seen what can happen. Something's not right with that lake. Something's not right with any of this. I guess I'll know soon enough—

The rest of the day was hectic. The phone never stopped ringing. It was either a technician with a problem that needed solving, or someone from the White House wanting to know if everything was still on schedule. All the while, his thoughts kept going back to that day when he and Connie discovered the hole to nowhere. With all of the other things going on, no one had ever taken the time to explore what really had happened.

As weird as it was, it still wasn't weird enough to warrant a serious investigation. Not when two people had been killed in the beam tunnel. The fiasco in the lake would just have to wait its turn.

He was almost ready to leave for the day. His eyes watered and his stomach was sour from all the coffee he'd been drinking when his AI assistant's voice came over the intercom, informing him that he had visitors.

"It's really late, Susan, just make an appointment for tomorrow morning. I'm dead tired and I have more work to do tonight."

He started to pick up his jacket when his office door opened. Two men wearing long black trench coats and dark sunglasses came into the room.

146

"You've got to be kidding," he said, just loud enough that he wasn't sure if they'd heard him or not.

They walked to his desk and stood there, staring at him for a good ten seconds before they said anything.

One of them reached into an inside pocket and retrieved a wallet. He flipped it open and there, behind a clear vinyl cover, was an ID. It identified him as Don Singleton. The initials HAARP were on the ID as well, in bright red letters.

"We're sorry to barge in on you this way, Dr. Scott. I'm Don Singleton and this is my associate, David Meyer. We'd like to have a few words with you about what's been happening here, if we may."

"Can't this wait until tomorrow, gentlemen? I've been up since five this morning and I have a staff meeting in less than two hours."

"No, it can't. But we'll only need a few minutes of your time. I have some papers that will explain why we're here. It would be in everyone's interest if you read them at your earliest convenience—tonight if possible. I think you'll want to meet with us before you begin testing PIP-II again."

The other man, Meyer, opened a briefcase and removed a small stack of what looked to be less than a dozen sheets of paper. The cover page of the stack had the same letters across the top that he'd seen on Singleton's identity card—HAARP. Directly under the letters, TOP SECRET was written in large black print. It looked like these were copies of the originals by the way the letters were streaked and blurred. The paper was of a cheap stock as well. It reminded him of the paper used in fax machines before inkjet models were available. It had that waxy look and feel. Meyer put the papers in a manila envelope, sealed the flap, and handed them to him.

As soon as he took possession of the papers, the men turned and started towards the door.

147

"We'll assume that you'll have read these by tomorrow," Singleton said without looking back. "We'll be in touch with you then."

Before he could reply, they were closing the door behind them. He stood there for a few seconds trying to figure out what exactly had just happened. If not for the papers he was holding, he might have been tempted to think that he had just dreamed this. He was certainly tired enough.

"Is everything alright?" His secretary's voice brought him back to his senses. He stuffed the papers into his own briefcase and walked out of his office.

"Everything's fine, Susan. I'll see you in the morning." With that, he headed for his car. In a few minutes, he'd be home. The first thing he'd do when he got there would be to get online and find out what the hell HAARP stood for. He thought he'd heard those initials before, but he couldn't quite place where or when. As he drove, he kept thinking about the two men who'd just visited him. They were right out of a "B" grade gangster movie.

"Men in Black," he mumbled to himself. Maybe they're not so strange after all. They fit right in with everything else that's been going on around here.

Chapter Seventeen

It only took Bill a few minutes to get to his house. He walked inside, dropped his bag, and went straight to his computer. "Hey, Iris," he said to his AI assistant, "bring up a browser and search for HAARP."

Almost instantly, the screen filled with results. HAARP – High Frequency Active Auroral Research Program. Bingo.

He remembered reading something about the project years ago, but hadn't realized it was still in operation. He clicked on the first link: https://haarp.gi.alaska.edu/. It was HAARP's home page. Just like Fermilab, HAARP had its own public portal. There were categories for General Information, Technical Details, Photo Index, News Articles, Research Activity, the Ionosphere, and even a HAARP Cam. That sounded interesting. He clicked the camera icon and was presented with a live image of an antenna array, the Alaskan sun setting behind a forest of metal towers. There were several inches of snow on the ground. The caption read, "Photos are taken at periodic intervals throughout the Alaskan daylight hours." That explained the snow—Alaska, of course.

He browsed through the categories, noting the similarities to Fermilab's own site. The webcam was a nice touch. He made a mental note to suggest something similar for the Fermilab homepage.

The phone rang. "Bill." It was Tom Nelson, calling from the Feynman Computing Center. "We've just started the meeting. I hated to call, but I was afraid you might have forgotten about it."

"Hi Tom, glad you did. Something came up and I lost track of the time. I'll be there in about ten minutes. Thanks for reminding me. See you shortly."

Bill bookmarked the HAARP homepage and started to leave. Then, on impulse, he did something he rarely did: he powered down his computer. It usually ran 24/7, but tonight, with those "TOP SECRET" papers in hand, he felt a little more cautious. He slid the envelope under the couch—no real reason, just a hunch that if they really were top secret, they shouldn't be left out in the open.

The meeting was straightforward. Mostly it was just reaffirming what everyone already knew and making sure all teams were on the same page. There were reports from various contractors: everything was either on schedule or already finished. Several upgrades had been made to the lighting and monitoring systems, all tested and working. As director, Bill had to be there, but the meetings bored him to death.

It was 9:15 when Bill got back home. He looked at the dark screen of his monitor and chuckled. *What the hell was I thinking? This cloak-and-dagger stuff is all in my head. Those guys were from another research facility, not the CIA. They probably just left me some information about a project overlap. I'm not getting enough sleep. No wonder I'm paranoid. I'll be seeing aliens next.*

He turned the computer back on and sat on the couch as it booted. He was tired—over sixteen hours on the clock and only one meal all day. He reached under the couch for the envelope. It wasn't where he'd left it. Now he was starting to get worried again. He got down on the floor and looked under the couch. There it was, but way off to the right. *That's odd,* he thought. *I was sure I put it under this end.* He tried to recall: *I turned off the computer, turned to the couch, reached down, slid the papers under. Here they are, anyway.*

Bill sat at the computer and started to log in, but his eyes hurt. He really didn't feel like staring at a screen any longer. *I'll continue this tomorrow,* he thought. *I've had enough excitement for one day.*

He decided to go to bed and browse through the papers before falling asleep—if he could keep his eyes open. He didn't realize it then, but he wouldn't be sleeping anytime soon.

HAARP – TOP SECRET

There were only a few pages in the documents the "men in black" had left. Still, the words TOP SECRET couldn't help but get his attention. As he removed the paperclip, he felt like a spy in a James Bond novel. That feeling quickly faded as he read the cover sheet.

Dr. Scott,

My name is Dave Glaspie. I'm a scientist involved in research at the HAARP facility in Gakona, Alaska. Actually, I'm only one of several hundred—myself and several colleagues have reason to believe that HAARP might have something to do with a problem you had in a recent test of the PIP-II accelerator. Normally, I wouldn't get involved in someone else's project without a prior invitation, but many of us feel that you should know of our experiments and how they might have influenced your test.

Let me start at the beginning. HAARP stands for High Frequency Active Auroral Research Program. HAARP was commissioned as a joint project between the US Navy and Air Force in 1990, working in conjunction with the University of Alaska. Basically, we conduct research on how radio communications are affected by the various layers of ionized gas in the upper atmosphere.

Much of our work consists of modifying these layers using an array of specially designed radio antennas. The first 18 of an eventual 180 antennas was brought online in 1995. As additional antennas were brought online, the overall power of the system increased exponentially. The building phase of HAARP was completed earlier this year. All 180 antennas are now in operation.

The main research at HAARP is supposed to be the study of the interaction of charged particles in the ionosphere with radio waves propagated from the earth. While this is in fact a large part of our research, it's only one of a series of projects HAARP scientists are working on. Many of which are secret and purely military in nature.

I'm sorry to be boring you with so much detail, but I think you'll appreciate it later on. It's important you know exactly what HAARP is capable of.

HAARP's antenna array is what's known as an "upper atmospheric heater." It actually heats sections of the ionosphere by saturating it with over three billion watts of focused radio waves. This has just become possible since the full complement of antennas went online. Without going into why this is desirable, let me tell you some of the possible military uses of this technology.

Weather modification, communications disruption, VLF and ULF submarine communications, mental disruptions, wireless power transmission, Earth-penetrating VLF and ULF transmissions... these are just some of the projects being undertaken by government scientists.

The public knows very little about the research being performed here because it's hidden under the blanket of the National Security Act. But the entire site is financed by the DOD and DARPA, so you can imagine the influence that the military has in the work being performed here. There are plenty of documents on the Internet if you need additional convincing of the government's involvement in the military aspects of HAARP.

The reason for our contacting you is, we heard about the problems you experienced during the last test of the PIP-II accelerator. Especially when it was noted that PIP-II was running at full power without drawing any energy from the electrical grid. I have the answer as to how that was accomplished.

You see, one of the experiments we are working on here is the transmission of power to anywhere on earth without the use of wires. This was first postulated by Nikola Tesla in 1891. Great strides have been accomplished by HAARP in doing what Tesla set out to do but was not able to because of his limited finances and materials.

HAARP is capable of shaping the molecules in the ionosphere into a plasma mirror so that enormous amounts of electrical power can be converted to microwaves and then beamed to anywhere on the face of the earth. This power comes from the millions of amperes of electrical energy produced by the sun and delivered to the earth by the solar wind. Once here, it's captured in the magnetic fields of the Van Allen radiation belts surrounding our planet.

It's not enough to just transmit that power; you also have to have a receiver on the earth that can convert the microwave energy back to usable electricity. We believe that somehow the PIP-II complex picked up this energy and was able to use it. We were conducting experiments in shaping this mirror at the same time you were running your tests.

HAARP's antenna array focuses over 3 billion watts of energy into a small region of the upper atmosphere. It's about four kilometers thick and twenty kilometers wide. While this sounds like a large amount of energy, and by human standards, it is—it's still minuscule compared to the energy supplied by the solar wind every second. The amazing thing is, this beam can control thousands of times more energy than we are producing.

Think of it this way. HAARP performs like a BJT transistor. A small change in the voltage on the base/emitter (our RF beam) causes a huge change at the base/collector junction (ionosphere). We tap into the charged particle streams captured by the earth's magnetic fields and redirect part of this energy to the ground as microwaves.

We think that somehow, the PIP-II accelerator was able to lock onto and use this energy when it was running free. That's where the TOP SECRET comes in. Someone at the DOD or DARPA noticed a correlation between the timing of events at Fermilab and those of our initial test with the full complement of antennas. I'd guess we were both breaking new ground at about the same time.

I only have a limited knowledge of particle physics, but I know that PIP-II requires an enormous amount of energy. I believe that HAARP provided that energy for a short period of time. How it was converted from microwaves to actual electricity though, is beyond me.

There's one other thing we may have in common. You may or may not want to comment on what I'm about to say, but I feel that it could be important.

We are very careful about when we turn on our transmitters. We have our own radar system and monitor the surrounding skies constantly to be sure that no planes are in the vicinity of our RF stream. There's actually a failsafe built into the system that will shut down the transmitters if a plane is detected within a five-mile perimeter. Somehow, just after we'd brought all 180 antennas online, a small private jet flying at 27,000 feet managed to avoid triggering the failsafe and flew directly into the center of the RF beam. We followed the plane's path on radar. It was flying at 425 miles an hour at the time of contact. At that height, it was nowhere near the prime focus of the projected RF beam and should not have been affected other than a possible malfunctioning of its navigational equipment for a few seconds.

Yet, something unexplainable happened. It disappeared. I mean, it totally vanished. It didn't crash. It didn't explode. It didn't leave any debris. It just ceased to exist. We have the radar record stored on disk. It shows the plane as it approaches the RF beam. As it makes contact with the beam, it just disappears from the screen.

That's not all. At the exact time the plane disappeared, three additional blips showed up. One was at 21,000 feet, directly below where the plane was last seen. The other two were above it at 30,000 and 41,000 feet.

The really weird part is—the radar echoes showed them to be solid objects almost a quarter mile in diameter. They stayed on the radar screen for approximately five minutes.

The one at the lower altitude was the first to go. A few seconds later, the blip at 30,000 feet started fading. Then the one just above it. It took about twenty seconds for each of them to disappear. It was as if they just faded away. They didn't move in relation to where they first appeared. The radar returns just got weaker until they were gone.

I noticed that there were some very strange events surrounding the last PIP-II test as well. Something about water running in a stream that seemingly came out of nowhere. And the deaths—I'm wondering if these events aren't somehow connected. It's hard to say what such high energy fields might produce, or what kind of Pandora's Box they might open.

I'd like for you to meet with Meyers and Singleton as soon as possible. We have other information you'll be interested in. We have an object that appeared one day by the antenna array that just hangs in the air. We have no idea what it is, or where it came from. I'm sure you know things that would be of value to us.

We are going behind the DOD's back by contacting you in this manner, but right now I'd rather put my trust in scientists than the military. The documents I've included go into much more detail (excluding the military's involvement in HAARP's special projects of course) explaining the disappearance of the aircraft and the anomalies surrounding it. They don't mention the possibility of PIP-II running on our wireless power transmission though. I don't think the DOD wants anyone to know how close they are to perfecting that technology. This is so classified that the DOD isn't putting anything in writing. Not even with a TOP SECRET classification.

I hope to hear from you soon. We are running diagnostic and alignment tests every day now and will continue to do so for at least another couple of months. I'd like to set up a meeting with you and any others that might be sympathetic to our cause.

Sincerely,
Dave Glaspie

Bill was totally taken aback by what he'd just read. No one would have guessed in a million years that PIP-II had tapped into a military experiment in Alaska to transmit power wirelessly. That didn't seem possible. Yet, here was confirmation from a scientist working on the project, saying they were conducting power transmission tests at the same time PIP-II was seemingly running on nothing.

He was wide awake now. He started thinking about the other things going on at HAARP. Weather modification, communications disruption, VLF and ULF submarine communications, mental disruptions—HAARP sounded more like a weapon of mass destruction than a research tool. He'd need to be very careful about how he handled this. Mental disruptions—hell, that's mind control on a global scale. And how the hell did this Dave Glaspie character know so much about what was going on at Fermilab?

He thumbed through several sheets, each stamped "TOP SECRET – CLASSIFIED." They supplied more detail to what Glaspie had mentioned. It seemed the DOD had known all along that HAARP was the probable cause for the free running of PIP-II. They just didn't want to bring it up because it would expose how close they were to perfecting wireless power transmission.

He was up now. He couldn't sleep if he wanted to. It was still early—about 10:00. He decided to bring HAARP up on the Internet again and see what else he could find.

The first thing he did was type HAARP into the search engine. Damn, over a million hits. Apparently everyone knows about HAARP but me. He'd already been to HAARP's homepage, so he decided to click on some of the other pages. There were so many; he started with one that looked the most controversial: "HAARP: High-Frequency Vandalism in the Sky." That sounded straightforward enough.

The page was a review of the book, "Angels Don't Play This HAARP." The first topic that caught his eye was HAARP Boils The Upper Atmosphere. So this is what he meant by an "ionospheric heater." He read on—opposite of a radio telescope, lifts areas of the ionosphere, Star Wars technology, submarine communications, Earth-penetrating tomography, weather modification, mental manipulation, wireless power transmission. There it was again. Wireless power transmission.

I think I should back up and start at the beginning—with Tesla. Everywhere I read, Tesla's name keeps popping up. So he changed directions and typed, "Nikola Tesla" into the search engine. This produced over a million hits. Just for the hell of it, he tried "Thomas Edison." Edison's search produced even more. That's odd. I'd have expected Edison to have several times more hits than Tesla. Everyone's familiar with Edison, but how many people have ever heard of Tesla? Maybe scientists are just now starting to realize what Tesla was doing a century ago. When you think of it, pretty much all of Edison's inventions have already come to pass. Tesla was so far ahead of his time, it's taken a century just for science to catch up. Hard to believe Nikola Tesla was born just five years before Lincoln became president.

He refined his search: "Nikola Tesla wireless power." That still produced hundreds of thousands of hits. He devoured the information, even though there were contradictions. Several articles stated Tesla was the inventor of the fluorescent light, when in fact, a Frenchman was. Tesla invented the high-frequency coil that made the light much more efficient.

Tesla gave spectacular demonstrations, holding a fluorescent lamp in his hand, turning on the Tesla coil, and the lamp would light—no wires. He was already transmitting wireless power in the late 1890s.

It was at Wardenclyffe in New York where the real research took place. Tesla built a massive transmitter in a mushroom-shaped tower, two hundred feet tall. Below, a well was dug 120 feet deep and twelve feet square. A steel shaft ran from the bottom of the well to the top of the tower, over three hundred feet in length. That was twenty-two feet greater than the distance from home plate to the right field fence at Yankee Stadium. This behemoth was to be Tesla's finest accomplishment—but it never came to pass.

Tesla, unlike Edison, wasn't as interested in making money from his inventions. That may have been his downfall. At the time, Tesla had entered into a deal with J.P. Morgan, who bankrolled Wardenclyffe. In return, Tesla was supposed to be working on transatlantic signals—something Marconi would later do using Tesla's ideas and patents. But what Tesla was really working on was the wireless transmission of power. He wanted to distribute electric power to any point on earth, free of charge.

The costs of building Wardenclyffe rose almost as fast as the tower itself, and when Tesla came to Morgan for more money, Morgan refused. He wanted to know why things were going so slowly and how the radio transmitter was coming. Tesla was forced to explain he was also working on wireless power. When Morgan heard this, he cut Tesla off. Free wireless power was the last thing a businessman like Morgan wanted. He threw his resources into Marconi's work using Tesla's patents. Tesla was able to acquire another benefactor, but only to pay off debts. He struggled for the next ten years, finally turning over the Wardenclyffe deed to cover expenses.

Luckily, he was able to test many of his theories before losing the property. Lightning-like flashes were often seen from the tower. Arcs of electricity would exceed 100 feet. To this day, no one has produced this kind of power display. There are stories of people seeing sparks jump from their feet to the ground as far as 25 miles away when the tower was in operation.

The tower was finally destroyed and sold for salvage in July of 1917.

Tesla, Bill thought. *One of the most important geniuses of all time and I've hardly even heard of him. It's only because of him that I have this computer. All of this, and he was born before Lincoln was president.* Bill rubbed his eyes and stretched. It was really hitting him now. *I've got to get some sleep.*

Bill put his computer in "hibernation" mode and headed off to bed. Tomorrow, he'd have to contend with his duties at Fermilab as well as meet with the "men in black." But for now, the only thinking he wanted to do was in his dreams.

Chapter Eighteen

Dave Glaspie was worried. He knew that the experiments being performed in the upper atmosphere were causing considerable problems around the world. It was a dilemma he would have to learn to live with. HAARP wasn't the only facility working with ionospheric heaters. There were several others as well—Puerto Rico, Norway, the big dish at Arecibo, and most notably, Russia, all had projects underway of a similar nature.

He was sure, though, that it would be years before anyone else would come close to developing the techniques they were pioneering. For one thing, HAARP had more power than all the other ionospheric heaters combined. Only the U.S. government had pockets deep enough to fund a project of this magnitude. It was the hidden resources—the Black Ops budgets—that provided the money used to develop the nation's most secret projects. And HAARP had a prodigious appetite.

What he really wanted right now was to meet with Bill Scott personally. He was sure that the disappearance of the plane, the three blips picked up on radar, and the strange things happening at Fermilab were all connected. But security at both facilities had been increased to the point where this was quickly becoming an impossibility. It looked as though he would just have to communicate through his associates.

Earlier this morning, he'd discovered that HAARP's antenna array was being reconfigured to provide maximum energy for another wireless power transmission test. The test was being scheduled for the following week. If he was right, this would take place around the same time that Fermilab would be going back online. This was no great surprise to him. If he'd connected the dots between Fermilab's PIP-II running off-grid and HAARP's wireless power transmissions, his peers were surely aware of it too. They probably not only knew of it—they approved of it. Maybe they wanted to see if it would happen again. If it did, then they'd want to know why. The only way to find out would be to duplicate the conditions that caused it in the first place.

He needed to get the new testing schedule to Meyer and Singleton before they met with Dr. Scott. Passing classified information over great distances posed a unique set of problems. First, there was a good chance he wouldn't know the location of the people needing the information. Second, sending it by encrypted email was not a good idea. Email is notorious for being intercepted, even in 2030. He also knew that as additional people became involved, it would be even harder to get this information to all of them. With HAARP located in Alaska and Fermilab in Illinois, there was already a serious problem of distance. It would not be at all unusual for others of his group to be in Europe, or for that matter, anywhere in the world.

What was needed was a place where information could be hidden and encrypted, yet available to anyone who knew where to look for it. Luckily, one of the members sympathetic to their cause was a cybersecurity specialist with a penchant for data encryption. He suggested that the information should be encrypted and stored on the Internet. This way, anyone in the world with the correct address and password would be able to download and decipher it. He also suggested a place to hide it that would be in plain sight, and available to everyone.

It was ingenious. They'd use their own website to deliver the information. HAARP's webcam, which took pictures of the facility and broadcast them over the Net, was the perfect vehicle. The webcam was pointed toward the high-frequency antenna array, updating every 20 minutes during daylight hours. Just before sunset, the camera shut down and stored the last picture it took, then broadcast it continuously until the following morning. It would be possible to hide a message within the individual pixels of this picture—an encryption process known as steganography.

The message was hidden in the unused pixels of the image and hardly affected the quality at all. Only those who knew a hidden message was there would be any the wiser. His operatives would only need the decoding software and password to decipher it. To everyone else, it would look just like any of the other pictures taken by the automated webcam.

There were rumors that terrorists had been hiding information encoded in pictures on auction sites for years. With millions of images online, it would be nearly impossible to find a single picture being used for covert communication. HAARP only provided one picture, but who would ever suspect it of containing hidden information?

Just like HAARP itself, things are often not what they appear to be.

On Wednesday, just two days before testing was to begin again, Bill received a phone call from Connie. She had finally heard something about his fish.

"Good morning, Bill."

"Hi, Connie. My assistant said you had some good news for me."

"I received a call from the people at Woods Hole a few minutes ago. It was a pretty amazing phone call. It mostly consisted of, 'Where did you say you got this from? Are there any more? Can we have additional samples? Are you sure that's where it came from?' More questions than answers. But finally, I got some information on what it might be."

"Don't keep me wondering. What is it?"

"They don't know."

"What!"

"I'm sorry. I mean, they couldn't tell me what it is, exactly. They kept saying that its DNA is unlike anything they've ever seen before. I mean, it's not just the sequences, it's the DNA itself. That's the problem. The DNA isn't really—DNA. I know that doesn't make much sense, but that's what they said. It's similar, but not the same."

"How can a living organism have no DNA?"

"That's what they'd like to know. That's why all the questions about where it came from. I think they realize that it may not be from the Earth at all. This may be the first time that we actually have proof of life existing outside of our own planet."

"I figured as much. I guess when I caught the damn thing, I thought it looked like something out of a science fiction movie. You've just confirmed it."

"Are you still needing me at the lake Friday?"

"Yes. So far, everything's running on schedule. I'd like for you to get there between 2:30 and 3:00."

"Fine. The weather report looks promising. Carol and I plan on spending a nice afternoon outdoors. I'm sure we'll enjoy it."

"I hope so. I know I'm being overly cautious—but I want you to be careful. I can't imagine anything bad happening. There's just something about that lake that worries me."

"We'll be careful. I'll call you if I see any aliens."

"Don't wait for that to happen. Call me when you get there and again when you leave. If anything looks out of the ordinary, call me immediately. Oh, and have fun on your picnic."

The next two days would be long and stressful. Bill stood at the apex of the pyramid, his stamp of approval necessary for virtually every important decision. Responsibility was no stranger to him; since his college days, he had invariably found himself at the helm of every project he joined. At Fermilab, he was one of only three individuals with the authority to halt testing at a moment's notice. So far, everything was progressing even better than planned.

While Fermilab adhered to its schedule, HAARP faced considerable challenges. For several days, scientists there had been radiating a region of known terrorist activity in Central Asia. HAARP transmitted powerful high-frequency electromagnetic waves into the upper atmosphere, where they were converted to low-frequency (ELF) waves and beamed to the other side of the world. These waves formed the active component of an enhanced ground-penetrating radar (GPR) system, with Afghanistan as the primary area of interest. The GPR enabled scientists to detect tunnels where hostile forces might conceal troops or weapons caches, information they would then relay to the military. This covert application stemmed from technology Tesla had proposed in a patent during the early 1900s.

The technique wasn't unique to HAARP; GPR had been in use for years, typically utilizing planes and satellites as radar platforms. However, HAARP's ground-based antennas were tens of thousands of times more powerful than those relying on older technologies.

Transmitting a signal deep into the Earth demanded enormous power. Plane and satellite systems, limited by available power, could only penetrate a few meters underground. HAARP employed an entirely different approach, harnessing the energy inherent in the Earth's electrical fields to power their probing. The potential for limitless power existed, though this remained one of HAARP's pioneering endeavors. Even in these early stages, HAARP's antenna array could reach hundreds of feet into the Earth, with the possibility of unlimited depth as more power was applied.

Oil companies worldwide would pay billions for the ability to view the Earth's interior without drilling. They could pinpoint exact locations of oil reserves, eliminating dry holes. Precious metals could be located, even within mountain cores. The potential benefits to humanity were enormous, matched only by the staggering military applications. The frequency used in GPR closely mirrored that of human brain synapses—7 to 9 Hz. The implications of tuning GPR to exactly mimic brain waves and directing it at human populations remained uncertain, though many suspected such experiments might already be underway.

HAARP's technology had transitioned from testing to real-world applications during its use by President Bush Sr. in Desert Storm. Those early experiments in detecting underground anomalies had demonstrated the potential of this powerful technology.

While most problems associated with manipulating the upper atmosphere were well understood, unexpected issues still arose. Various atmospheric layers often proved less homogeneous than anticipated. Sunspot activity posed the greatest challenge, wreaking havoc on the Van Allen radiation belts and causing enormous fluctuations in the Earth's electrical potentials. Complete polarity shifts had been observed during these plasma storms. Sunspot activity followed a 22-year cycle, peaking every 11 years—a phenomenon first noted in the early 1700s. Though the science behind sunspots remained inexact, sun-orbiting satellites had provided previously unknown data about solar composition. Current theory suggested that as the sun approached its sunspot cycle maximum, massive magnetic storms occurred deep within its interior. When these storms reached the surface, they manifested as sunspots, some larger than several Earths combined. These dark, cooler spots resulted from tangled magnetic force lines.

When magnetic lines snapped or separated, enormous flares of plasma—many times the size of Earth—were ejected into space. If aimed towards Earth, these ejections could trigger a multitude of problems. The charged plasma particles flowing from the sun were captured by Earth's magnetic force lines. As the plasma excited gas particles in the upper atmosphere, it caused them to glow, creating multi-colored displays in the night sky. The specific colors depended on the affected gases. These displays, known as the Aurora Borealis or Northern Lights, could be visible as far south as Texas during periods of extreme energy.

A highly charged ionosphere complicated HAARP scientists' efforts to control the shaping of their high-altitude reflector. They struggled to maintain the stability of the projected parabolic reflector.

Three and a half billion watts focused on a relatively small area of space generated plasma reaching millions of degrees. Controlling plasma at such temperatures proved exceptionally challenging. On Earth, it could be contained by magnetic force lines, but managing this force in the ionosphere presented problems that scientists were only beginning to comprehend.

At 3:31 A.M., the day before Fermilab was scheduled to go online, HAARP experienced its first shockwave. Though always considered possible, no one truly expected it to occur. The potential consequences were catastrophic: destruction of their facilities and loss of life within several hundred miles. While discussed in HAARP's early developmental stages, the topic had since been largely ignored.

The event that unfolded that morning offered merely a glimpse of what was possible, yet it demanded everyone's attention—even those who had dismissed its likelihood.

The unthinkable transpired, if only for a fraction of a second. With little warning, the incident began and ended almost instantaneously. After six hours of operation, a voltage transient caused a power spike to the antennas. Sensors on several instruments surged into the red zone, triggering alarms throughout the facility.

The master power meter recorded an unprecedented influx of energy into the array, far exceeding what was being transmitted into the ionosphere. The exact amount remained unknown; the power overwhelmed the recording instrument, pushing it completely off-scale. For a while, it seemed a very expensive piece of equipment would need replacement. Ultimately, recalibration sufficed.

What had occurred was deemed impossible by most, though a few scientists had voiced concerns from the outset.

Post-analysis revealed that the electron beam emanating from the antennas had ionized the surrounding air, transforming it into a conductor. Normally an insulator, air under specific conditions of humidity and pressure had provided the perfect conduit between one of the magnetic force lines and Earth itself. For a fleeting moment, billions of amperes of electrical energy surged between Earth and space. Had this persisted for more than a few millionths of a second, HAARP would have been obliterated.

The prevailing belief had been that this scenario was impossible due to the vast radiating area of HAARP's antenna array—several thousand square feet, far more than could be ionized by the antennas' radiating power.

Evidently, not only was it possible, but it had happened. A contingency plan existed for such an eventuality, requiring only a few days to implement. It involved magnetic shielding. While the antennas were already grounded, the radiated energy could also be magnetically shielded as it left the transmitting antennas. This shielding needed to extend only for the first sixty meters—a precaution that, in hindsight, should have been taken from the beginning.

Within 72 hours, the magnetic shielding was in place, and authorization was given to resume normal antenna array operations. Unfortunately, the only way to verify the solution's effectiveness was to run the array at maximum power. Even then, the exact atmospheric conditions present during the conduit's opening couldn't be replicated. Unknown variables would always exist. One certainty remained: if the fix proved inadequate, the consequences would be catastrophic.

Chapter Nineteen

Finally, the day arrived. By 6:00 A.M., the place was buzzing with technicians. This was actually the second crew; a skeleton team had been working throughout the night, prepping the PIP-II accelerator and DUNE detectors for the big test. If everything went according to schedule, the critical phase—where the beam generator would start firing charged particles at the detector—was set to begin just before noon.

As the hours ticked by, tension in the control room rose faster than the outside thermometer. Coordinating hundreds of people, both on-site and remotely, was no easy task, requiring considerable care and planning. Everyone was on edge, eyes flicking between digital dashboards, AI status reports, and the ever-present wall of live video feeds.

Around noon, Jim Depina, one of the technicians monitoring the bank of cameras within the beam tunnel, thought he saw something unusual as images flashed by on the monitors. It was on camera number 15, located about three hundred meters from the tunnel's entrance and to the left of the DUNE service elevators. He adjusted the camera using the joystick, centering the image of interest on the screen. Zooming in, he could see what appeared to be liquid dripping from one of the superconducting magnets.

There shouldn't have been any liquids in the area. The only liquid in the entire beam tunnel was the liquid nitrogen being pumped around the magnet's coils, and it was only in liquid form when cooled to almost 200 degrees below Celsius. If it were to leak, it would revert to gas immediately. It wouldn't flow at all. This looked more like... water.

Water was one of the things he'd been told to watch for. Everyone associated with the beam tunnel had heard of incidents where water appeared with no discernible source. It only seemed to show up during testing. If this was what it appeared to be—it was happening again. He left his post to report his discovery.

"Dr. Scott," Jim said, hesitant to bother the project director at such a busy time.

"Yes, what can I do for you?"

"I'm Jim Depina. I control the cameras that monitor the beam tunnel. I've just imaged what appears to be water dripping from one of the superconducting magnets. I thought you'd like to know about it."

"Are you sure it's water?"

"I can't be certain without a sample, but it appears to be. It's not condensation because there's too much of it. It's not just dripping; it's more like a constant trickle. I'd guess it would take several minutes to fill a liter jar, but it's definitely not from condensation."

"Thank you, Mr. Depina. Go back to your station and let me know if the flow increases. I'm going to send someone from maintenance to take a sample and check the situation up close. Keep an eye on him, if you would."

"Yes sir. I've already assigned that monitor to local status. It will display this one screen constantly."

Bill thought that things had been going too smoothly. It was about time for something to gum up the works. He hadn't expected this, though. Water—where the hell did it come from, and why did it only appear when PIP-II was in operation? He got on the phone with the maintenance department and told them to get him some samples. He also instructed them to give the area a cursory investigation to see if they could determine the liquid's source. They were told not to spend any more time than necessary, as a test was underway. What he really wanted was the sample. He wanted to see for himself what this water from nowhere looked like.

By 1:30, the tests were well underway. PIP-II had been put in motion just after noon. The power indicator stood at 45 percent. The liquid dripping from magnet 71 had indeed turned out to be water, at least as far as a hands-on visual inspection could determine. As usual, the source was not discovered. Within an hour, two more magnets were found to have water trickling from their housings. Again, the source could not be determined. The trickle appeared to be coming out of the wall where the liquid nitrogen lines were attached. The problem was, there was no crack or hole in the wall. It seemed to be coming out of the wall itself. In none of the cases was the amount enough to worry about. If it continued at this rate, it would eventually reach the drains on the tunnel's floor. Other than someone slipping on it, it wasn't a concern. But its presence was just one more thing that Bill had to take into consideration. In the back of his mind, he worried.

At 2:00 P.M., he decided to give Connie a call. He needed a break from the day's stresses and wanted to see if she had started for her picnic yet.

"Hi, Bill. So—how's the test going?"

"I need a break! I wish I could join you. I got here about six this morning and I've not stopped running since. I thought I'd give you a call and relax for a few minutes. Have you started for the lake yet?"

"Actually, we've been here for about an hour. We both decided that we'd like to get some sun; it's a lot stronger in the middle of the day. Everything here is beautiful. It's cool, but the sunlight really warms you up. The lake's got a slight ripple on it, there's just a bit of wind blowing from the west. I think they must have cut the grass within the last few days. It's only about an inch high and feels like a carpet. Carol says, 'Hello' and that we're available for this kind of work anytime."

"Tell her I'll see what I can do. I'm glad you're enjoying yourselves. I know one thing; I'll sleep like a baby tonight. This will go on until about midnight, unless we have problems. In that case, they'll either stop the test early or continue until they find out what the problem is. Either way, it will mean more work for me. Right now, everything's running as planned. There have been a couple of surprises, but that's why we conduct these tests. Listen, I'll not call again unless something happens that might concern you. Enjoy your afternoon. If you can, plan on staying until 4 or so, and be sure to call me if something suspicious happens."

"We're fine. Don't forget about tomorrow. We're going to get back to our sunbathing. I won't bother you unless something warrants it. Good luck with the test. I'll talk to you tomorrow."

Bill hung up the phone. He'd only been talking for a minute or so, but he was glad to get a break from the stress surrounding him. He didn't know it, but his day was about to change for the worse. Things were about to get very exciting at Fermilab.

Chapter Twenty

It was exactly 3:25 P.M. according to the digital display on Bill's desk. He knew that for a fact because he had just made an entry into his computer and had glanced at the clock. He'd been updating his digital logbook two or three times an hour since he checked in, nine and a half hours ago. Most were just trivial entries: "everything is on schedule" or "no problems have been encountered." Most entries were just a sentence or two in length.

The only entry worth reading was the one concerning the discovery of water once again. It was only a short paragraph though; there wasn't really much he could say.

At 3:25, he was preparing to make another entry because a critical point in the test had been reached. The PIP-II accelerator was now operating at the 90% power level. They would hold at this level while a mandatory systems check was made to ensure that everything was working properly. This would take about thirty minutes. Somewhere between 4:00 and 5:00 P.M., PIP-II would be brought to full power. If all was well, it would remain at full power for the next 24 hours.

Bill had only written a few words in his logbook when his office door was thrown open and two men in black full-length trench coats rushed in. Hats pulled low over their foreheads, they resembled spies from a Marvel comic book.

Not now, he thought, as he dropped his stylus. He leaned back so far in his ergonomic office chair that he almost tipped over. I don't have time for this.

"How the hell did you get past secure—" they cut him off before he could finish his sentence.

"An important message is online from HAARP." It was Singleton who spoke first. Being the bigger of the two, he also did most of the talking for the pair. "Bring the HAARP picture up on your computer. You need to decipher the message on their website."

"Are you two crazy? I'm in the middle—No; I'm at a critical point in bringing PIP-II online. We go to full power in less than an hour."

"I know, we've been following everything going on here since noon. What I have to say may influence the remainder of today's test."

"Who are you two, anyway? You come in here like you own the place. You tell me about this HAARP project and how it has an effect on Fermilab's power supply—you come and go, seemingly without authorization. You're never stopped or checked by any of the security staff—I don't even know if you are who you say you are! In fact, who the hell are you?"

"Suffice it to say, we have complete authority to do whatever we feel needs to be done in the operation of this facility. I'm not at liberty to divulge that authority at the present time, but you'll be told when the need arises. I'm sorry to be so blunt, but this is a matter of national security. Just be assured that we have the power to stop this test, if need be.

Now, if you would, bring up the picture we talked about earlier on HAARP's webpage. The one transmitted by the webcam. I want you to read the information hidden in the encryption."

"I can bring it up, but I can't decrypt it. That software is on my system at home but not here in my office."

"The software has been installed. If you'll bring up the webcam, I'll give you the password to unhide and run the software."

"You mean, you've been on my computer and installed software without my knowledge? How can you do that? How did you get the passwords to get into my computer? Who are you?"

"I'm sorry Dr. Scott, but for now that information is strictly need-to-know, and you're out of the loop. I assure you, you'll have all your questions answered in good time."

With that, Bill started to search for HAARP in his browser, but Singleton stopped him.

"It's in your 'favorites.'"

"What? I've never brought up HAARP's webcam on this computer."

"I know, but it was added to your 'favorites' at the same time the steganography software was installed."

Bill opened his browser, clicked on 'Favorites,' and, sure enough, there was a link called "HAARP Webcam." He'd never noticed it before. He was sure he didn't put it there.

Clicking on it, the picture of the antenna array came into view. He centered the cursor over the picture and clicked on the right mouse button. A menu appeared. One of the choices was "save picture."

He left-clicked the mouse and typed in HAARP_CAM.

The software asked him to name the picture before he saved it.

"There, I have it saved. Now how do I view the secret message, if there is one?"

Mr. Singleton looked over Bill's shoulder at the image as it appeared on the screen. "Go to your Start menu and click on All Programs."

Bill did, and a list of the software appeared.

"Now, click on Accessories and then System Tools." Again, another menu came up.

"Click on Disk Defragmenter and the steganography program will start."

Apparently, the software had been installed in a hidden partition on the hard drive. It had been given the name of a common but rarely used disk utility program.

Bill clicked on the Disk Defragmenter icon and, sure enough, the steganography program loaded immediately. Before it completed loading, a box came up asking for a password to continue.

"icebox180."

"What?" Bill asked.

"icebox180." Mr. Singleton repeated. "That's the password to bring up the program. It's a combination of a word, all lowercase, and a number. The number is how many active antennas there are in HAARP's antenna array. Memorize it."

Bill typed in the password and the program finished loading. "I guess we'll see if this thing works."

"It works!" These were the first words spoken by the other half of the dynamic duo since they'd entered the room.

Bill clicked on the file containing the picture he'd just downloaded from the HAARP website. The hard drive LED came on as it accessed the file. In a few seconds, the picture appeared on the monitor. Bill knew how to run the software, as he'd already tested it on his computer at home.

It took the computer a few seconds to scan the entire file and unlock the code. It was pretty amazing to see the message appear as if by magic. All three of them gathered around the monitor as the letters scrolled across the bottom of the screen. Bill became so engrossed in what he was doing that he totally forgot about the test. The message was from Dave Glaspie, and the time stamp said it had been sent about three hours ago. It read—

Dr. Scott—at approximately 5 P.M. Central Standard time, the tests you are currently conducting will be interrupted by a computer malfunction at the Feynman Computing Center. This will cause a loss of data collection that will last for three minutes exactly. It's imperative that you don't try to shut down PIP-II during this time. During this outage, a link between Fermilab and the antenna array at HAARP will be established. This will in no way affect the results of your tests, nor be harmful to equipment, or personnel, at your facility.

Mr. Singleton and Mr. Meyer will be assisting you in case a problem should arise. You will understand the need for all this secrecy soon.

David Glaspie.

Bill looked at the clock on his desk. It was 4:08. According to Dr. Glaspie, there would be a computer failure in 52 minutes. What the hell has all this cloak and dagger business got to do with Fermilab? A week ago, he'd never even heard of HAARP. Now, it seemed like HAARP and Fermilab were joined at the chest like Siamese twins.

"Dr. Scott." The gravelly voice of Mr. Singleton caused him to look up though he was still in a stupor, not quite believing this was really happening.

As he spoke, Mr. Singleton reached down and clicked the close button on the program. In a few seconds, the Desktop re-appeared. "There's no need to worry about erasing the history files, Bill. I can call you Bill, can't I? It looks like we are going to be spending a lot of time together. Anyway, your computer has had some modifications made that will automatically erase where you've surfed on the Internet. Any downloads will also be forensically deleted so they can't be reconstructed at a later date. Just use it as you normally would, but remember, anything you save—won't be—saved that is."

Bill just sat there, staring at his computer.

"Bill—I think you'd better get back to the test. I'm sure there are things that need your attention. We'll be here to help if you need us. You won't always see us, but we'll be around. And don't forget. At 5 o'clock, something will happen that might be a little out of the ordinary. It will only last for three minutes, and then everything will be back to normal. You can look surprised, and be sure to look like you're doing something, but just remember—everything is under control."

Bill could hardly believe this was happening. He was supposed to be in control of everything going on at Fermilab. Not someone he didn't even know two weeks ago. And who was this Dave Glaspie? He knew he was some kind of a big-wig in Alaska, but how could he be pulling strings here? How could anything he was doing thousands of miles away affect the tests at Fermilab, and what would that effect be? This was just a little too weird. He'd believe it when he saw it. For now, there were things he needed to be doing. He got up and left his office without so much as a, "goodbye, kiss my ass, or whatever." If something was going to happen, there wasn't much he could do about it anyway.

He couldn't keep from watching his digital clock as it clicked off the hours, minutes, and seconds. It was synced to the atomic clock in Colorado. At 4:59:00 he stopped. He stood and watched the clock as it counted down to 5:00 P.M.

He looked around for Singleton and Meyer, but they were nowhere to be seen. He figured they were close by. At 4:59:30, he realized that he was clutching his fingers into a fist. He couldn't remember having ever been so nervous. And then it was 4:59:50. The seconds counted down, one at a time.

The numbers on the digital display crept forward: 04:59:55, 04:59:56, 04:59:57, 04:59:58, 04:59:59, 05:00:00, 05:00:01, 05:00:02, 05:00:03. Nothing had happened. Where were those idiots? He'd have them both thrown out of here as soon as he could get one of the security guards' attention.

05:00:07 – The lights dimmed visibly across the entire complex. The display monitoring the transfer of data to the Feynman Computing Center started flashing, "Malfunction" across the screen in bright red letters. It sounded an audible warning as well. The computers at the Feynman center were offline. Something had interrupted the data flow between the main detector and the supercomputers.

What happened next was really strange . A pale blue light fell over everything, bathing them in an eerie glow that screamed that something bad was about to happen. Bill noticed that when he touched something, a weak, just barely visible aura of multicolored light seemed to emanate from his fingertips. It reminded him of when he was a junior in high school and he'd first discovered the art of Kirlian photography.

For Christmas, his parents had bought him a Kirlian photography kit from Edmund Scientific. He set up a darkroom in the basement and experimented with taking pictures of auras surrounding living things. Along with photos of plants, leaves, and even vegetables, he acquired quite a collection. He stopped when he about electrocuted his girlfriend. It turned out that the Kirlian process wasn't all that safe, and Edmund Scientific pulled it from their catalog the following year.

The auras he'd photographed back then looked exactly like the ones he was seeing now, but without the need for a Tesla high voltage power supply or film. You could actually see the colors with the naked eye. Thinking back to those early photographs, no one ever really proved if there was any meaning to the various colors produced by the Kirlian technique.

There were certainly some interesting theories. He wondered if they were being immersed in some kind of high energy field right now, and if that might be the cause of the auras he was seeing. They were brightest when he touched a metal object though when he looked closely, he realized that an aura could be seen around everyone. It just happened to be brighter if the person was touching something that was grounded.

The shimmering light wasn't bright enough to be a problem, though it did tend to interfere with anything displayed in light blue on the monitors. The monitors! He'd been so caught up in what was going on that he hadn't looked at the other displays. He took a quick glance at the central bank of monitors, but none were showing any warning flags. Only the one monitoring the link to the computing center was affected.

Singleton and Meyer were still nowhere to be seen. This was exactly what the message said would happen. It seemed that HAARP and Fermilab shared an invisible power cord. What else did they have in common?

Bill wondered what the scientists at the DOD were thinking of all of this. Key displays were linked to DOD scientists by way of the Internet so that they could offer immediate assistance if needed.

Because of the problems associated with the last test, many other plans had been put into action. To augment Fermilab's security, local police and State Police had plans in place to block all access to Fermilab at a moment's notice. Military security had been beefed up as well. There were 14 additional Military Police on the grounds, along with the normal contingent of hired security. No one was taking any chances that a terrorist might try to sabotage the facilities again. Assuming, of course, that it really was a terrorist that had caused the previous problems. Bill felt pretty sure this was a total pile of crap.

Security had been operating at a near lockdown since the last test. The presence of the military was more felt than seen. Bill knew they were there, lurking in the background. Most of the time they were like shadows. Some of the scientists didn't like the idea of the military being so closely involved in what they considered were civilian projects.

Bill wondered what was going on outside of the control room. Was security, even now, locking down the complex? He looked at the clock again, 05:02:12. Two minutes had passed. It was strange how calm everyone was. Most of those around him had also been here the last time something like this happened. Well, not quite like this, but just as strange. That last time everyone was busy trying to figure out what was going on. They were checking then double-checking every monitor and readout, comparing notes, sharing ideas, trying to come up with answers. This time, they just stood there. Nobody did much of anything. They had blank looks on their faces, as if things were just too surreal to warrant being afraid.

Then, in an instant—the bluish light faded and the lights came back up to their original intensity. The alarm coming from the Feynman computer monitor fell silent, and the display returned to normal. Data was being transmitted again. It seemed like everything was back to normal. Bill looked at the clock, 05:03:07. Exactly three minutes had passed.

Even though things seemed the same, the occurrence of such a disturbance would mean that the remainder of the tests would have to be canceled. Bill was just about to give the order to start shutting things down when an assistant brought him a specially encrypted cell phone.

"Dr. Scott. I'm General Howard. I'm calling from DARPA headquarters in Maryland. I've been in contact with the scientists overseeing the test you're conducting and they'd like you to know that everything on their end has gone according to plan. They hoped the advance warning came in plenty of time and that there were no problems encountered at your facility. They also recommend that the test NOT be canceled.

Of course, it's your call as the Director, but the recommendation for continued testing comes from a very high source. Are there any questions?"

"Yes General, I'd like to know why, if I'm truly in charge of these tests—why I wasn't informed that there was going to be an 'incident,' long before the few minutes of warning I actually received? I'd also like to know—"

"I'm sorry Dr. Scott, but I'm not the one you need to be talking to, and that person isn't available at the moment. All of your questions will be answered in good time. Right now, I'm sure you'll want to take the advice I've given you and continue with the testing. Have a good day."

With that, the phone went dead. Bill was beginning to feel like he was just a pawn in a game he didn't remember joining. He'd been the Director here for over three years. He'd never had his authority questioned before. It had always been his call if a test should go ahead or be canceled.

Before he had a chance to say anything, Mr. Singleton appeared. "I hear you're going to continue the testing."

Bill stared right through him as he handed the phone back to the technician who gave it to him. "I guess that's the plan. It seems that there are those in high places that want it to continue."

"Good. Mr. Meyer and I are going to check the premises to make sure that nothing—shall I say—unusual has appeared."

Bill wasn't sure what he meant by that. Was he talking about the water in the beam tunnel, or something more ominous? It was the way he said it, more than what he said, that bothered him.

As Mr. Singleton turned to leave, Bill thought he saw Meyer talking to several technicians that had gathered by the doorway leading to the elevators. Bill remembered the tech monitoring the cameras imaging the beam tunnel. Depina, he thought to himself. He made his way to the back of the control room where the tunnel monitors were located.

As he approached, Depina saw him and started to stand. "Dr. Scott. I hope what just happened wasn't anything serious."

"No, I don't think so. Has anything unusual happened in the beam tunnel?"

"No, only those three incidents of water and they are barely a trickle. One of them might have even stopped; it was down to a slow drip. Nothing else has shown up. Are you expecting something to happen?"

"No, but this is an area of interest. I think there may be one, possibly two people going in there soon to inspect the tunnel firsthand. If they do, can you follow them on your monitors? I'd like to know if they find anything."

"That's no problem at all. I can do just about anything with this setup. I'm surprised they'd want to do a personal inspection without checking with me first. I can check the entire tunnel out in seconds. What are they looking for?"

"I have no idea. I'm not sure if they are even going. I just have a feeling that they might. There must have been a good reason to have installed such a sophisticated monitoring system. Let me know if anything interesting happens."

"Yes sir. I have recording capabilities as well, so I can save a record of everything for you if you'd like."

"That would be an excellent idea. Record everything they do."

As Bill made his way back to his office, he conferred with other technicians along the way. Everyone wanted to know what had happened, but none of them were finding any problems in the devices they monitored. All was well, as far as he could tell.

Shit! Connie and Carol may still be at the lake. He dialed Connie's cell phone.

"Hello?" Connie answered.

"Connie, are you still lakeside?"

"As a matter of fact, we are. But we're getting ready to go. We started to leave about twenty minutes ago. We were listening to the top 20 country countdown and decided to stay until we found out what the number one song was going to be."

"Has anything happened in the lake?"

"Well, I don't think so, though there was something a little weird that happened just as we started packing up our things. It must have been just after 5:00, because the number one song had just finished playing. It was 'Fastest Gun Alive' by Toby Keith."

"Great song, but what happened at the lake?"

"I wasn't going to bother you. I'm not sure it was anything at all. As I looked out over the water, I'd have sworn that it had acquired a bluish tint. Carol noticed it too. It's still pretty bright out here, the sun hasn't dropped below the tree line so I thought it was probably just a reflection of some kind. It only lasted a few minutes, and then it was gone—if it was ever really there at all. I hated to bother you with something so trivial. Does this make any sense to you?"

"Yes, it does. I think you did see something. I don't know what it was, or what caused it, but it was real. I'll explain later when I see you. For now, it would probably be best if you go on home and stay in for the night. We are going to continue with the tests. I'll probably not get out of here until midnight at the earliest."

"I'll be up late. If you get in before 1:00, give me a ring. Take care and try not to get too stressed out. I'll help you unwind tomorrow in Chicago. If you still feel like going, that is."

"I'll feel like going alright. I'd go right now if I could. I've got a lot to tell you, but I'm not sure how much of it I can without getting you too involved. It seems like you, Carol, and Tim are the only ones I can trust these days. I'll call you if I get out of here at a reasonable hour, but don't count on it. I'll save the interesting stuff for tomorrow."

The testing continued as planned. Around 7:00 P.M., PIP-II was brought up to full power. The first experiments involving the crashing of protons against various substrates in the DUNE detector began at 9:47. All was going well. The majority of technicians had left by 11:00 P.M. when the night crew came in. Only a few of the original crew were still here at this late hour. They were about to call it a day as well. Even though PIP-II was running at full power, few experiments were being conducted. The main objective now was to let the accelerator operate at this level for 24 hours to make sure that everything was performing as expected.

Around midnight, Bill and the other scientists who had been here since six in the morning decided to call it a night. Eighteen hours was enough. When Bill got home, he thought about giving Connie a call. But he was so exhausted he decided against it. He just wanted to close his eyes and sleep. This had been the most stressful day of his life. He was asleep as soon as he hit the bed.

He didn't even set his alarm. He'd wake up when he woke up. Unfortunately, that would turn out to be much sooner than he'd hoped. At 3:20 A.M., there was a knock at his door. A few seconds later it turned from a knock to a pounding. Before he could even get his pants on the door opened.

"Dr. Scott. I'm sorry to wake you, but it's urgent that you come back to the facility." It was Lieutenant Donaldson. Bill hadn't seen him in over a year. He'd thought he'd probably been transferred to another facility. When did he come back, and what kind of problem had come up now?

"What time is it?" he asked, wiping the sleep from his already burning eyes.

"It's 3:21, sir. We need to get back to DUNE immediately. There's been another incident. This one wasn't planned."

"In the morning?"

"Yes sir, you've been sleeping a little over two hours. Here, I'll help you gather your things."

"What things?"

"You could be there for quite a while. You'll need your personal items—toothbrush, deodorant, and shaving utensils. Clothes will be provided as needed."

"You're telling me I'm going to be living there—in the control room?"

"No, not in the control room—I don't think so anyway. But the base, excuse me, the facility, has been locked down. No one goes in or comes out of the complex without a direct order from the commander. The facility is under military control as of midnight."

"I must still be dreaming. Wake me up, will you?"

"Believe me, Dr. Scott, you are awake. At 9:00 P.M. last night, all but about 200 technicians, scientists, and other necessary people were evacuated from the facility. You were so busy, you never noticed it happening. The only personnel left on the grounds now are those deemed necessary by DARPA and the National Security Council."

"What's this all about? Do you know if Dr. Baker is still here?"

"I'm not at liberty to say, sir, but I'm sure your clearance will enable you to find the answers to all of your questions. Right now, I need to get you to the control room. You're needed there."

The ride back to DUNE was uneventful. As they pulled into the parking lot Bill noticed the lights were turned off. He thought that this was strange. They were always on all night long. He assumed they were on timers. He also noticed that there were several soldiers standing at the entranceway. As he surveyed the area, he spotted others. The place seemed to be under heavy guard.

The Lieutenant pulled the vehicle into the Director's parking space. "Please, follow me, sir."

"Lead the way, Lieutenant. I hope they have a lot of coffee brewing. I think I'm going to need it."

"I'm sure they'll have whatever it takes to keep us all alert and at our most productive, sir."

Chapter Twenty-One

"Dr. Scott! We're so glad to see you." Bill couldn't believe it. Here was the last person he wanted to encounter.

"Mr. Singleton. Why am I not surprised to find you still here? I'd have thought you'd be sound asleep in your cave somewhere—dreaming of cloaks and daggers. I'll bet Meyer's here too, disguised as a normal person."

"I'm glad to see you're awake and in good spirits. I'm afraid you're going to need all the humor you can muster. We have a... situation."

Bill didn't like the sound of that. With the military guarding the doors, the place evacuated, and Singleton and Meyer seemingly in charge, the situation must be totally out of hand.

"So, what's the problem?"

"I believe you already know Mr. Depina?" As he said that, Singleton motioned with his right arm to someone at the back of the control room. Bill recognized him immediately. It was the technician who had been monitoring the beam tunnel during yesterday's tests. As Depina came forward, Bill noticed how exhausted he looked. At least he got to leave early last night, Bill thought. He probably got twice as much sleep as I did.

"Good morning, Dr. Scott," Depina mumbled, nearly dropping the stack of digital printouts he'd brought with him.

"Good morning. Does this have something to do with the beam tunnel?"

Singleton spoke next. "Right now, it has everything to do with the beam tunnel, but I'm afraid that may change at any time. Depina has something I want you to see. There's been a breach in the beam tunnel, but we have no idea what caused it. He has the whole thing recorded on disk. It will take about half an hour to watch it all. In the meantime, I'm gathering a security team to take samples, if we can get to them. That will take place around 4:30. Thank you, Mr. Depina. Bill will be with you in a few minutes."

As Depina returned to his station, Singleton turned back to Bill. Looking around to ensure no one could hear him, he spoke softly. "You are the Director here, and these people are used to hearing you give orders. As far as your people know, you are calling the shots. This is now a military matter and most likely a National Security issue. As of midnight, I have complete authority over all personnel, both civilian and military. At 5:00 A.M., you'll receive a call from Senator Walker—I believe he's a friend of yours. He'll fill you in on the legal aspects of what's happening, along with instructions as to what your role will be in the chain of command. Tim Collins will join you later today to handle the news media."

At least something good was happening. Bill had wondered why Tim was a no-show for yesterday's tests. It was obvious now that someone had been pulling strings.

"I'm glad to see that Tim's still in the picture. I've also been working with a marine biologist, Connie Baker. Is she still in the complex, or has she been evacuated?"

A smile appeared on Singleton's face. "Your lady friend will be joining us later today. Her assistant stayed on as well. We're not sure what all we're dealing with, so her services may be needed. We're converting several offices to makeshift living quarters. Only a small group will actually be staying in the building, probably fewer than 15 people. About 40 people—scientists, technicians, and maintenance—are still on the grounds, excluding security, of course. This group will be pruned even more as needed. We'd like for some of them, you included, to be available at a moment's notice. So you'll be bunking in here for the next few days."

At first, Bill was glad to hear that Connie was going to be staying. Then, he thought better of it as he wondered how dangerous this might turn out to be. There were usually as many as 2,000 people working here. If there were only 40 left, and that number might go even lower, what the hell was going on?

Others were vying for Singleton's attention, so Bill decided to wander back and see what Depina had to say. As he made his way to the back of the control room, several technicians and scientists gave him questioning looks. It was obvious that they were concerned and probably completely in the dark. He doubted that any of them had any idea of what was happening.

When he saw Depina, the technician was hunched over his console, tapping on a series of colored touchscreens. "What have you got to show me?" Bill asked, as he gazed at the bank of displays monitoring the beam tunnel.

"I've set up monitor number one, the black one on your left, for playback. One of the automatic cameras started recording these frames just before midnight last night. What causes it to be triggered is kind of a complex process, but basically, any time the image on one of the monitors changes—that's to say, if something moves in the camera's range of vision—the software shifts from a passive to an active mode and recording begins. The images are updated every few seconds and saved on disk for later analysis."

"I remember when we installed this system, but I never knew much about it. I just recall it being expensive."

"Well, it's a state-of-the-art surveillance system. Look at this picture. Remember when the leaks first showed up and water started dripping from the housing around three of the magnets?"

"Yes, but you said that within a few hours the leaks had stopped, or nearly so."

"That's correct. When I left for the night and put the system into auto mode, none of the leaks were a problem. Two of them had stopped, and the third was nothing more than a slight drip. About midnight, the leak around magnet number 88 intensified. Here's the image I recorded just before I left for the evening." Depina tapped another button, and the image on the display faded as a new one took its place.

Bill looked at the image and could see that the housing was wet, but no trace of running or even dripping water could be seen.

"Now, look at this image. It's time-stamped 11:48:31 P.M. Something has gathered around the spot where the water was first discovered. It looks like... soap suds."

Bill compared the split-screen images. What he saw on the new image did indeed appear to be bubbles. They covered an area almost the size of a basketball and encased the upper left side of the magnet's housing.

"Any idea how long it took for these bubbles to appear?"

"Well, the camera takes an image every 20 seconds. But not all images are saved. Only if something has been determined to have changed does the software start saving the images. If we go back and look at the time stamps, we can deduce how long it took before the images started being saved. This will also tell us how long it took for the mass to accumulate on the magnets."

"I'd like for you to do that, Mr. Depina, and let me know as soon as possible."

"I've already done it. It took about thirty-five minutes for the mass to grow from nothing to what you see here."

"And when was this image taken?"

"Two minutes before midnight."

"That's almost five hours ago. What does the mass look like now?"

"Singleton told me to keep this monitor turned off until you got here so no one else would see it. Here's a live shot of the magnet."

Bill could hardly believe what he was seeing. The entire wall around the magnet was covered with what looked like soap suds. Zooming in, he could see that up close, they looked more like small mirrors—no, rings—of varying sizes. Some were not much larger than the buttons on his shirt; others were up to an inch in diameter, though there could easily be larger ones inside the mass.

He could also see that the whole thing was vibrating, ever so slightly. He guessed that what he was actually seeing was growth. It was growing before his eyes. It was approximately seven feet wide and maybe eighteen inches above the magnet's housing. From there, it was solid all the way to the floor.

"My God!" Bill exclaimed. "What in Sam Hill is it?"

"Nobody seems to know. There are similar masses where the water showed up on the other magnets, though none of them are anywhere near this size."

"Has anyone tried to get a sample of it?"

"No. There have been other, apparently more pressing matters."

"You've got to be kidding. What else has happened?"

"I'm afraid you'll have to ask Mr. Singleton about that. I've been glued to these monitors since I came back last night."

"Thank you, Mr. Depina. Get back to me if there's any activity in the other masses, or if anything changes with this one. Anything at all!"

"Yes, sir. Oh, sir, there are at least three other people trained to operate this system. Could you see if I could possibly be relieved? I've been here for 21 of the last 24 hours."

"I know how you feel. I'll look at the schedule and see if I can get you some relief."

"That would sure be appreciated."

With the conversation over, Bill returned to his office, hoping to run into Singleton or Meyer. When he got there, his phone rang. "Dr. Scott?" A young female voice surprised him.

"Yes, this is Bill Scott."

"Please hold for a call from Senator Walker." He'd forgotten that the Senator was supposed to call him. He glanced up at the clock. The Senator was late, but it didn't really matter. A few seconds later, Senator Walker came on the line.

"Bill, I'm sorry to be so secretive about what's going on and for springing Singleton and Meyer on you like I did. But it couldn't be helped. There are things happening that are beyond my control."

"Good morning, Senator. Yes, I think I just got a glimpse of one of them in the beam tunnel."

"Good, you've seen that. Then you can understand what I'm talking about. I'm afraid that this has become a national security problem. What you saw is only the tip of the iceberg."

194

"If it's weirder than that, I can't imagine what else is going on."

"Listen, you're going to be sharing control—well, 'share' is not exactly the word I'm looking for. You're going to appear to be in control, but in reality, you'll be taking orders from Mr. Singleton. He'll be taking orders directly from the White House. Don't feel badly. You're going to be spared a lot of responsibility that you really wouldn't want on your shoulders.

You're not going to just be a talking head, though. You'll still have a lot of say in the running of the accelerator. Necessity warrants a military figure at the top right now."

"I figured as much. What exactly will I be doing?"

"Singleton will fill you in on your responsibilities later. Just follow his orders, and everything should be fine. These are trying times. We are involved with something that has never been encountered before in the history of man. All bets are off. We play the cards as they are dealt. While I'd love to be there with you, we all have our own roles to play. You're going to have a place in history, Dr. Scott. Enjoy it."

With that, the phone went dead. Bill knew that from now on, his contact with the outside world was going to be limited to the proverbial slim and none.

Chapter Twenty-Two

Swishhhh...swishhhh...swishhhh...

Bill sat there for a moment, wondering if he was actually hearing something or if it was just his heightened imagination. The sound was barely audible, like air escaping from a tire with a nail in it, coming in short bursts of about three seconds each. He couldn't tell where it was coming from; it seemed to be everywhere and nowhere at once.

A few seconds later, his door opened, and Meyer stepped in. "Hello, Dr. Scott." A wide smile was plastered across his face, reminding Bill of the Joker from the old Batman TV series.

"You're awfully cheerful considering all that's going on."

"I'm just putting my best face forward, so to speak."

"Do you hear something that sounds like air escaping from a tire?"

"Yes. It started a few minutes ago. Everyone is trying to figure out where it's coming from. Word is, it started at Wilson Hall about an hour ago. We have people stationed all over the complex, and it's only audible in certain places. It seems to be spreading along the beam tunnel in a counterclockwise direction."

"What do you think it is?" Bill asked.

"I have no idea—escaping gas maybe? Escaping from where, or what, who knows. It's no louder than a whisper, and twice as soft. That's not why I came in here, though."

"I know, you're lonely and needed someone to talk to."

"Funny. Listen, I know that all of this is happening so fast it's hard to keep up with. I mean, in just a few hours, you've been replaced as the Director of Operations. Well, not exactly replaced, but your authority has been seriously diminished. Even so, you still have a very important role in the decision-making. The military may be in control, but we know virtually nothing about how this gigantic piece of machinery works. We're going to need your expertise in everything concerning it."

"Gee, thanks, and I thought I was just a talking head."

"Plus, you have the respect of the remaining scientists and technicians working here. They'll be much more likely to confide in you than in strangers. So, even though we have the final say, we won't make any strategic moves without consulting you first."

"So, what is your next move?"

Meyer sat down in an office chair facing Dr. Scott. "We're getting ready to go into the beam tunnel to see if we can get some samples of the 'soap suds,' as everyone is calling them. These will be flown to DARPA for study. Another team will be exploring the tunnel in the opposite direction. Have you been brought up to date on what's happening there?"

"I've seen the video of the soap suds and heard that other 'anomalies' have been seen, but I have no idea what they were referring to."

"It's probably just as well. You might not want to stay here if you'd seen what's stalking the rest of the tunnel."

"I don't think I like the sound of that," Bill said. "Just what exactly is it that you'd rather I not see?"

"I've already said more than I should; that's why Don—Mr. Singleton—does most of the talking. He's stretched tight as a piano wire right now, though. You'll find out soon enough. Tim Collins is scheduled to meet with you and some of our security people at 9:00 A.M. to craft a statement for the press.

The whole complex has been posted 'off limits' to the public until further notice. State and local police are guarding the entrances and patrolling the outer boundaries. Military police are responsible for the grounds and buildings. All are armed with orders to restrain anyone not on a guarded list of names. Be sure you have your ID badge visible at all times."

Bill had several questions, but before he could ask, Meyer's phone buzzed—a secure, encrypted device. Meyer glanced at the screen and recognized the number immediately. "Hello, sir. Yes, sir. I understand, sir. I'll get right on it. No, sir. Goodbye, sir."

He closed the phone and stood up. "I'm afraid I'm going to have to cut this short, Dr. Scott. I'm sure you have questions, but problems have come up that need my immediate attention. Either Mr. Singleton or I will get back with you as soon as possible to bring you up to date on the situation. Be as vague as you can at the press meeting. Mr. Collins will be brought up to speed as well. Like you, he'll need to know what's happening so he'll know how to spin it for the media. Good day."

Before Bill had time to say anything, Meyer was closing the door. At least he had a good idea now of where he stood and what was happening. He still had an important role in things. He was still the Director and was still at least partially in charge of running the accelerator. He wondered how much his authority would count if he were to order it shut down.

Not much, he surmised. Not if the powers that be thought otherwise. He'd settle for that. He had no choice in the matter anyway. As the Senator had said, "I'm saving you from a lot of responsibility that you really don't want."

Swishhhh...swishhhh...swishhhh...

What the hell is that? He turned his head, got up, and walked around. No matter where he walked, the sound always seemed to be coming from somewhere else. Being able to hear it so clearly but not being able to tell where it was coming from was frustrating. It was another one of those mysteries that he'd just have to live with. He sat back down and pulled up the Internet on his computer. Just for the hell of it, he brought up another image from the webcam at HAARP. He thought he'd check and see if any additional messages had been sent. He might as well get used to this spy stuff as it was all around him. Damn, there was one. He wasn't sure if it had anything to do with him, though.

They must be using these images to message people everywhere, he thought. The message read, "The Blips are back, and they are larger than before."

He knew what it meant. It was referring to the blips that had appeared just after a plane had flown into the antenna's beam at HAARP. He remembered reading it in the papers that Singleton and Meyer left with him. Apparently, they had returned.

Looking through the glass partition in his office, he could see that something was happening in the control room. Several of his colleagues were gathered together and looked to be having a lively discussion. He figured he'd better check it out. He just hoped they wouldn't ask him anything he couldn't answer, which right now was about anything other than his name.

"Here's the Director." They gathered round him. "Dr. Scott, what the hell is going on?"

That's just what he didn't want to hear.

"Hello, gentlemen." It was too late to dodge them now.

"I'm not going to lie to you; I really don't know. I was called in about 3:30 last night because some problems had turned up concerning the accelerator. From what I've seen so far, there's much more to it than that. I'm sure you've noticed that we're working with a skeleton crew. Don't expect to see many more being added, either. It looks like those of us here are going to be here for a while."

"Is it safe?" one of the group asked.

"I don't think we're in any great danger. We have plenty of protection. I'm sure you've seen the armed security people at every corridor."

"Don't you mean armed military personnel?" The voice came from the edge of the gathering as a young technician approached the group. "Are we prisoners here? Can we leave if we want to? I have a wife and child that I'm sure are wondering why I didn't come home last night. I tried to call them a little while ago, but the phones were out of service. I borrowed a cell phone to make the call, but one of the security guys saw me do it and confiscated the phone, saying all communications had to go through Captain Rider at Wilson Hall."

So Captain Rider is back again. Bill hadn't seen him since the last test. He wasn't surprised to hear he was back, though. After all, he is a member of the military.

"As I said, I just got here a little while ago. I know there are certain procedures that take precedence if a major problem has occurred. It's obvious that something major has happened. I wasn't aware of the phone situation. I'll look into it as soon as I can. For now, I think it would be best if we all just do our jobs and let the military handle things."

Another technician spoke up, "That's fine for those who don't have families, but I'm sure my wife is worried to death. At the very least, she'd have expected a call from me. This wouldn't be the first time I've had to stay overnight. But it is the first time I've not called her to let her know where I am."

"I understand. I'll get in touch with Captain Rider immediately and see what's going on. I'll have an answer for you within the hour."

That seemed to calm everyone's nerves. They all went back to work as Bill stepped back into his office. He watched them through the one-way mirror looking out over the control room. They were still talking among themselves, but they were not as agitated as they had been. Bill picked up his phone (probably the only one in the control room still working) and dialed the extension for Fermilab Security at Wilson Hall.

It only took a few minutes to explain to Captain Rider the need to contact the families of those still here and let them know that they were alright. It was agreed that those remaining could call their families themselves soon, but that phone conversations would be monitored, and talk of anything happening here would be strictly prohibited.

Bill delivered the message and handled all of the questions asked of him like a pro, not once acting like he was concerned with their safety or well-being. In reality, he was worried about both.

Chapter Twenty-Three

At 8:45, there was a knock on Bill's door. "Come in." Tim Collins entered. "I thought I'd get here a few minutes early if you're not busy."

"No, Tim, that's fine. It has been a hectic morning though. How about a cup of coffee? That's about the only thing this morning I can depend on being here."

"Sure, I'll take two creamers and two Sweet-n-Lows, if you have them."

"I forgot. You only like coffee if you can't taste it."

"I'm not much of a coffee drinker, but I can use all the caffeine I can get."

Bill poured Tim a cup and mixed in the condiments. "Yeah, I know what you mean. Did you know that Connie and Carol are here too?"

"No, I didn't." It was easy to tell that Tim was quite surprised. "I wonder why they were allowed to stay on?"

"Singleton said it was because they didn't know what they might run into, and Connie's skills might prove useful. I don't know about Carol, unless they thought she was part of the team."

"Singleton—what do you know about him?"

"Not much. I only met him a little while back. At first, I thought he was just a messenger boy. That amateur-looking spy get-up, the trench coat and dark glasses, gave me the impression that he was some kind of clown. Now, I'd say it's part of the disguise. It puts people off and tends to make them think he's not to be taken seriously. I'm including Meyer here as well. That's a mistake that works to their advantage. They cultivate it well. I guess you know that Singleton is running the show?"

"Yes. I attended a meeting yesterday morning and was brought up to date on the changes being undertaken. I was also told that there was going to be a thinning out of those remaining on site, but I never dreamed it would be this thin. They must have known that something was going to happen during that test. They told me I wouldn't be covering it, but I would be needed today."

"That explains how they got everyone out of here so fast. I guess they started evacuating people yesterday afternoon. They must have expected something was going to happen last night and wanted their plans in place before it did."

"I saw vans coming and going all afternoon. I'd say they had things pretty much the way they wanted long before midnight."

Swishhhh swishhhh swishhhh

Bill cocked his head to one side. "There's that sound again. I think I've gotten so used to it that it's just another noise blending into the background. For some reason though, it seems louder."

"I don't know if it's any louder, but it bothers the hell out of me. I'm sensitive to sound anyway. I think I can hear a spider crawl up a web. I heard it started at Wilson Hall."

"Yeah, that's what Meyer told me a few hours ago."

Tim got up and walked over to the one-way mirror. He was much too nervous to sit for more than a minute or two. "I've been thinking about this most of the night. I'm going to spin this as if it was a possible terrorist attack. I'll say the whole thing started with a rupture in one of the liquid nitrogen tanks. Maybe have a terrorist responsible for sabotaging the tank. Allude that several suspicious devices have been discovered scattered about the complex. That would account for the military presence and the evacuations as well. It should buy us a few extra days until somebody can figure out what's really going on. I hate lying to the public, but they're not yet ready for the truth. Hell, we don't know what the truth is ourselves!"

"That's for damn sure. Listen, have you been told about HAARP?"

"HAARP? No, this is the first time I've heard of it."

"I won't fill you in now. It's too long of a story. I'd say they don't want you to know about it if they haven't mentioned it to you by now. This goes all the way to the top. When you get a chance, look it up on the Internet. It's spelled H-A-A-R-P, with two A's. Act like you've never heard of it if someone brings it up. I'd rather them not know that I was the one who clued you in."

"It sounds important."

"It is. I think it may play a part in everything that's going on here. The press meeting is scheduled to start in a few minutes. After the meeting, I'll fill you in on what I've been able to find out. It's far too complicated to do right now, and I don't want to be interrupted once I get started."

"If it's as good as you say, I'm sure it will be worth the wait."

Before Tim could sit back down, the door opened and three men entered. The media had arrived. DARPA wasn't wasting any time in getting something out to the press. He wondered if any of these three were in the government's pocket.

From their ID tags, it looked like two of them were from national television networks and the other was from the New York Times. There was a small conference room at the rear of Bill's office. Tim did most of the talking. Bill cut in when the topic concerned technical issues about the tests. The key was to downplay everything. That wasn't the easiest thing to do. Not after he mentioned the word "terrorist." Tim hated using that word, but it was the only way he could justify all of these military types standing around.

The meeting lasted about 20 minutes and seemed to go well. It looked as though they bought it, including the crack about the sound they were hearing. He told them it was pressurized liquid nitrogen escaping from one of the damaged holding tanks. They all said it sounded like air escaping from a tire. Bill agreed—smiling broadly. With the meeting over, everyone left but Tim and Bill.

Unless something drastic happened, Tim figured it would be three to five days before they'd be back with more questions. He just hoped things would be back to normal by then. They'd know how well their spin had worked by the reaction it received on tonight's news.

Bill was about to fill Tim in on the HAARP connection when Meyer cracked open his office door.

"Got a minute?"

"Don't you ever knock?" Bill growled. "Sure. What do you need?"

Meyer stepped into the office along with two individuals wearing full bio-suits.

"I'm getting ready to send a team into the beam tunnel to take a sample of the—substance."

"You mean the soap suds."

"Yes, the soap suds. I'd like for you to inform everyone that testing will continue as planned until further notice. Everyone is to remain at their assigned positions. Only short bathroom breaks will be permitted.

I'd say we'll be less than an hour in the tunnel. We're planning on gathering samples and getting the hell out of there. If you want to watch what's going on, have Depina transfer the video feed from the beam tunnel to your computer."

"Can I do that?"

"Yes, as Director of Operations, your computer was patched into the audio/video console when the monitoring system was initiated."

"I'll have him do that."

The men in the bio-suits turned and walked out the door. Before Meyer could leave, Bill called out to him.

"Have you seen the latest image from the HAARP cam?"

Meyer looked over at Tim, wondering if he had any idea what HAARP was all about. Tim had a blank expression on his face.

"No. Was there one?"

"I just happened to bring it up for shits and giggles and saw the image had changed. It read, 'The blips are back and they are larger than before.'"

"I'll inform Mr. Singleton. The team will be entering the beam tunnel at 1100 hours. I'll tell Depina to send a feed to your computer. It looks like he's going to have to wait a while though, until he's relieved."

Meyer left, leaving the door slightly ajar. Tim walked over and closed it. "You may have just let the cat out of the bag. Did you see the way Meyer looked at me when you mentioned HAARP?"

"Yes, I did. I probably shouldn't have said that while you were here. You won't believe all the spy stuff that's going on. I mean, there are encrypted messages being sent over the Internet, top-secret papers being smuggled into the complex, armed guards stationed at every turn, DARPA taking over the entire operation. Who knows what else is going on, or what those soap suds really are."

"Or where they came from," Tim chimed in.

Bill started filling Tim in on how he first met Meyer and Singleton, and how HAARP had entered the picture. About fifteen minutes into his rant, he happened to glance at his computer screen. He noticed a square yellow icon flashing in the toolbar. It looked like a miniature television set. He clicked on it and a window popped up about the size of a deck of cards. He could tell the image was coming from the beam tunnel, but it was hard to make out any detail from such a small image. He double-clicked on the picture and it resized to a full-screen display.

"Looks like we're online," Bill said.

Tim came around to Bill's side of the desk so he could get a better view of the monitor.

"Technology—isn't it amazing."

There was a menu at the bottom of the display that read, "scroll to zoom." Bill positioned the cursor over a section of the display and rolled the scroll button on the mouse. The image immediately zoomed in on the area under the cursor and expanded it to full screen. He found that he could move the image, changing his point of view as he pleased.

"That stuff really does look like soap suds," Tim said.

"I guess it was aptly named. I wonder when the guys in the bio-suits will get there."

"It shouldn't be long now. I'd hate to have to wear that getup any longer than necessary. It looked hot as hell."

"I wish I had a little more zooming power. If I could get a little closer, I might be able to figure out what that stuff is made of."

"Maybe once the guys get there, they'll hold some of it up to the cameras. Say, can you talk to them from here?"

"I doubt it. I'll be amazed if I'm even able to see them from here. Depina probably can, though. That setup is incredible. I'm sure there are microphones on the cameras. In fact, I know there are. I remember seeing an audio icon on the playback he showed me this morning. So sound can be recorded as well. I don't know if you can talk back to anyone though."

"Some microphones can double as speakers; it just depends on how they were designed. Are there any other options on your computer?" Tim asked.

"Looks like I'm limited to zoom, pan, and record."

Suddenly, a dark shape blocked out the image on the display. Bill had the zoom set to maximum when the bio-team arrived and someone walked in front of the image they were viewing. Bill rolled the scroll button backward and the image zoomed out to wide angle. Now they could see all three of the bio-team members. They had several devices with them. Tim was pretty sure that one of the objects was a Geiger counter. Another looked like it had a display screen on it. Probably some kind of recording device. They also carried two cylindrical bright yellow tubes, each about eighteen inches long with handles attached in the middle. Written on the side of one of them were the words, "WARNING-HAZARDOUS-WARNING," in large red letters. Above the words was an emblem of a black skull and crossbones. When they got a better view of the second cylinder, they could see that it had the same markings.

Bill hadn't noticed it before, but there was a slider at the bottom of the frame surrounding the display. It resembled the volume control on Windows Media Player. It was set to the lowest position. He took the mouse and moved it to the right, as far as it would go.

The speakers came alive with the sound of the men talking. They were describing what they were seeing, much like a doctor would while performing an autopsy.

As he thought about what he was witnessing, he couldn't help but feel in awe of all that was going on. Here he was, observing something that has never been seen before, live and in color, and in the comfort and safety of an office cubicle. Jackie Gleason would have said, "How sweet it is!"

As Bill watched the display, it suddenly zoomed in on a small section of the soap suds.

"What happened? I didn't do that."

Tim leaned over Bill's desk, almost touching the video screen. "I just realized what's going on. You've been zooming and panning the image on the display, but you're not controlling the actual camera. I'll bet only Depina can do that. You've just been exploring the image he'd selected. Otherwise, we'd all be trying to control the camera at the same time."

"You're right. The camera has been displaying the same image all along. I've just been exploring different sections of that image. Depina obviously moved it this time. I wonder why he zoomed in on that section?"

"Wasn't there only two guys in bio-suits when Meyer was here?" Tim asked.

"Yes. They must have picked up another person along the way. I noticed that one of the suits was a slightly different color."

"Turn up the volume. Let's hear what they have to say."

Bill had clicked the mute button earlier. He clicked it again and voices appeared. The camera pulled back about that time and they could see all three of the men in the tunnel again. Bill was right, one of the suits was a much lighter color. It was also made differently.

"If I'm right, you won't be able to use the containment vessels you brought with you. I think this is going to be an entirely different kind of substance than you've ever worked with before."

Bill couldn't tell who was speaking because everyone's face was covered. He thought it was the guy in the odd-colored suit.

"Jim, I'm going to try something. I want you to record it. I've brought a couple of items with me that will confirm, or deny, my hypothesis." With that, the man in the odd suit (Bill was right, it was him talking) picked up what looked to be a Louisville Slugger.

"That's a baseball bat!" Tim said. "I wonder what he's going to do with that?"

The image zoomed in so that it was only on the guy in the suit holding the bat.

"I'm going to touch the soap suds with the end of this bat. If it does what I think it will, you'll see the bat disappear." As he brought the heavy end of the bat near the soap suds, the camera zoomed to a close-up. The image wasn't nearly as fuzzy now. Bill had only a few pixels to work with, but the optical zoom was working at the camera's full resolution. As the bat touched the soap suds, it seemed to sink right into them. The man in the suit stopped and pulled it back out. Except, there was nothing there to pull out. It was like someone had cut it off.

"I'm going to try one more thing, then I'll tell you what I think is happening."

With that, he picked up a steel rod. It was about an inch in diameter, and maybe three feet long.

"This is stainless steel. It's one of the strongest metals known." The camera zoomed in as he brought the metal rod near the soap suds. At first, he just touched the edge of the suds, barely probing them with the rod. He pulled back, and part of the rod was missing. Then he plunged the rod into the suds until there was only about a foot between his hand and the soap suds. When he pulled back, the rest of the rod had vanished.

"This is very similar to what Rider and Madison reported happening when they probed the mysterious floating circle they found during the last accelerator test. I think I know what's happening, but I don't understand how. Let me look at the structure of these soap suds more closely."

He bent down and picked up the device with the video monitor and handed the probe attached to it to one of the other men. He told him to hold it about a foot over the top of the soap suds but warned him to be very careful to not get any closer.

Looking at the display he said, "From a distance, this substance looks like soap suds, but when magnified, it appears to have a crystalline structure. I can only get a 10X magnification without a solid probe support, but even at this magnification, I can see that it's made up of thousands of small, circular, no, make that many-sided—let me see if I can count them. I believe there are 18 sides to each structure—an octadecagon. The walls seem to be bound together, but I don't know how tightly. I'm going to try an experiment."

With that, he opened a small metal box marked "tools" they had brought with them, picking out a hammer and a cold chisel. He walked over to the edge of the magnet's housing where the soap suds had formed in a thin layer. They looked like a sheet of bubble wrap. As he moved behind it, he made a discovery.

"There's a definite front and back to this thing. This is the same thing Rider and Madison found when they encountered the floating disk. When they first saw it, it was invisible from the rear. But later on, the back side became transparent."

"I know what he's talking about," Bill said. "During the first test, there was a report about a small round object floating in mid-air. You could see into it from one side but not the other. Captain Rider and Sgt. Madison were the two who discovered it. They said it grew to softball size within half an hour or so. They also said they could see a moving image in it, and that it was like looking through a window.

The consensus was that most people don't think it ever existed. They said it was probably a hallucination brought on by stress, or by being in such close proximity to the superconducting magnets."

"I remember reading the report, but the details evade me now. I'm afraid I was also one of those who didn't believe it at the time. Now, I'm not so sure."

"Mr. Hammond, I have you on the screen, but there's not enough light behind the soap suds to pick up much of what you're doing."

Depina's voice was coming through the speakers much louder than the others.

"I guess we now know who the guy in the odd suit is. Where have I heard that name before?" Bill asked.

"The only Hammond I know of is a molecular scientist who works for Bell Labs. I wrote an article for Future Technology about him three or four years ago. He'd developed a way to organize Mitochondrial DNA molecules using sound waves instead of electrical currents. It was a revolutionary idea, but it never really caught on. He was kind of a scientific rebel if I remember right. Brilliant, but not much of a team player."

"That's OK Jim; I'm going to see if I can get a piece of this material to break away from the main body. Listen, you two had better get farther back in the tunnel, just in case this happens to shatter. The parts could be deadly."

The other two guys backed out of the camera's view. When they were no longer in sight, Hammond took the hammer and gingerly tapped at the back edge of the sheet of soap suds. Nothing happened. He struck it a little harder. Again—nothing.

"This has a very solid feel to it. I might not be able to break it with a sledgehammer."

He centered the cold chisel about an inch from the edge and struck it solidly. A metallic sound, similar to that of a cowbell being struck with a leather hammer, filled their speakers. A piece of soap suds about as wide as a quarter and maybe five or six times as long broke away from where he'd struck his blow. The piece moved so slowly as it broke free that it almost seemed to be floating. No, it didn't almost seem to float, it was floating. It was moving about a foot every twenty seconds, and tumbling. It must have been lighter than air because it never dropped at all in elevation. It took it almost five minutes to reach the other side of the beam tunnel.

The camera couldn't focus on where it was going to strike the wall of the tunnel because it was going to hit almost directly underneath it.

All three men were following it as it approached the impact with the tunnel wall. They were standing within a few feet of it when it impacted. The irregular shape of the projectile was critical as to what damage would be done. The translucent side, the side that resembled soap suds, came in contact first.

The walls were made of reinforced concrete. As the piece touched the wall, it melted into and through it. It was spinning very slowly on its axis. The concrete never slowed its forward motion at all. It was like it hadn't encountered anything. It was not until the back of the object, the opaque side, touched the concrete that it stopped.

It was Hammond who spoke first. "If that object had not been spinning so that the rear side would eventually come forward, I don't think anything would have stopped it. This is some kind of matter never encountered on Earth. It doesn't belong here. God help us if it gets into the wrong hands."

"Dr. Hammond." It was Depina. "I think you'd better look at the area where the soap suds broke away."

Hammond hurried back to where his hammer and chisel still lay on the floor. "What the—" His words hid the astonishment he was feeling. Cracks were appearing everywhere. The soap suds were starting to separate into sections of various sizes. A small section had snapped off at the point of impact, but the shock wave had continued on throughout the rest of the structure. It was starting to unravel the matrix holding it together.

"We've got to get out of here—NOW!" Someone else was speaking, but because of the suits, Bill couldn't tell who it was.

"I came for a sample and I'm going to get one." This was Hammond's voice.

"I think I have a way to capture a piece of this stuff." With that, he reached back into the toolbox and brought out a dull black object. Bill couldn't tell what it was, but it looked to be about a foot long. It might have been made of wood, or metal. They watched him as he opened a tube of something and smeared it on the end of the object.

Then he moved to the rear of the soap suds. He placed the object he'd smeared the substance on against the back of one of the sections that was about to separate from the main structure. The section he'd chosen was about the size of a paperback book. He held the object against it for 15 to 20 seconds, and then turned it quickly to his right, breaking it free.

"I hope this glue holds," Hammond said, as he made his way around the left side of the soap suds. "I don't think any more sections will break free without help. There are cracks everywhere, but it looks like it's going to hold together. We'll need someone to come back later and spray a coating of contact cement over the entire back of this thing. Everywhere he can get to anyway. That should keep all of the sections together until we can figure out what we want to do with them."

"Good job, gentlemen. Let's go show the grown-ups what we've discovered. I'm sure they're just dying to play with it."

"Looks like you're right about his being a rebel," Bill said.

"You can be that way if you're good enough, and I've heard he's the best."

Hammond and the two others made their way back to the elevators in DUNE without further complications. Hammond led the way, holding the death-on-a-stick well ahead of him. There were several scientists waiting for him as he stepped out of the elevator.

Amazing, incredible, unbelievable. Each scientist had a different exclamation, but they were all valid. What he'd brought back was something that none of them had ever seen before. It was attached to a stiff piece of rubber tubing by a special adhesive, very similar to common household super glue.

Up close, everyone could see the crystalline structure of the soap suds. "We may have to get a new name for this now that we've got a better idea of what it is," This came from one of the scientists examining the substance, from a distance of a few feet.

"Soap suds is good enough for me. I wouldn't know what else to call it," remarked another scientist.

"How about the Blob?" said a third. "I just hope this doesn't turn out like the movie." That lightened up the mood a little.

Hammond spoke up. "Did all of you see what went on while I was collecting this?" They agreed they had.

"Good. Then you know what it can do. Or maybe you don't. I don't think you could see it as it entered the wall. Let me give you a demonstration."

With that, he walked over to a table in the lab where a large metal vise was attached to the table's edge. "The back of the soap suds is solid, though I was able to break this piece off, using a hammer and cold chisel. The chisel focused all of the hammer's energy onto a small area. The only piece that actually separated from the main body was the one you saw float across the room. It wedged in the wall when the rear of the piece struck the concrete."

"As you can see, I'm able to hold this easily with the rubber tubing. The soap suds are practically weightless. I'm going to sacrifice this vise for the demonstration. Watch, as I touch the front of the soap suds to the vise."

With that, he placed the soap suds perpendicular to the vise and about two inches below the top of it. Next, he moved it towards the center. Every part of the vise that the soap suds touched just disappeared. He pulled it away, leaving a smooth finish to the metal, as if it had just been freshly cast. Absolutely nothing had changed on the soap suds.

The scientists didn't know what to say. They just stood there astonished. "It didn't take any effort at all to cut through that vise. Actually, 'dissolved' might be a better choice of words.

If you magnify the soap suds, you'll see that each 'bubble' is about a quarter inch in size. I saw some on the main mass that were almost twice this size. If I had a small enough object, I think I could push it into the center of the bubble without harming it. I'm basing this on a report I read about what happened during the last test of the accelerator. It's the sides of the bubble that do the damage. If I'm right, only a part of the metal in that vise was dissolved. The rest of it went into the bubble. From there though, I have no idea what happened to it. We'll be able to tell more when we can get this mounted and we're able to run some experiments on it.

By the way, the bubbles aren't really bubbles as you can see. With magnification, I was able to determine that each one has 18 sides."

They were in one of several laboratories located in DUNE. A much larger lab was being readied where they could perform a batch of experiments on this unworldly substance.

One of the scientists spoke up. "We could sure use more than one piece of this stuff. We need several, or we'll be forever running tests, one at a time."

Hammond realized that before it was asked. "The main structure is already fractured. I'll send someone back to gather as many pieces as he can. It would probably be a good idea to seal the back with adhesive too, so that more of these pieces don't break away on their own. This stuff is too dangerous to have just floating around. We might get three or four more pieces, more than that is just too risky. You'll have to make do with them."

Both of the military officers that had gone with Hammond earlier volunteered for the job. "Two might be better than one. It will be easier to bring back the samples. I'll have a secure area prepared in the other lab for four additional specimens. That's all we can handle right now."

The two officers started to put their helmets back on when Hammond stopped them. "No need for that. The tunnel's clear. I had an instrument with me that analyzed the surrounding air and it was fine."

Chapter Twenty-Four

Bill and Tim didn't know what was going on with the "soap suds" once the team left the tunnel. They'd have to wait for an update—there were other things to worry about.

Tim decided to borrow Bill's back office to update his logs. He had his ultralight laptop with him, so he'd work there and then sync the files to the main system. The entire Fermilab complex, grounds and all, was now blanketed by encrypted wireless mesh towers. You could get online anywhere, and Tim was networked to the Feynman Computing Center, where the instrument logs were stored. Still, he kept a copy on his laptop and another on a quantum-encrypted USB "jump" drive, just to be safe.

Bill was overdue in checking with his fellow scientists to see how well the PIP-II accelerator was performing. No warnings had sounded, so he was pretty sure there hadn't been any problems. They'd been operating at maximum power for over twelve hours. If no issues arose, they'd continue at full power for a 72-hour stretch, then shut down, compare notes, and run a full analysis. If all was well, the next test would last for a week or more. If all went according to plan, there would be no limits to the running time. It wasn't unusual for modern accelerators to run continuously for a year before scheduled maintenance.

Bill had hardly gotten started when Depina came running up. "Do you want a feed from the beam tunnel redirected to your computer?"

He told him he'd been watching the video all morning and had other work to do.

"This is different. Another group is going in the other direction in just a few minutes. That's where the monsters are."

Bill wasn't sure he'd heard that right. "Monsters—there are monsters in the beam tunnel?"

"Well, that's what they're calling them. I don't know if they're really monsters or not. Sometimes the cameras go dark, and I can't see a thing. Other times, strange shapes have appeared, even before the testing began. 'Monsters' just kind of stuck, like 'soap suds.'"

"When is this going to take place?"

"In just a few minutes. Singleton is leading the group."

"Singleton again. How many are going into the tunnel?"

"I don't know, but I'd say eight to ten, and well armed. I saw them suiting up outside the elevators. Not bio-suits—body armor."

"Transfer the feed to my computer. Who else is receiving these feeds?"

"I can only assign them to three places—your computer, the systems controller at Feynman, and a special link just labeled 'admin.' No idea where that is. Of course, all feeds are transmitted to DARPA headquarters. From there, who knows."

"I'm headed back to my computer now, Mr. Depina. Hook me up."

When Bill got back to his office, he told Tim about the conversation. Of course, Tim was as anxious to see these "monsters" as Bill was. He pulled up a chair and they both waited for the beam tunnel feed to appear. It took less than a minute.

The feed had just started when Bill's phone rang.

"Dr. Scott."

"Yes, this is Dr. Scott."

"Dr. Scott, this is Major Thompson. One of my security team just reported something unusual at the lake near the dam. I'd like you to hear what he has to say firsthand. He's on the line now. I have additional men en route. His name is Corporal Davis."

"That's fine, Major, patch him through."

"Dr. Scott!"

"Go ahead, I'm listening."

"I'm sorry to bother you, sir, this is Corporal Davis. I'm at the pumping station on the lake. Do you know where that is?"

"Yes, Corporal, I'm familiar with the pumping station."

"Something strange is happening here, sir. I'm not quite sure how to explain it. The water around the intake pipe is boiling."

"What do you mean, it's boiling?"

"I don't know. Maybe it's not actually boiling, but it's bubbling and churning like water does in a pot. It looks like it's boiling to me."

"Are you alone?"

"Yes."

"Call for backup and get me a picture. Is there any change in the water's color?"

"No, it looks the same as everywhere else. But there are huge bubbles coming up to the surface and exploding in a shower of droplets that are reaching me on shore. Sometimes it looks like a geyser gone mad."

"Forget calling for backup, I'll get someone over there right away. I'd come myself, but we have problems here of our own. Help is on the way, Corporal. Call me back when they arrive, or if something else happens."

"Yes sir, thank you."

Bill informed Tim of the activities at the lake.

"That lake has accounted for a lot of mysteries lately. Whatever happened with the hole you and Connie discovered?"

"Nothing, as far as I know. There have been at least two different teams exploring it, one included some Navy SEALs. Whatever they found, they kept to themselves. I asked once, and was told it was classified. They made it pretty obvious—unless you were part of their group, don't waste your time asking questions. So I didn't."

"How could you, the Director of Operations, not be in their group?"

"I'm a civilian. Everything's been under military control since the last test. It's probably been under military control since the beginning—we just didn't realize it."

The speakers on Bill's desk sprang to life.

"Privates Benson and Richardville, you're to take the lead. Everyone listen up. No one steps outside of their path. I don't know what we might find this time. Those of you that were here last week know the dangers. Don't be shocked if you see things you've never seen before. You could see anything down here. Keep your weapons ready, but don't use them unless you absolutely have to. These walls are made of reinforced concrete, and bullets have a way of bouncing back at you. For God's sake, don't get separated from the group. Stay together, and keep the talking to a minimum."

"OK, get the shield up and let's get moving."

As Bill and Tim looked on, Bill spoke first. "Do you see what he's calling a shield?"

"Yes, it looks like a modified version of the contraption Captain Rider mentioned in his report—the famous balloon detector. I wasn't sure if it was real, or just something they made up."

"Oh, it was real alright. He improvised it on the spot. It was pretty ingenious when you think of it. This looks like it's just a more sophisticated version—and about three times as wide. I wouldn't think it would be much help against monsters, though. Then again, what do I know about monsters?"

"Shit, I almost forgot." Bill dialed the extension for security at Wilson Hall. He had them send some officers to lakeside to help out Corporal Davis, including someone with a remote television camera. He wanted to see what was going on there himself. They could patch the remote into the Wi-Fi system. He'd be able to view the transmission on his computer. They may not have all the answers, but they did have the technology.

Depina was in constant contact with Singleton as the group moved through the beam tunnel. He was watching the cameras ahead of them so he could report anything suspicious before they stumbled into it. The beam tunnel was a big place. It would take the group at least two hours to explore it all.

"Mr. Singleton, in approximately another 100 feet, you'll find a 10 to 12 foot section of the wall covered with soap suds. It will be on your right as you approach magnet 837."

"Thank you, Mr. Depina. We'll be watching for it."

Tim spoke. "Magnet number 837. I've forgotten; how many of these magnets are there, anyway?"

"One thousand, and all of them superconducting."

"Damn, that's a lot of magnets."

"Several hundred million dollars' worth! Magnets are the only thing keeping the plasma from striking the wall of the guide tube. Without them, the plasma would melt through the tubing like molasses."

"It's easy to forget, sitting here in these comfortable surroundings, that there's over a trillion electron volts of energy, racing at nearly the speed of light, just a few dozen meters away."

Bill's phone rang again. "Dr. Scott."

"Yes, go ahead Corporal."

"Sir, something else is happening now. The water seems to be rising, as well as swirling and churning. You won't believe this, but the surface seems to have a bulge in it, directly over the area where the pipe from the pumping station is located. It's the strangest thing I've ever seen."

"Oh, I can believe it. I have help on the way, including a cameraman. Just hold your ground. They should be there shortly. Let me know when they get there. Be sure the cameraman transmits a live feed over the Wi-Fi connection. I saw this once myself, Corporal. You're not going crazy."

"What was that all about?" Tim asked.

"That was Corporal Davis, at the pumping station. He's got more problems at the lake. There's water coming up from the bottom in enough volume to cause a bulge on the surface."

"That's an intake pipe. Is he sure of what he's talking about?"

"I saw it happen once myself, though it only lasted a minute or so. Hopefully, this won't last long either. We'll be able to see it ourselves as soon as security gets there and sets up the remote. That should be any time now."

"This I'd like to see."

It had been a strenuous morning. Bill wondered what the afternoon would bring. It didn't take long to find out. He thought he heard a commotion outside his office, but before he could get up to go see what it was about, his door burst open and Meyer came running in.

"Have you seen the noon news on WLS?" WLS was the number one television station in Chicago, now streaming globally.

"No. I haven't had the television on all morning."

"Well, turn it on. I'm glad you're here too, Tim. I'm going to need your help. We have a situation."

Tim looked puzzled. "Which situation might that be? There seems to be several to choose from."

"I'm talking about the news chopper filming the lake down by the pumping station."

"I wasn't aware of any news chopper filming anything. You say it's from channel 9?"

"Yes, WLS. It's on right now. Here, look!"

The television was just coming on. Bill switched it to channel 9, which was actually 44 on their cable. There was a live shot of the lake. The water did seem to be boiling but it was probably just gas escaping from some underground reservoir. Several people with guns were standing on the bank, watching it. The news-cam zoomed in on the frothing water. The reporter was talking about how the place was almost deserted, and locked up tight. Adding that military personnel were the only ones to be seen. The cameraman panned over the complex showing a parking lot with nothing but Hummers in it.

"We've got to get a lid on this before there's a public outcry. They get nervous whenever something happens at a place where they think bombs are being made."

"This is a research center, not a bomb factory," Bill said.

"Tell that to someone who doesn't know an atom from an apple. Most of the public thinks that places like this are where weapons are either being built or designed. Somebody's tipped them off to the fact that we evacuated the premises last night. I can't believe they weren't invited along with the other media this morning. I mean, WLS is a superstation and they're practically in our backyard. What a screw up that was."

"We've got to stop that live feed. If one of the networks picks it up, this place will be overrun by media," Tim said.

Bill was turning up the audio with the remote as he spoke. "Look at that water bubbling. Isn't that steam starting to come off of it? No wonder they went live with the video."

"Say, maybe we can use that," Tim said.

"Use what?" Meyer asked.

"The part about the boiling water. It looks enough like it's boiling that we might be able to claim that some kind of hot spot has appeared under the lake. Maybe we could say a volcanic chimney is heating the water and we evacuated everyone just to be on the safe side. That just might work."

"I like it," Meyer said. "We might actually be able to use this footage to our advantage. Only, I've seen about enough of it. I'm calling in the National Security card. I'll have that video shut down in less than a minute. I'll also see if I can get the chopper to land. You can give them an exclusive, on the hot-spot theory. That will help smooth things over for canning the live video."

Meyer stepped out of the office and called someone with the authority to stop the news transmission. Then he set up a meeting with the WLS reporter.

"I wanted to see what was going on at the lake, but I didn't think I'd see it on the noon news," Bill said.

"I need to use your conference room again, if you don't mind. I've got to figure out how I'm going to explain this in a way that might actually sound believable."

"Good luck with that. Let me know what you come up with. I don't want to quote something only to find that you've said the opposite. We need to be together on this."

Meyer stepped back in Bill's office and told him that things were taken care of. The WLS reporter would meet Tim within the hour.

"Tim's working on the story right now. They can use my conference room for the meeting," Bill said.

"Not a good idea. There are too many other things going on here that a snoopy reporter might get wind of. I've set up the meeting at Wilson Hall near the atrium. I'll let Tim know when the reporter gets there. I'll buy him as much time as I can."

"Fine, call him here when you're ready."

Meyer hadn't been gone five minutes when Depina poked his head into the office. "I was told you wanted a second video feed."

"I don't know who told you, but yes. Can that be done?"

"Sure. I just received a signal from a portable remote camera transmitting from somewhere on the lake. I assume that's the feed you're talking about. They told me you wanted it patched into your computer."

Bill watched as Depina brought up the video feed on the monitor. "This will only take a minute. I'm setting this up for a split screen. The lake video is on the right, the beam tunnel on the left. If you click on either image, that feed will go full screen. Each feed has its own icon on the desktop. You're good to go. I've got to get back to my monitoring."

"Thanks. You're making my life a lot easier."

"No problem. That's what I get paid for." Depina closed the door behind him. Bill turned down the sound on the television. When he glanced at the picture, they were giving last night's baseball scores.

I guess Meyer got the story pulled, at least for the time being, Bill thought to himself. As he viewed the feed from the lake, he could hear someone talking there as well. Actually, he was picking up the audio from both displays. He clicked the "mute" icon on the left image, cutting out the audio from the beam tunnel. This split screen was OK, but having only half a screen left a lot to be desired. He clicked on the right image and it zoomed to full screen. He also turned up the volume control.

"Are you getting this?" asked Corporal Davis.

His voice came over the speakers, loud and clear. "I've got it, but I don't know what I'm seeing," Bill said.

There was no answer. What the hell am I doing? he thought to himself.

He could hear Davis over the camera's microphone, but he couldn't talk back to him.

Feeling like an idiot, he sat back and watched the monitor. Davis wasn't even talking to him. He was talking with one of the security men.

"There are five-inch high waves on the lake, and there's not a bit of wind. Have you noticed that the water's rising?" Davis continued.

"I hadn't paid any attention to it. There's an overflow about a hundred yards up the bank. It should take care of any excess, but where's the water coming from?"

"It's coming from somewhere near that intake pipe. Ever see those old submarine movies, where they're dropping depth charges into the ocean, and when they go off the water bulges on the surface, just before it breaks through and explodes?"

"Sure."

"Well, look about 70 yards from shore, and a little to your right. See that bulge in the water? It's not big, maybe six or seven inches, at most. You can tell by the motion of the bubbles that water is coming up in huge quantities. It takes a lot of water to make a bulge like that."

"I see it now. I hadn't noticed it with all the turbulence. Could the intake pipe be backing up?"

"Not a chance. It only takes in coolant water for the heating systems. I don't know where all that water is coming from, but it's been bulging like that for at least an hour."

Bill couldn't make out the bulge they were talking about. There wasn't enough resolution in the video feed, but he could easily see the turbulence. It did look like water boiling in a pot. Maybe Tim's story about an underground hotspot would be believable after all.

His phone rang. "Sorry to bother you, sir. This is Sgt. Finley, with Security in Wilson Hall. I'm trying to find Tim Collins. I was told he might be in your office."

"Yes, he is, Sgt. Hold on, and I'll patch you through to him."

Bill put the phone on hold and called back to Tim. He was sitting in the conference room with his head in his hands.

"Tim, catch line three."

When he saw Tim reaching for the phone, he transferred the call to line three. It was only a minute or so before Tim headed off to Wilson Hall. As he went by Bill's desk, he dropped off the notes he'd been copying.

"Here's the basic spin I'm giving to the reporter."

Bill quickly looked it over. It was only a few paragraphs.

"Okay, if anyone asks, this is what we're going with. I wish this would have happened earlier. Those other guys are going to be pissed as hell that we didn't tell them too."

"I'm going to call them as soon as I talk to the WLS reporter. I'll tell them we were trying to keep this secret until we knew more about it, but WLS sent a film crew and I had no choice but to break it now. They'll be pissed, but they'll get over it. I doubt that they've filed their reports yet anyway."

"Hot springs in Northern Illinois. Do you think anyone will buy it?"

"It's as good as anything else I can think of. On such short notice, it's all we have. I see you've got the feed coming in from the lake. I'll get a digital copy of what WLS has already broadcast. We'll probably have to deal with the locals next. If anyone saw that news story, the whole town will be up in arms about the evacuation. They'll want to know why they weren't notified. If it isn't safe for the scientists, why aren't they being evacuated as well? There's going to be a lot of repercussions when this goes nationwide. I just hope we can figure out what's really happening and get this place back to normal before all hell breaks loose."

"I couldn't agree with you more. If you get time, stop back later this afternoon. We didn't get to complete our discussion on the HAARP connection. I wonder where we can get something to eat around here, now that the place is a ghost town!"

"That's what's the matter with me. I haven't eaten since last night. I'm starved. I won't be any longer than I have to be with that reporter. After I give the other guys a call, I'll find out where we can get some food. If you want to wait that long?"

"I only had two hours of sleep last night. Take care of business and I'll find out where Connie and Carol are," Bill said.

"Maybe we can all have a late lunch together. I'll call you just before I head back."

"I'll be waiting for your call."

As Tim left for Wilson Hall, Bill sat staring at the boiling and frothing lake. It reminded him of when Connie and he were washed ashore. Even more water was rushing up from underground then. It made a wave high enough that it carried their boat to shore like a surfboard.

This was similar, but not quite the same. There was smoke, or something that resembled it, coming off of the water in several places. It actually did look like it was boiling. What the hell is going on here? he thought to himself.

He clicked the "_" on the display to minimize it. The desktop reappeared. Next, he clicked on the icon to bring the beam tunnel display back up. He noticed that the sound was muted, so he clicked the "speaker" icon and the sound came on.

Depina was talking to Singleton. "I don't understand it. I was watching the picture when it just went blank. Neither camera is working. I'm showing power going to them, but no picture. I have audio, but I'm not hearing anything."

"Which cameras are you talking about?" Singleton asked.

"It's the two just beyond the soap suds."

"We're almost to the soap suds now. I don't see anything unusual, yet."

"Damn!" It was Depina again. "Now I've lost the next camera too. That's three cameras in a row that have lost their images."

"Is it possible that it's some kind of electrical problem? Maybe it was a surge, or something to do with the test that's running. I mean, we are at full power. I swear I can feel the pull of those magnets in my bones."

"It could be any of several things. It's just weird that it's happened to three cameras in a row. If I didn't know better, I'd say someone covered up the lenses."

"If they did, they turned the lights off too," Singleton said, sounding worried.

"We just passed the soap suds and the tunnel ahead is getting darker. I think the overhead light is out."

"That would explain why I'm not getting an image. If there's no light, there's no image. But who turned the lights out?"

"I didn't know there was a switch," Singleton said. Then, thinking to himself, Of course there's no switch. The lights are controlled in two ways. There's a switch by each elevator that controls additional lighting in the staging area, but each individual light doesn't have an on/off switch.

The entire lighting system is under computer control. The computer overrides all manual switches whenever the accelerator is in operation. Basically, the lights are almost always on. The only way to turn off just one is to manually remove it. Or break it.

Only Singleton and Hudson were in direct communications with Depina. As they neared the darkened section of the tunnel, Hudson told everyone to turn on their flashlights. He looked at Singleton for an indication of what to do next.

Singleton realized what he wanted, and spoke up. "Let's stop right here. I want to talk with our lookout before we go any farther. Listen, Depina, what about your ears?"

"My ears?"

"The microphones on the cameras. Have you picked up anything over the microphones?"

"No sir, I've got the volume turned to full but I'm not hearing a thing. Nothing but static anyway. Sounds like an electrical storm from miles away. It's just background noise being amplified by the electronics."

"Are you sure?"

"Yes sir. I get the same thing from every camera if I listen to it at full volume. No! Wait a second, I do hear something. It's coming from the microphone on the second camera. It sounds like—well, like someone is moaning. It's really low. I can just make it out. It sounds like something between a groan and a growl. Here, I'll patch it into your headset."

"I hear it. It's just barely above the noise level."

As they listened, it got louder. It was continuous. There was no break in the sound as you'd expect if it really was someone moaning. Then it got even louder. So loud that Depina barely got the volume turned down before it burst their eardrums. Singleton and Hudson tore the headsets from their ears. It was normally so quiet in the beam tunnel that the sound in the headsets was deafening.

The moaning sound reverberated throughout the beam tunnel. Everyone tensed up. Flashlights were replaced with automatic weapons. Handguns were drawn and ready to fire. Several in the group put their hands over their ears to shut out the sound. It was so loud that it was painful.

Bill had overheard the entire conversation and the moaning coming over his computer's speakers. He had his monitor displaying the image from the beam tunnel at full screen. His face was no more than a foot away from the monitor as he tried to make out something at the front of the image. It was too dark.

The men in the tunnel backed up a few steps. The moaning was so loud they couldn't tell if it was coming closer, or if it was stationary. Depina was no help, either. He was hearing the sound equally loud from all three camera microphones. He still had no image, other than the one near the soap suds, where the team was located. The men looked scared, and Singleton figured they were about to break and run. He knew he had to do something, fast.

He reached into his bag of tricks and withdrew a package of five light sticks. These were not your normal, run-of-the-mill light sticks. They were government issue, guaranteed to light up the world light sticks. The kind an outfit used when they wanted to blind an enemy that was overrunning them at night. He tore open the package, breaking the seal on the first one by bending and shaking it.

In less than a second, the chemicals started mixing, turning his hand into a glowing inferno of light without the presence of heat. He ran to the edge of the darkened tunnel and threw the light stick as hard and as far as he could. Then, he broke the second one, ran a little farther, and threw it too. It was so bright that his pupils closed to a pinpoint.

He could hardly see any more now than when he was in total darkness. He turned around, bounced off the side of the tunnel wall, and ran back to his men. They were yelling encouragement to him. His eyes hurt, he was following their voices more than anything else. They were watching him in amazement.

The tunnel ahead had gone from pitch black to flashbulb bright.

"Depina—what do you see now?" Singleton cried out.

"Still nothing, sir."

"How the hell can that be? I just lit that section up like an arc welder!"

"I don't see a thing. Everything is just like it was. Maybe someone did put something over the lenses."

"SHIT!" Singleton screamed. "We've got lights. We've got weapons. Let's go see what the hell's making all of this racket. Benson, Richardville, you've still got the lead. We're right behind you."

The light given off by the light sticks was at least ten times brighter than the lights overhead. Benson and Richardville picked up the shield, and the rest of the group fell in line behind them. Weapons drawn, their flashlights were now back in the holders they wore on their belts.

Singleton was third in line. "Talk to me, Depina. Do you hear anything?"

"Nothing but that incessant moaning."

"We'll be up to the first camera in another minute or two. I'll give it a once-over before we go on."

"Fine. If the video is working you should see a red LED glowing right next to the camera lens."

"There's more soap suds off to our right!" Singleton yelled to the men behind him.

All of a sudden, the groaning sound stopped. At almost the exact same time, the first light stick went out.

"What the—" Benson said.

They stopped, dead in their tracks. The other light stick was bright enough that they still had plenty of light to see by. Then, a few seconds later, it too went out.

"The government better get their money back," Singleton said. "Those sticks should have lasted at least 30 minutes each."

They were looking into darkness again, but only for a few seconds. The darkness flickered between dark and light as the overhead lights were trying to come back on.

The flickering got shorter until the lights came back on for good.

"Are you getting this Depina?" Singleton asked.

"Yes sir, I don't know why the moaning stopped, but I'm sure glad it did."

"Not the moaning, the lights. The lights are back on."

"I'm still in the dark, sir."

"Okay, we're going to continue into the tunnel."

They had only gone about ten yards when Singleton first noticed the camera. It looked like someone had poured a can of tar over it. Something thick and gooey was dripping off of the lens onto the floor below. It ran from the lens in a two-foot glob, looking for all the world like a frozen, black icicle. On the floor, the goo was so thick that it looked like a stalagmite. It was about six inches high at the center.

"I see why you're not getting any pictures. The camera lens is covered in black gunk."

"That may be why the sound is so low, too. Though, I didn't have any problem picking up that God-awful moaning."

"Sir?" It was Richardville. "Just ahead, about 10 o'clock. I believe I see something." It was hard to see at first because it was almost directly below the light in the ceiling. As his eyes adjusted, Singleton was able to make out a circular object, seemingly floating just behind the now depleted (so much for the guarantee) light stick. This thing was big and circular. Two, maybe three, men could easily step through it at the same time. It encompassed a large part of the tunnel. He was familiar with the reports of similar objects being seen during the last test, but none of them had been anywhere near this size.

"Don't, under any circumstances, touch the outer edge of this thing," Singleton warned his team. "Make sure you know where the edges are at all times."

As they approached, they realized that they could see inside of it. It was as if they were peering through a picture window. They could see what looked like sand, but it wasn't the color that it should have been. It had a bluish tint to it. Everything inside of the window had a bluish tint to it.

There were some plants growing in the sand, but they didn't recognize any of them. They resembled a cross between a cactus and a rose bush. Flowers and thorns covered the bulk of the plants. Both were much larger than anything they'd ever seen before. The flowers were about the size of a dinner plate, and the thorns were more like mini-spikes. The plants were probably twenty feet inside the window. Singleton guessed the tallest to be about fifteen feet in height, with a trunk more like that of a tree.

The strangest thing by far was the sand. It was being picked up and swirled, as if blown by an alien wind. It was actually more like dust than sand. Hell, it might have been snow. As it swirled, some of it floated out of the window and settled on the men.

They backed up in unison; this wasn't a window at all. As they got closer, they realized that it only resembled a window because a window was something they were all familiar with. Something they were used to seeing. This was a doorway, an opening into another world. Or another dimension. Whatever it was, it didn't belong here. The more they stared, the more they thought, we don't belong here either!

Singleton couldn't help but think how truly weird their situation was. Here they were, a group of men who would feel just as comfortable on the front lines in Iraq as they would sitting in their own living room—standing in a small tunnel just a few feet away from a plasma conduit, charged to over a trillion volts of energy, and staring into God knows what—surrounded by what appeared to be bubbles that could cut through the hardest substances known. What was this place? What were they doing here?

A tap on his shoulder brought him back to reality. Richardville was trying to get his attention. "Sir, there's something moving beneath the sand."

Singleton looked hard at where Richardville was pointing. Sure enough, it did look as though the sand was shifting. Looking around, he saw a pry bar leaning up against one of the magnets. It was about 30 inches long and probably weighed four or five pounds.

"Everyone stand back," he said. "I'm going to throw this through the opening and see what happens."

"Try and hit that lump under the sand," Richardville said, pointing to a place near one of the larger plants.

"Good idea. I think I can get it that far."

Singleton tossed it with an underhand motion. It spun wildly, end over end. His aim was off to the right by just a few feet, and the pry bar hit the plant about a foot above the base—pointed end first, piercing it like a spear.

"Damn!" Singleton said. "If I was trying to hit that thing, I'd have missed it by a mile."

They all stood there, waiting to see if anything would happen. It didn't take long. The lump under the sand began to move towards the plant. As it was only a few feet away, it took two, maybe three seconds to totally surround the plant. The plant began to vibrate—slowly at first, then more violently. The pry bar was buried deep in the plant, with no chance of shaking free. A few seconds later, the plant, along with the pry bar, disappeared beneath the ground. It looked like one of those cartoons where a gopher yanks a shrub underground. It was almost comical.

As they watched, the sand seemed to roll, and what looked like bubbles began to appear at the surface. Each one threw a small amount of sand into the air as it burst. It was like watching large air bubbles breaking the surface of a calm lake.

Suddenly, there was a roar from under the sand that made the alien desert tremble. Sand rose off its surface like mist on a pond.

The plant shot up and out of the ground, rising about thirty feet. Trailing it was a large amount of fine blue sand that gave the impression of an exhaust plume streaming behind the engine of a rocket.

No one was really sure about what happened next; it happened so quickly. Suffice it to say, they all ran as fast as they could back towards the elevator. No one was thinking about the danger of running into any floating soap suds.

They didn't even try to follow in each other's footsteps. They ran, not stopping until they reached the elevators. There they stood—listing—not moving until they were fully convinced that they were not being followed.

What had happened? The consensus was that something had either thrown or shot the pry bar back through the portal, barely missing the top of their heads. They agreed that it had come from the same region where it disappeared. It was little more than a blur as it whizzed by.

It hit the side of the tunnel with such force that it knocked a chunk the size of a brick out of the reinforced concrete. The pry bar continued on its journey, finally coming to a stop about twenty yards from where it first made contact with the wall. The one-inch thick bar was bent near the center at a 30-degree angle. Singleton reached down and grabbed it as they ran by.

Depina soon had them on the cameras that were still working. He had heard the roar but didn't have any idea what had made it. He verified that they were not being followed, at least not by anything that the still-working cameras could detect.

But only a few seconds after he'd just told them the tunnel was clear, he came back online, his voice shaky and somewhat distorted. "Sir, I've just lost another camera. It's the one coming back toward the elevator. I can hear noises. I think you'd better get out of the tunnel, immediately."

Chapter Twenty-Five

As events unfolded at Fermilab, emergency measures already in place were put into action. DARPA activated a full-scale evacuation plan for the entire town of Batavia, along with everyone living within a five-mile radius. Batavia's population had grown to about 27,000, and with the surrounding area, at least 30,000 people were to be moved out.

Airspace was also being tightly controlled, though not as effectively as authorities would have liked. Fermilab was simply too close to Chicago to keep everyone away. The major airlines were notified, and commercial air traffic was rerouted around the quarantined airspace. But in such a congested region, it was nearly impossible to control the hundreds of small business and private aircraft. Drones and news choppers were a constant threat, and the FAA was scrambling to keep the skies clear.

Highways leading into Batavia were cordoned off and opened only to official vehicles, while the lanes leading away from the city remained open. By the end of the day, the town would be locked up tight. The National Guard set up roadblocks on seldom-traveled dirt and gravel roads, usually used only by farm vehicles. State and city police were on hand as well, but it was clear the main thrust of the operation was under Federal control.

Bill had no idea all of this was taking place. He hadn't talked to Tim in over an hour, but even Tim didn't realize the seriousness of the quarantine. The government was taking no chances that whatever they were dealing with could spread beyond the Fermilab complex. This was, after all, a matter of national security. This wasn't a terrorist threat—it was contact with an alien entity. The orders to cordon off the area had come directly from the White House. There was little doubt that what they were dealing with was of alien origin. This was the long-awaited first contact. So far, it had not proved to be a friendly one. Things would only get worse.

As Bill sat there, glued to his monitor, his cell phone rang. It was Connie.

"Bill, I'm sorry to bother you when I'm sure you're busy, but I don't know what we're supposed to be doing. Carol and I have been sitting in an office for almost four hours now. Every time we ask someone what's going on, they just say to wait here and someone will get back to us. We're starting to get hungry, and we're tired of sitting in these office chairs. Is there anything you can do?"

"I don't know. You wouldn't believe what's been happening. Where are you, anyway?"

"We're in an office on Level 1. I think there was a number on the door. Carol, would you get it for me, please?"

Carol turned the door handle only to find it locked.

"I can't believe it. We've been locked in!"

"I'm sure it's for your own safety. There are some very strange things happening around here. I'll get someone to bring you something to drink and some sandwiches. I'll also see if I can't get you moved to more comfortable quarters."

"I may as well make some phone calls while I'm here, and see if anyone has had any luck identifying our fish."

"Sorry, but the phone system is closed to all outside calls."

"You're kidding. What's going on around here?"

"I can't tell you over the phone, especially my cell phone. I think I'm one of the few who even has a cell phone, and that may be by mistake. I know they took everyone else's. I'll explain everything when I see you— which may be a while from the looks of things. I'll try and get you brought up to the main level. I don't even know where I'm staying yet. I've been in my office since before daybreak."

"Just don't forget us. We're hungry, tired, and starting to get a little worried. Scared, even."

"You'll be alright. There's plenty of security here. That's about all that is here—security, a few scientists, and some media people. I'll get back to you within the hour to make sure you've gotten something to eat. Just hang in there. That's all I'm doing right now, too. Hanging in."

"Thanks, Bill. It looks like our weekend plans are off. I feel like a caged animal. I can't remember ever being under lock and key before. Just don't forget us. I'll talk to you later. Goodbye."

"If nobody has shown up in an hour, call me back. I'll do all I can to get you up here on the main floor. Take care, and tell Carol to hang in there too. Goodbye."

Bill hated the fact that he'd totally forgotten about Connie and Carol. So much had been happening, though, that it wasn't surprising. He didn't know what he could do about their situation, but he'd try.

About fifteen minutes passed. Tim poked his head in the door. "Have you got a few minutes?" he asked.

"Time is the one thing I do have. You'd think that the director of this place would be busy as hell. Not so. Come on in."

Tim had just been brought up to speed on all that was happening outside. He was going to give a nationwide, live interview for the six o'clock news later in the day. They were still using the "hot springs" spin, but that might have to be changed before he went national.

Bill brought Tim up to date on the events happening in the beam tunnel, and Tim relayed what was going on outside. This was turning into something for the history books. Once the news broke that contact had been made with an alien presence, all hell would break loose. The government was trying to keep that bottled up for as long as they could. From the looks of things, it wasn't going to be much longer.

Bill told Tim about Connie and Carol's plight. He couldn't leave his office, but he figured Tim had gathered enough contacts that he should be able to get them the help they needed.

Tim had plenty to do, but he also wanted the girls to be safe and close by. He left in a rush, making them his next agenda. It was a good thing that Bill didn't go because as soon as Tim closed the door, his desk phone rang. It was Meyer.

"Bill, have you looked at the data coming from the detector lately?"

Bill had been too intrigued watching the drama unfolding in the beam tunnel to have kept up with the numbers being generated by the detector.

"No, I've been too busy with other things."

"The scientists at DARPA have been monitoring it closely. They say something remarkable is happening—something to do with the amount and type of particle collisions. I'd like you to check it out and let me know if you have any ideas as to what's going on."

"I have several instruments that are not connected to the DARPA facility. I'll gather a summary of their readings and send them along to your guys. Say, I need a favor."

"Sure, if I can help."

"There are two colleagues that have been locked up since this morning, and I'd like to have them moved up here, next to my quarters."

"Connie and Caroline?"

243

Bill was surprised—but didn't let it show. "Yes, how'd you know?"

"Just call it a lucky guess. I'm sure I can arrange that. Consider it done. Oh, and Bill—I know you are probably feeling like a cog on a wheel, but believe me, you are not going to be left out of the loop. It's just that we haven't needed your expertise until now. When we need it—you'll know."

"Thanks, I needed to hear that. I'll get right on that data from the detector. Goodbye."

"Goodbye."

He wouldn't have to worry about how Tim was getting along now. He'd taken care of the girls' problems. Now, he was ready to get back to doing the work he was familiar with. After all, he was a scientist, not a paranormal detective.

Looking at the numbers on a printout, he could see why the scientists at DARPA were puzzled. Most of the tracks under study were common to anyone who was accustomed to reading the footprints of particle collisions, but some of these tracks just didn't look right. They were seeing more collisions than the models had predicted.

Somehow, something seemed to have strengthened the mass of particles being fired around the ring. The density of the beam had been greatly enhanced. With what, he hadn't a clue. For some reason, "dark matter" popped into his head. Dark matter is the as-yet-unproven matter that supposedly accounts for 75% of the missing mass in the universe. He thought it would be best not to add his suspicions in his report to DARPA. He'd let them bring it up if they wanted.

As he gathered data for his report, he happened to notice what appeared to be a live transmission from DARPA's headquarters on one of the nearby monitors. This surprised him because he didn't realize that this was even possible. Why would they have a feed into the control room, but not into his office?

The discussion taking place was between one of DARPA's scientists and Reverend Tower, a minister of some renown. Apparently, DARPA had decided to take a few outside individuals into their confidence and get their views on what was happening. He decided to sit down and watch a little of the transmission.

"My God! You're telling me you think this is an alien contact?" the minister asked.

"Nobody knows for sure, but that's the general consensus. You've seen pictures of the 'portals,' as we are currently calling them. I can't imagine anywhere on this planet that these things might be coming from. The Secretary asked that we bring in several religious scholars and garner their opinions. Maybe one of you will be able to help in explaining what they are."

"What we're looking for is information. Is there anything you can think of, something you might have read, something that seemed impossible, or unbelievable, that might give us a hint as to what's happening here?"

Reverend Tower's background was of the Judeo-Christian faith. He was chosen because of his extensive knowledge of ancient biblical documents. He was also one of the first scholars called upon to help with the deciphering of the famous "Dead Sea Scrolls." The two men came from entirely different backgrounds, each a little cautious as to where their conversation might lead, but both realizing the importance of this meeting.

"I'm afraid I'm not as much of a believer in other dimensions as you are, Dr. Walter. In my faith, there are only three planes of existence—the Earth, which we know to exist, Heaven, and Hell. The last two fall under the realm of religion. Of course, I realize that there are many places in the universe that were never mentioned in the Bible."

"How do you scientists put it—something about there being more stars in the heavens than there are grains of sand on the earth? I too have seen the wonders photographed by the Hubble telescope, and have often wondered what these distant worlds must be like, and if there are other planets such as our own. When God created the universe, did He also create other worlds filled with people like us, or were all those wonders created just for His own personal glory?"

The two men said nothing for a time, each lost in their own thoughts. What was happening at Fermilab was something that neither of them could explain. It was Dr. Walter that broke the silence.

"I don't denounce the existence of God."

That took Reverend Tower entirely by surprise.

"I know that many scientists are deeply religious men, but I was told that you were not listed among them. Have the events happening here somehow changed your way of thinking?"

"No, Reverend. My God and your God may well be one and the same, but I think of him in a different manner. You see, I've read the Bible too. You wouldn't think that someone with my reputation would believe in the Bible as fact, and to be truthful, some of it, I find almost ridiculous. I'm not going for the tale about Jonah and the Whale, for instance. There are many other wonderful stories that I consider to be just that—stories."

"Many of my beliefs are contradictory to biblical teachings. I believe in the theory of the 'Big Bang.' I think the universe formed from a singularity. I don't think God created it, as it says in the Bible, in seven days. I believe that someday, scientists actually will discover how the universe came to be. Theories such as Strings, or the enhanced version, Super Strings, or an offshoot called M-Theory, are getting close to the answers right now. These theories take into account other dimensions. I have a feeling that what's happening right now may be a merging between these other dimensions and our own."

"Still, I can see the possibility of a God creating or causing these events to take place. And while I don't accept most of the biblical stories as fact, I do believe that Jesus Christ was a God, or the Son of God, as Christianity would have it. I also believe that the miracles Christ was said to have performed really happened, probably just as they were written. Yet, it wasn't magic, or even technology that allowed him to perform those miracles. I think that Christ came from the stars. An entity that was part of a race that has evolved for millions, maybe billions of years. God is as good a name as any to give such a being."

"I'm at a loss for words, Doctor. How can you say that you are a believer, and also be an agnostic? That doesn't make any sense."

"I guess it's the definition of the term 'God' that makes the difference. My 'God' and your 'God' may not be all that different. It's the way we relate to him that makes the difference. That's true among other religions as well. That's why there are so many different denominations of Christianity. You all read from the same text, but interpret the meanings so differently that many of you won't even talk to one another. Why is that? No, don't answer yet. I'm not a biblical scholar, but I do know a few things about the Bible. I used to hear the saying, 'Not one word of this testament shall be changed' or something to that effect. Then I find that the Bible has been changed dozens of times over thousands of years. Mostly to appease whichever Pope, or King, happened to be in power at the time."

"The last and most popular change occurred during the reign of King James, in 1611. That's why our present version is known as the 'King James Version.' Or should I say, 'one' of the present versions. There seems to be several varieties around, depending on what flavor of faith you happen to be akin to. Catholic, Baptist, Protestant, Lutheran, etc. Even these main line religions have their offshoots."

"What about the dozens of other religions around the world? Buddhist, Hindu, Mohammad, Islam, Confucius, Mormon—each with their own sub-denominations. Plus all the loony cults whose followers are forever committing suicide. I believe in the existence of God, of a greater power... I just don't believe in organized religion."

"Some things don't have easy answers, Doctor. I can only tell you what I've learned from my own experiences, my own values and beliefs. If you are so skeptical of organized religion, how can you say you believe in God?"

"Because my God, or Gods, have to exist. Evolution will produce Gods. Think of the miracles that were accomplished in the Bible. In fact, what does the word miracle really mean? A miracle is just something that happens that we can't explain—yet."

"When Cortez invaded South America, the Aztecs thought he was a God. They had an ancient belief that foretold of a white-skinned man who would come and be their leader. They called him Quetzalcoatl."

"He had a beard; they had never seen such a thing before. He also had firearms. To these natives, a weapon such as a gun was a terribly frightening thing. They were scared to death of it, and rightly so. Cortez and his soldiers were able to kill at a great distance. Of course, it was their diseases, smallpox mainly, that eventually all but wiped out the native population."

"The truth of the matter is—these invaders from across the sea had an advanced technology. Even today, when we encounter primitive peoples such as in the rain forests of South America, they look upon us as Gods. Any sufficiently advanced civilization will be looked upon as Godlike by those on a lower technological ladder. Those performing impossible feats of 'magic' will be called a God by people incapable of understanding how these feats were accomplished."

"I believe in God, because I've come to realize that we, Mankind, will eventually evolve to a point where we will be able to perform all of the miracles in the Bible through our technology. We are seeing this happen, even now. We've made tremendous advances in medicines allowing the average lifespan to double in the last century. Science is moving forward at an exponential rate. We are not just doubling our knowledge; we are tripling and quadrupling it at a staggering pace. When computers become truly conscious, and capable of doing their own thinking, we'll see thousand-fold increases in the advancement of knowledge every few hours. Someday, we'll probably merge with our machines. That is, unless our machines don't want to merge with us."

"Think of how far we've come in the last century. We can't even begin to imagine what will happen in the next. What about the next thousand years? The universe is somewhere between 13 and 14 billion years old. A million years is not even a blink of an eye when you think of it in these time scales. Where, along the evolutionary ladder, are those beings that had a ten billion year head start on us? Where have they gone? Are they Gods?"

"Every one of us is composed of 'Star Stuff.' All the heavy elements in the universe came from the cores of exploding stars. Stars that died billions of years before our sun condensed out of the cosmic gas that formed it. You said you've seen the pictures returned by the Hubble. Scientists understated when they said there are more stars in the sky than there are grains of sand on the earth. The truth is, the universe is composed of more stars than we ever imagined. More than we can ever hope to comprehend."

"It appears that planets are quite common, too. If that were not enough, new theories are being proposed that suggest this may not be the only universe. There may be as many universes as there are stars. Parallel universes, multi-dimensions, space and time warps—concepts that once existed only in the minds of science fiction writers may no longer belong in the realm of fantasy."

"Respected theoretical physicists such as Michio Kaku are proposing that our present universe may have come about because of a collapse in a universe that consisted of either eleven or twenty-six dimensions. It's the theory of supersymmetry, the theory of Strings. It's the first theory that allows all of the nuclear forces and Einstein's theories involving relativity to fit together. For the first time, a theory of 'everything' is being constructed. If it turns out to be correct, our universe is just like a bubble in a bubble bath. We have neighbors everywhere."

"Reverend, I believe that Gods must exist. Gods who have the power to cause all we see around us to have been created. What I can't bring myself to believe is that these Gods, or this God of your Bible, would be so selfish, so conceited, as to have us bow down to him on every occasion, and to punish us with everlasting torment if we don't. How could anyone of such a superior intellect treat those he is supposed to love in this manner?

Throughout history, there have been those who have demanded such obedience. Kings, conquerors, dictators— we call them tyrants! Many have ruled in such a manner, and all were hated by those they ruled over. Or should we consider ourselves so much lower than God, that we are but mere cattle, to be led whichever way our Master wishes us to go?"

"So many things in your Bible make no sense at all. The Creationists tell me that the earth is only six thousand years old. Then where were the dinosaurs during that time? Why have we found the bones of earlier species of man? Neanderthals, Peking Man, Java Man, and Australopithecus? Their bones are similar, yet obviously different from our own. Many of these later bones came from the same sediments as modern Homo Sapiens, a clear indication that they once walked the earth together. Earlier species of man, Hominids, died off. Or were eradicated by the wiser Homo Sapiens we were becoming."

"Creationists talk of a flood that covered the world, but when Noah finally landed on solid ground, he discovered other people. Where did they come from, and how did they survive a watery grave?"

"What about the ice cores? They clearly show layers of snow that have fallen for hundreds of thousands of years. Or the decay of radioactive elements used in dating rock samples, from both the earth and moon? All of these point to an earth that is billions of years old. Six thousand years is ludicrous. It's claims such as these that cause people to doubt the important issues."

"Well, I for one, don't believe in the six days of creation and the six-thousand-year-old Earth, but I do think that God created the universe and all the things in it—including us. He did it in his own good time. Maybe time in Heaven is not measured as it is on Earth. God knows no age. Time for him doesn't exist. We measure time because we are finite. We live our lives based on a beginning and an end. God knows no beginning or end. Time is not relevant to him. Six days, or six billion years, is of no consequence."

"I believe the six days of Genesis were given to mankind as something he could understand. It's taken us thousands of years to acquire the knowledge we have, and we are only now beginning to understand how the universe is structured. We are like babies in God's eyes, just beginning to explore the universe around us. We are discovering that the universe holds more secrets than we can ever begin to appreciate. So yes, I respect the wonders that science has explained, but I still see the hand of God in them. I think these portals are just another fabric in the cloth that God has woven. Not all of God's creations were intended for the well-being of mankind. This may be one of those whose purpose is to cause us harm."

'There are more things in Heaven and Earth, Horatio, than are dreamt of in your philosophy.'

"Shakespeare wrote that line hundreds of years ago, but it's as true today as it was then. Maybe even more so. There have been more scientific discoveries made in the last 50 years than in all previous years combined. Man is accumulating knowledge at an astounding pace. Yet, we find we've only scratched the surface of understanding. Every question we answer raises a hundred new questions. There is but one true answer, and it will be found in religion, not science. Science has made our lives easier. It has allowed us to live longer, and to enjoy those extra years of life. But it will never give us the answer to 'why' we are here, or 'who' we are. Only God can answer those questions."

"I don't know where the portals come from, or why they are here. I've never read anything that might explain them in any manuscript, ancient or modern. I don't know how to destroy them, or even if we should. I do know that as much as man strives for answers, he'll never find them without first finding God."

"As it says in 1st Corinthians 1:19, 'For it is written. I will destroy the wisdom of the wise, and will bring to nothing the understanding of the prudent.' So much for man's knowledge in the eyes of God."

Bill was mesmerized by the conversation he was listening to. He knew he felt much the same as the scientist, but as he listened to the reverend speak, he also realized what a profound influence his Christian upbringing had on his life. He may be a scientist by choice, but he was still a believer in his heart. If he were pressed, he wasn't sure who he'd side with in such a discussion.

His concentration was broken by the sounds of voices. It was Connie and Carol. He gathered his printouts and picked up a portable USB drive that contained the same information, only in a digital format that could be encrypted and transmitted to DARPA over the Internet.

"Ladies!" he called out, startling the women who hadn't seen him from their perspective.

"You scared the bejeezus out of me. I was expecting to find you in your office. Thank you for getting us out of that one-room prison," Connie said.

"I'm sorry. I heard you talking and thought you'd seen me. Have they told you where you'll be staying?"

"No, they just said to find you and you'd take care of everything."

"I don't even know where I'm staying," Bill said.

"That's just great. We still haven't had anything to eat, but that took second preference to getting out of that place."

"My office is right around the corner. Let's go in and see if we can figure out where you're going to stay. I'll see if I can get some sandwiches. Did you happen to see Tim? He was trying to rescue you too."

Carol entered the conversation. "No, we haven't seen much of anyone since we were locked in that room early this morning."

"He'll be back shortly. There's a lot of pressure on him right now. He's handling all of the media and press assignments, and you can imagine what that must be like."

Bill thought for a moment, then said, "There's a small rec-room down the hall on the right. No food, but there are a couple of vending machines with coffee and soda. I think there are two stationary bikes and several stair steppers in there too. It doesn't get much use. There are showers and bathrooms there as well. That's the only room I know of that has a shower. I don't know what they were thinking, locking us out of our quarters and expecting us to live in offices. What do they expect us to sleep on?"

The door opened and Tim walked in. His eyes widened as he saw the two women.

"No wonder I couldn't find you. You're here."

"Your powers of observation are amazing," Carol said.

"So, how'd you get here, and where are you staying?"

"Bill pulled some strings. We don't have any idea where we're staying, though."

"Bill," Carol said. "Is someone doing laundry back here?" She was looking in the doorway of the back office.

"No, we haven't gotten to that point yet," Bill halfheartedly laughed. "Why?"

"Well, it looks like soap suds are all over the floor. I thought your washer might have overflowed."

Bill and Tim's faces turned ashen white as they looked at one another. They ran to the back office where Carol was looking, confused.

There, covering most of the back wall, was a layer of the so-called soap suds. They were moving too—inching their way forward toward the door. As they watched, they could see that they were oozing out between the filing cabinets.

"When did this happen?" Tim asked in a voice that only Bill could hear.

"It wasn't like this an hour ago. Let's check the other offices and the route to the outside. We don't want to get trapped in here."

"We need to tell the girls what's happening. They need to know what this stuff is, and not to get near it," Tim said.

"Why don't you fill them in while I make a quick check outside? I'll make sure that the exits are clear. I'll be back in a few minutes. Then we can figure out what to do, and where to go."

"That sounds good to me. Hurry back. I don't like this at all."

Bill turned and started for the outer office door. As he passed Connie he practically whispered, "Tim will fill you in. I'll be right back. Don't go near that back office." He continued on, not waiting for an answer. Connie knew that something was seriously wrong. It scared her when Bill left in such a hurry. She figured that these soap suds were at the heart of it.

Chapter Twenty-Six

Bill returned after fifteen minutes of searching the adjacent offices, not seeing any sign of more of the strange, creeping "soap suds." It was odd that they'd only appeared in his office, but so far, that seemed to be the case. Stranger still, he hadn't seen anyone else during his search. Just a few hours earlier, the place had been buzzing with military personnel, scientists, and techs.

He wasn't sure where they should go, but it was clear they needed to leave the control room soon. Still, he felt he should probably stay—at least as long as the PIP-II accelerator was still running. The others could find a safe place, and he could join them later. For now, he needed to survey the rest of the control room and make sure the soap suds hadn't invaded it as well. As far as he could tell, they were only in his back office.

First, he needed to get hold of Singleton and let him know their situation. Of course, Singleton was up to his neck in his own problems.

The lake had undergone another transformation. It had turned a lurid lime green and was still bubbling like a witch's cauldron. At times, things could be seen swimming in it, causing wakes several inches high. Whatever was making these wakes had to be as large as seals—maybe even larger. They were fast, streaking through the thickening water as if in search of prey. The surface of the lake was dissected by them.

Three portals had formed on the north side of the lake, hanging in the air about thirty feet above the water, forty to fifty feet apart. Occasionally, one would dump what looked like green syrup into the water, which would boil as it touched the surface. There might have been more portals under the water.

The smell coming from the lake was sickeningly sweet, almost overwhelming. Maybe that was why insects were beginning to arrive in great numbers. The scent carried for miles. Bees especially were attracted, and huge flocks of birds were starting to arrive as well—perhaps drawn by the insects, perhaps by something else. Whatever the reason, they were arriving by the hundreds.

The strangest thing happened when birds landed on the water. Normally, birds might land at the water's edge and splash around, but rarely would they venture into deep water. Now, crows, sparrows, robins, doves, starlings—even a few hummingbirds—were seen sitting far from shore.

They didn't crash into the water. They landed softly, as if on a branch, barely making a ripple. Then, after a few seconds, they simply sank—even the ducks. Several Canadian Geese were seen to land, swim for a few seconds, and then sink, as if someone had pulled the drain plug in a boat. Their heads were the last to go, still in the same position as when they were swimming. It was eerie. No fight, no fright. Everything that touched the water just sank, as if it was the natural thing to do.

Except—sometimes—when one of the larger birds touched down, a wake would be seen heading directly for it. These birds didn't sink slowly. They were dragged under. In the blink of an eye, they were gone.

There were other anomalies, too. For a while, there had been a vortex near the overflow, as if a hole had opened in the lake's bottom, sucking everything into it. Any debris floating on the surface disappeared down the vortex.

In another part of the lake, the top arch of a portal could be seen rising about twenty feet above the water, the lower half submerged. It was in the deeper water, about a hundred yards from shore. From the looks of the current flowing out of it, any water being lost to the whirlpool was being replaced by this portal. The water level in the lake ebbed and flowed. At any one time, it was hard to tell which side was winning. It just depended on the time of day you checked it.

Every once in a while, a wake would emerge from this portal. Sometimes large, sometimes small, but always moving quickly—like a torpedo in an old war movie. Sometimes, several wakes would move off in all directions, but they all seemed to originate from this portal. It was as if they were searching for something—birds, maybe?

Then Bill had an idea. Maybe that hole in the bottom of the lake that he and Connie had discovered wasn't a hole at all. Maybe it was a portal lying horizontal on the lake's bottom, and they had dropped their sounding device through it—into an alien ocean. No wonder they never found the bottom. There wasn't any.

No one ventured onto the water. There were several boats tied to the shoreline, but no one seemed interested in investigating. Who could blame them?

The rest of the complex was changing as well. The grounds that had been covered with trees and thick prairie grass were almost unrecognizable. By mid-morning, the trees looked as if they were dying, their limbs drooping. Leaves started falling, soon covering the ground. Not like in autumn, though. In autumn, the leaves would first turn warm brown, then splashes of red, yellow, and orange. These leaves were still green, full of chlorophyll. They didn't look dead—they looked dried up. Later in the day, they fell with greater ferocity, raining down and covering the ground like a living green carpet.

Strangely, the pines weren't affected at all. There were dozens of pine trees on the complex, and they seemed as healthy as ever. Soon, they would stand out against the backdrop of bare, leafless limbs.

The prairie grasses didn't seem to be bothered either, though being so low to the ground, it was hard to tell if they were experiencing any problems. They grew thick on the protected grounds, their only enemy the buffalo that continually kept them in check.

The buffalo—where were the buffalo? It's hard to hide forty-three full-grown buffalo and three calves. They were nowhere to be seen. Upon further inspection, it was found that a fence had been knocked down on the east side of the complex and the entire herd had broken free. This had never happened before. Something must have spooked them during the night, causing them to flee. These were huge animals. Tearing down a wooden fence didn't pose much of a problem, but not a single buffalo had ever gone missing before.

The truly amazing part of all this is that no one heard them leave. Yet the place was crawling with military personnel, supposedly guarding the complex. If they hadn't noticed a herd of buffalo tearing down a fence, what the hell else had they missed?

Bill's desk phone rang. It was Singleton.

"Bill, I want you to gather together everyone that's still in the control room. I'm going to send one of my people to lead you out of the building."

"I've been trying to reach you. There are soap suds in my back office."

"I'll have you out of there soon. Are you near your computer?"

"Yes, I'm standing right beside it."

"I want you to log onto the HAARP cam and see if there are any new updates. I have a feeling that our problems, and theirs, are one and the same."

"Just a second. I'll bring it up. There's no one in the hallway. Where is everyone?"

"All of the guards were called in to help lead the few remaining civilians out of the complex. The control room was the last place we planned to evacuate. Make sure everyone's with you so we can get you out at a minute's notice. How about that image at HAARP?"

Bill wasn't thrilled about being the last to leave, especially since Connie and Carol were still here.

"Connie, Carol, and Tim are here with me. I think Depina may still be manning the cameras, but I'll have to check on that. I want to be sure they all get out of here. I can stay if you need me to."

"Are you sure that all of the guards are gone? I was thinking that we left one sentry guarding each elevator," Bill asked.

"I didn't see anyone, though there could be a guard on a lower level. There's no one on this floor, though."

"Don't go any lower than the first floor in the elevator. Especially don't go anywhere near the beam tunnel. Something's down there, and it's not friendly. Just remain in your office until I can get someone to help you. You don't want to be walking the corridors unarmed at this point."

"Alright, we'll sit tight until we hear from you. If the soap suds spread into this office, we'll have to leave. Hold on, the HAARP website is coming up. A new image has been uploaded. I'm unscrambling it now."

The others gathered around the monitor. Tim knew about the hidden messages, but the women had no idea what was going on. Two images appeared on the monitor. One was a picture of the antenna array. The second was a clone of the first, except this one had writing in the center of the image.

ALL HELL HAS BROKEN OUT. THE THREE BLIPS HAVE MERGED INTO ONE. HALF OF THE STAFF HAS DISAPPEARED. EVERYONE IS AFRAID. THE ANTENNAS ARE STILL TRANSMITTING. SEVERAL PEOPLE ARE DEAD OR MISSING. WE NEED HELP!

Bill thought to himself, *we need help too*.

"Bill." Singleton's voice cracked a little as he spoke. "There are things happening at HAARP that you need to know about. Fermilab and HAARP are tied together in more ways than you realize. DARPA has a huge investment in the technologies being developed at both complexes, and they'll stop at nothing to make sure that these technologies are not jeopardized. What we've encountered is totally alien. I'm relying on your help, and Tim's, in dealing with it."

Bill wasn't exactly sure what Singleton was talking about, but he had a pretty good idea. He'd read about the controversies surrounding the HAARP project. He knew that Tesla's ideas and patents were being developed there.

He was sure that PIP-II had been drawing power from HAARP when it was off the electrical grid.

Now he wondered how many of the other claims—mind control, weather control, the ability to cause earthquakes, the ability to make people sick with radio waves—how many of these projects were under development at HAARP, too? How many of them were already being implemented?

"I'll do what I can. Right now, I'm worried about the safety of the people with me. Is there anything else I need to know concerning our present plight?" Bill asked.

"Just gather everyone together. Most people have already been evacuated. If you have to leave, be sure to let me know when and where you're going. I'm below you in one of the science labs. D-33, I think. We've made some startling discoveries. I'll fill you in when I can. There are seven of us here, but I can't spare anyone right now. Give me 90 minutes or so."

"OK, I'll call you if we decide to leave. I don't know where we'd go, though. Goodbye."

Bill turned and walked to the back office. The soap suds were still bubbling around the filing cabinets, but they hadn't advanced any farther as far as he could tell.

Tim was filling Connie and Carol in on how the message was hidden in the webcam image when the office door opened.

"Hello. Can I join the party?" It was Depina. "I just looked down on the floor of the detector, and the place is deserted. The test is still ongoing, isn't it? The guards—they're all gone. Where is everyone?"

Bill was glad to see Depina. Not knowing what they were up against, he figured the more people in their group, the better their chances of getting out of this unscathed.

For the next hour, they exchanged information. Bill had seen some of what had happened in the beam tunnel and had a good idea of how dangerous the soap suds could be. Depina was able to fill him in on the things he'd missed, but he knew practically nothing about what was going on outside.

Bill didn't know a hell of a lot either, but he told him what he knew. One thing they both agreed on—they wanted out of there, and as quickly as possible.

The day was growing short. Bill estimated that there might be about three hours left before sunset. He wasn't sure if that was a good or a bad thing. Hidden in the darkness, it would be harder for someone—or something—to find them. But that worked two ways. It would also be harder for them to spot something hiding. The grounds offered a lot of nooks and crannies to hide behind. Those unique sculptures took on menacing shapes at night. He was hoping someone would get here before it got dark and lead them out. He had his doubts, though, that this would happen. That 90 minutes Singleton mentioned may as well have been 90 hours.

There wasn't much they could do but wait, so they decided to turn on the television and see if Fermilab was still in the news. The meeting this morning should have put an end to any additional news coverage. Bill turned to channel nine, WLS. Even though this was an all-news channel, he didn't really expect to see anything. What a surprise to see, "Special Report – The Crisis At Fermilab," flash across the screen along with live shots of the complex.

Several portals could clearly be seen hanging in the air above the lake. The lime green color looked even weirder on television. A reporter in the background alluded to the possibility of an alien presence, and how the military had cordoned off a five-mile area around the town of Batavia. Sure enough, military vehicles were seen blocking every entrance to the town. The overhead shot made it look like the place was under siege.

Bill switched over to CNN, and again, there they were. Apparently, the story had broken several hours ago when the portals were seen and photographed by a small aircraft. The pictures were leaked, or sold, to the news media. So much for Tim's meeting this morning.

"We've been talking to the wrong people. All we needed to do was turn on the TV," Tim said.

"I doubt that the media has many answers, but they do have a great view of the action. I wonder how many choppers are up there? I'll bet it's a zoo outside. Every news agency in the world will be covering this story. Aliens—terrorists—portals to other worlds—it's the story of the century."

Bill was at the computer now, punching up a direct video feed being transmitted 'live' from the lake.

"I'm sure they'll all want the story, but I'll bet the government has this place locked down tight. I'd be amazed if there's more than one news chopper in the air. They'll have to let at least one in because the public will demand it. But they won't open the airspace any more than they have to. All of the media will have to share the same video feed. Did you notice that the video was the same on both channels? I'll bet if you go to the other networks, you'll find the same feed there too. I'd also bet that the military is piloting that helicopter, and that the feeds are being heavily censored before they're released to the public. Live isn't always as 'live' as it looks. They don't seem to be blocking out much, though," Tim said.

It was Connie who spoke next. "That's what scares me."

"What do you mean?" Bill asked.

"If they are allowing this much to be shown—then what are they not showing?"

They looked at each other for a few seconds. You could feel the tension in the room, as they thought about what Connie had just said. Then they remembered Singleton's words—*There's something in the beam tunnel, and it's not friendly.*

Depina had told them about the sounds. They had scared the hell out of him just hearing them over the speakers. And of how the crowbar had been bent, and thrown so hard that it knocked a chunk of concrete from the tunnel's wall. Of the way the men had run from the portal like little children. Grown men—armed men—men who were used to war and fighting. They were scared. Not so much of something they'd seen, but of what they hadn't seen. Or what they might see.

Bill broke the silence.

"I don't think there's anything more we can do here. I mean—this test is a farce. There's no one left to monitor the equipment. It's still running. I couldn't shut it off if I wanted to. I'm not sure it even will shut off. DARPA is controlling it, anyway. There's just the five of us as far as I can see."

"Call Singleton and tell him we want out of here. There's no reason for us to stay any longer," Tim said.

"OK. I think you're right. I'll stay if he wants, but you four need to get to somewhere safe. I don't know why I should stay here either, though. About all I can do is check for more messages from HAARP, and I can do that from any computer."

Bill dialed Singleton's cell phone. It rang—but after the fifth ring, the voicemail picked up.

"You've reached Don Singleton. I'm sorry, but I'm unable to answer the phone right now. If you'd like to leave a message, please wait until after the beep and then speak slowly. If you'd like to leave a callback number, press the pound sign."

So much for that. Bill didn't want to leave a message, at least not the kind of message that Singleton would want to hear. The situation was too urgent, too complex to be condensed into a voicemail. He needed to speak with Singleton directly, to convey the gravity of their predicament and the pressing need for immediate action.

Chapter Twenty-Seven

"How hard can it be?" Tim asked. "We go down the hall, get on the elevator, take it to the main floor, find the entrance, and haul ass. If we're lucky, we might run across a guard or two along the way."

"That sounds easy enough—but what do we do once we're outside? It's almost two miles to the front gate. Who knows what we'll run into along the way? It'll be dark in about two hours. We should easily reach the front gate before then, if we don't have any trouble. If we do, we'd be stuck out in the open, in the dark, with no way to defend ourselves," Bill said.

"It's either that, or we stay here and hope someone comes to get us," Tim replied. "I don't think I'd care to be outside in the dark. This place is spooky enough in the daytime; I can't imagine being here at night."

"What if the lights in here were to go out?" Carol interjected.

"I'd be terrified!" Connie exclaimed.

"I hadn't thought of that," Bill mused. "I have a flashlight in my desk, but we need more than one. Let's go through some of the other offices and see if we can find more. Connie and I will start on the right, the rest of you go to the left. There are only six or seven offices on this floor, but there are a lot of desks. We'll meet back here when we're finished. If we can't find more flashlights, we definitely won't be going anywhere after dark. Pick up any candles if you find them too, and anything else that might come in handy. We might be stuck here for a while."

The hallway was brightly lit, but it was still creepy. Usually, this place was bustling with people. The AI-controlled building system still played a continuous stream of elevator music through the ceiling speakers, the songs all running together and sounding like one long dirge. Everyone complained about it, but nothing was ever done to change it. Announcements occasionally broke the monotony. It was quiet now, though. Only their footsteps could be heard, echoing down the hallway while their voices bounced off the wood-paneled walls.

The offices were unlocked and looked as though the occupants had left in a hurry. Books were lying open, papers were scattered about the desktops with more lying on the floor. It looked as though someone had been searching through them, found what they were looking for, and left the rest where they fell. There was a spilled cup of coffee on one desk, the caramel-colored liquid staining a neatly stacked ream of paper that apparently was never touched.

Connie found a flashlight in the first desk she came to, but that was the only one in the office. Tim had better luck. He remembered that just left of the elevator, there was a small room where the maintenance crew stored cleaning supplies. In a cabinet over the sink, he found a box of candles. Plugged into AC receptacles were two rechargeable LED flashlights—heavy-duty models, with 12-volt batteries. If fully charged, they should easily burn all night, especially on the low power setting. He also found a rake and a shovel. He hadn't planned on doing any gardening, but they might be able to use these as weapons if they actually had to defend themselves. He didn't really want to think of that happening, though.

He looked around a little while longer but didn't find anything else of value. He'd left Carol and Depina in the office next to him. He could hear them opening and closing desk drawers. He figured he'd better get back and show them his treasures.

The entire excursion took about 30 minutes from the time they left Bill's office until they returned. It had been a successful trip. They'd managed to find four flashlights, eight candles, two transistor radios, an assortment of candy bars, crackers, chewing gum, a rake, a shovel, and all the canned drinks they could want. At least they'd have light, and something to snack on if they decided to spend the night.

Once they settled back in Bill's office, they realized how hungry they were. It had been hours since they last ate. Connie doled out the candy bars, each getting two, along with a package of crackers. There was a water cooler in the control room, and they'd raided the coke machine, so they had plenty to wash them down.

This would hold them over for now, but they knew they'd not be getting much sleep tonight, and it wouldn't be long before they'd be hungry again. Now they had to decide if they were going to stay where they were, or try and make it to the front gate before nightfall. It was a little under a two-mile walk. Since the average person walks about three miles an hour, they should be able to make it easily before nightfall. Bill figured they had a little over an hour's light left.

"Bill," Tim said, "Why don't you try Singleton one more time? He might have freed up someone by now. He originally said 90 minutes. I'd feel much better if we had an escort."

Bill dialed Singleton's cell, but with the same result. All he got was Singleton's voicemail. He also checked the image on the HAARP cam, just in case it might have changed. Nothing different there, either.

"I figure we have a little over an hour of daylight left," Bill said. "I guess we should take a vote."

Before anyone could answer, Connie screamed.

She was staring at the back office. No one had paid any attention to it since they returned. They had completely forgotten about the soap suds.

It wasn't the soap suds that had scared Connie so badly. The door to the back office was wide open. Clutching partly to the doorframe but mostly to the wall, was what looked like a giant slug. A snail with no shell. Its body, at least as much of it as they could see, was about two feet long. It had a pair of antennae attached to what must have been the head, and they were swaying slowly, sampling the air much like a snake's forked tongue.

Its skin glistened in the fluorescent light, solid black in color, and so shiny that had you been standing right next to it, you would probably have seen your reflection. It was like looking into a living mirror.

Then there were the eyes. At the end of thin stalks each about six inches long, were four eyes. They too were swaying in the air, taking in all of their surroundings.

As they watched, another slug—if "slug" was even the right word—appeared at the bottom of the doorway. This one was much smaller, ten to twelve inches at most. It looked similar to the larger version, except its color was a milky white. Still another crept into view behind it, about the same size and color. They moved slowly, inching their way along with a rippling motion. They didn't leave any slime trail like a normal slug might leave.

The larger slug was almost entirely inside the office now. As it got closer, it looked more like a leech than a slug. It was long, and maybe four to six inches thick. In a few more seconds, it had cleared the doorway and was making its way along the wall. Bill guessed its length to be about four feet. As it inched along, its body would contract and then expand. With each contraction, it would move four or five inches forward. It reminded them of an inchworm crawling along a branch.

As soon as this slug had cleared the doorframe, another one took its place. Then one appeared at the top of the doorframe. Apparently, they could stick to the ceiling as easily as the walls. Bill wondered if the smaller ones would turn black, too, as they grew.

The five of them stood there, mesmerized by what they were seeing. They didn't seem to be in any immediate danger. These things were obviously slow. They would be able to outrun them at a walk. For now, they just stood there, gawking.

"Do you hear something?" Carol asked. She was the closest to the slugs, though by only a few steps.

"I don't hear anything," Bill said.

"Me neither," Connie said, standing just behind Bill.

"I hear something," Depina chimed in. "It sounds like tiny bells. Very high pitched, almost a constant tone. It sounds like the ringing of sleigh bells off in the distance."

"I still don't hear anything," Bill said.

"I do now," Connie exclaimed. "Listen, it's them. They're making the sound." She moved closer to Carol, and they both moved a little closer to the slugs.

"That's close enough," Bill warned, not wanting them to go any nearer.

"There's more than one sound. I think it's the smaller slugs that we're hearing now," Carol observed.

Then, a much louder sound chimed in with the tiny tinkling. It still sounded like a bell, but it was definitely louder, and the tone was much lower in pitch. It really did sound like someone ringing a bell. Even Bill heard it this time.

"It's coming from the slug on the wall. I can see vibrations along its back when it's ringing," Bill said.

Connie was near enough that she could see into the back office, and when she did she gasped. "The whole office is full of them! And the soap suds are gone. These things seem to have taken their place."

"That settles it," Bill declared. "It will be close, but we have flashlights. We're going to head for the front gate. If we're lucky, we'll run into some guards along the way. We can't stay here any longer. Who knows what these things might do. They may be slow, but if there are enough of them, they could trap us in here. Carol, you and Connie carry the extra flashlights and candles. Tim and I will bring the rake and shovel. I'll try Singleton one more time. If I don't get him, I'll leave a message on his voicemail saying that we've left for the front gate. Depina, you lead the way."

Taking one last look at the slugs, they left Bill's office and entered the hallway leading to the elevator. From the light shining in through a window, they could tell that they didn't have a lot of daylight left.

When they reached the elevator, they stepped inside and pushed the lobby button. There were two levels below the lobby: level 1, where most of the laboratories were located, and level 2. The beam tunnel and main floor of DUNE were on level 2. When they'd last talked to Singleton, he said he was working in a laboratory on level 1.

As the elevator approached the lobby, they expected to hear the announcement of the floor over the elevator's sound system. It never happened. They realized that the elevator music was gone, too.

"What happened to the crappy music we're always complaining about?" Tim asked.

"I don't know," Bill replied, poking the lobby button again with his finger as he spoke.

The lobby light on the floor indicator lit, but the elevator didn't stop. It just kept going down. A few seconds later, the level 1 light came on—again, without any announcement.

"I don't like this," Connie said nervously. "Isn't there any way that you can stop this thing? Where is it taking us?"

Bill continued to push the lobby button. Next, he pulled out the red "emergency stop" switch, but that didn't do anything either. The elevator slowly continued its descent.

They were starting to panic. The next stop would be the beam tunnel, and they all remembered Singleton's last words: *Don't go near the beam tunnel. There's something in there and it's not friendly.*

That was exactly where they were headed, and they had no way of stopping it. As they watched, the level 1 light went out, and a few seconds later—the level 2 light came on. Soon after that, the elevator shuddered and came to an abrupt stop as it settled on the floor of the beam tunnel.

Bill was frantically switching between hitting the lobby button and the close door button. Neither seemed to do anything. Before anyone could say a word, the elevator doors started to open.

The first thing that hit them was the smell. It was like someone had broken a bottle of perfume, and the air was soaked in it. It was almost overpowering. Yet, there was something in the smell that was almost intoxicating. It was a conundrum of sweet and sweeter. If you breathed through your mouth, you could almost taste it. The senses were overwhelmed.

As the doors opened wider, fear began to set in. The fear was even stronger than the smell. It gripped them like a claw. The light in the tunnel was dim, almost non-existent. The overhead light was on, they could see where it was located in the ceiling, but the light was being filtered through what looked like thin filaments of green, almost black moss. It hung everywhere. Some of it was so long that it touched the tunnel floor. In other places, it was only a few inches in length. The only place that wasn't covered was the area close to the inner wall, next to the beam tube. There wasn't a bit of green anywhere near the magnets or the tube itself. The rest of the tunnel, though, had green fungus hanging everywhere.

As they watched in amazement, Bill was the first to speak. "Look at the stuff hanging from the light fixture. There can't be any wind in here, but it's moving."

"Maybe there's an air vent next to the light," Connie suggested.

"No, I don't think so," Tim interjected. "The ventilation shafts are located near the floor. They installed the shafts and the drains at the same time. I remember reading about the tunnel's construction when I first decided to take this job. I wanted to learn as much as I could before I started writing about it."

"Then what's making those filaments move like that?" Bill asked.

"I think they are moving on their own. Maybe they are growing," Connie theorized.

"It's hard to tell in this light, but it looks like all of this stuff is moving. It looks like a plant, but who knows? It might be some kind of lichen. I've never seen anything like it."

"What do we do now?" Depina spoke up. "We can't stay here forever. If this elevator isn't going to move, we need to find another way to get to the lobby, or at least the floor above this one. There must be some stairs nearby."

"There are," Bill confirmed. "They're right next to the elevator. They go all the way to the top of the building with an entrance at each floor."

Bill took a step out of the elevator and stopped. He looked in all directions, but all he could see in the dim light was green filaments hanging everywhere.

"I think it's safe," Bill said. "I can't see the door to the stairs, but I think I see the lighted 'exit' sign above it. Everything's covered by this stuff. I'm glad we brought the rake. It's just what we need to free the door."

Tim came out next, shovel in one hand, and rake in the other. Connie and Carol followed. Depina stood in the doorway and watched. The elevator's light was much brighter than the one in the beam tunnel and only his silhouette could be seen. He stood there, watching, as the other four approached the exit light, just barely visible through the mossy filaments that engulfed it.

Bill took the rake from Tim and placed the sharp teeth just under the exit sign. He could feel a bump as the teeth found the space between the doorframe and the door. He pushed against the door, and pulled with a downward motion, tearing away a section of the filaments. It revealed a swath of red as the door appeared underneath. Bill continued his downward motion until the rake struck the floor. Then, he slid the rake to the right, shaking it firmly in order to free it from the mass of broken filaments. This worked well. He cleared a path about a foot wide from the top of the doorframe to the floor. A few more swipes, and the door would be free.

Before he got the rake back to the top of the doorframe, the filaments on the sides of the path he'd just cleared started creeping toward each other. As he watched, more filaments came to the aid of those he'd just torn down. He placed the rake at the top of the door again, hoping to tear at the filaments before they could grow back together, but this time they held fast.

He pulled, but his rake was stuck. No matter how hard he tried, it held firm. Then he saw why. The filaments were starting to spin their way down the rake handle. Only the first few inches were covered at first. Within seconds, they'd moved several inches down the handle.

"Tim, grab on and help me."

Tim and Bill had both hands on the last few feet of the rake. They pulled with all their might, but the rake wouldn't budge. The filaments were now almost halfway down the rake handle.

"Watch out!" Carol screamed.

Bill and Tim jumped back together, and it was a good thing, too. The filaments that Bill had dragged to the floor had gathered with others, and were within a few inches of reaching Bill's shoe. He let go of the rake, and it just hung there, waving in the air.

"Look at the ceiling," Depina said. "The moss, or whatever it is—it's moving. It's coming toward you."

They all looked up. It was hard to make out. The light was even dimmer now, as more moss began to cover it. It was soon obvious that the moss was moving, and in their direction.

"We've got to get out of here," Connie said, her voice trembling with fear.

"Try the elevator again," Bill shouted to Depina.

"I've been doing nothing but that—it's why I stayed here," Depina replied, frustration evident in his tone.

"Then we've got to make it to the next elevator. This one's not going anywhere, and there's no chance of us getting through that door. The next elevator is this way," Bill declared, his voice filled with determination.

Bill pointed his flashlight down the tunnel. The light cast a narrow beam, barely illuminating anything beyond its path. The moss absorbed the light instantly, leaving hardly any reflection.

Suddenly, a loud clang echoed beside them! They jumped in unison as the rake bounced off the floor, its sharp teeth nearly grazing Connie's ankle. The moss that had been holding it had inexplicably released its grip. Bill shone his light back toward the door, revealing it completely hidden behind a living coat of thick, undulating filaments.

He picked up the rake, grateful to be holding something that at least resembled a weapon, even if it hadn't been much help so far.

The moss above them seemed to sense their impending departure, dropping down fine filaments that felt like eerie spider webs.

"Let's get out of here before this stuff attaches itself to us like it did to the rake," Bill urged, his voice laced with urgency.

They hastily brushed the filaments from their hair as they hurried away from the area.

Bill led the way, calling out instructions. "Stay close to the wall. The moss doesn't appear to like being next to the beam tube. Maybe it's the magnetic field that's keeping it away. Whatever it is, just stay next to it."

The group lined up behind Bill, with Depina bringing up the rear, clutching the shovel. Though they all had flashlights, only Bill's remained on to conserve batteries. As they walked, the darkness intensified. The moss that had covered the overhead light by the elevator now obscured all the lights, leaving Bill's flashlight as their sole source of illumination.

The tunnel, claustrophobic even when brightly lit in its usual pumpkin orange hue, now felt downright terrifying with only a small corridor to navigate and practically no light to guide them.

"Depina," Bill called, glancing back momentarily while keeping his flashlight trained ahead.

"Yes?" Depina answered.

"Turn on your flashlight and shine it to our left. I hate to use up the batteries, but I can't tell what's there, and it's just too damn scary not knowing."

"I thought you'd never ask," Depina replied, relief evident in his voice.

Depina wielded the other rechargeable flashlight, capable of focusing into either a sharp beam or a wide-angle floodlight by rotating the collar on the reflector. He opted for the floodlight. Even at its lowest setting, the light wasn't particularly bright, but it provided the group with a comforting sense of awareness of their surroundings. Without it, they felt as if they were squeezing through a small, dark tunnel—which, in fact, they were.

The surreal atmosphere was intensified by the eerie lack of sound. Normally, sounds amplify as they bounce off hard surfaces, like singing in a fiberglass shower. However, the moss covering the tunnel acted as a near-perfect sound absorber. Sound, like light, was instantly absorbed, leaving no reflections. Unless one was looking directly at the person speaking, they were unlikely to be heard. Even then, voices sounded like whispers, forcing everyone to practically shout to be understood.

"How far is it to the next elevator?" Connie asked, her voice tinged with anxiety.

"I'm not sure," Bill admitted. "I've only been down here a couple of times, and we used golf carts then."

"I didn't see any golf carts," Connie noted.

"They're usually parked next to the elevators, but I didn't see them either. They must have been left at the next elevator. There are six in total, two for each elevator," Bill explained. "See those numbers on the walls? If we had a map, those numbers would tell us our exact location in the tunnel. If I remember correctly, it took a little more than ten minutes to get from DUNE to Wilson Hall. The carts probably travel at least twice as fast as someone walking, and we're not making very good time, all cramped up like this. I'd guess we're half an hour, maybe forty minutes away."

Connie's heart sank at this news. She had been hoping the next elevator was just around the bend. Of course, in a circular tunnel, the bend was continuous.

They walked for about ten minutes in tense silence when suddenly, Bill came to an abrupt halt, causing the others to bump into each other to avoid collision.

He switched off his flashlight and turned to the group. "Depina, douse your light!"

Depina, sensing something was amiss, had already extinguished his flashlight before Bill finished speaking.

They stood motionless in the darkness for a few seconds, then Bill whispered into the ear of the person behind him. "I hear something up ahead. I'm not certain, but it sounds like someone talking. Pass it on, quietly."

As they stood there, their eyes gradually adjusted to the darkness. They could make out the faint glow of an overhead light struggling to penetrate the moss encasing it. They also discerned a dim glow ahead of them.

Knowing that neither light nor sound could travel far in these surroundings, they deduced that whoever was ahead must be just around the bend.

"Someone's up ahead," Bill whispered. "I can't make out what they're saying, but I'm sure it's human voices. Let's wait here for a few minutes and see if we can figure out who it is and what they're saying."

So there they stood—five people in the dark, each holding onto the arm of the person in front of them. They barely breathed, their concentration entirely focused on deciphering voices that were only audible when listening intently.

"It's Singleton," Bill announced, cupping his hands around his right ear to form a funnel. This significantly increased the surface area for sound waves to reach his ear, collecting and directing them straight into his auditory canal.

"I'm certain it's Singleton, talking to someone. I don't hear anyone else, though. Maybe he's on his cell phone."

"I didn't think cell phones worked in the tunnel," Tim remarked.

"They usually don't," Bill replied. "But who knows? Stranger things than this are happening. Wait here. I'm going to go ahead and make sure it's him."

Bill left the others standing in the darkness as he switched his flashlight back on. He had only walked a short distance when the sound grew louder. Now he could distinguish other voices. He decided to announce his presence, not wanting to startle anyone and risk getting shot.

He called out, "Singleton—it's me—Bill Scott."

Singleton looked up, surprise evident in his voice. "How the hell did you get down here?"

"I've got four other people with me. Give me a few seconds, and I'll be there."

As Bill approached, a group of men came into view—three, four, six in total.

"Am I ever glad to see somebody. I thought we were alone down here," Bill said, relief washing over him as he neared the group gathered around what appeared to be a Coleman lantern.

"I've got Tim, Depina, and the girls with me," Bill continued. "Some kind of strange creatures appeared in my office. They resembled slugs or leeches of some kind, but they were enormous. A couple of them were at least four feet long. We decided to make a break for the front gate, but the elevator didn't stop at the lobby. It took us down to the beam tunnel, and we've been trying to find our way out ever since."

"Same here," Singleton replied. "We were conducting experiments in a lab on level-1 when the soap suds appeared and threatened to trap us. We had to knock a hole in the wall and escape through a side office. When we tried to go up in the elevator, it took us down instead. We have a few weapons, mostly side arms, a few flashlights, this lantern, and some candy bars. We've been stopped here for over an hour, trying to decide our next move."

"I'm going to get the others. I'll be back in a few minutes," Bill said.

He turned and walked back down the narrow corridor, keeping as close to the inside wall as possible. The power emanating from the superconducting magnets made the hair on his arms tingle. As far as he knew, the tests were still ongoing as if nothing had happened. It was clear that the magnets had never been shut down; the whine of thousands of volts of electricity flowing through their coils was audible.

It took only a few minutes for Bill to reach the rest of his group. He briefed them on what he'd learned as they walked to join the others. Now their group was eleven strong, but this presented an unexpected dilemma. Who would lead them? Bill was the director, but Singleton held the real authority. Or would they take a vote? Majority rules. Did it really matter? Did they truly need one person in charge?

These questions were never put to the test. Before introductions could even be completed, the same sound that had terrified Singleton's first group rose up behind them. It seemed to originate from where Bill's group had just been, and it sounded alarmingly close.

The last time, it had started as a low moan and crescendoed to the volume of a freight train. This time, it began like a freight train and escalated to the deafening roar of a space shuttle launch. In the confined space, the sound was painful, almost debilitating. It was so intense that it induced vertigo, causing several of them to lose their balance. Clasping their hands over their ears did little to muffle it. The low, throbbing moan penetrated every part of their bodies. They could feel it in their stomachs as well as hear it with their ears. It lasted about thirty seconds before stopping as abruptly as it had begun.

Everyone was stunned. Some had fallen to the floor, dizzy and disoriented. Others leaned against the inside wall of the tunnel for support. One person had vomited. If the sound had persisted much longer, the consequences could have been dire. It took at least five minutes before they were able to function normally again. For the moment, Singleton and Bill assumed joint leadership.

It was clear, though, that Singleton would have the final say in any disagreement. Bill was content with this arrangement, not wanting the responsibility for all these people anyway.

Their next decision wasn't difficult. They had only one choice—to get away from whatever had produced that horrifying sound. They formed a line, heading towards Wilson Hall. Singleton led the group, with Bill and his party bringing up the rear. Depina was the last in line, keeping his flashlight permanently trained behind them. The last thing he wanted was for something to sneak up on them. He divided his attention equally between looking ahead and behind, though at this rate, he'd soon be nursing a sore neck.

Every third person had their flashlight on. The tunnel seemed less intimidating when things weren't hidden in shadows.

"Strength in numbers," Bill thought to himself, though he knew this kind of reasoning might not apply to their current situation. Nevertheless, he found comfort in it.

They had only gone a few hundred feet when suddenly, they were blinded by a light that appeared on the floor ahead of them. It was a portal. Just the top of it protruded from the floor, partially covered by fine moss. It was far enough to their left that there was no danger of someone accidentally stepping into it. Had it been closer, it could easily have severed someone's foot had they stumbled into it. As with the soap suds, it was the edges of the portal that posed the greatest threat.

They gathered around the strange phenomenon, several of them experiencing a portal for the first time. The portal's location made it even more bizarre. Since only the top foot or so was visible, peering into it was like looking through a window at something just beneath the floor. But it wasn't just under the floor—it wasn't under anything. They were gazing into another dimension, another time, and it terrified them.

The view was limited due to the small visible area. Like the portal Singleton had seen earlier, it revealed a reddish-brown desert with plants scattered randomly across the terrain. A light wind kicked up fine dust, some of which fell onto the floor before them. The scene was so bright that they couldn't help but squint as they peered into it. Their pupils had dilated while walking in the dim light, and when the portal appeared, it was as if someone had turned a searchlight on them. Their eyes gradually adjusted to the glare.

This was Carol and Connie's first encounter with a portal, and they were captivated by it. The idea of seeing another world, completely alien to their own, was something humans had dreamed of throughout history. Now, they were actually doing it.

"We'd better move on," Singleton said, though he, too, could have stared into the portal for hours. "We've got to be careful and examine every step. You haven't seen what these things can do."

With that, he asked Depina if he could borrow his shovel for a moment. Depina handed it over.

"Let's make this a little more useful as a weapon," Singleton said.

He took the shovel and placed the metal blade against the edge of the portal. Where the shovel touched the edge, the metal simply dissolved. Singleton was able to shape the shovel into a point, transforming it into a makeshift spear.

"Thanks," Depina said, admiring his newly forged weapon.

"Just remember, the edge of these portals will cut through anything just as easily. That goes double for a foot. So be extremely careful where you walk. Everyone follow the person ahead of you, and don't wander out of line," Singleton warned.

"This is a pretty big portal, but they come in all sizes. They can be much larger, or smaller than a dime, and they can appear anywhere. We've already lost two people. They were unfortunate enough to walk into a dime-sized one. Just follow the person in front of you, and you should be fine."

The fascination that Connie and Carol had felt moments ago was replaced by a sense of foreboding. What were they getting into? Connie had been part of several deep-sea diving expeditions and had thought those were terribly dangerous. But this—this was something else entirely. Something she couldn't quite comprehend.

Even so, it was exhilarating. "This is what life is all about," she thought. It's amazing how much you appreciate life when you're in a position to lose it. This must be the rush that people experience when they scale mountains, drive race cars, and base-jump off buildings. The adrenaline was definitely kicking in. Fear makes you feel alive. It's not the same as watching a scary movie, where you know the danger isn't real. This is the real thing.

"Let's move on. We have a long way to go, and the pace is going to be much slower now," Singleton said as he led the way. His flashlight was set to flood position to illuminate as much area as possible.

Depina brought up the rear again. His thoughts dwelled on what had made that awful moaning sound behind them. Maybe something had fallen into a portal, he thought. No, we couldn't be that lucky.

As they walked, Singleton noticed a change in their surroundings. The moss covering the ceiling was growing thinner. The outline of an overhead light became clearly visible. The next light had only a small section covered in green.

They turned off their flashlights. The moss that had covered everything was nearly gone, and they could see again. It looked as if it had died. There were piles of it on the tunnel floor, several feet deep in some places. It had turned from a dark green to a pale gray. What little moss remained alive was hidden in crevices and behind pipes. It had frayed gray filaments where it was exposed to the light.

Yet, it couldn't have been the light that was killing it. There must be something different about this part of the tunnel.

Singleton thought this would be a good place for them to stop and rest. It was wonderful to have light again. Now they weren't confined to the few feet next to the inside wall.

285

They could actually walk around and stretch out a bit since they no longer had to worry about bumping into something. For this, they were all grateful.

Chapter Twenty-Eight

Bill turned to Depina, motioning for him to come closer.

"What do you think about the moss? Any idea what could have killed it? I don't see anything different here than anywhere else."

"Maybe whatever killed it has gone," Depina replied thoughtfully.

"Does it feel a little cooler to you? I could swear the air feels either cooler or drier. Something's different; I just can't put my finger on it."

Depina pondered for a few seconds. "Now that you mention it, it does seem a little cooler. Let's ask Singleton if he's noticed a change."

When they looked, Singleton had disappeared. Apparently, he'd walked on ahead to scout the next section of tunnel. Before they could follow, he came running back.

"I know what killed the moss."

"We have an idea, too," Depina said.

"It's the cold. The moss can't take the cold. There's a leak in one of the cryogenic lines cooling the next magnet. Liquid nitrogen is boiling out of a split seam. It's downright frigid as you get near it. Even a slight drop in temperature must be deadly to the moss."

"We figured as much, but didn't know what was causing the cold," Bill said.

"I wonder how close we are to the next elevator. Even if it isn't working, the door to the stairs may not be covered. Hopefully, we can get into the stairwell."

"I think we're getting close," Singleton said. "I hadn't even noticed the temperature change here, but it was still enough to kill the moss. I'm sure the tunnel on the other side of the leak will be moss-free as well. What we don't know is if the cold reaches as far as the elevator. I guess we'll know when we get there."

The group stood talking, enjoying the light for the next ten or fifteen minutes. It was Bill who made the suggestion that they move on and see how far this moss-free stretch extended. He also repeated the warning about stepping into a portal, to make sure everyone stayed in a tight line while they were moving.

It was about time they had some good luck. They passed beside the leaking cryogenic line with no problem; the gas bubbling up from it was nitrogen, an inert gas that makes up 78% of the earth's atmosphere.

As they approached the next light, they saw one of the electric golf carts and knew the elevator had to be nearby. It was. There was just a tiny bit of moss on the cart, but they were at the boundary where it was starting to warm up, and the moss was beginning to make a comeback.

Only a few strands of moss were covering the elevator doors. These were easily removed. Bill punched the "up" button. Actually, it was the only button since this was the lowest floor the elevator went to. The floor indicator above the door showed that the elevator was sitting at the lobby. It seemed to take a long time before the L-1 light came on. They began to wonder if the elevator was moving at all. No one was sure if the power was still on. The beam tunnel lights had battery backup, but the elevators would be dead if the main power was off. The PIP-II accelerator seemed to operate on its own power (transmitted from HAARP, no doubt), so its still being in operation didn't mean much.

Eventually, the L-1 light did light, so the elevator had to be coming down. It just seemed to be taking forever. The L-2 light was next. The elevator would be there in a few more seconds. Ding. There was a soft chime as the elevator announced its arrival.

They waited. After a few seconds, Singleton spoke. "There's something wrong. The doors aren't opening. Depina, see if you can wedge your blade between the doors while Bill and I try to force them open."

Depina wedged the makeshift blade between the doors and pushed as hard as he could, throwing all of his 187 pounds into it. The modified shovel slid between the frozen doors, all the way to the handle. Next, he twisted and pried with the blade, opening the doors just wide enough so that Bill and Singleton could get their fingers in between them. Two other men grabbed the doors as well, and they all pulled at the same time.

As the doors started to open, they peered into the dark cavity, but there wasn't enough light to see anything. The elevator's overhead light was either burned out or turned off. With only a few inches of open door to look through, they couldn't tell what, if anything, was inside. The doors seemed to be jammed. They were moving, but with a lot of resistance. Then, they broke free—slamming against the sides of the elevator with a loud thud.

With the doors wide open, the dim light from the tunnel flowed into the elevator. What they saw made them cringe. The elevator was thick with moss. It looked like spinach. It had a wet sheen to it and seemed to be moving.

The elevator light was probably on, it was just blotted out by the moss.

Bill caught a glimpse of something white on the floor and aimed his flashlight toward it. In a carpet of living, rippling moss, he thought he saw a hand. The fingers were just barely visible, and contrasted sharply against the dark green filaments. As the moss rippled, it forced the hand up and into view. It was severed at the base of the wrist. Bones, tendons, and blood vessels were dangling out of it.

The moss moved in waves. The hand rode on the crest of these waves like some obscene surfer as it moved from one wall to the other.

It was the most frightening thing Bill had ever witnessed. While this bizarre event was taking place, the moss along the edges of the elevator started to creep outside, sending streamers of green filaments that attached themselves to the outer wall. In less than a minute, the moss had covered the "Up" button that Bill had just pushed. The whole group watched in horror, as the dead hand seemed to be waving to them as it traveled on its endless living conveyor belt.

Then, suddenly—it stopped. A few seconds later, the moss pulled back into the elevator as quickly as it had come out. The moss on the floor stopped its undulating motion as well, and the hand sank back into the filaments.

"It's the cold," Bill said. "It doesn't like the cold."

As they watched, the doors began to close. Only the right door was stuck. Apparently, they had pulled it off its track when they forced it open. The other door closed normally, but the right door kept jerking, like it was hitting something.

There was another "ding" and the elevator vibrated slightly, then started up to a higher level. They watched as the L-1 light came on. A few seconds later, the Lobby light lit up. During that whole time, no one had said a word, no one dared. But they all remembered Bill's last words. Their lives might soon depend on them. "It's the cold. It doesn't like the cold."

"The stairs," Depina said, breaking the silence. "Let's see if we can make it up the stairs."

He was already standing next to the door leading to the stairwell. Like the elevator, there were only a few strands of moss he'd have to deal with. One fairly large strand was hanging from the exit sign. He knocked it away with the modified shovel and pulled on the door. It opened easily.

It was pitch black inside. The lights were out, which was not a good sign because they, too, had battery backup. Bill and Singleton turned their flashlights towards the door at the same time. "What do we do now?" Depina asked, standing in front of the open door. He was staring at a wall of moss that had completely covered its entrance.

"We keep going," a new voice called out from the rear of the group. "There are two maintenance hatches in the back section of the tunnel. They were put in so that technicians could access the tunnel without having to go through Wilson Hall or DUNE. They are also part of the emergency plan, in case of fire or breach of the beam tube."

"Who are you?" Bill asked.

"My name is Carl. Carl Richardville. I was assigned to fix the leak in the cryogenic line we just passed. We knew about it this morning, but I never got the go-ahead to fix it. I ended up here with the others when the elevator failed."

"How familiar are you with the tunnel?" Singleton asked.

"I know it like the back of my hand."

"Why the hell didn't you say something before now?"

"I learned a long time ago that the less you say, the better off you are."

"Are you military?"

"No. I'm a tech working for Arlington Corp. My specialty is cryogenics."

"How far is this hatch that you're talking about?"

"We're at 723." Richardville pointed to the number on the wall. "The first hatch is somewhere around 960, give or take a few numbers. I'd say we are about a quarter mile away."

"Will it be easy to see?"

"It should be, as long as this damn moss isn't covering it. We should probably start looking, though, when we get to 955. Just in case. I don't think we'll miss it."

Before anyone else could speak, the sweet-smelling air turned sour. It smelled like rotten eggs, or meat that had been lying in the sun for a few days—lots of meat. The mix of the two smells was nauseating.

Then they heard it—a cross between a growl and a moan. It had to be close, probably within a few feet of rounding the bend behind them. They moved as one, heading towards the hatch that Richardville had mentioned. Bill was leading now, though he was soon passed by two of the guards. No one wanted to be in the rear.

Within seconds they had thrown caution to the wind and were almost at a run. Thirty yards later, the tunnel grew dark. The chill in the air was gone, and the moss had returned. This slowed their progress to a fast walk. Everyone that had a flashlight turned it on. They pressed against the inner wall once more, as the moss was blocking most of the tunnel.

Singleton shouted to the group. "Stop!" His voice was absorbed by the moss. He yelled again—as loudly as he could. "Everyone—stop! Now!"

And they stopped. Some of them bumping into the person ahead of them—but they stopped. As they did, a roar came from behind them. That started them off again, this time running even faster than before. They ran for about 50 yards, when there was a scream from either Carol or Connie. It was hard to tell in the dim light.

It was Carol. The person in front of her had stepped out of line and into a maze of moss hanging to their left. It wrapped around him, snaring him instantly. The moss gripped him tightly, not allowing him any chance of escape. In seconds, it had covered his arms and head, severely restricting his breathing.

He was trying to call for help, but he could hardly breathe, let alone cry out.

Depina was the first to get to him, and he hacked at the moss with his shovel. The blade came to a sharp point, but the edges were dull as cardboard and didn't have much of an effect on the moss. It continued to envelop the man's body. It was forming a cocoon around him and as it did, it pulled him deeper into the darkness. Here the moss was as thick as a heavy carpet, and moved as if a strong wind was blowing it. He disappeared deep into the folds while the others looked on in horror. In less than a minute, all they could see was a clump of moss where the man had been. Then, he was gone—lost in a sea of rippling green filaments that seemed to wave slowly, beckoning them to join him.

They stood there, not knowing what to do. Something horrible was behind them, and now the moss which had previously only been an annoyance had proved deadly. Who knew what was up ahead? Or what was going on outside of the tunnel? What if they reached the surface only to find that it was even worse up there?

They began to move again—towards the hatch. Not at a run this time, not even at a fast walk. They moved slowly. With every step they thought about what they'd just seen—each of them replaying it in their heads like a bad movie.

Bill took over the lead without realizing it. Richardville was second, with Singleton well back in the bunch now. He wasn't afraid to lead, but he wanted to think and not have to worry about what they were walking into. He was thinking about HAARP, and what was happening there. He was thinking about things that only he and Meyers were privy to. He was wondering if he should tell Bill why the PIP-II was still running. Why it would only be shut down as a last resort. He wanted to be alone to think—but being alone wasn't an option in this situation.

Bill was thinking, too. Thinking of how he'd gotten into this mess to begin with. Thinking of how things had gone so terribly wrong. Thinking of Connie, and how their relationship had matured in such a short time. Wondering if she realized how much he'd become attached to her.

He was also thinking about what they were going to do next, and what was wrong with Tim? He'd hardly said a word since they left the elevator. It wasn't easy trying to find answers to the unanswerable.

Even though in deep thought, he kept a sharp lookout toward his surroundings. Seeing the moss swallow their companion had left a vivid impression of what could happen to any of them. He felt responsible for the group, though he knew he shouldn't. No one could have predicted what they were experiencing now. He was just another person, trying to get out of here alive.

As they walked, they were once again overcome by the sweet smell of flowers. The 'rotten eggs' sulfur smell was behind them. Bill thought to himself, if the rotten smell was coming from whatever was making that moaning sound, we seemed to be able to keep in front of it. Maybe it was like the slugs, slow moving.

Images flashed through his mind like home movies. Oblivious to the people behind him, he was in a world of his own, a trance of sorts, his body on autopilot, his mind soaring. He continued in this way for another five minutes, before something broke him out of this heightened state of consciousness.

"Bill!" It was Singleton. "Bill!" He had made his way to the front. No small feat, considering he had to pass people without moving them out of line. It was a tight squeeze, getting around someone without stepping into the waiting tentacles that would love to make him their next meal.

"We need to get to a computer."

"Are you crazy?" Bill asked. "We're nowhere near a computer. We'll be lucky if we can even get out of here."

"No, we are near one. I was just talking to Richardville and he told me that there's a maintenance room next to the escape hatch that consists of several rooms. They keep supplies in it—tools mostly, and spare parts for the maintenance of the magnets. There's also a computer. He's almost positive that it has Internet access, too."

"You've got to be kidding. I could strangle that damn Richardville. What the hell else is he not telling us?"

"He's a strange bird, alright. I asked him if there was anything else in the tunnel that we should know about, and he just shrugged his shoulders.

"I'll bet if there was a bottomless pit ahead he wouldn't mention it until one of us fell in. Then he'd say, 'Sorry, but no one asked me about it.'"

"If we can get to a computer, we can find out what's going on up above. I'd hate to step out on the surface and get squashed by a giant bug, or something."

It was hard to talk as they walked because their voices died so quickly. Singleton closed the gap between them a little more.

"I also need to find out what's going on at HAARP. I'm sure you've wondered how HAARP figures into all of this. The thing is—you only know a small part of it."

"I surmised that HAARP supplied the power while we were off-grid," Bill said.

Singleton was shocked. "You obviously know more than I thought you did. How'd you figure that out?" Bill's stature had risen considerably in the last few hours.

"After you gave me the Top Secret reports, I got on the Net and researched all of the controversies thought to be going on at HAARP. One of them was Tesla's proposal for the wireless transmission of power. It wasn't hard to put two and two together and figure out that something was providing power to the PIP-II when we were offline. It sure wasn't batteries."

"You only know the half of it. All the shit that's happening around here now—the moss, the slugs, the portals—it all started at HAARP. I've been investigating these phenomena for over a year. That's the reason I was sent here to begin with. It's also why I have so much authority. Even though these things started at HAARP, the bulk of the manifestations have occurred here. Meyers was also there at the beginning, but he hasn't been with the organization as long as I have."

"And what organization might that be?" Bill asked.

"DARPA," Singleton replied.

"I figured as much. It's not that I'm against DARPA; it's just that, this isn't supposed to be a government-run facility. It was becoming pretty obvious, though, as DARPA always seemed to control what was being studied."

"That's because the government is paying the bills. Yours is not the only civilian organization that's under DARPA's control. Look at NASA. The public thinks they are controlled by the private sector, but when it comes to which projects are funded and which are shelved, DARPA has the final say. As long as you agree with what the government wants, you can call yourself anything you wish. Public, civilian, private, whatever—but if Uncle Sam is paying the bills, he's pulling the strings, as well."

"So how long has this symbiotic relationship been going on between HAARP, Fermilab, and DARPA?" Bill asked.

"Since the beginning, only DARPA was called something else back then. It was about ten months ago that power was first successfully transferred to Fermilab. Setting up the receiving equipment without anyone realizing what was happening was a major coup for our people. No one here was ever the wiser."

"That's about the time our problems started," Bill said.

"It's been a little over two years since that first portal appeared at HAARP. I'll never forget it. Everyone came out to look at it. It was just hanging in the air, right next to the antenna array. The entire complex was cordoned off until it disappeared, only to come back a week later in a slightly different place. It wasn't like any of these, though. I'm not even sure it's the same thing. It's more of a solid cylindrical object that's totally opaque. It's small compared to some of the portals we're seeing here. Nothing approaching this size had ever appeared at HAARP, until one night when a small plane flew into the transmission beam. Seconds later, three huge portals appeared."

They were talking so softly that no one else could hear them.

"That original portal is still hanging there. We've conducted hundreds of experiments on it, but we don't know any more now than when we first started. It's just there."

"The portals that appeared later, and probably the ones mentioned in that last transmission, are more like those we're seeing here. They're transparent with an alien landscape inside of them. If they've merged into one, I can only imagine how big it must be. We need to get to that computer so I can contact DARPA and see what's going on."

They had only walked a few minutes when Richardville shouted for them to stop.

"Something must be up; this is the second time he's spoken without being spoken to," Bill said.

"I think we are near the hatch," Richardville said.

"I don't see anything," Bill said, as he shined his flashlight on the opposite side of the tunnel—revealing nothing but a wall of slowly undulating moss.

"I'm sure of it. It was across from the magnet with the red X on it, and this magnet has a red X. We had been having a lot of trouble with high-frequency resonance in the windings, and somebody put an X on the cover to remind us to check it occasionally. I'm positive that this is it."

"If it is, then we're going to have a problem finding the hatch and the maintenance room. The moss is worse here than anywhere I've seen yet. It might not have gotten inside of the hatch, though. It should be sealed tight from this side. The only way the hatch would be compromised is if the moss came in from the surface," Singleton said.

"I think I can clear the moss," Richardville said.

"He did it again. That's three times now without being prompted," Bill said.

Not reacting to Bill's comment at all, Richardville continued on.

"I believe I heard you talking about how the cold had killed the moss. I can remove the cryogenic hose and send a blast of liquid nitrogen directly into the moss. There was just a small leak before and it killed it for several hundred feet. This will be more like a snow blower."

"Can you do that?" Bill asked.

"Of course I can. That's what I do. I work on the cryogenic lines. There's a valve right here," (He shined his flashlight on a blue valve a few feet from the base of the magnet) "that shuts off the coolant flow. I'll turn it off, and then remove the hose where it connects to the magnet. It's stiff, but flexible enough that I can bend it and aim it towards the moss. Then, I'll turn the valve back on and send a stream of liquid nitrogen splashing against the tunnel wall. It should kill the moss instantly. I'd say it will clear it for a hundred feet in both directions."

"Is it safe?" Singleton asked.

"Well, I wouldn't want to keep it on for more than a minute or two. The section of moss that died early on in the tunnel was killed by the cold coming from a small leak. The liquid was barely bubbling as it turned back into a gas. This time, it will still be in a liquid state as it leaves the hose. Within a few seconds, it will start turning back into a gas. A freezing cold gas that will kill everything it touches, even us, if we were near enough. So you'll need to move everyone away from here while I'm working. I can control the volume of flow with the valve. I'll give the moss a good dousing, then hook the hose back to the magnet. The magnet won't function in a superconducting mode without it. The oxygen in the air will be thinned for a while, because of the amount of nitrogen mixing in with it. I'd say we ought to keep everyone out of here for at least half an hour to give the air time to stabilize."

Richardville was proving to be more valuable than anyone had expected. Without him, they'd have never known about the escape hatches or the maintenance room. Now, he was providing the solution to getting into them, something they'd have otherwise been unable to do.

"What can we do to help?" Singleton asked.

"Just get everyone behind the bend until I come and get you."

"You got it. Good luck."

Singleton ordered everyone to retrace their path back from where they'd come. They did a 180; Depina now leading the way, something he wasn't used to doing. They walked until Richardville's flashlight could no longer be seen, and then they stopped. Only Depina and Singleton kept their flashlights turned on, lighting the tunnel ahead and behind them.

Richardville had never felt so alone. He was not prone to claustrophobia, but confined to such a tiny space, and with total darkness all around him, it was enough to give anyone the creeps. He shined his light on the opposite wall. The moss was rippling like waves on the ocean—almost as if it knew what he was going to do. The silence was unnerving. He could hear his heartbeat and realized it was racing. He had a dozen tools in his tool belt, but the only one he'd need was the adjustable wrench.

He closed the valve feeding the liquid nitrogen to the magnet. With the coolant stopped, he realized that it had been making an almost imperceptible sound as it flowed around the magnet's coils. Even that was gone now, and the sound of his own breathing reverberated in his ears.

He placed the mouth of the wrench over the titanium fitting binding the intake hose to the magnet and started to unscrew the outer flashing when something caught his attention. It was faint, but he was sure he heard it. He stopped—and listened. Bells—it sounded like someone ringing a bell. He listened for a few seconds more—then it was gone. He was sure he'd heard it, though. Maybe, he thought, maybe, the sound was traveling through the cryogenic system. It might have originated on the other side of the tunnel, and I only heard it because it's so damn quiet.

He didn't give it any more thought as he went ahead and removed the cryogenic hose. He had about a three-foot section to play with. The hose was similar to hydraulic hose. Wire reinforced, it was able to withstand several thousand pounds of pressure though, in this case, it was only being subjected to about 150 PSI. But considering that the liquid flowing through it was just a few degrees above absolute zero, it had to be some quality stuff. I'll bet this stuff cost a fortune, he thought to himself.

He had a pair of heavy leather gloves with soft sheepskin linings attached to the left side of his tool belt. He would need them in order to keep his hands from freezing. He was able to hold the hose, and his flashlight in his left hand as he turned the valve with his right. As it began to open, liquid nitrogen spewed from the end in an arc, flowing farther as the pressure increased.

Soon, he had a stream shooting all the way to the back side of the tunnel. Everywhere it hit—the moss froze solid. Within seconds, the liquid started bubbling as it turned back into a gas. The frozen moss dropped from the ceiling and shattered against the concrete floor, breaking into dozens of pieces in the process. Moss on both sides of the stream turned grey and died. In thirty seconds, he could see the hatch cover and the maintenance door, and he directed the spray towards them. The tunnel was turning from green to grey before his eyes. He wasn't keeping track of the time like he should have and before long, the air started to thin. It was getting hard to breathe. He turned the valve to the off position.

It was time to join the others. He could hook the hose back up when they returned. He was coughing now, the air thinning even more as the liquid on the floor turned into gas. As he started towards the others, he shined his light once more along the wall opposite him. The moss continued to turn grey before his eyes, dropping in clumps with a thud to the tunnel floor. The maintenance door and the escape hatch were completely clear of moss, other than a few dead strands hanging from the door handles and handrails.

He had done well, he was proud of himself. The others would appreciate his efforts too. Without him, they'd have had little chance of clearing the moss, and they desperately needed to get to that computer.

Richardville had accomplished all he could here as he continued back down the tunnel towards the others. As he walked, it became easier to breathe. He didn't realize it, but had he not stopped when he did, he might have died from asphyxiation.

It was only a few minutes before he saw the glow from Singleton's flashlight. They waited until he reached them before asking how things had gone, but they could tell by the look on his face that his plan had been successful.

Thirty minutes passed before they started back to the hatch. The air, even at this distance, had a chill to it. They'd gone less than fifty feet when they noticed moss dying along the inside wall. Long before they reached the hatch, mounds of moss could be seen lying grey and lifeless, scattered about the tunnel floor.

Opposite the magnet with the X on it, they saw a hatch and a door where there had only been a wall of moss before.

They cleared a path to the maintenance room door by kicking the dead moss to one side with their feet.

Singleton was the first to get to the door. Bill was right behind him. Depina and Richardville checked out the hatch. The rest of them stayed put, keeping a watch down both sides of the tunnel, just to make sure they didn't have any unexpected visitors.

Singleton turned the handle on the door and pulled it towards him. It opened easily. It was pitch black inside, but there didn't seem to be any moss along the door's edge. That was a relief.

Bill shined his flashlight into the dark room. It cast shadows on the furniture and desks.

"I don't see any moss," Singleton said, as his light merged with Bill's.

"Me neither," Bill said.

Singleton took a step into the room, finding the light switch on the wall next to the door. He flipped it on and the room lit up with the cool brilliance of white LED panels. The bright light spilled out into the beam tunnel and was a welcome sight to those who were waiting. Sometimes, waiting is a lot harder than actually doing something.

Depina and Richardville decided that it might be better to wait until the maintenance room was fully explored before they opened the escape hatch, so for the time being, they stayed where they were.

Bill followed Singleton's lead, exploring the various rooms that branched off from the main entrance. There were four rooms in all, counting the room that opened into the tunnel. Two of the rooms were full of boxes, which were labeled and looked like they probably contained parts for replacement and repairs.

"There doesn't seem to be anything usable here," Bill said, as he browsed through an inventory sheet attached to a clipboard hanging on the wall.

The next room was small, and obviously what they were looking for. Two monitors were suspended from the ceiling, but neither was turned on. They were probably attached to cameras that guarded this section of tunnel. There was a shortwave radio sitting on the only desk, alongside a wide-screen LCD monitor. A computer tower was sitting on the floor beside the desk. There was also a telephone, something they hadn't expected, on the right side of the monitor. A mouse and keyboard completed the computer accessories.

An intercom hung on the wall, just to the left of the doorway. There was a green light blinking next to one of three entries written on a white label. Printed on the labels were Wilson Hall, DUNE, and Feynman. It was the Wilson Hall entry that was blinking. Singleton pressed the button next to the blinking light and spoke into the combination speaker microphone.

"Hello? Is anyone there?"

When he let up on the button, the blinking light went out, but only static could be heard coming through the speaker.

"Well, I tried, anyway," he said, talking to himself.

He looked down, and saw three rechargeable flashlights plugged into AC sockets next to a filing cabinet.

"We can never have enough of these." Again, he was thinking out loud, but Bill heard him this time.

"Enough of what?" he called out from the other room.

"Sorry, I was talking to myself. I found three more rechargeable flashlights."

"Any sign of a computer?"

"Yes, and it looks like it could be exactly what we're looking for. There's a shortwave radio here, too. It might be of use to us as well."

"Great," Bill said. "There's nothing in here but boxes of replacement parts. The main room looks promising though."

What Bill was referring to as the main room was the first room they'd entered. It was also the largest of the four rooms. On one side, it had a refrigerator, microwave oven, and a large rectangular table that seated eight people. Several cabinets hung over a stainless steel sink set in a fake marble countertop.

Bill walked over and opened one of the cabinets. It was stuffed full of canned goods. He checked the other cabinets, and they were equally well stocked. Next, he looked in the icebox.

"I don't see anything to eat, but there must be a couple of cases of soft drinks, mostly diet, and a dozen or so bottles of mineral water. There's even a few beers in the back."

"It sounds like we won't have to worry about starving, anyway. We could hold out in here for a week or more. When you get a chance, go tell the others. I'm sure they'd like something to eat and drink."

"There's another door back here, next to the icebox."

Bill opened it slowly, shining his flashlight inside as soon as it had opened wide enough.

"It's a bathroom. No tub or shower, but there's a sink and stool. We have all the amenities of home."

"That's good, because we might be staying here for a while."

"I'm going to check out the computer," Singleton said. "Let the others know what we've found, but tell them to give me a half an hour or so before they come in. If the computer's online, I'd like to have some privacy before the whole group gets here. I can shut the door, but I'd still like a little while alone."

"I'll keep everyone away for thirty minutes. Most of us haven't had much to eat or drink though, so it will be hard to keep them at bay for much longer."

"That will be fine. If the computer's not online, I'll let you know right away, and you can bring them on in. If I'm not out in a few minutes, you'll know I'm on the Net."

"Let's hope I don't see you for a while then."

Bill left Singleton on his own, walking outside and shutting the door behind him. When the others saw him come out, they gathered around him, curious to know what he'd found. They were excited when he told them of the food and a working bathroom. He didn't mention the computer, phone, or shortwave radio. They'd find out about them soon enough, anyway. He didn't need anyone trying to "phone home" right now, though that might be a real possibility in a little while.

Richardville figured that this might be a good time to connect the cryogenic hose back to the magnet. He left a small leak in the connection though, so that the temperature would stay a little cooler here than in the rest of the tunnel. That should keep the moss at bay, he thought to himself.

Back in the maintenance room, Singleton reached down and turned on the computer. It wasn't the newest model; the OS splash screen appeared on the monitor—Windows 12, patched and running in "offline mode." In about a minute, the desktop materialized. The first thing he noticed were the security and anti-malware icons. This was a good sign that the computer was online. He'd know soon enough. He clicked on the browser icon. It took the system about 20 seconds before the Fermilab homepage appeared. He was online!

Next, he typed in the address to HAARP's website to see if any new information had been uploaded to the antenna array picture. A few seconds later, the array was displayed, along with the date and time of the last update.

"Damn," he muttered to himself.

He had the website up, but he had no way to decode it. Whatever was hidden in the image would stay hidden.

"Shit! I can't believe I've gotten this far and still don't have the information I'm looking for. Technology can really be a pain in the ass sometimes." He knew he would be able to log onto DARPA's website though, and that would be just as good. He didn't need decrypting software there, just a password.

He typed in DARPA's web address, and in seconds the familiar DARPA login screen appeared. He entered his name and password, and the screen went blank for a few seconds. Then it returned to the login screen again. What the—

He typed in his name and password a second time and hit the 'continue' icon. The screen went blank again, but after a few seconds—he was back at the login screen. This doesn't make any sense, he thought to himself. Maybe the third time's a charm. He tried it once more, making sure that the caps lock was off and that he was hitting the right keys. The login screen came up this time, too, except underneath the login box, in bright red letters, it said, "You've exhausted your login tries. Please contact a system administrator to confirm your name and password."

"Shit!" This was becoming a habit. "I'm positive that this is my login and password. I've been using the same one for over a year." Then, it dawned on him. In cases of a national emergency or if the database is compromised, all passwords will need to be changed. He'd read that a thousand times but never thought much about it. Now he wished he had.

Apparently, something had happened that was serious enough to invalidate everyone's login and password. There wasn't much he could do about it right now. Logging in without the proper name and password was impossible.

There were other ways he could find out what was going on now that he had Internet access. He typed www.cnn.com into the address field. All of the major news organizations had websites. CNN just happened to be his favorite.

"Shit!" This seemed to be his answer for everything lately.

He watched as they showed an overhead view of the Fermilab complex. There didn't seem to be anyone left. No tanks, no guards, no cars, no trucks, no vehicles of any kind. Everyone had gone. The only living thing he saw as the pictures flashed by was a lone bison. It seemed content as it randomly grazed on the prairie grass. How he envied that bison. A banner ran across the top of the page, stating, 'Fermilab Evacuated – Alien Presence Feared.' Another headline read, 'Several Dead In Alien Attack.' He read the story and discovered that nine soldiers had been killed, and four more were missing in a confrontation with something that had emerged from a portal near Wilson Hall.

They showed a blurry image of some kind of creature, but the whole thing had happened in the dark of night, and not much could be seen of the incident. The article ended with—of the 25 soldiers involved in the attack, only twelve returned to tell about it.

Other articles told of portals appearing throughout the complex, accompanied by pictures of the alien landscapes that could be seen within them. One picture of the lake showed nine portals, either in the water or hanging above it. Close-ups of the surrounding grounds showed that the moss that plagued the tunnel only affected a few areas on the surface. The night time temperature was probably still cold enough to stunt its growth. He was surprised that it wasn't cold enough to kill it altogether.

As he read, it became clear that things on the surface had taken a major turn for the worse. In only a few hours, the entire complex had been evacuated. There wasn't even a skeleton crew left. He wondered if anyone realized that they were still here, imprisoned in the beam tunnel. DARPA surely knew that he and Meyer were here. They might not be admitting it, though. Where the hell was Meyer, anyway? He hadn't seen him since early this afternoon. There were too many people here for them all to be ignored. There must be a mention of them somewhere, but he couldn't find it.

Everything revolved around the Alien presence. That started him thinking—if everyone thinks this place is deserted—that would open a whole lot of military options in ways of dealing with the situation. Maybe that's why we aren't being mentioned. We might be sacrificial lambs, if it came to it. Singleton's thirty minutes were about up. As he sat there contemplating what to do, he thought he heard something. There were few things in this tiny office that could make any noise.

The fan in the computer's power supply made a little whirling sound, but that wasn't what he heard. He looked up at the intercom, but it was turned off. At least none of the station lights were blinking. He stood up and looked around the room, trying to find where the sound had come from. It had been very faint. Maybe he hadn't heard it at all. Maybe it was just his mind playing tricks on him. After all, who would be ringing a bell down here?

"Ladies first," Carol said as she made her way toward the bathroom.

"I'm next," Connie chimed in, walking close behind her. When Carol opened the door, they saw that it was hardly big enough for one person, let alone two. "Ok, I'll wait," Connie said.

A line formed at the table, where bowls of soup and spaghetti were being served. Even though there were dozens of canned goods in the closet, most of them contained either soup or spaghetti. Several people sat at the table while others gathered along the opposite side of the room. A couch and recliner awaited them. "This beats the hell out of standing in a cramped tunnel, not knowing if something is sneaking up behind you." This was another voice Bill couldn't identify. Probably another technician, he thought.

Conversations took on a party atmosphere. Their present situation was so different from what they'd been experiencing the last several hours, it was easy to forget they were still in a lot of danger. You couldn't blame them, though. They had full bellies, a restroom, a reasonable amount of safety, and a renewed hope of getting out of here. Just a few hours earlier, they didn't know if they had a pot to piss in.

For the past hour, Singleton had been surfing the net, trying to find out what was happening.

He didn't like what he was finding. He'd been so caught up in trying to find breaking news about their situation that he'd entirely forgotten about the telephone.

"Shi—" He caught himself. He picked up the phone and punched the button on one of the three lines that were listed on the touchpad. Nothing. He tried the other two with the same result. No dial tone. No static. Nothing. I didn't really think they'd leave the phones on—then again, they left the power on, and the computer connected—

He sent fourteen emails to friends and colleagues. It wouldn't be long before he got some replies. Any of his colleagues would be able to get him reinstated with DARPA. He'd also left a message for Dave Glaspie at HAARP. Before he signed off, he added his email account to Outlook so he could check his email easily. Password protected, of course.

He decided to turn on the overhead monitors. An image of the tunnel appeared immediately. The cameras seemed to be located just outside of the entrance. One showed the tunnel to the left, the hatch clearly seen in the upper part of the image. The other covered the tunnel to their right. The leak that Richardville had left in the hose connection could be seen. The escaping gas looked like a tiny cloud of smoke. It was nice to have eyes outside of the entrance. Now they wouldn't need to post a sentry outside in order to know what was happening.

It was 10:21, and they were all tired. Singleton thought that someone should watch the monitors throughout the night. They were going to get some sleep tonight and try the hatch in the morning. Even though the main room was large, there was only one couch and recliner to sleep on. There wasn't a blanket, or even a rug to be found. The floor was made of the same concrete as the tunnel, and it was cold. They gave the two women the recliner and flipped a coin to see who would get the couch. It was crowded, but they found that four of them could squeeze onto it without piling on top of each other. The rest of them used the cardboard boxes that the spare parts were packed in to insulate themselves from the cold of the floor. They'd seen homeless people on television sleeping on cardboard boxes. It wasn't very comfortable, but it worked.

Bill took the first watch. It would give him a chance to use the computer for a while as well. Singleton gave him his password and told him to wake him if he received any emails. He'd be taking the next shift and figured he'd surely hear from somebody by then. The shifts were one hour each. Just long enough for a person to get on the net, make contact with a friend or loved one, and then get back to sleep. All while keeping an eye on the monitors, though no one really expected to see anything now that the moss was taken care of. Tim's turn came about 4 AM. He'd hardly said a word to anyone but Carol in hours.

With all the commotion and intrigue going on, no one had said much to him, either. It seemed like Bill and Singleton were pretty much running the show. With Richardville stepping in as he had, he didn't feel like he was needed. He wasn't just along for the ride, though. He was hired to chronicle the events taking place here, and that's what he was doing. His notebook was filling up quickly. He had been taking notes of everything that had happened since yesterday's meeting in the security office.

Sitting here watching the monitors gave him the opportunity to review what he'd written. It had been a long time since he last wrote in longhand. All he was doing though, was jotting down reminders to help him remember what had taken place. He would fill in the details later on his computer. As he reviewed his notes, he intermittently looked up at the overhead monitors. When he looked this time, he was shocked to see that the left one was black. He sat back and stared at it. The right one looked fine, and nothing unusual was seen in the display, but the left one was black. It was still turned on—the power light was lit, anyway. He stood up and found the on/off switch. It was on the rear of the monitor. He flipped it off and waited a few seconds. He'd had to do this occasionally on his home computer when it locked up for some unknown reason. Resetting the power seemed to fix a lot of problems.

He turned the power back on, but it didn't help. The monitor was still as black as the inside of an icebox. He sat back down, wondering if he should wake Bill or Singleton. Before he could decide, a shadow settled over the other monitor. Shadow may not be the best way to describe it. It kind of went fuzzy, and the image vibrated a little. Then, it too was black. Now he knew he'd have to wake someone.

"Bill! Wake up."

Bill woke from a deep sleep, and it took him a few seconds to realize where he was.

"What's the matter? Is it 6 o'clock already?"

"No, it's about 4:30. Something's happened to the monitors. First one, then the other, went black."

Bill was still groggy and wasn't exactly sure of what he was hearing.

"Both monitors went out? Did you turn them off, and back on? Maybe the fuse blew? Is everything else on? How about the computer? Is it on?"

"Everything else is fine. They went out one at a time, first the left one, and then the right. The computer is on the same circuit, and it's fine."

Bill was awake now and sitting up. "You'd better wake Singleton. He'll want to know what's happened." Tim woke Singleton, and the three of them sat at the table, drinking diet cokes and discussing the situation. "I wonder if the monitors went out, or the cameras?" Bill said.

"I'd say it's the cameras. Didn't you say that the image vibrated just before the picture went out?" Singleton asked, as he pushed the diet drink away. He'd much rather have had coffee this early in the morning.

"It kind of vibrated for a second, like someone had bumped the camera, then it just went black."

"That does sound like something bumped the camera. Maybe the power was turned off to them? Depina should know. He's the camera expert."

They woke Depina and told him what had happened. Now, four of them were awake and functioning. It wouldn't be long before everyone would be awake and wondering what was going on.

"I wasn't even aware of these cameras," Depina said. "They're not included among the ones under my control. They seem to be connected here only. I gave the monitors the once over when I first saw them. They looked like they were added on a whim. The installation was sloppy. The wires were not attached to wall plugs like they should have been. It looked like someone just drilled a hole and ran them through it. I never noticed the cameras. I wonder if they were purposely hidden from view."

"Why would they even need cameras? All that's in here is spare parts," Bill said.

"Somebody obviously added the cameras as an afterthought. Maybe they wanted to know what was outside, while they were inside," Depina said.

"You might be right about that. Why all the food, unless someone thought they might have to be shacked up here for a length of time?" Singleton asked.

"Along with a bathroom, kitchen, and communications—this would have made a great bachelor pad in my younger days," Tim said. "If someone has been staying here, they wouldn't have wanted to make it too obvious. I doubt if anyone comes to this part of the tunnel often. You could probably hide in here for weeks without anyone being the wiser."

"That would explain all the food, but who would go to the trouble of putting in the camera system? Who'd have access to that kind of equipment?" Singleton asked.

"Maybe the communication equipment was already here. I mean—the intercom to Wilson Hall and the Feynman Computing Center. That had to have been installed when the place was built. The Internet lines were probably put in at the same time, along with the telephone. It's only the cameras that were added later," Depina said.

"That sounds more like it, but if someone was living here, where'd they go? That still doesn't tell us anything about what happened to the cameras," Bill said.

"What if someone was trapped in here, by the moss? It was totally covering the outside door when we got here. I doubt if anyone could have gotten out until we freed them," Tim said.

"But we didn't see any sign of anyone living here when we opened the door. No mess, no opened food containers," Singleton said.

"Did you notice the trash compactor, next to the bathroom door?" Bill asked.

"What trash compactor?" Singleton answered.

"It looks like a regular cabinet with a cutting block on top, but it's a trash compactor. My sister has one just like it," Bill said.

"I'll be damned, I see it now. I never paid any attention to it. I just thought it was another cabinet. I'll look and see if there's anything in it," Singleton said.

He walked over and opened the fake drawer underneath the counter top. It hid three controls, labeled, "open – close – compact." He pressed the 'open' button, and a small electric motor turned a screw that forced the front of the unit open. It allowed the user to view the trash bag inside, and remove and replace it when necessary. Singleton could see that the bag was about half full. The cans it contained were crushed flat. Someone had been using it.

"I think we may have interrupted someone," Bill said. "What if somebody was staying here and studying what was going on, reporting back to someone else—"

"DARPA probably," Singleton broke in.

"Someone like DARPA," Bill confirmed. "He'd have access to the tunnel almost anytime he wanted, and with the cameras, he could do it from a safe distance. He'd also have all the supplies he'd need if he had to stay here for an extended length of time."

Depina got up and walked to the door. "He may even have been here when we first arrived. He could have been watching us the entire time. Perhaps he was trapped by the moss and escaped when Richardville freed the door. We waited a while before we returned." Depina said as he walked back to the table. "Did anyone happen to look at the tunnel door?"

"No," they all said in unison.

"I didn't either," Depina admitted. "But I just checked, and it's been reinforced. It's a steel door to begin with, which isn't unusual for a storage facility, but look at the door frame. See the brackets attached to each side? There's a steel brace located alongside the door. It can be lowered between the brackets, but only by someone on the inside. The only reason to have this kind of lock is so that someone inside can block the door, even if the person outside has a key."

"Or," Depina continued, "you want to block something on the outside that a regular lock might not stop. That brace would make it nearly impossible to force the door open."

It was almost 5:30 now, and there was no way any of them could go back to sleep. They were a little apprehensive, though, about opening the door. Everyone knew there had to be a reason for the monitors going black.

"Why don't we venture outside and have a look before we wake the others?" Bill suggested.

"That's a good idea. I'd like to examine those cameras," Depina agreed.

Bill opened the door slowly, cracking it just enough to peek outside.

"It looks okay," he said, opening it fully and stepping out into the tunnel. "It's clear. You can come on out."

They walked over to the first camera.

"I'll be damned!" Bill exclaimed, looking up at the towel hanging over the lens. "I guess we were right. We did have a visitor."

"I bet whoever it was got trapped in here," Depina said. "And I'd wager he escaped through the hatch, or he's still inside it."

"I just hope you can't lock it from the inside," Singleton said. "I couldn't care less what happened to him, as long as he didn't lock the damn hatch. Right now, it's our best way of getting out of here."

"There's only one way to find out," Tim said. "Let's check the other camera, then try the hatch."

"Maybe we should wake the others first," Bill suggested. "They should know what's going on, too. It concerns us all."

"I'll go get everyone up," Tim volunteered. "Give me about ten minutes."

"Great. We'll check out the other camera while we're waiting, then we'll all meet at the hatch," Singleton said.

Singleton, Depina, and Bill walked over to the other camera.

"Just like the first one," Bill said, pointing to what looked like a handkerchief draped over the lens.

As they stood there, the only sound that could be heard was the hiss of gas escaping the loose fitting where the nitrogen hose connected to the magnet. A cloud of vapor rose above it, dissipating before it reached the arc of the ceiling.

In a few minutes, the rest of their party came stumbling through the open maintenance door, groggy and still tired. They gathered around the hatch.

Bill spoke first. "I guess I should lead the way. Keep a light on the opening when I crack the hatch."

There were three rungs he had to climb before he reached the hatch. He studied it closely before turning the wheel that sealed it shut. It reminded him of a hatch on a submarine, only this one opened up instead of out. The wheel spun easily.

"It doesn't seem to be locked," he reported.

Tim and Depina had their flashlights trained directly on the hatch as Bill pushed it upwards.

"It's not heavy at all. I wonder what it's made of?"

It opened much easier than he expected. It must be counterbalanced, he thought. His flashlight reflected off the roof of a small room just inside the opening.

"No sign of any moss. I'm going on in."

317

Bill grabbed hold of a handrail just inside the hatch and pulled himself up. He looked around but didn't see anything dangerous. He motioned for some of the others to join him.

"There's not a lot of room up here. Why don't one or two of you join me, and we'll see if we can make it to the top." A metal ladder was attached to the wall, and another hatch was above it.

Singleton was next in line, then Richardville. It was really too small for any others to come up comfortably. Singleton guessed the room to be about six feet square, with a ten or twelve-foot ceiling. There were seven rungs between the floor and the next hatch, each about 18 inches apart. Bill stepped on the first rung and then climbed up to the top. This hatch looked similar to the first one. It was about two feet in diameter with a wheel in the center. He held onto the top rung with his right hand, turning the wheel with his left. It turned just as easily as the first one, but when he tried to swing the door open, it wouldn't budge.

"It won't open," he said.

"What do you mean, it won't open?" Singleton asked.

"I mean, it's stuck."

"Well, try harder. Wait a minute, and I'll come up and help."

"It's no use. I don't think it's stuck. It's locked. You can try if you want, but I don't think you'll have any luck."

Bill climbed down, and Singleton took his place. While Singleton was climbing, Richardville studied the back of the first hatch. There was a lock with a bolt that could be slid into place so the hatch couldn't be opened from the bottom. The bolt was a good half-inch in diameter. There was no way they could break it, not in the confined space they were working in.

"Shit!" Singleton said. "It's locked tighter than a drum."

They climbed back down and gave the others the bad news.

"I know how we can open the hatch," Richardville stepped forward. "I'm pretty sure that I can open it. There are tools in the maintenance room. I saw a drill and some bits earlier. If both hatches are the same, then all we need to do is measure where the bolt fits into the lock on the first hatch, then drill out that spot on the second. That should cut the bolt in half."

Who is this guy? Bill thought to himself. First, he tells us about the hatches and the maintenance room, then he kills the moss with the liquid nitrogen, and now he's found a way to open the escape hatch. Maybe he should be the one in charge around here!

While Singleton and Bill measured the lock on the first hatch, Richardville went back to get the drill and bits. It was a Black & Decker cordless drill with an extra battery. There was no way of knowing how much charge the batteries had in them or how long they'd been sitting unused. He hooked the extra battery up to the charger and took the drill and bits with him. When he climbed back through the escape hatch, Bill was just coming down the ladder. He'd marked an X where Richardville was to drill.

"I measured as carefully as I could. I think you'll be able to drill through the hatch lid easily. It's less than a quarter-inch thick, but the bolt is a half-inch in diameter and it will try to turn on you. I put an X where the center of the bolt should be," Bill said.

"I'll start with an eighth-inch pilot hole. Once that's through, I'll follow with the half-inch bit. That's the largest one in the toolkit," Richardville said.

It wasn't an easy place to use a drill. He had to hang on to a rung with one hand while holding the drill in the other. As if this wasn't hard enough, he also had to keep upward pressure on the drill at the same time. It was imperative that he keep the hole straight, too. If he was off by even a slight bit, he'd only drill through part of the bolt.

Bill's mark was right on the money. As the bit broke through the hatch, it struck the bolt dead center. The bolt was hardened steel and didn't drill nearly as easily as the hatch had. After five or six minutes, Richardville tired, and Bill took his place. It took nearly ten minutes to get the pilot hole drilled. The battery was still going strong, though.

Once the pilot hole was drilled, Richardville put in the half-inch bit and widened the hole. If this worked, the locking bolt would be cut in half, and the hatch would open easily. This wider hole took more time to drill, as a lot more steel had to be removed. The battery died about halfway through the bolt. Depina retrieved the spare battery and placed the depleted one back on charge. Bill was doing the drilling when the bit finally broke through.

"I'm through!" Bill shouted to Richardville and Singleton.

"Can you push the hatch open?" Singleton asked.

"I'm pushing, but it's still not opening. Wait, it's moving—it acts like it wants to open, but it's just opening a crack."

"Try this," Richardville said as he climbed up the ladder and handed Bill a hammer.

Bill struck the bottom of the hatch near the locking mechanism, and it opened a little wider. He smacked it again, this time as hard as he could. The hatch gave a little more.

"It's open!" he exclaimed.

He pushed up on the hatch, but it wasn't light like the first one.

"This thing's heavy as hell," he shouted.

It was all he could do to force it open. Something was blocking it. He pushed with all his might. Whatever was blocking it fell away with a thud, and the hatch opened easily. He shined his flashlight into the space above him. As far as he could tell, it was identical to the one they were in now. He reached for the handhold to pull himself up and touched something cold. It was a hand, the fingers locked tightly in a death grip.

"Someone's up here," he called to the others below.

"Find out who it is and why they locked us out," Singleton said.

"I don't think he's going to tell us anything. He's dead. Son-of-a-bitch!"

"What's the matter?" Singleton asked.

"It's Meyers."

"It can't be Meyers. He's not supposed to be in the tunnel."

"It's Meyers, alright."

"Are you sure he's dead?"

"Pretty sure."

"Can you tell what killed him?"

"No. Not in this light. I wonder if he was the one hiding in the maintenance room."

"That's hard to say. I've known him for a little over a year. He's always been straight with me. I know he had a top security clearance and access to highly classified information. If he was working for someone else, he sure had a lot of people fooled. I'll get a rope or extension cord, and we can lower his body down to the tunnel floor where we can get a better look at it. Maybe there'll be something on him that will help us figure out what happened."

"Before I do anything, I'm going to climb up to the next hatch and see if it will open."

Bill climbed the seven rungs and turned the hatch lock. He said a prayer as he pushed up on the hatch.

"It's open!" He lifted it high enough that he could look outside. "The sun's shining. We're free."

As Bill climbed down to the chamber floor, Singleton poked his head through the hatch.

"Damn, that's Meyers, alright. Here's an extension cord. Tie it under his arms, and we'll lower him down to the next level. Then we'll get him down to the tunnel floor. Maybe we can find out what killed him."

Chapter Twenty-Nine

There were no apparent marks on Meyers' body or tears in his clothing. For all they knew, he might have died of a heart attack. His wallet contained $136 in cash, a California digital driver's license, and a DARPA identification card. There were no photos, no slips of paper, nothing personal.

Unbeknownst to Bill, Meyers had carried a .32 caliber Beretta, hidden in an ankle holster. Singleton removed it before they lowered him to the tunnel floor. Singleton himself carried a similar weapon, except his was a .22 long rifle caliber—smaller, but with a much higher velocity, a favorite among professional assassins for its silence and precision.

With the discovery of the body, everyone gathered around. The mood shifted from shock to relief as they realized the escape hatches were open—they could finally get out. As they discussed what to do next, a new sound began to fill the tunnel.

Shhhhhhhh. Shhhhhhhh. Shhhhhhhh.

They all recognized it instantly. A few seconds later, a portal appeared about thirty feet away, twice the size of a basketball.

The hissing continued as another portal appeared, then another. They were popping in and out of existence all around them. Some were only the size of a dime, while a few had water flowing from them. The volume of the hiss was proportional to the size of the portals.

Panic set in. Mixed among the hissing were the sounds of tiny bells. The bells grew louder and deeper in pitch, soon drowning out the hissing. Then, something happened that terrified them all.

"Get out! Get out of the tunnel!" The voice screamed in their heads.

They looked around, but couldn't figure out where the voice had come from. It seemed to emanate from everywhere and nowhere, popping into their minds as if by magic. Now Carol understood what Depina meant when he said he'd heard a voice telling him to use the hose to kill the moss. She heard it too. Everyone did.

"Look at the hatch!" one of Singleton's men yelled. "The hatch is blocked!"

All eyes turned upward. Hanging just below the hatch and blocking it completely was a portal. Not exceptionally large, but big enough—about the same size as the hatch, but perpendicular to it.

Bill looked over at Richardville. "Use the hammer and see if you can move it out of the way. Just be careful not to strike it near the inner edge. Try hitting it from behind first, or from the side. We just need to move it about a foot, maybe fifteen inches."

Richardville picked up the hammer and climbed the three rungs to a good position. First, he struck it from the rear. It didn't move at all, but it did make a ringing sound.

Several in the group wondered if this was the source of the bell sounds. The sound was close, but not quite the same.

Next, he struck the edge face-on. It was like hitting an anvil. There wasn't the slightest movement. In frustration, he struck the portal from the rear again, this time near the edge instead of the center. This off-center blow caused it to start spinning. It spun so fast it almost seemed to disappear. A breeze wafted from it several feet away, but it remained directly under and blocking the hatch entrance, spinning like a top.

"What now?" Richardville asked.

"You may as well join the rest of us," Bill said. "It's probably not a good idea to be so close to that thing." As he spoke, the hissing continued, and portals popped in and out of existence all around them.

"Ahhggg!"

Before Richardville could reach the tunnel floor, a wet gurgling sound came from the rear of the group. They all turned to look, and the horror of what they saw was sickening. One of Singleton's men was holding his hands to the right side of his head, blood pouring from between his fingers. The entire right side of his face had been cut off, as cleanly as if he'd stuck his head in a bandsaw.

He stumbled, trying to reach out for help. Blood streamed down his arms and poured from his elbows. Then, he closed his remaining eye and fell backward. His hands dropped away, making no effort to block his fall. The back of his head smacked the concrete floor so hard that part of his brain oozed from the cavity where his ear had once been.

Lying at his feet was what looked like half of a mask, an eye staring blindly toward the ceiling. A portal had opened inside his head, cutting off his right ear, eye, most of his nose, and splitting his tongue and chin evenly. The portal's bottom edge had slashed into his throat, slicing his windpipe and choking him in the process. He was dead before he hit the ground.

Everyone looked around, afraid they might be next. There was no way to know where the next portal might appear. They were popping in and out of existence every few seconds now. As they stood there, watching in terror, they again heard the ringing of bells. The sound was coming from the hatch. They looked up and saw what appeared to be two drumsticks protruding from the opening. They were black and waving slightly in the air. In another few seconds, the head of a slug appeared, its eyes waving on stalks as it looked in several directions at once. The drumsticks had been its antennae.

As they watched, another head appeared, then another. Soon, the entire hatch opening was filled with antennae and eyes, all waving back and forth in the same rhythm. The bell sounds intensified as the additional heads appeared. Then something remarkable happened.

The sounds suddenly synchronized. What had once been a cacophony turned into a single tone. It was loud but pleasing to the ear. The tone seemed to put everyone at ease, replacing their fear with a calm, relaxed feeling, as if an anesthetic had just been injected into their systems. Something else happened too: the portals began to disappear. One by one, they vanished, with no new ones taking their place. The first to disappear was the portal blocking the hatch, the one closest to the slugs. It seemed to fade back to wherever it had come from.

They looked at each other, then at the slugs, who were now hanging from the hatch like giant snakes waving in the wind. At any other time, such a sight would have sent them running in all directions, but for some reason, it wasn't frightening to them now. They shared the same feeling: these things were not going to hurt them. They had come to help.

After a few minutes, all the portals had disappeared except one. The one that remained was the one that had appeared earlier—the one from which the creature Depina had killed with the liquid nitrogen hose had crawled out.

This portal didn't seem to be affected by the slug's tone. Maybe it was too far away, or perhaps it was just too damn big. Once the other portals had gone, the tone softened and became a cacophony of sounds again. Then the sounds softened until there was only the sound of a single bell ringing.

"You are in great danger." The voice appeared in everyone's head.

"Your machine has opened a conduit between dimensions and caused a breach in the space/time continuum. You must shut it down and cease your experiments. We only have limited power in this dimension to help you. You must understand the consequences of your actions. You could doom your entire planet to destruction."

Before anyone could say anything, the slugs pulled back from the opening, all moving as one. It seemed to be a reflex action, as if they were trying to get away from something. As it turned out, they were. Bill was the first to see it. Coming out of the only remaining portal were two more of the creatures that Depina had killed earlier. They crawled onto the concrete floor and stopped, apparently disoriented in this new world of hard surfaces. All they had ever known was the soft feel of sand.

"Everyone, get into the hatch. We'll be safe on the surface," Depina hollered.

Connie was the first up the ladder and through the hatch. The two lights in the tiny compartment were on, but they didn't seem to be putting out much light. It was just bright enough to see where the rungs of the ladder were, so she wouldn't have to climb in the dark. As she pulled herself up, she realized where all the light had gone.

There, clinging to the walls, were hundreds of slugs. They were blocking most of the light. The room was alive with them. The only clear area was next to the rungs of the ladder. She knew they were not going to harm her, but the sight of them was so repulsive that she had to fight off her fear.

They reminded her of sea slugs she'd seen on the ocean floor—scavengers that live off the remains of dead creatures that sink to the bottom. It was hard for her to shake this image from her mind. She closed her eyes, her hands tightly gripping the rungs as she climbed to the next level.

Carol was only a few steps behind her. When she saw the slugs, she wasn't afraid at all. She watched the living wall of eyes and antennae with great amazement. If she could, she'd have stayed in the chamber for hours. She realized she was in the presence of totally alien creatures, and she wanted to study them—learn from them. She followed closely behind Connie, but she couldn't take her eyes away from the slugs clinging right beside her.

327

What are they thinking about me? she wondered. I must be quite a sight in their eyes.

There were still seven people in the tunnel when the creatures began to move toward them.

"Go! Go! We don't have any time to lose!" Bill shouted, pushing the men to the front toward the ladder.

Depina was next, with Richardville right behind him. It didn't take them long to get into the hatch. Two from Singleton's group were next in line. The creatures from the portal were beginning to get accustomed to their new surroundings and started crawling in their direction. They realized what they were seeing might be prey, and they began to move much faster.

"Hurry, those things will be on us in a few seconds!"

Bill knew there was no way he or the guy in front of him was going to make it into the hatch in time. He thought about trying to make it back to the maintenance room, but that wouldn't work either. Then he heard the sound of bells again, louder than ever before. In a few seconds, they coalesced into one single tone so loud it hurt his ears.

Everyone clasped their hands over their ears, trying to blot out the noise.

Shhhhhh. Shhhhhh. Shhhhhh.

A portal was appearing right before their eyes, only a few inches in front of them. The creatures were almost upon them. The portal covered most of the beam tunnel. It was different from the others; it was completely translucent. It was only because they were inches away that they could see it at all. In a few more seconds, the creatures would be on top of them.

The creatures never saw the portal as they lunged at the men. Their tusks were raised high, ready to plunge into the prey standing before them. And they did. Reared up on four of their back legs, they came down hard, driving their tusks into the prey as they always had. Only this time, there was no prey there. They came down on nothing. And because there wasn't anything there to stop them, they tumbled forward and disappeared. They'd fallen into the space between dimensions—a place with no boundaries, no up or down. They didn't die; they just ceased to exist as we know it. They were neither dead nor alive. Like Schrödinger's cat, they were both.

Bill's heart nearly stopped when the creatures dropped down on him. They had disappeared just inches away from his face. He thought at first that he had died, that this was what death was like. Then he realized what had happened. The slugs had caused the portal to appear, and the creatures had fallen into it. Once again, the slugs had saved their lives. As the tone grew weaker, the portal began to shrink. Its translucence turned opaque, then to a pale blue before it faded away entirely.

The two men just stood there—watching, not saying a word. Their hearts pounded from the ordeal they'd just been through.

Slowly, they started to climb the ladder and pull themselves into the hatch opening. Bill was the last to go.

"Bill."

A voice called to him before he could mount the second step. At first, he thought it was one of the slugs calling to him in his head. Then he realized he knew that voice.

"Bill, back here. I need to talk to you." It was Tim Collins.

"Where the hell have you been? I thought you went to the surface with Carol."

"No, I had some things to do. I've been in the maintenance room all along. I saw what happened on the monitors. I've been writing about what's been going on here. If we didn't make it, I wanted to leave a record of what we've seen."

"We're going to make it. There's nothing blocking our exit now."

"No, not anymore. Thanks to the slugs—though we shouldn't be calling them slugs anymore. They're Thoreins."

"They're what?" Bill said.

"Thoreins. I've learned a great deal about them, and what's been happening here. Don't ask me how—it just came to me. I've written most of it down. At least, all that I could in the time allowed.

Basically, what's caused all of this is that the proton stream in the PIP-II beam tube has set up a resonance that's allowing parallel dimensions to merge with our own. I don't understand it all, but it's got something to do with sympathetic vibrations.

Think of a string vibrating at a certain frequency. Say, middle C on a piano for instance. If this vibrating string is placed in the vicinity of another string of the same length, it too will start vibrating at that same frequency. This happens because the natural frequencies, or wavelengths, of the two strings match. The second string absorbs the radiated energy coming from the first, setting it in motion too. It vibrates in sympathy with the first string.

These strings don't have to be the exact same length. They might be multiples (harmonics) of each other.

The Thoreins told me that there are eleven dimensions separated by a slight shift in space and time. If enough energy is present, and it's vibrating at the right frequency, dimensions can merge together. The PIP-II is producing that energy and at the right frequency. The portals we see are openings into these other dimensions."

"So, what can we do to close them?"

"We have to shut the PIP-II down before the dimensions merge permanently. The Thoreins won't allow that to happen."

"I don't think I like the sound of that," Bill said.

"You can't blame them. We could well destroy their world, too."

Bill wasn't sure if he understood all of this, but it did sound possible. Considering everything else that had happened, it even sounded probable.

"So how do we shut it down? We tried turning off the power grid, but that didn't work. When we get to the surface, maybe we could explain the problem to DARPA and have it blown up."

"We can't do that. An explosion could rupture the thin membrane dividing our reality and the others. The Thoreins told me how to shut it down—that's not the problem. The problem is where the power is being generated from—"

"HAARP," Bill said.

"Yes, and that's where we have to go. Fermilab is a firecracker. HAARP is a nuclear bomb. HAARP has the potential to unleash the electrical energy stored in the ionosphere and bring it down to the earth—billions of amperes of electricity. It would be like setting off thousands of hydrogen bombs."

"So, how do we stop the PIP-II without explosives?"

"With this." Tim held up a small wrench.

"You've got to be kidding."

"No, it was the Thoreins' idea. All we need to do is to unscrew a liquid nitrogen line going to one of the superconducting magnets. The system is a closed loop. With the line wide open, enough coolant will escape to cause the magnets to lose their superconductivity. At that point, the containment field in the beam tube will collapse. When that happens, the particles will no longer follow the curve of the tube. They will interact with the tube walls."

331

Bill broke in. "They'll melt through the tubing, and the whole thing will come to a grinding stop. No explosion. Just a total system meltdown. The tubes will be destroyed."

"You've got it."

"How long will this take?"

"I'd say two or three hours, four at the most. Long enough for us to be out of here for sure."

"Let's do it."

Bill headed for the hatch while Tim proceeded to unscrew the liquid nitrogen line that Richardville had already loosened. When it was free, he wedged it between the wall and the magnet and opened the valve to full force. Once that was done, he joined Bill in the first chamber. Bill was waiting for him, to be sure he didn't have any trouble.

"How did it go?"

"No problem. Just listen to the gas escaping."

There was a roar coming from the open hatch.

This was the first time that Tim had been so close to the Thoreins. As he looked around, he wondered which one of them had spoken to him, or if they all acted as one. It might be that they share the same consciousness. They only stayed there for a few seconds. They were determined to get to the surface. As they opened the upper hatch, they took one last look at the other beings—beings who were obviously far more intelligent than themselves.

On reaching the surface, they didn't find what they had expected. The sun was shining and the air was warm. There was a damp, almost wet mist that seemed to roll over the landscape. They could see portals off in the distance. The Thoreins wouldn't try to remove them until the particle accelerator was completely destroyed. Tim held a briefcase under his arm.

Singleton told his two remaining team members, along with Richardville and Depina, to head for the front gate and see if they could find a vehicle so they could all get the hell out of here. He said that they'd be along in a few minutes. As far as he knew, they would be.

Tim looked at those remaining and told them that he needed a few minutes alone. There was something he had to do. He stepped back into the open hatch and climbed down to the floor of the upper chamber. Once there, he opened the briefcase, took out a stack of papers, and started writing. He wrote for about fifteen minutes. Twice, Bill called to him to see if anything was wrong.

Next, he took the manuscript and wedged it between the lower hatch lock and the door. It reminded him of when he'd discovered Meyers, lying in the exact same spot. He knew it would be found after they were gone.

I'm finished; it's time to get back into the sunlight.

"So, that's it." General Russell laid the last page back in his lap, stretched, and noted that the sun was starting to brighten the skylight. "They did make it to the surface and free of the beam tunnel. But where did they go once they got there? And why haven't we found any trace of them after two weeks of intense searching? All four of the people that were with them said they were fine when they left them. They said that Tim needed to do something, and they'd be along as soon as he was finished. That was the last they saw of them. Obviously, leaving these papers was his intention. What happened next though? What caused them all to vanish? I guess I need to read this again; maybe there's something I'm missing, something hidden between the lines."

General Russell wanted to start from the top again, but he was tired. It had been a long day, and now, even the night was coming to an end. He went to bed, but his mind was still racing. He dreamed of monsters, portals, and beings from other dimensions. After several hours of tossing and turning, he finally fell into a deep state of REM sleep. This lasted only a few minutes when suddenly—he woke up. Startled!

"You will be called."

He sat up, frantically looking from side to side. He was sure that someone was in the room with him. Sweat beaded on his forehead. Sunlight poured in the windows, illuminating every square inch of the master bedroom. He knew he had heard it. He sat there, listening—cocking his head, trying to perceive any sound that might still be lingering in the quiet that surrounded him.

Then, he realized he did hear something. Just above the sound of his breathing, just slightly louder than his heartbeat, he heard the faintest tinkling—of bells.

The Sequel
Fermilab II Paradox
(PLAYING ON THE STRINGS OF HAARP)

(PREVIEW)

Bill, Connie, Carol, Singleton, and Tim stood together, gazing out over the grounds of the Fermilab complex. What should have been familiar was only partly so. Here and there, a building or a statue reminded them of where they were, but much of the landscape was barely recognizable. Covered in shifting shades of green and brown—sometimes both at once—it looked alien and threatening, as if the world itself was caught between realities.

"Step into the portal."

The unmistakable voice of the Thoriens filled each of their minds, accompanied by the now-familiar Shhhhhh Shhhhhh Shhhhhh—

A portal appeared to their left, nearly twenty feet in diameter. Its base was buried in the ground, eliminating any chance of accidentally stepping on the edge. The portal was similar to the one that had saved them in the beam tunnel: nearly translucent, beautiful even, with a faint aquamarine glow tracing its outer rim.

Inside, a snow-white mist swirled, obscuring whatever lay beyond. There were no words to adequately describe it. They walked up to the face of the portal and just stood there, peering in. A chill came over them—not fear, but a physical cold, sharp and bone-deep. The air in front of the portal was frigid.

"Please, enter the portal."

Again, the voice echoed in the center of their minds, coming from nowhere and everywhere at once.

They looked at each other, then back at the portal. Bill and Connie stepped in together. Carol, Tim, and Singleton followed. Seconds later, the portal faded to nothing.

They could see each other, but little else. They walked forward, their footsteps muffled. After a few minutes, the white mist began to clear. In an instant, they were no longer in the portal at all. They stood on firm, snow-covered ground, the portal now floating lazily above them.

Behind them, a sound rose—the buzzing of thousands of bees. They turned to see what it was.

"I don't believe it," Bill whispered.

"Where are we?" Connie asked. "And what are those things?"

"Antenna arrays," Singleton answered, his voice steady.

"One hundred and eighty of them, to be exact," he added, not needing to count.

Tim was the last to speak. "We're right where the Thoriens want us to be—we're at HAARP."